Away with the

by

Vivienne Tuffnell

All characters in this novel are fictitious.
Any resemblance to persons living or dead is purely coincidental.
However, concerning the fairies, I am saying nothing.

For my husband Nigel,
with love and thanks.

Chapter 1

Isobel could pinpoint the exact day, even the exact moment when her life began its inexorable slide from amiable muddle to downright anarchy and dangerous chaos. She had a number of occasions to choose from, but the real moment stood out like a light on a dark night.

It wasn't the moment when Mickey, her husband of three weeks said somewhat apologetically,

"I hate to tell you this, Izzie, but I have a terrible feeling that God is calling me to become a minister."

It was, however, a supremely incongruous moment, as anyone less like an embryonic priest she couldn't imagine. He was lying on their brand new leather sofa, more or less naked, and was holding out a wine glass for a refill, and she had topped it up with a shrug and had merely remarked, mildly,

"Well, you could have told me that before you married me!"

"I know. I tried. There never seemed to be the right moment," he said, apparently contrite, and had set down his glass and pulled her onto the sofa to christen it a second time.

It wasn't the moment late on a dull Wednesday afternoon when her brother Simon had phoned her, incoherent with grief and confusion, to tell her that their parents were both dead; had in fact died in the strangest of suicide pacts so contrary to anything they had ever done or said that even now, six months later, Isobel couldn't look at their urns without a burning of sudden rage and couldn't think what she could do with those ashes if she wasn't allowed to chuck them on the compost heap as her every emotion told her to do.

It wasn't the moment when she woke up one morning, counted, then counted again, and realised that not only was she pregnant, not unusual in itself, but that she had passed the twenty week mark she'd never got even close to in previous brief pregnancies, and that the chances were she was actually going to have a baby at the end of this.

Nor was it the moment when the stag stepped out into the headlights of her car.

It was the moment when she straightened up, caught a glimpse of herself in the mirror over the bathroom sink, and totally failed to recognise herself. She'd stood there, her feet bare and wet, and gazed at the face staring back at her and wondered who was looking at her. It had not been a nice moment at all.

It had come on the day when her daughter Miranda, now just over two years old, had flooded the house and called the emergency services, and in one of those little master strokes of irony Isobel was to come to recognise much later, she'd done it all wearing a fairy costume. The outfit, which Isobel regarded as an abomination and refused to allow her to wear except on high days and holidays, had been a gift from Simon's wife, and consisted of an absurdly frilly pink dress sewn all over with shimmering sequins, with a set of pink gauzy wings which shed glitter over everything to such an extent that Mickey had celebrated Communion with specks of it on his cheekbones, raising some unwholesome questions in the minds of the more imaginative in the congregation. To top off the whole horrible outfit, there was a pink magic wand with a tinsel covered star on the end. Isobel hated the damn thing, but somehow, Miranda had that day managed to dress herself entirely unaided and Isobel was too tired from a broken night with the baby to bother making her change. Dealing with the inevitable tantrums of an excessively bright and self-willed two year old was actually more exhausting than being up at night with a four month old baby who thought two in the morning was a great time to have a one-to-one with Mum. That morning, Isobel's nipples hurt, her eyes felt gritty and her back was aching, but she still had work to do, so as soon as Luke was snoozing serenely in his rocking crib, she grabbed her easel and paints and started work while Miranda was happily floating round the house singing to herself in a mindless, tuneless croon, apparently turning everything into clouds of flowers as she informed her mother from time to time.

Isobel set to work to try to finish the painting she'd promised would be finished three weeks ago; a series of photographs were pegged to the top corner of the easel and she laboured with tired eyes to try and capture the light in the eyes of a child on a swing. Miranda was lost in her own little world, and when she did speak to her mother, it generally only required responses like, "Yes, darling," to keep her happy.

She'd decided some time ago that she was better off using acrylic paints as not only did they dry faster, they could be washed off with plain water, not something to discount when small fingers seemed to get everywhere, but today, she wished she could have used oils, as they seemed to give a greater brightness to the kind of details she was trying to perfect. She sighed; first thing that morning, she'd caught herself in her materials cupboard with the lids of the bottles of turpentine and linseed oil undone, inhaling softly and losing herself in a nostalgic haze. Poppy seed oil gave a lovely sheen, especially when you were doing faces filled with light and happiness, but linseed today had a perfume that made her think of garlic bread and red wine, of drunken lunches only a few years ago, and not, as Mickey suggested, of cricket bats at the start of the season.

"Must have a wee," Miranda said abruptly, and ran off up the stairs, waving that wretched wand.

"Don't forget to wash your hands," Isobel called and then got lost in the painting.

Luke snuffled in the crib, reminding Isobel of another reason why she couldn't use oils and the accompanying mess and stench of turpentine and linseed oil. She moved her foot and the string round it rocked the crib until the snuffling subsided and was replaced by the soft sound of deep sleep. She tried to concentrate, while keeping an ear out for noises upstairs. The toilet flushed. Miranda had decided to toilet train herself shortly after the arrival of her baby brother Luke. She'd stood and watched her mother change a particularly vile nappy and had stood thinking for some time.

"Nappies are for little babies," she said. "I'm not a little baby. Why do you make me wear nappies, Mummy?"

Isobel had been astounded at that; and even more astounded at how fast Miranda had become first clean and then dry, with minimal involvement from her or Mickey. However, it did have disadvantages. The holding power of a minuscule bladder meant that any trip of more than half an hour had to be meticulously planned around where public loos were located and which of the department stores had loos accessible to a pushchair. It meant that Isobel rarely went out any more at all, unless it was to one of those groups for mothers with small children, where such concerns were the norm, or she went alone, when Mickey was able to be with the children for a few hours. Though while Luke was still being breastfed, Isobel's excursions were limited by that, and she was usually summoned home by a frantic call to her mobile, to arrive back to find Luke red faced and screaming with hunger and her own breasts about to explode.

She sighed again, and wiped away a drop of sweat that was running down her face. Even though it was June, it was still quite cool and she wondered why she was sweating. Another drop fell, this time onto the painting, and distracted, she looked up.

Water was running from the light fitting and dropping like an indoor rainstorm, and for the first time, Isobel could hear running water.

"Oh shit," she said, and very calmly, unhooked Luke's string from her foot, moved her easel away from the dripping water and hurtled upstairs.

The bathroom seemed to have turned into a domestic version of Niagara Falls; the taps at the sink were full on and water was spilling out onto the floor, now almost an inch deep in water. The bath taps were on too, but fortunately the bath had not quite filled yet. She tried to turn the basin taps off, which took some time as they had been jammed on, and then turned the bath taps off too, and then turned to see Miranda, standing daintily on the plastic step stool she used to reach the sink or the toilet. Her bare feet were wet but the rest of her was dry and she was happily waving the wand at the taps. When she was the look on her mother's face, she said,

"It wasn't me; the fairies made the taps get stuck. I was using magic to make them stop," and skipped off down the stairs, leaving wet and twinkly footsteps behind her all the way.

Isobel stood silently looking at the devastation around her and was very glad of her daughter's strategic retreat, because it meant that first she wasn't tempted to throttle her, and second, because she wasn't going to be there to hear her mother's very colourful language as she tried to bail the bathroom floor into the bath with a bath toy like a seaside bucket. She soon gave up with that and ripped up the bathroom carpet and heaved it into the bath to drain while she attempted to mop the sodden wooden boards beneath with all the already damp towels that Miranda had used to make an island around her step.

After ten minutes, Isobel's hands were red and aching from wringing out wet towels and the floor still looked like a lake, so she fetched the mop and began to use that. At least she could do that standing up. The doorbell rang.

"Go away, I'm not in," she snarled under her breath and for a moment the charm seemed to work and nothing happened, beyond Luke waking up and beginning to grizzle. Then the doorbell began to ring as though someone had taped it down.

"GO AWAY!" Isobel yelled. This was really not a good time for someone to call to see the vicar, unless of course they were psychic and had come round with their wet'n'dry vacuum cleaner.

As soon as she'd yelled, Luke's crying intensified and had become his usual enraged bellow of indignation that he had been ignored for more than ten seconds, and not only did the ringing not stop, someone started pounding both on the front door and the back door simultaneously.

Isobel hurtled down the stairs and flung the front door open, ready to yell at whoever was making her life a misery, but the words of anger died in her throat. There was a scared looking policeman standing there.

"Mrs. Trelawny? We had an emergency call from this number and all we could hear was a screaming baby," he said. "Is everything all right?"

A second policeman, who'd obviously been at the back door, now appeared and stared at Isobel. Luke's crying had settled into his "I can do this all day if I have to," mode, and Isobel felt her own eyes fill with tears.

"No, I'm not all right," she said, feeling her lower lip tremble childishly. "But it's nothing you two can do anything about. Domestic disaster."

The first policeman was clearly concerned over Luke's crying.

"May we come in?" he said.

Isobel shrugged and stepped back and let them in, and went straight through to the living room to pick up Luke and at least assure them that the baby was crying for very ordinary reasons. She was holding a now quiet Luke when she saw what Miranda had been doing while she'd been mopping the bathroom.

The phone was lying off the hook, so it was now clear who had made that emergency call, but Miranda was standing at Isobel's easel, brush in hand.

"I've finished your painting for you, Mummy," she said and beamed at them all.

Isobel nearly dropped the baby. Six weeks' intermittent work had now been erased with what was for two years old, a brilliant piece of painting. Isobel sat down on the sofa, her knees weak and felt the first tears begin to fall. A drip from the ceiling fell onto Luke's face and set him crying with surprise. The two policemen stood there, looking embarrassed and helpless, and said nothing. Miranda put the brush, the handle thick with paint into her mother's hand, and Isobel stared at it, and passed it from hand to hand, spreading the paint randomly all over her own shaking hands.

"As you can see," Isobel said thickly. "This is a purely domestic disaster, nothing criminal or dangerous. I think my daughter must have called 999."

The second policeman bent down and put the phone back on its receiver and then put the whole thing back onto the little table near the door.

"That was very clever of her," he said, uncertainly.

"On the television," said Miranda calmly, "They always tell children that if they are in trouble to call 999."

"Not this sort of trouble," Isobel said, wiping her eyes with the side of her hand and getting paint into her eyes. "Oh, God, now what have I done. That hurts!"

The policemen were glad of something they could do, and helped Isobel wash the paint from her eyes, and when they'd made certain that there was no real reason for them to be there, they made their way to the front door. Isobel followed them and Miranda was in the process of running after them when she caught her arm and stopped her.

"Now, Miranda," she said. "You've wasted the time of these two nice men. What do you say to them?"

Miranda looked gravely at the two young men and considered her options. Despite having a formidable vocabulary and excellent diction, she had some time since worked out that on certain people, cute worked a hell of a lot better than clever. Waving her wand graciously at them, she curtseyed and lisped,

"Sowwy!" and frolicked back up the stairs.

"I can only concur," said Isobel. "Sorry!"

"Mrs. Trelawny," said the first officer. "Would you mind me offering you some advice?"

She looked at his young earnest face and wondered if she had ever been that young.

"If you like," she said, uncertainly.

"Try to prioritise," he said. "You're obviously exhausted. Your little girl is a real handful and you don't look like you're coping. Painting is a nice hobby but maybe when the kids are a bit older...?"

Isobel managed to smile and thank him but once the door was shut, she went back upstairs and returned to mopping out the bathroom muttering under her breath,

"I'm a professional bloody artist not some useless amateur."

She mopped and mopped till the floor was as free of water as she could manage and she knelt down and began to dry the boards with one of those magic micro-fibre cloths that hold huge volumes of water. When she straightened up, she saw herself in the mirror and wondered who it was looking in at her. She took a minute or two to realise that it was a mirror not a window and that the tired, grey looking face with boring mouse-coloured hair cut to be long enough to cover the piercing scars on her ears but not long enough to tie back, belonged to her, and a sense of horror swept over her and she began to cry in earnest now.

"Where did I go?" she asked herself in the mirror, so shocked that she no longer looked the way she imagined she looked.

She hadn't missed the dreadlocks when she'd had them cut off three months before Mickey went to theological college; they'd been a nightmare to keep clean and they'd itched too. She hadn't really missed all her many, many earrings, and even now, most of the holes had healed up without trace; after all in over seven years nearly every cell in her body had replaced itself. Even so, she'd kept her hair to this length for years just to hide her ears, even if there wasn't much to hide now. Her eyebrow piercing had healed and so had her nose piercing, but she still had her own image filled with details like that, even though no one now knew anything about them. She'd drawn the line at neat little pearl studs in the only holes left open in her ears, but she'd even stopped bothering with the arty, dangling earrings she'd usually worn; babies and earrings can be a painful mix.

What she couldn't get over was the fact that the face staring back at her didn't look like her at all. Surely her hair had a better colour than that dull shade a house mouse would be ashamed of? Surely it shone more than that? Why had her eyes turned to this shade of mud when they should be amber? And why were there shadows under her eyes that made her look hollow-cheeked and deathly?

"I've got to do something about this," she said to her reflection and flung the wet cloth into the bath with the sodden carpet that didn't look like it was worth saving anyway.

The doorbell rang again and Isobel slowly went down the stairs to answer it, hoping it wasn't anything important.

They'd only been in this parish a few weeks and they were still getting a lot of the social calls that ate into daily life, and meant that Isobel's life often consisted of answering the door to parishioners who wanted to meet their new minister and his wife and children. Mickey, of course, was out most of the time, and Isobel floundered at times dealing with people when she was in the middle of something, but had somehow managed to stay on the right side of politeness.

It was Mrs. Hall, a middle aged lady who Isobel had a feeling was probably in charge of the flower rota or something of the sort.

"Hello Isobel, you're looking well. Is the vicar in?" she said breezily and Isobel felt her hackles rise at the obvious insincerity.

"No, sorry, he isn't," Isobel said. "He's out all day, I'm afraid. I can't ask you in; we've had a flood. The taps got jammed and the bathroom got flooded."

"That's OK, I don't need to use the bathroom." Mrs Hall said and began to push into the hall. Isobel stood her ground and Mrs. Hall found herself in the uncomfortable position of either needing to shove Isobel out of the way or of backing off. She backed off, looking puzzled.

"Sorry," said Isobel, managing a nice smile. "It really is like the Somme the morning after. I'm sure you wouldn't want visitors if you'd just had the morning I've had. I'll let Mickey know you called. Was it anything in particular?"

"No, nothing special," said Mrs. Hall. "If you need any help, you will just ask, won't you?"

Isobel managed an even nicer smile.

"It's all under control now, but thanks. I appreciate it," she said. "It's just going to take a bit of time to sort out. See you soon."

When she'd shut the door, Isobel went back to where Miranda was playing quietly with her baby brother on the living room floor and stared at her ruined painting and wondered what the hell she could do. She eventually decided that Miranda's additions were still damp enough to wash off, even if it took off what she'd added today, so she took the whole canvas upstairs and using the shower spray managed to wash very lightly until the extra paint her daughter had put on was washed away and the painting was restored to how it had been when she'd started work that morning. So at least one thing has been salvaged from the chaos of the morning, even if the bathroom carpet was ruined. She took the painting and its easel and left it in a corner of her and Mickey's bedroom to dry and bolted the door from the outside and went down to get lunch ready.

That evening, over a grown-up dinner of Chinese chicken and noodles and a bottle of red wine, Isobel told Mickey about her horrible day and wept into his black shirt when they snuggled up on the sofa later.

"Do you think this is post-natal depression?" he said after a while and a lot of tissues. "I mean, you were pretty low after Miranda, and you did lose your Mum and Dad while you were still expecting Luke. It's only natural you'll feel low sometimes."

"Low? Low?" wailed Isobel. "I couldn't get much lower if I went potholing. I have six commissions to do and I never get the time or space to do them. If I don't get them done even near to when I said I'd do them I may lose them. And I never get the time to do any *real* painting any more. It would be bearable with the kids if I didn't get the parish hammering on the door the whole time."

He was thinking about it, she could see that.

"Maybe you need a studio," he said.

"Yeah and how are we going to manage that? Childcare and a studio? On what I earn, never mind your stipend? I don't think so."

She buried her face in the dark soft leather and sobbed.

"No, I've been thinking," he said. "Maybe we can manage it. Look, the sale of your parent's house is going through any time soon. I know it'll be split two ways between you and Simon, but there'll be a lot there. Not enough to buy a house for us outright, maybe, but enough so we'd only have a small mortgage. What about looking for a small place somewhere quiet that we can use as a holiday home and we can have for when I retire? If I ask around, I reckon there are a few people who'd help out with the kids during the week if you went off to this small place to get on with painting. Even weekends too sometimes. I know it's not perfect, but it might help enough to get you through this."

Isobel sat up abruptly, and gazed at her husband in wonder. He had glitter from his daughter's preternatural wings on his nose and his lips had a purplish stain from the wine, but right now, he looked good enough to eat.

"That's a brilliant idea," she said. "But in the mean time, I have an even better one."

"Which is?"

She put her hand on his thigh and leaned over to kiss him.

"This," she said, and just then a thin wail of infant irritation floated down the stairs.

"Damn," said Mickey and watched as Isobel levered herself out of the sofa and padded upstairs. He waited for some time, and after almost an hour he finally went upstairs to look for her. She was sprawled in the big armchair in Luke's room; the sleeping baby lay in her lap, her shirt was open, her nursing bra adrift and milk was dribbling down her stomach. She was fast asleep. He took his son from her lap and put him in his cot and then with a much greater effort, eased the mostly asleep Isobel to her feet and guided her along the passage to their own room, held back the duvet and helped her slide into bed. She raised her eyes sleepily to him.

"Where were we?" she said.

"It'll keep," he said and tucked her up. She was snoring softly before he reached the light switch.

Chapter 2

The next morning, Isobel felt a lot more like herself, partly because she'd had the first unbroken night she'd managed in heaven knows how long, and partly because, after a day like that, life can only get better. It was Mickey's day off too, which made things easier at the best of times. Today he told her to get on with the painting and leave all the rest to him, so she set up in the spare bedroom and worked solidly all day till the light went, only stopping when Mickey brought Luke to her to feed and when he brought her sandwiches and tea. By eight o'clock, the painting was finished and so was she. She signed her name in the corner and breathed a sigh of satisfaction and went to wash her brushes, taking care to bolt the door when she left, just in case Miranda had another art attack.

Both kids were in the bath, almost obscured from sight by a mountain of fragrant bubbles. The carpet was gone. Mickey was sitting on the little plastic step stool, one arm supporting Luke.

"You aren't supposed to use that much bubble bath," Isobel said. "Let me guess: did our resident fairy princess run the bath?"

Mickey shrugged.

"Once it's in, you can't get it back in the bottle," he said, unconcerned. "I chucked that carpet in the bin; it stank. I thought I might sand and varnish the boards instead."

Isobel leaned against the basin.

"Good idea," she said. "I got it done, you know. I didn't think I would but I have. Thanks for giving me a clear day; I don't know what I'd have done otherwise."

Mickey scooped Luke out of the water to show her the foam beard and moustache he'd put on him and the baby shrieked in protest at being removed from the water.

"Have you thought any more about my idea?" he said.

"I assume you mean about buying a house somewhere and me use it to work from?" she said. "Yes, I have. If I can find the right place, not too far away from here, then yes, it might be a goer. I haven't got the faintest idea where to start looking though."

"We'll think of something," he said. "OK, Miranda, time to get out."

"It's Princess Miranda," said the froth-coated fairy. "And I don't want to get out."

"If you get out now, Mummy will read you a story," Mickey said and Miranda thought about it.

"Were you going to read me one anyway, Mummy?" she asked.

"Nope," said Isobel. "You've got to a count of ten to make up your mind."

Isobel walked out of the bathroom counting in a slow and patient manner, but before she got to eight, she was accosted by Miranda in a big pink towel looking anxious.

"Does it count even if I haven't got my jammies on yet?" she asked.

"Get them on as quick as you can and I'll think about it," Isobel said and watched her daughter race to get into pyjamas.

Miranda fell asleep before the end of the story, and Isobel went to give Luke his last feed and then, smelling of milk and baby bath, hurried down stairs to where Mickey was washing dishes accumulated from the whole day.

"How was your day?" she asked, grabbing a tea towel.

"Great," he said. "It was wonderful to do all the things you do every day. I'm just glad I only do them once a week. I have my suspicions that Miranda is some sort of changeling, or else she's just hopelessly precocious. When I went to the park, there were lots of mums who knew Miranda, by the way. I assume they're your cronies from Mother and Toddler Group."

"Mother and Terrorist Group, you mean," Isobel said. "I don't know where people get the idea that it's good for small children to play together. Some days, I think this is where world wars really start."

"You're probably right," he said. "Are you making any friends yet?"

"Sort of," she said evasively.

She wasn't quite sure how to explain to him that many of the people even in the last place had not been friends exactly. They were all in the same boat: at home with small child or children. You ended up banding together if not for comfort exactly, then for something very like it. Often she had nothing in common with the other mums and mostly that didn't matter one bit; she went to coffee mornings and activity mornings and it filled the day with other voices than those of her own personal tyrants and it stopped it becoming so overwhelming that she lost all sense of her own identity. But most of her sort-of friends would only suggest a bit of retail therapy to sort out her current batch of blues and she knew that not only did they not have the kind of cash that made such an excursion to the shops possible or enjoyable but that from previous experience, the relief only lasted as long as it took to unpack the shopping bags and put it all away.

Isobel looked at the clock and then at the telephone and thought about ringing the one friend she had made while Mickey had been training, and then remembered the row they'd had a few weeks ago and knew she couldn't break the ice and ring her first. It had been one of those rows that seemed to blow up out of nowhere. Chloe was blunt, irritable and with enough personal demons to populate a small corner of Hell, but Isobel had liked her from the first moment they'd met, sensing in her a kind of kindred spirit that would rather die than give in. The trouble was that Chloe could be as hard on others as she was on herself, and while she was unremittingly supportive of Isobel in most things, she'd go very quiet if Isobel ever complained about how hard things had become with two small children. Isobel knew from experience that this meant that Chloe was doing her level best not to comment on it, but almost a month ago, she'd been in the midst of a batch of real post baby blues, and had had a good old fashioned moan about the kids, and Chloe's resolute silence had got on her nerves and she'd pushed her into commenting.

"Well, for God's sake, Isobel!" Chloe had snarled. "What do you expect? That's what life's like with kids. Why do you think I don't have any? You can be forgiven for the first; no one knows till they've tried. But having a second so close is just asking for trouble. I assume you've worked out what causes it by now? Good. Well my advice to you is invest in some decent modern contraception or else keep your legs together now you know what comes of it."

Isobel had slammed the phone down at that; furious and betrayed, she'd wept for half an hour before metaphorically crossing Chloe off their Christmas card list and getting on with things.

"It's not as if I expected her to be able to help," she said to Mickey when she told him what had happened. "I just wanted a bit of insincere sympathy."

"Ah well, you know Chloe," he'd said. "She'd rather shoot herself than be insincere."

"I'll buy her the bloody gun, then," Isobel had snapped and had drawn a line very firmly through Chloe's name in her address book.

Tonight though, she'd have put up with Chloe's acerbic comments just for the chance of talking about something other than nappies or child development or the latest offers at the Early Learning Centre.

She finished drying the plates and was putting them in the cupboard when the phone rang. Mickey answered it, looked a bit surprised and then passed the phone to her. A familiar voice filled her ears.

"I know you can't see me, but rest assured I am beating my chest in the prescribed manner while I say this: mea culpa, mea culpa, mea maxima culpa," Chloe said. "I'm a horrible, evil-minded bitch and I deserve to be shot for the things I said. I'm such a coward, I'd never dare have children because I know I'd never manage half as well as you have."

"Are you drunk?" Isobel said, trying not to laugh.

"Nope. But I could try if it's going to make things better between us. I could get myself arrested for drunk and disorderly behaviour if it'll make you forgive me. I'm not worth listening to at the best of times so I certainly wasn't worth listening to then."

It was a tacit admittance that things had been decidedly difficult for Chloe at the time of the row; she rarely admitted when things were getting tough.

"Of course I forgive you, you daft bat," Isobel said. "I was going to phone you but you beat me to it."

"Liar, liar pants on fire," Chloe said.

"I was thinking about it anyway," Isobel said. "Anyway, how's things?"

"They've been better," Chloe said. "But I don't want to talk about it. How are you?"

"Could be better," Isobel said, and told Chloe the saga of the previous days events and listened to her friend roar with laughter.

"You should have got the bobbies to make you a cup of tea," she said finally.

"No way," Isobel said. "Neither of them looked old enough to be trusted with hot water!"

Chloe roared with laughter again.

"Mickey thinks we should buy a small place somewhere in the country so I can sneak off and paint," Isobel said when they'd both calmed down. "Somewhere we can go for holidays and then retire to. I'm not sure. What do you think?"

She heard her friend sigh and knew that she'd somehow exasperated her.

"It's a bloody brilliant idea you idiot," Chloe said finally. "I can't think of anything better. Just make sure it isn't too close or else your parishioners will be able to track you down even when Mickey's supposed to be on holiday."

"I've no idea how to start looking," Isobel said. "I don't know where I even want to live."

"That's easy," Chloe said. "I'd be willing to bet there are websites devoted to this sort of thing. Probably called Dream-homes dot com or something like that. It's easier if you don't have a preference. You'd just have to give approximate range, like no more than two hours drive from where you are now and there'd be dozens of places. Go and have a look, see what you can find. I assume this means your brother has found a buyer for your parent's house?"

"Yes," said Isobel and felt sad suddenly.

Chloe seemed to pick up on this.

"Come on, don't let that get to you again," she said briskly. "Unless you really want to begin properly, that is?"

Isobel felt herself begin to sweat. She found thinking about her parents' death too hard still and she really didn't want to talk about it.

"Nah," she said. "I'm going to bottle out of it again, if you don't mind."

She heard Chloe's chuckle and relaxed again.

"Fine; don't blame you," she said. "Quite honestly, if I were you, I'd save that nice bit of angst for when you've got time to go to pieces. Look, I just wanted to grovel and get forgiven, but I'm going to have to go now. I've got a lot on at the moment but I just wanted to check you're all right."

"Yeah, I'm fine," Isobel said. "It's good to hear from you. You take care, now and don't work too hard."

"As if," said Chloe, and rang off.

Isobel put the phone down and smiled.

"Well, at least that's sorted," said Mickey, seeing her face. "It was about time one of you made the first move. Is she all right?"

"Not sure," Isobel said. "You know what she's like. She never tells you if anything's really wrong unless there's anything you can do about it. I swear she gets more secretive every year. I mean, look at when she retrained. She didn't tell me what she was doing till it was all done. She said it was in case she couldn't complete the course because of her leg; she didn't want anyone to know she was doing it so she didn't have to tell anyone she'd failed to finish. Daft cow."

Some years previously Chloe had broken her leg very badly in a stupid accident; even now she had something of a limp and being too proud to admit to being permanently crippled she had turned it into a cross between a sort of swagger and a Marilyn Monroe sway that gave her one of the sexiest walks Isobel had ever seen.

"She does reckon your idea was a good one though," Isobel added. "I may have a look on-line tomorrow and see what I can find. Obviously we can't do anything till the money's through and Luke's been weaned, but there's no harm in looking, I suppose. I was wondering: may I have the car tomorrow? I want to get that painting to its rightful destination before something else happens."

"Yes, but you'll have to take the kids," Mickey said. "I've got a funeral and I don't really think one bellowing baby and one anarchic fairy princess will give it the right tone."

"What time is the funeral?"

"Three."

"If I drive over first thing, can you mind them for an hour or so? I just don't like the thought of them in the car with it. Call me superstitious but I just don't want to risk it."

"Fine, I'll do it," he said, sounding reluctant.

"Look, mate, that's three hundred quid sitting in our spare room, and I want it out and paid for before another disaster happens," Isobel said crossly. "Or you can drive it over if you prefer. I just want rid of the damn thing."

"OK, OK, keep your wig on," he said, waving his hands at her in protest. "Take it over. I'll mind the kids. Tomorrow morning is quiet anyway."

She leaned over and kissed him.

"I'll give her a call to say I'll be bringing it over in the morning," she said. "I don't want to get there to find she's out. I also need some directions. I know roughly where I'm going but not exactly."

"Just don't get lost," he said and grinned. "I really don't want Tinkerbell up there at this funeral."

*

The following morning, Isobel gave the painting a quick spray with sealant and wrapped it first in a layer of bubble wrap and then in an old blanket she kept for such a purpose and then put it carefully in the boot of the car and set off. It felt very odd, driving along without either squawks from the baby or an endless running commentary from Miranda but after a few miles, Isobel felt suddenly much more relaxed.

It took more than an hour to get to the home of her client and when she saw the house, she had a bit of a shock. Somehow she had imagined her client to be in the same bracket as her parents, well-to-do middle-class: not short of cash but not rolling in it either. When she pulled up on the immaculate gravel of the drive, she rather regretted not having charged more, especially given the fact that she'd had such a lot of trouble with the painting even without the kids' endless interruptions. She wrestled the canvas out of the boot and staggered over to the door and rang the bell and waited. The distant sound of the bell ringing far off in the depths of the house had something of a Hammer House of Horror feel, and she giggled nervously, wondering if she would be greeted by a butler.

Her client opened the door; a smartly dressed businesswoman, her grey hair set in rigid, beautiful waves and her face made up to take ten years off her age unless you looked too closely. Her face broke into a smile that didn't quite reach the eyes.

"Ah, Ms. Trelawny, good of you to get here so promptly," she said. "Do come in. Is that my painting? Excellent. I can hardly wait to see it."

Isobel followed her in, and her host turned into a room that could only ever be called a drawing room. Elegant and well proportioned, the room had French windows that stood open to a stone terrace that Isobel could just glimpse. An easel stood waiting for the painting and Isobel undressed the canvas and set it neatly to be viewed. She hated this bit. If she didn't like it, she'd still have to pay the balance, but Isobel hated the embarrassment of people who tried to haggle at this stage.

The woman's face seemed to freeze with shock, and she drew her hands instinctively up to her face, covering her mouth as her jaw dropped.

"Yes," she breathed. "Yes. This is just how I imagined it. When I saw your work at that exhibition, Ms. Trelawny, I just knew you were the artist for me. This is perfect. Just perfect."

She stared at it, rapt. Her eyes were shining with what looked like tears of joy and her face was split by a real, living smile.

"Glad to give satisfaction," Isobel said. "It was a lot harder to do than I thought it would be. My usual portrait work is much less imaginative. Here I had to combine a number of elements."

The woman continued to gaze at the picture. It showed a scene of apparent domestic contentment; the garden was filled with flowers, and she was depicted pushing a small boy, her grandson, on a swing hanging from a branch of the huge cedar tree Isobel could just see from the window. Fair enough, but the scene had never happened. There was no swing, the child had never been here and Isobel had concocted the picture from a set of photographs. She had been under the impression that the child and his parents were abroad; and she had also sensed the kind of conflict so common in families where one grandparent is somehow excluded.

Isobel stepped away to let her client enjoy the moment. She went closer to the open French door to enjoy the breeze and get a better view of the tree. Something bright red caught her eye; on the terrace a child's bicycle lay on its side.

"Is your grandson visiting?" Isobel said. "I'm sure he'll be pleased to see his picture. Maybe you could get someone to really put that swing up for him."

The woman turned and Isobel felt that horrible little jump you get when you know you've said the wrong thing entirely. Her make-up had been ruined by tear tracks ploughing through the beige powder and the crepe-like texture of her skin was suddenly much more apparent.

"He's been dead ten years," she said, but her voice was brisk and without a tremor. "I bought him the bicycle for his fourth birthday. They were going to come here but they never did. He died of meningitis a week before his birthday. I wanted, as I said to you, a moment of his life that never happened to be created on canvas so that I can sometimes imagine what it would have been like. You have captured that moment just as I pictured it. I cannot thank you enough."

She rummaged in an elegant beige handbag for a chequebook and began writing in a fast, italic script and tore it off and passed it to Isobel.

"You've already paid me half," Isobel said. "This is too much."

The cheque was for five hundred, not the three hundred she was owed.

"Not at all," said the woman. "You mustn't sell yourself too short, Ms. Trelawny. I consider what I have paid you an absolute bargain. You have changed history, at least for one small moment. In this picture, I did finally get to play with my grandson, as I always wanted to. Thank you."

Isobel drove for ten minutes in a state of suspended mental animation, barely able to take in what had happened. When it finally began to hit her, she pulled over into a lay-by and howled for five minutes till her own make up was ruined and she looked like a panda with smears of mascara and eye-liner in the shadowed area under her eyes. When she'd finished crying, she scrubbed her face with tissues and drove the rest of the way home refusing to think about it at all.

Mickey was alarmed when he saw her.

"Did she not pay you then?" he asked.

Isobel shook her head.

"No, she liked it so much she paid me an extra two hundred," she said. "But it turns out the grandson wasn't abroad at all. He's dead. I had to create this moment in time that never happened, and she was so grateful she cried. I don't think she'd ever got to play with him. I don't even know if she'd ever even seen him in the flesh. I am such an ungrateful cow. I am going to be such a good mother from now on and never, ever moan about them again. Where are they?"

"Both asleep," Mickey said. "I took them swimming."

"That was brave!"

"Tell me about it. Do you really do that every week?"

"Yep."

"You deserve a medal," he said. "I've made some lunch for when they wake up. Are you hungry?"

"Ravenous," Isobel said. "Just let me get this slap off properly and I'll eat."

Over lunch, Isobel was still pensive and Mickey thought it wiser not to ask any more, but she brightened up when the children joined them, even when Luke threw up his whole feed over her shirt.

"It's about time this little man started on solids," she said. "Might stay down better then."

But as he went out, Mickey saw the look in her eyes as she watched Miranda play and he sighed and shut the door. There's only so much one man can do, after all.

Chapter 3

The day that Isobel's parents died, she had reached that lethargic, elephantine stage of late pregnancy when anything is too much effort. Getting out of a low chair was hard work, and Mickey had begun joking that he was going to get her one of those ejector seat chairs that they make for the elderly and infirm. She had actually been sorely tempted to tell him to go ahead and get one; that afternoon she had sunk so far into their squashy leather sofa that she had been almost incapable of extricating herself unaided and when the phone had rung it had been Miranda who had brought her the entire phone, having been told off on a number of occasions for answering the phone herself and confusing or even freaking out whoever was calling.

"For you, Mummy," she said and delivered the ringing phone into what little remained of Isobel's lap, and ran off.

Isobel sighed and picked up the receiver.

"Isobel? You've got to come straight away; I can't do this on my own," said Simon, his voice cracking and lurching.

Isobel sat up as straight as the sofa and her bump would allow.

"What is it, Simon? You aren't making any sense," she said, but feeling that small chill of alarm that would reappear for many months when the phone rang late in the afternoon.

"They're both dead," he said, and she could hear him start crying. Her immediate thought was for Katy his wife and their little daughter, Jodie.

"Who are? Simon, calm down and tell me what's happened," Isobel said, swinging her legs off the sofa and struggling to her feet.

It didn't take long to get the gist of what had happened, though the full details took a lot longer. The previous day, their father had phoned to ask Simon to come over when he finished work the next day. This wasn't unusual in itself; Simon lived relatively close to his parents, and would often drop by on his way home from the secondary school where he taught English. It *was* unusual for his father to request it. But Simon hadn't thought anything of it; his parents had been on a long winter break to Crete and had returned the week before and Simon hadn't yet been over to see them, and he assumed that his father wanted to pass on to him a bottle or two of foreign booze. When he got there, he was surprised to see that the house was in darkness, but the car was parked up on the drive. He'd gone round to the back as usual and found taped to the back door a note for himself.

He had opened it assuming that his father had been obliged to change his plans and they were probably down at the local pub waiting for Simon to join them. It was no such thing; in his father's neat handwriting, Simon was told quite bluntly that when he read the note both of them would be dead.

"I didn't want you to just walk in and find us," his father had written.

Simon had not gone in, but had phoned the police and an ambulance and then when the police had confirmed that they were indeed both dead, Simon rang his sister. By the time Isobel got there, some hours later, Simon was sitting at the big polished dining table, eyes reddened and his face pale.

She didn't hug him; they rarely hugged, but she rather wished she could bring herself to hold him but sensed that he would break down again if she touched him. She'd had trouble getting into the car and even more trouble getting out and her back was aching, but so far the whole thing had yet to sink in properly. Their father had left them each a proper letter, telling them quite why they had done this dreadful thing, and yet somehow, leaving Isobel none the wiser.

It turned out that Simon had known but hadn't told Isobel that their father had had a brush with leukaemia. He hadn't been able to conceal it from Simon who saw his parents more or less weekly, but Isobel hadn't seen them for months and rarely talked to either of them on the phone and had assumed that her father was retiring because it was time to retire, not because he had a health problem. The leukaemia had been treated, with apparent success, and he was in remission when unknown to both Simon and Isobel, their mother had been diagnosed with the onset of Alzheimer's disease. On their return from Crete, it became clear that their father's remission had been prematurely diagnosed and the illness was about to stage a real comeback.

"And so," wrote their father, apparently without emotion. "We had to make a decision about what we should do. I had been told that I was unlikely to survive a second brush with the leukaemia, and that would have been acceptable had it not been for your mother's diagnosis. She could have lived for many years, but not without a huge amount of help. It would have been cruel to expect either of you to take her in. At your respective stages in life, neither of you are in a position to care for an elderly woman with dementia. The other alternative is not acceptable either: to sell the house your mother and I worked so hard to pay for to fund care in a private home and then when that money is exhausted, have your mother placed in a NHS care home where the standard of care is not always what one would hope for. Rather than have you faced with any of these awful choices, your mother and I have decided that rather than cling, in my case to the vestiges of my life, and in hers, to a diminishing half life where her soul slips away in dribs and drabs, we will leave life with as much dignity as a morphine over-dose will allow and leave you all our assets to divide equally between you. This is our last gift to you."

He had gone on, in their respective letters, to state how proud he was of their individual achievements, and how much he and their mother loved them and asked them for forgiveness for doing this without telling them in advance.

"If I had told you, you would have tried to stop us," he wrote. "Your mother, in her better days, has agreed to this, having some idea of what the rest of her life may be like has decided that to go knowing her own name is better than what might lie in store for her. I am aware that breakthroughs in medicine happen every day, but rarely in time for those whose lives stand on the very brink and I am not a fool. I know my days are numbered and I wish to spare myself and my beloved wife, and yourselves too, the pain of deaths drawn out beyond what is decent."

Isobel lay on the bed in Simon and Katy's neat anonymous spare room and fought with the fury she felt welling up inside. She'd been in no state to drive home and Simon had taken her back to his house, where, after a brief call to Mickey, she'd flopped down on the bed and fallen deeply asleep for half an hour, craving oblivion. She'd have asked for a double or triple gin if she'd not been so hugely pregnant, but Katy her own eyes puffy from crying, had made her hot chocolate and loaned her a nightie. She could hear Katy downstairs, cooking the supper, and Jodie playing in the living room, and she felt so lonely.

After a while, Katy came up with a cup of tea.

"How are you feeling?" she asked.

Isobel struggled to sit up and took the tea.

"Not too bad," she said. "Angry, mostly. Are you OK?"

Katy shrugged.

"Now the shock's worn off, yes, I'm OK," she said. "I knew about Roy having leukaemia, obviously, so I'd got the idea that maybe he wasn't going to be with us for ever. And Wendy had been more than usually scatty lately so that wasn't as much of a surprise as it might have been. But it must be tough for you."

Isobel stuck out her bottom lip in unconscious imitation of her daughter's sulky look.

"I'm an orphan," she said. "What really bugs me is I never got the chance to say goodbye and I never got the chance to say I'm sorry."

"Sorry? Sorry for what?" Katy asked, horrified.

"For existing, I sometimes think," Isobel said. "I wasn't a good daughter sometimes, you know."

Katy sipped her own tea and looked at her hands, clearly thinking about what she should say.

"OK," she said. "But then, they weren't perfect parents either, were they? Look, everyone causes their parents some trouble when they're in their teens and twenties. It's part of flying the nest; I think it's called individuation. Until you really break away, you can't develop. I know your dad worried about you."

"Dad wanted me to do science and become a pharmacist," Isobel said, crossly. "I didn't. He thought I was a drop-out till I married Mickey, all mixed up in the Bohemian arty crowd. He even accused me of being on drugs, once. Even getting married, I cocked it up and deprived Mum of the frilly meringue wedding she wanted for me. The only thing I ever did right was get married to Mickey and start giving them grandchildren. And they could even be bothered to wait six fucking weeks to see this one make its entry into the world."

"I think you've got it wrong," Katy said nervously. "Your Dad was only worried for your welfare, you know. And as for the wedding thing, well, Wendy had enough fun helping me and Simon with ours. I even wore the meringue! Your Dad followed your career, you know. He had a book of cuttings and things about your work."
"Won't have been a very big book," Isobel said morosely.
"Bigger than you'd think," Katy said. "He showed it to me; every exhibition, every review, every mention. He'd got them all, I think. He told me that you were getting to be something of a known name in the art world; he said that it would be a matter of luck whether or not you made it big. And he was proud of the fact that you worked on the other stuff, the portraits and things, to make ends meet. He was always a pragmatist, your Dad; this suicide is about as pragmatic as it gets."
"I suppose so," Isobel said, slowly, trying to digest what Katy had told her. She couldn't somehow imagine her father keeping a scrapbook about her work.
"Look, you must be starving," Katy said. "I know Simon will be, but we'll all have to make the effort to get him to eat. I've done lasagne, and salad and chips and Death by Chocolate courtesy of the freezer shop. Let's go and eat. I've opened a bottle of red wine."
Isobel knew Katy was trying very hard to be cheerful when she was herself desperately sad and she swung herself off the bed.
"I reckon I can risk half a glass," she said, and Katy steadied her as she got up.
Between them, they managed to coax Simon to eat a decent dinner and watched him fall asleep on the sofa with Jodie curled up on his knee. Katy carried her daughter up to bed and came and sat in the kitchen with Isobel till two in the morning when Simon woke and came through for a glass of water to find them still up and talking. He looked grey with red-rimmed eyes, but he was looking a bit less wild-eyed.
"I think I'll ring in sick tomorrow," he said. "There's going to be a lot to do. I don't think it's fair to get you to do much of it, Izzie, is it?"
Isobel patted her huge stomach.
"Not really, given the circumstances," she said. "Look, if you drop me back at my car tomorrow, I'll get off home for the time being. Ring me about anything, won't you? Make sure he does, won't you, Katy?"
Katy nodded and they all trooped off to bed, but Isobel had lain for hours thinking about what Katy had said, and later, much later, when they'd begun going through the house, Katy had found the scrapbook and given it to Isobel. It was another thing she could hardly bear to look at now, and Mickey had put it in his filing cabinet, next to the two urns of cremated ashes that Isobel couldn't decide what to do with. Her father's will had stipulated cremation but had stated that it was up to Simon and Isobel what should be done with the ashes afterwards. Simon had so far had no useful ideas, and Isobel's only suggestion had shocked Mickey so much that he had hidden the urns from

her in case in a moment of furious grieving she might actually go and tip the contents on to the compost heap at the bottom of the garden.

So the urns continued to sit at the back of a filing cabinet drawer, waiting for inspiration to strike Isobel. At the moment, it seemed more likely that lightning would strike her first.

Chapter 4

It took some weeks before Isobel got round to looking at websites about houses, and she found herself overwhelmed with choice and began to despair of ever beginning to narrow down the field enough to be able to actually look at houses. She also found that she couldn't get her head round the various complexities of price, location, distance and so on, and she usually ended up with a headache and a bad mood when she'd spent a precious hour trawling the net. Eventually she found a site that had the friendly little words, "If in doubt, just give us a call."

That decided it; she scribbled down the number and the following morning, with both children in plain view for obvious reasons, dialled the number and waited, expecting one of these horrible, "You are held in a queue" type messages.

A real, live human voice answered her after a few rings.

"Hello," said Isobel, her heart suddenly beating too fast as though she were ringing a secret lover. "I've been finding the website far too confusing and I wanted to speak to a real person who can unravel things for me."

"I'm Matt," said the voice at the other end. "How can I help you?"

"I'm looking to find a small home in a quiet location," Isobel said. "It's a bit complicated, so I'll try to explain."

"Fire away," said Matt, who sounded vaguely amused.

"I need to find a house maybe an hour or two's drive away from my current home," Isobel began. "I'm a professional artist, but because I have two small children, as you can probably tell from the noise in the background, I'm finding it hard to get any work done from home. I've come into a substantial amount of money and since my husband is a clergyman, we don't own a house, so we are looking to find a house we can use for holidays and then retire to. The idea is that maybe one day a week I go to this dream cottage and work undisturbed and then spend the rest of the week playing Mum. So it has to be within a certain distance of our current home, and also within a certain price range."

"That's fine," said Matt. "Now, when you say quiet, how quiet do you mean? As in relatively quiet or really quiet? Are we talking deep rural, or suburban or just a nice little house at the quiet end of a city?"

Isobel had thought about it at night, rather wistfully.

"Oh, deep rural," she said. "Lots of trees and fields and stuff. The kind of place where it would be nice to spend a week in the summer, but not tourist stuff."

"OK, I get the general idea," he said. "If you could give me your current location and your price ceiling and the maximum distance you're happy to travel, I can feed that into the machine and see what happens. Can I take your phone number and I can call you back? It can take some time."

Isobel gave him the details he'd asked for and sat biting her nails waiting for him to call back. After about half an hour the phone rang and she snatched it up.

"Right we have a number of properties on our books that might well fit the bill," he said. "Shall I email the details to you so you can have a good look at your leisure and then you can call me back about any that you think might be worth a closer look?"

Isobel spent most of that evening, when both children were in bed, looking carefully through the properties he'd earmarked for her, and both she and Mickey were starting to get quite excited about the whole thing.

"Some of these sound just so amazing," she said. "You wonder why people are selling them at all."

"They're meant to sound fantastic," Mickey said cynically. "They have to make them sound better than they are. Bijoux: read tiny, no room to swing a cat. Tranquil: nothing ever happens, or else it's on the main flight path to Heathrow and they hope you don't notice. Needs some work: it's a wreck. Charming period cottage: you'll have trouble getting permission to do anything other than wash the windows. Mind, they do sound lovely. But I don't think you can really tell till you've actually seen them. I reckon there's maybe six we should look at; the rest are beyond what we can afford if they need renovation as well, beyond what my DIY skills can hope to tackle. That one is really cheap, though, and it only needs minor work and redecoration. I wonder what's wrong with it."

Isobel leaned forward and had a look.

"Does look nice," she conceded. "It's got a huge garden, too. That is a silly price. I wonder why."

She asked Matt why the next day.

"It's been on our books for a while," he said. "I think it's maybe a bit too isolated for most people's tastes, and the garden is big and very overgrown. It's a nice cottage; but rather plain, I suppose. No one's done much with it beyond the basics of plumbing and electrics and the roof and so on. The kitchen is very basic and the bathroom not much better. Silly me, I'm supposed to be selling it to you, not talking you out of it. Were you thinking of seeing it?"

"Yes, there were a few we wanted to have peep at and that was one of them," Isobel said. "I just wanted to know why it seemed to be such good value."

"The owners dropped the price recently; I think they need the money," he said. "Shall we make arrangements for you to see some properties then?"

"Yes," said Isobel decisively and felt very scared suddenly. It all seemed very real and horribly grown up, buying a house. It didn't feel like something she would do at all.

*

Isobel hadn't wanted to go and view properties on her own but there didn't seem any alternative. Mickey was team vicar in their new parish, which meant that he was the junior partner and under the command, so to speak, of the team rector, and he was unwilling at this early stage of their unequal partnership to jeopardise the relationship by taking more time off than was easily explainable. House hunting didn't seem to come under the banner of legitimate time off. Isobel managed to get a friend from the local Mother and Toddler group to have Miranda for the day the first day she went off to look at houses, but since Luke was still being breastfed, she had to bring him along. It was less of a problem since he was still static, still in nappies and apart from a small amount of the weird gruel that was baby rice, didn't need real food. Taking Miranda with her would have been more than her nerves could stand: endless stops to use the toilet or the hedgerow, endless requests for drinks, for food, for entertainment and attention, not to mention the hassle of actually looking at houses while trying to ensure she didn't escape or destroy anything.

Luke was a quiet baby when his sister wasn't around to poke him awake and Isobel relished the chance to drive with a tape of her own choice playing. The kids' songs and stories on tape that Miranda loved probably reduced her mother's driving skills exponentially as the hours of a long drive went on, till reaching journey's end was maybe more a matter of Providence than of anything else. The first house was a disappointment; it was far more dilapidated than the specifications had shown and Matt, who had met her there had the grace to be apologetic about it when they had extricated themselves from the owner who tried to distract them from the damp patches on the living room wall by pointing out that the view from the window was lovely.

"Nope," she said, when they got away. "Definitely not. And it's right on a main road too, with all this lot thundering past day and night. I don't think so."

She tucked Luke back into his car seat.

"Is there another one within range, or shall we call it a day?" she said.

"There's that one that you were saying seemed very cheap," he said. "I have the keys with me. It was at the very limit of your distance requirements though, so it's maybe forty minutes away from here."

"You've got the keys?"

"Yes. Didn't I say it was empty? I should have done. No chain, either, available for immediate occupancy. Do you want to have a look?"

Isobel considered. Luke would need feeding in maybe an hour if the tightness of her bra was anything to go by; she could feed him when they got there and then he might doze in the baby sling while she looked round.

"OK," she said. "But the baby will need feeding when we get there so you'll have to wait a few minutes before you show me round."

"No problem," he said and they set off again in convoy.

Isobel realised that they were getting into real countryside by the proliferation of trees and the narrowing of the roads till they were bucketing down a one-track road along the top of a valley. A long way below she could see a river glittering in the summer sunlight, like a trail of diamonds in the deep lush green of the valley. She wound down the window and took a deep breath and smelled only the green smell of living trees and grass.

"Promising," she said to herself and followed as Matt's car pulled off the road and down a little lane with a ditch on either side of the road surface. There was a snort and a wail from Luke as he woke up and realised his tummy was empty.

Matt's car rolled to a stop as a gate blocked the lane and Isobel pulled up carefully behind him. She got out as Luke's wails became louder and went to Matt's car.

"I'll be about fifteen minutes," she said.

"Bring the bottle," he said.

She gave him the look she gave people who assumed such things and went back to her car, climbed into the back seat and plugged Luke in. At least this way she never had to make up bottles and worry if they were going to go off in hot weather like today. She watched as Matt lit up an impatient cigarette, and began pacing.

"Your problem, mate," she said softly and swapped the baby to the other side.

When Luke had fed and had fallen asleep, she strapped him into the sling, taking care to tuck a cloth between his face and her shirt, to catch any bloops that might occur and then caught up with Matt.

"Ready now," she said and smiled at him. "Just be glad I didn't have to bring my daughter too. This was the easy option, believe me."

He smiled nervously, and opened the gate. The path had long been overgrown and indeed the gate was held on with orange bailer twine, but the scent of honeysuckle and bramble flowers was inviting even if they had to pushed back tendrils of each to reach the cottage. Many of the blackberries were fruiting already though none were ripe yet. She glanced up from the ground and saw the cottage for the first time. Whitewashed outer walls were greenish from algae and moss and the windows were as dull as slate, reflecting little of the brilliant sunshine, and the paint was peeling off the front door a little.

"It does look a little dismal," he said, uncertainly. "But empty houses often look like that. And summer makes all the weeds grow and with nobody to cut them back, it soon gets overgrown. A few hours work and this would all be manageable."

Isobel ignored him and gazed at the cottage in wonder. It was like some sort of fairytale cottage that had been lost in time and forgotten about. A rampant pink rose rambled so madly around the door that her hair became tangled in it while she waited for him to unlock the door. The heat of the day was becoming oppressive and she had a bet with herself that the floor inside would be grey stone flags worn with age and cool to the feet. He managed to get the door open and stepped back to let her in.

She'd won her bet; the floor was made of grey stone flags, small and slightly uneven from long wear. The air smelled musty but faintly floral as if someone had left one of those rather chemical air fresheners in a window to be warmed by the sun; she could also smell dust and a slight trace of mushrooms.

"The entrance hall," he said grandly, and then looked round the small dull space and grimaced. "Who am I kidding? OK, just bear in mind that nobody has lived here for some time. The last owners bought it as a holiday cottage but seldom used it. Then they came to retire here and found it too quiet. That's why they need the money fast, to pay for the house they've now got. The damp smell is just that smell you get in all old places when they're empty. The damp course is in order, I can assure you."

"OK," said Isobel uncertainly. "I'll leave that sort of thing to the survey. Just show me round; don't try to sell me it or I might get bored and walk out. Let me get a feel for the place."

"Do you want me to just shut up?" he said anxiously and she felt suddenly sorry for him. He seemed very young and not terribly well suited to the job.

She gave him a distinctly maternal grin; no need to give him the other kind in case the poor kid thought she was hitting on him.

"Probably best," she said. "You can tell me anything useful but cut out the hard sell stuff. It doesn't work on me."

"Fine," he said, and seemed relieved.

She walked through the long passageway that connected front to back, glancing in at the doors that opened off it. Halfway along, the stairs began. They were uncarpeted and each stair had such a thick layer of dust on it that they might have been covered in dirty flour.

"How long is it since anyone viewed this place?" she asked, curiously.

"Someone came six months ago," he said. "But they never made it up the path."

That was strange; such a cheap price, you'd think that buyers would be pounding the path weekly.

"Why?" she asked.

He looked uncomfortable.

"Not really sure," he said. "It happens sometimes, a place sort of stays on the market, people get used to seeing it. When it's been on a while, the assumption is there must be something wrong with it that we're trying to hide."

"And is there? Anything wrong with it, I mean?"

He looked even more uneasy at her directness.

"Not that I know of," he said.

Isobel shrugged.

"I don't suppose you'd lie to me," she said. "But take it as read I'll be bloody annoyed if I find that you have."
He seemed actually a bit distressed at this.
"Mrs. Trelawny, please," he said. "I honestly don't know of any good reason why this place is still on the market and so cheap."
Isobel's quick ears picked up on that.
"Any good reason," she repeated. "So you do know of reasons, just not sensible logical ones? Yes? Am I right?"
He looked at his shoes, for all the world like a small boy caught out in some sort of mischief.
"It's silly," he said, and stopped.
"Go on," said Isobel encouragingly, but with the faintest hint of a threat in her voice.
"I've taken a few people here," he went on. "Every time, they get excited about the price, but when they see it, they sort of go off the boil."
"Do you mean, see it, as from the lane or the garden. Or as in having been shown around?"
"Shown around," he said. "It's a bit dismal, what with being empty. I suppose that's all it is."
Isobel knew he was still hiding something. She gave him her brightest grin, the one that made her look briefly and disconcertingly like a hungry shark.
"Come on," she said. "'Fess up. You know you want to. You know you'll feel so much better once you do."
He actually scuffed his shoes on the ground, his head lowered so he didn't have to look her in the eye.
"They reckoned it was haunted," he said in a sudden rush. "It's rubbish, I know that, and you know that. But they all thought it was great till they got inside and then they all said it was spooky and they wouldn't want to be here after dark."
Isobel roared with laughter.
"Is that all it is?" she said. "I was expecting subsidence or worse. Nah, ghosts don't bother me. I'm a *mother*: you can't scare me. And bear in mind my husband's a clergyman. We'd have no truck with ghosties and ghoulies and long-leggedy beasties or things that go bump in the night. Bell book and candle. No worries!"
She could hardly believe her luck that it had only been a matter of superstition that had kept this house on the market and at such a low price.
"All right," she said. "Either that's meant to be a very bizarre selling point you're trying to con me with, or I've already heard the worst. Let's have a proper look round."
She walked into the kitchen, and looked round the almost empty room. There were a few antediluvian cupboards and a steel sink by the window, and the stone floor was dirty, as if the last occupants had not been bothered to scrub the floor before leaving. A tiny corner of the kitchen window was broken, enough to have admitted nesting birds.

A neat round nest had been made on the high wooden shelf next to the window, but nothing remained in it when she lifted it down but a few fragments of eggshell. The window was very dirty too, smeary and laden with cobwebs filled with ancient desiccated bundles that had once been flies. Dead flies lay at the bottom of the window and all across the sink and draining board. Beyond that, there wasn't much else in the room but dead leaves on the floor and that strange sweetish smell. She didn't think it was air freshener now; it was much nicer than that, a sort of sappy green smell like trees in the sunshine in very early spring, or that Aspirin smell of wet willow leaves.

"It doesn't have mains gas as you'd expect," he said helpfully. "But you can get Calor gas delivered. It does have the correct fittings for an electric cooker though. I know the kitchen looks awful, but just think: you could have a kitchen from scratch. No putting up with the one that was already in the house because it's too expensive to replace."

She gave him another look of irritation.

"I may be a mother and a housewife but please don't patronise me," she said. "I am also a professional artist. I don't spend any more time in any kitchen than is strictly necessary, and I doubt it will be any different here. I shall probably buy some bog standard units from IKEA and put my mother's welsh dresser over on that wall."

He looked suitably cowed but he didn't say anything and she felt sorry for him again.

"Oh, never mind," she said and sailed out of the kitchen in search of the living room.

At some stage in the past, someone had knocked down the walls between living room and dining room to make one large room with windows at either end. The dining room end, as she thought of it, had windows overlooking the front garden, but the living room end had a broad expanse of window and of French doors overlooking the back garden. The light was streaming in through dirty glass and lighting up the whole room. Dust danced in the golden beams of light and Isobel felt a surge of real enthusiasm.

"I like this," she said softly. "The light is good, very good. It'd be even better with clean windows."

Ancient green velvet curtains were pulled back as far as they would go on the tracks, and stupidly, as she quickly realised, Isobel gave them an experimental tug to see if they were still viable. It took several minutes for Matt to extricate her coughing and spluttering from them. The material tore under his hands as he tried to pull it from her and when Isobel's face emerged, filthy with dust and cobwebs, she did look rather pale.

"Damn thing seemed to jump on me," she said, brushing herself and the still sleeping Luke down. "It's me for a bath then. Is the water still connected?"

"No, it's not," Matt said. "Is the baby all right?"

Isobel glanced down and smiled.

"Yep, not a whimper," she said. "Can't say that for his mother, though. I definitely gave a bit of a squeak when that happened. Mind you, I was daft touching them. They look like they're about a hundred years old. That's real velvet too, not this modern stuff. They'd have cost an absolute fortune new."

She gave herself a bit of shake and glared at the dark pool of crumpled fabric.

"If that's the sort of thing that happened to other visitors, then I guess I can see why they had a problem," she said. "It was a bit sudden and alarming."

She looked round the deserted room. A vast amount of dust had been raised by her wrestling match with the curtains. But dust was only dust. A decent hoover and maybe an ioniser would deal with that. In each of the rooms there had been a fireplace but they were both boarded up now with squares of chipboard. She went over and touched one. It had been taped in place but the tape had turned dark yellow with age and the board obligingly fell into her hand. It was a reasonable size for a fireplace, not big enough for a child to climb up but not far off it. The remains of the last fire lay damply in the grate, a few charred bits of wood and grey ashes and the skeleton of a bird that had been trapped down there behind the board. The bones lay white amid the grey ash and the beak looked like that of a dove or a pigeon; a few stray feathers that hadn't rotted moved slightly with the breeze from the chimney pot high above.

"I think the chimneys are both still open," Matt said from behind her, making her jump slightly. "There are fireplaces in all three bedrooms, and even one in the bathroom."

"Where is the bathroom?" she asked, pushing the board back, covering the sight of the dead bird.

"Ground floor, next to the kitchen," he said. "You've got reception rooms on one side of the hall, kitchen and bathroom and a little utility room on the other. Upstairs there are three bedrooms and one little room that has been converted to a loo and a shower by the current owners."

Isobel shrugged. That was good. Two loos were always better than one, especially when there were children in a house.

"Let's have a look then," she said and he led her uncertainly back into the hall, past the kitchen and into a small room next to it. It contained nothing but an old Belfast sink and electric points and those funny little taps you get to connect a washing machine to. A small window let in virtually no light; leaves seemed to be growing over most of the window, letting in only a few gleams of daylight. Still, you don't need much light in a room that is used only for boring things like laundry, she told herself. Next to it was the bathroom proper.

A big old enamel bath stood on four clawed feet, brass taps tarnishing and a big lime-scale trail from the taps, even though no drips were falling now. There was a sink on a white pedestal, and a loo. A shower cubicle in frosted glass stood to one side. The floor was the same smooth worn stone flags, but one stone had been removed to make a drain, covered with a grill, so that it would be possible to wash the floor and have the water drain away rather than have to mop endlessly. There was a somewhat larger window, filled with modern frosted glass. The room felt surprisingly cold and she thought, how nice it would be to have a long soak in that tub, with a fire lit in that neat little fireplace and candles all around. A few potted ferns and some deep green sumptuous towels and mats would make it the perfect bathroom.

"I'd like to see upstairs," she said, and jumped at how her voice seemed to echo in the empty room. "Do you think those stairs are safe?"

"Nothing wrong with them that a dust pan and brush couldn't solve," he said robustly and led the way.

The stairs creaked so much she started giggling and commented that it felt like being in a Scooby Doo cartoon.

"Are you sure they're safe?" she asked as they reached the top. "I wouldn't like to turn round and find them collapsing behind me?"

"Mrs. Trelawny, I am as sure as I can be the whole place is safe," he said, rather irritated. "OK, be my guest and have a good poke around."

The bedrooms were entirely deserted, apart from a half-mummified mouse lying on the mantelpiece in the master bedroom. Isobel eyed it rather severely and Matt looked away.

"Show me an old house that doesn't have the odd mouse," he said. "They come in during the winter, places like this, when it's cold. This one probably died of old age."

There was a small room off the landing that she imagined had once been either a dressing room or perhaps a linen cupboard and was now fitted with loo, sink and shower. There was no window, and there was an empty light socket hanging from the ceiling and a second pull that Matt said controlled an extractor fan. Isobel stood looking at the rather bleak, utilitarian little room and imagined it with candles and heaps of nice thick towels; she wondered if it might be possible to fit a second bath, one of those short deep tubs.

The bedrooms all had creaky wooden floors, sanded and varnished, and she found herself imagining rugs spread out on the floors of each room. The master bedroom as Matt termed it, had windows at either end of the room: she could just see the old brass bedstead that had been her parents' bed and was now hers. For the moment it was being stored in Simon's garage along with a whole load of furniture that wouldn't fit in her vicarage and that Simon and Katy didn't either want or need.

"It's nice," she said softly to herself, and found a rather strange almost atavistic feeling of needing somewhere of her own. She'd never owned her own home; the church houses she'd been living in these last years were never truly her own, and suddenly the thought came to her that here she could do what she wanted; there would be no one to comment on what colours she chose to paint walls. When they'd moved to Mickey's current post, for the first week or two of visits, she found that people continuously assessed how they had the furniture, what colours they'd chosen, and so on. She'd been particularly irritated about the comments that there were so few pictures on the walls.

"But Isobel," Mrs. Hall had said, as if in protest. "We all understood you are an artist. I thought you'd have your own pictures on the walls for us to admire."

Isobel had smiled, and gently explained that she tended to sell most of her paintings and that was why there were none on the walls.

"I do have a portfolio of photos of them, for reference," she'd added, just in case there might be a commission in the offing.

Now she gazed round the largest of the bedrooms, she thought, If I want to paint the walls of this room with a mural of trees and the ceiling dark blue with luminous stick-on stars, I bloody well can.

"Can I have a look at the back garden?" she said, and Matt jumped slightly. He'd been daydreaming and hadn't been taking any notice of her for some time.

"It is horribly overgrown," he said and they headed down the stairs and with difficulty, he opened the kitchen door and let her out into the garden.

She couldn't get very far, as the brambles and nettles and thistles had colonised so thoroughly there was no way through without a machete and a native guide. She could see that the end of the garden rose somewhat into a sort of hillock covered in trees and if she'd been obliged to give a quick succinct description, she'd have had to have said the garden was more like a wood and the cottage stood in a sort of clearing. It made her think of Briar Rose's cottage in the woods in the Disney film of Sleeping Beauty; there were hints of the sleeping castle what with all the brambles and briars too.

Luke gave a sort of snuffle and subsided back into sleep again and she realised he had been unusually quiet all day. Oh, well, that meant an interesting night for all of them if he'd managed to sleep most of the day away. She backed her way carefully back into the kitchen where Matt was waiting, nettling her legs in several places.

"I think I'd hire someone to help clear the garden," she said.

"So you are thinking of buying it?"

He sounded surprised.

"I'm going to go home and think about it," she said. "And then I'm going to bring my husband to have a look at it and then I shall think some more. And if in the meantime, you find another buyer, then it obviously wasn't meant to be for us. I shall call."

Isobel drove home with a growing feeling of excitement and elation that she couldn't put down to anything concrete and when she got home, tried to convey to Mickey as much as she could of what she'd seen.

"It's a shame you didn't take the digital camera," he said as she spooned baby rice into Luke's open mouth. He seemed terribly hungry, and had fed voraciously as soon as she'd got home and now demanded an extra bowl of the rice.

"I don't know where he's putting it," she said, admiringly. "Just as long as he doesn't just chuck it straight back up."

"I collected Miranda from your pal's," Mickey said. "She went to bed as soon as I gave her dinner. I would have thought she'd have woken up when you got in."

"Oh well, a bit of peace," she said. "That's if this one goes to bed. He's been asleep most of the day, so I don't have high hopes of that."

But when she put Luke into his cot, he gave the slightest of protests and went to sleep almost immediately.

"It's a good omen," she said.

Mickey gave a snort of amused derision.

"You know, Izzie," he said. "For a Christian, you don't half say some pagan things!"

Chapter 5

Luke was slightly unwell for the next few days, running a slight fever and coughing. His face seemed very red and Isobel, like a million mothers before her put it down to teething, but by the time Mickey's next day off came round, Luke had recovered completely and the whole family went to look at the rest of the houses on Matt's list. It had been disheartening at best; while one house had been pleasant enough, it had been too close to a railway line for Isobel's tastes, and the rest had just been overpriced for what they were.

"We can afford them, just," Isobel said on the way home. "But frankly I didn't like any of them enough to want to empty the pot for them."

"What do you want to do, then?" Mickey asked.

"I'd like you to come and have a look at the cheap cottage I looked at the other day," Isobel said. "It's a lovely setting; we'd have plenty of quiet there for holidays and it isn't too far from main roads so we could go out for the day if we wanted to. It's also cheap enough that we can buy it outright without worrying about a mortgage and I can use my savings for any work that needs doing."

Mickey said nothing for a while, thinking about it.

"You're pretty taken with it aren't you?" he said.

"It had character," she said. "And that couldn't be said about any of the others. And I reckon it's going for only about half of what they might get for it. Apparently they've lowered the price several times too, to try and get a sale. I could just see myself working there; the light was great."

"OK," he said cautiously. "I'll see if I can wangle tomorrow off too; can you ring that Matt guy and ask if he can take us round it tomorrow? Of course, it'll all depend on a decent survey. I bet something comes up with a proper survey that he hasn't been telling us about."

The following day they followed Matt up the lane to the cottage; he was seeming really quite excited about perhaps being on the brink of selling the company's white elephant, and Isobel was very amused by his attempt to stop himself going into salesman mode, since she'd made it quite clear there was a fair chance she'd just walk away if he tried that one on them. Mickey took a firm hold of Miranda's hand and kept that tight grip on her while they wandered from room to room, but it didn't seem to be needed. Miranda was unusually quiet and biddable, and Luke went straight to sleep in the sling, so that Mickey and Isobel could look round with almost no interruptions.

"Which room will be mine?" Miranda asked, when they went upstairs.

"Either of the two smaller ones, darling," Isobel said. "You can choose which. Big sister's privilege. If we do decide to buy this little house, we'll be coming here for holidays."

Miranda said nothing and just gazed around with huge eyes and an inscrutable expression.

"I like it," she said after a while. "Lots of fairies here."

"She means the tiny bits of dust dancing in the sunlight," Isobel explained to Matt whose eyebrows had been raised in silent query. "She calls those fairies. Mind you, she also calls dandelion seeds fairies and a good half dozen things besides."

"Kids, eh?" said Matt, awkwardly, with a slightly forced chuckle. "Such imaginations."

Miranda caught his patronising tone and looked at him very directly and said in a voice that sounded much older than two and a half,

"You mustn't laugh at me; the fairies don't like it."

"Sorry," said Matt, caught off guard. "I wasn't laughing at you."

Miranda looked hard at him.

"Yes you were," she said, crossly.

Matt shrugged and looked at Isobel and Mickey for assistance.

"She's got you there," Mickey said neutrally.

Matt looked at Isobel, who just grinned.

"How about if I gave you some chocolate?" he said, bending down to talk to Miranda. "Would that tell you I'm sorry?"

Miranda considered.

"Yes," she said happily. "Can I have it then?"

"It's in the car," said Matt.

"Are you going to get it then?"

Matt looked at Isobel helplessly, and conceded defeat silently and plodded despondently down the stairs and back to his car to retrieve the chocolate bar he'd put in to go with his flask of coffee. While he was gone, Isobel glanced at Mickey who had gone over to a window in the master bedroom and was gazing down at the tangled wilderness that was the garden.

"I reckon," he said. "I reckon that once we got rid of all the weeds, this'd be an easy garden to take care of. We'd just need to mow the grass every so often to stop the nettles and brambles coming back up. There aren't any real flowerbeds apart from the few right up next to the house; it'd be a woodland garden. I could maybe build a tree house for the kids."

He was apparently as taken with it as Isobel had been.

"There'll be loads of room for playing games out there; no neighbour's windows to get broken by cricket balls, no flowers to ruin," he said.

The garden at their vicarage had been planted up by a previous inhabitant with big flowerbeds full of roses and perennials and Isobel usually had trouble persuading Miranda that she mustn't pick the flowers, especially not the roses, after a number of sessions with the tweezers removing thorns from Miranda's hands and arms. Mickey had himself broken a neighbour's window a few weeks back while practising his bowling for the church cricket team. Clearly the chance of having space to muck about was as appealing to Mickey as much as it might to the children.

"So you like it then?" she asked, and he turned to her with a big grin.

"I love it," he said. "I just hope nothing horrible and expensive turns up with the survey."

"The only thing Matt said was a problem was other people have suggested it's a bit spooky," she said, and Mickey laughed.

"Spooky?" he said. "That's absurd. Cute little cottages in the country aren't spooky. Anyway, if there is a ghost, I know who to call."

"Yeah? Call the diocesan exorcist?"

"Nah. Ghostbusters!"

"I hate to tell you this, love and ruin your illusions, but that was just a film," Isobel said and Mickey was clutching his head theatrically in grief when Mat came back up with his chocolate bribe for Miranda.

"Is everything all right?" he demanded anxiously, obviously thinking that Mickey had been taken ill.

Mickey straightened up and grinned at him.

"Yes, everything's fine," he said, unabashed. "Just mucking about. I think you'll be pleased to know we are seriously thinking of taking this place. We'll just see what the survey says before we commit ourselves."

"Chocolate please," said Miranda imperiously, and a defeated Matt handed it over, and watched in puzzlement as she broke off the tiniest piece and laid it on the window ledge. She caught his baffled stare, and said, as if to an idiot,

"For the fairies. They like chocolate."

Matt looked at Isobel, eyebrows raised in silent query.

"I don't know where she gets this stuff from," she said. "She has a slightly older cousin, so maybe she tells her. I'm pretty sure we don't have any storybooks that say anything about fairies liking chocolate, but maybe she got it off the television. Just leave it; I reckon any mice will soon sniff it out."

But when they left the room to go back downstairs, Isobel changed her mind and went back to drop the fragment of chocolate out of the window, so that there was no excuse for mice to be charging around what she thought of as her new house. She stopped in puzzlement. The soft brown sliver had gone.

Oh well, maybe Miranda ate it after all, Isobel thought. You don't waste good chocolate; if I've taught my daughter anything it's the truly sacred nature of chocolate, and the sacrilege of wasting it.

*

The survey showed up nothing untoward and that clinched it; Mickey and Isobel decided to buy the house, and for the next few weeks, Isobel went round in a daze of shocked excitement until the formalities were over and then inwardly collapsed in a horrified reaction to spending so much money.

Mickey had been less concerned.

"Best place for the money," he said. "Property is always a good investment, whatever the market. You always have *something* to show for the money. What about if we go and camp there for our holiday? We can get a feel for what needs doing most urgently and ask around for someone local to clear the garden."

Isobel had to admit it was a good idea. Mickey's boss had school age children and had nabbed his summer break during the school holidays, leaving them with a fortnight at the tail end of September, not always the best time of year for camping. If they took the camping gear to the cottage, it would be a lot warmer and dryer to stay there, however basic the cottage still was, so she arranged for water and electric to be reconnected, though really that was little more than a few letters, and began planning their indoor camping trip with something like glee. Simon rang and asked what she wanted doing with all the stuff in his garage and that complicated the issue still further. In the end, he agreed to hire a van and driver and bring it all to the cottage for her and even help her unload.

"After all," he said. "I have high hopes that you might let us use the cottage for holidays sometimes so it's in my interest to keep you sweet."

"Cheeky sod!" said Isobel, amused. "Not that it isn't appreciated, mind. Why don't you and Katy and Jodie come too? There's enough room."

"Some of us have to work," Simon said. "I can manage a Saturday, though. But maybe we'll take you up on that for half term. I reckon I'll need a break by then."

He sounded so wistful that Isobel didn't know what to say.

"Yeah, whatever," she said eventually. "I'll email you some directions. It's a bit off the beaten track, so you'll need them."

"Sounds idyllic," he said and rang off.

"Idyllic," Isobel repeated to herself, thoughtfully. "Idyllic."

Maybe life was about to start to get that little bit easier, she thought, and went to air the sleeping bags and hunt out the camping pans.

*

Anyone who has ever gone camping with small children will know that you have to pack almost everything but the kitchen sink, and if you can find a collapsible, camping version of one, then bring that too. Their car was packed to bursting point and Isobel wondered how one extra baby could make such a huge difference to the payload, and they hadn't even packed the tent. It was the only thing they didn't actually need. Mickey had packed his tools, so that he could get on with some of the less demanding jobs.

"I hope you're going to be able to do some relaxing," Isobel said to him, but he just shrugged.

"When Simon turns up next Saturday with the three piece suite and all, and there's somewhere comfy to settle down for a few hours, I've got a damn good book I'm going to get read this holiday," he said. "Anyway, don't worry. No doorbell, no phone, no sermons; that's a holiday to me. I do quite enjoy pottering, you know."

The weather turned sour halfway there, and Isobel had a tiny smug smile at the thought that they were not going under canvas for a fortnight, with all the ensuing problems that entailed, of keeping Miranda occupied in wet weather, or simply of keeping their things dry and mud-free. The wet undergrowth gave off that spicy scent of approaching autumn and many of the trees they saw had begun to change colour, so that reds and russets and browns were sneaking into the green panorama.

At the cottage, Mickey got out of the car and opened the gate as wide as it would go and then shook his head, and went back to Isobel.

"I did wonder if we could get the car up close to the house but the weeds are stopping the gate opening properly," he said. "There's hard-standing under all that lot. Paving stones, I think. Once we've cleared it, we'll be able to park right next to the house. Come on, let's start getting stuff inside."

Isobel looked despondently at the unrelenting rain, and didn't move.

"At least we don't have to put up a tent in this," Mickey said. "If we get the kids' things in first, we can get them settled and then get on with the rest."

It took almost as long as setting up camp properly, and when the camping gas cooker had been set up on one of the rickety cupboards, Isobel thought longingly of tea.

"Damn," she said suddenly. "No bloody milk! I knew I'd forget something."

"We can have it black," Mickey said.

"Yes, but Miranda will need milk for bedtime, not to mention for the old Weetabix in the morning. And black tea makes me barf," Isobel said. "Look, I think there's a little shop in the village proper. I'll drive up and get some perishables like milk and bread, and maybe ask around if there's someone we can get in to clear the worst of the garden. It'd be good to at least have a bit of a look at what the neighbourhood is like."

Isobel reversed the car carefully down the lane rather than try to turn it in the narrow space between ditches, and drove slowly down to the heart of the village about half a mile away. There were a few small shops, and a garage, so she picked the bigger of the shops and went in. It was a small supermarket and while it didn't have the range of a city shop, it did have pretty much everything you might want by way of groceries. Feeling her spirits rise, she filled a basket with provisions and went to pay.

The woman at the till had been watching her.

"You wouldn't be the woman who bought Barrow Cottage, would you?" she asked, as she rang up the milk.

"I have just bought a cottage, yes," Isobel said. "But it's called Honeysuckle Cottage."

"That's what they called it," said the woman. "The people you bought it from. They gave it that name, on account of the honeysuckle that grows everywhere. But its real name is Barrow Cottage."

Isobel packed her shopping in her everlasting shopping bags made of woven hemp.

"Why's that then?" she asked, trying not to sound as curious as she was.

The woman laughed.

"On account of the barrow it's got in the back garden," she said. "I don't suppose you'd see it with all the weeds but it's there all right."

"It is pretty overgrown," Isobel admitted. "You don't happen to know of anyone we could get to come in and clear it? It's probably a bit much for us to do."

"There's a notice board over by the door with cards on," said the woman. "If I remember rightly, there's a few gardening contractors up there. Try one of them; they're all local lads, won't charge the earth for it."

Isobel drove home with the shopping and some telephone numbers scribbled on the back of a donated envelope, and told Mickey about what the woman had said while they waited for the kettle to boil. Miranda was in the main room playing and Luke was starting that funny grizzling sound that meant he was hungry but he'd give his mum a chance to at least have a sip of tea before he started crying properly.

"Why name a cottage after a wheelbarrow?" Mickey said, baffled. "That doesn't sound right to me."

Isobel shrugged.

"Nor to me, but that's what she said. Maybe it'll turn up when we clear the garden," she said and took a slurp of tea. "God, that's good. I thought that we'd ring these chaps later and see if there's any chance they might be able to fit us in while we're here rather than when we've gone home again."

"Good idea," Mickey said, and a wail from Luke made them both jump.

"I'd better feed him," Isobel said. "Stick the lid on my tea and I'll finish it in a minute."

Mickey came through with both mugs of tea and settled in one of their folding armchairs while Isobel fed Luke.

"I've found out how to turn the water heater on," he said. "But as there isn't any central heating, if it gets colder, I'm going to have to see if we can find coal from somewhere."

"There's a garage at the village," Isobel said. "They had sacks of coal outside. That'll do if we need it. I thought I'd try and get the kitchen clean first, and then the kids' room swept at least. What do you reckon we should do with the kids, though? I don't think we ought to leave her ladyship unattended for very long, not while the house isn't kiddy-proofed."

"If you're OK with being left with the scrubbing, I could take them both out for a walk for an hour or two," Mickey said. "Wellies and raincoats and the buggy for Luke. We'd have a great time. And that way maybe we'll get a good night's sleep if she's tired out."

"Sounds fine to me," Isobel said. "Somehow it doesn't feel like mine yet; maybe if I get bogged down with housework it will do. There's something so intimate about scrubbing a kitchen floor; best way to get to know a house, my mum used to say."

There! I've said it, I've mentioned my mum without either getting cross or getting upset, Isobel thought and grinned.

"Did you put the hot water on?" she said. "Because I reckon we're going to need plenty to get that hovel of a kitchen even half way clean and then some more to get me clean and de-ached later, never mind bath time for small people."

She shifted Luke from her breast and popped him down on the travel rug on the floor to make his usual swimming movements that were his attempts to crawl.

"Not long before he's off too," she said and retrieved her tea.

Isobel didn't consider herself a housewife except by default and had always maintained that only dull woman have immaculate houses. But today she scrubbed and rubbed and swilled and washed with a weird sense of enjoyment that her vicarage home never inspired in her when she was going about her chores there. She had to use a knife to chisel out ancient dried mud from between the stone flags of the floor; she wished she'd brought a stiff broom so she could have swept the worst to it away instead of the dustpan and brush she had remembered to bring. As she went along, she made a list of equipment she thought they'd need, as well as provisions they might get tomorrow. But by the time Mickey got back with a soaking wet Miranda and a sleeping baby, she'd made the kitchen a much better place and was well on her way to making the bedroom Miranda had chosen into a safer and cleaner place for a two and a half year old to spent her nights in. Mickey got Miranda some supper and spooned baby rice into a ravenous Luke while Isobel pumped up the single air-bed that was going to be Miranda's bed for the holiday.

"Mickey," she said, when he brought Miranda up to show her how her room was taking shape. "Do you think you could rig up something over the fireplace, so that there's no way we get hands up the chimney and soot everywhere?"

"I'll have a go," he said. "I can use some cardboard for the time being."

Miranda began her spinning dance, twirling round and round until she got dizzy.

"Can I have pink curtains?" she said. "Pink like my fairy dress?"

"Maybe," said Isobel. "But I don't think we'll bother with curtains just yet. Let the sunlight and moonlight and starlight in, eh? I bet the fairies would like that."

Miranda stopped spinning and gave her mother a hard stare, trying to assess whether she was being made fun of, and then began spinning again, until she fell over and began to cry.

"Sore!" she said, pointing at her reddened knees.

"I have told you not to spin and make yourself dizzy," Isobel said mildly, but picked her up and cuddled her anyway. "Now, how about a bath in the nice big bath downstairs?"

Miranda stopped crying as abruptly as she'd started.

"With the pink bubbly stuff?" Isobel suggested.

"Yay!" shrieked Miranda in a voice fit to melt earwax and Isobel trotted stiffly down the stairs to begin running a bath.

She discovered that she'd forgotten to pack Miranda's bubble bath and wondered how that would go down, so she let the bath run while she went back upstairs to ask if mummy's purple stuff would do.

"Pink is better," Miranda said, and then graciously added, "But the purple will do."

When Isobel got back to the bathroom, the water was still gushing out nice and hot and as she rummaged in her wash bag for the bottle of bath foam, she noticed that something was bobbing about in the water. She fished it out cautiously and saw that it was a strange little bundle of leafy twigs, twisted together to form a sort of green ball. It had the look of a curled up insect and she felt herself shudder involuntarily at the touch of it.

"I wonder where that came from," she said, and decided it must have fallen or blown into the bath when she'd had the window open earlier to get rid of the smell of bleach she'd sloshed down the loo.

She put it on the window ledge, intending to throw it out into the garden, as there wasn't a bin in the bathroom yet, and went to pour a smidgeon of her expensive scented essence into the water. Her hand seemed to slip and she put far more than she intended into the water, producing masses of bubbles and an overpowering scent of woodland violets.

"Oh well, we are on holiday," she said and resolved to buy more of Miranda's usual when they got to a proper supermarket and to treat herself to whatever was on offer.

Miranda and Luke played happily in the clouds of iridescent bubbles; Luke could sit up for himself now, and didn't need to be held the whole time, though obviously you didn't dare take your eyes of him for a second. When Mickey had taken Miranda up to her sleeping bag (pink!) and air-bed, Isobel took a little longer to stuff Luke into his sleeping suit, and she decided that she might be able to get a warm bath herself if she left the water and didn't take too long with Luke's bedtime feed. She could top the water up and ease some of her aches.

She was therefore very annoyed to find when she came back down to the bathroom that the plug had been pulled out and apart from a mountain of foam, the bath was empty.

"I didn't pull the plug," Mickey said when she accused him. "You must have done it yourself without thinking."

"I didn't," Isobel protested. "I deliberately didn't so I could use the water myself. Neither of them had wee'ed in the water, for a change so I thought I'd make good sound environmental use of the water."

"You must have caught your hand on the chain or something," he said. "Or else the plug doesn't fit properly and bobbed out."

Isobel shook her head.

"I'm sure I didn't," she said stubbornly.

"You must have done," Mickey said. "Anyway, let's get some tea ourselves. I'm starving."

After he left to go and start cooking some savoury rice, Isobel stared crossly at the bath and the twinkling lights of the dissolving foam. She went to throw out the bundle of twigs but it didn't seem to be there any more; it had probably fallen down and was lost in the shadows below the windowsill. Tomorrow she'd make a start on this bathroom, beyond the quick swill round the bath and cleaner down the loo. Now she thought about it, looking at the lime scale stains under the taps, she was quite glad she hadn't managed a bath herself; she'd have been staring at those marks the whole time and wishing she could get rid of them.

"Oh God," Isobel groaned. "I'm turning into my mother!"

Chapter 6

Isobel woke to brilliant sunlight streaming into the room through grimy panes; the air was cool but not cold and smelled of that glorious spicy smell of newly fallen leaves on the forest floor, before they get rained on and end up smelling of compost heaps. Luke was sleeping peacefully in his travel cot at the other end of the room, and next to her, Mickey was lying with his arms flung out, his long hair trailing across his face and across the pillows, snoring ever so softly. She sighed and wondered if she could manage to get to the loo without waking everyone. Not a chance, not with Miranda's bat-like hearing, not to mention the creaking floorboards of this place. Oh well, it wasn't that bad. She lay back to try and go back to sleep, and as she did so, she caught a trace of movement out of the corner of her eye from Luke's end of the room, fast movement, like a mouse or a spider. She raised herself up on her elbow and stared hard, trying to see what had moved and could see nothing. She'd had the same thing, late last night, sitting up with Mickey in the living room enjoying a glass of red wine. She'd turned and seen something move, but only at the very periphery of her vision, so that she was unsure if she'd seen anything. Mickey reckoned she was catching sight of the movement of her own hair.

"I find I think I'm seeing stuff, when I don't tie it back," he said. "I often see movement and it's only my hair."

"What if it is a mouse?" she asked.

"Hardly a huge problem. We can buy a few traps when we go to town, if that'll help," he said.

But now, lying in a sunlit bedroom, mice didn't seem such a concern at all, and she even felt slightly benevolent towards them, just as long as they didn't go in Luke's cot and wake him. She tucked her arms back into the sleeping bag, having tugged some of it back from Mickey, as the air in the room was cooler than she'd thought. Maybe one of the things they ought to get today was a couple of bags of coal, so that at least at night they could sit in front of a fire. It had been distinctly chilly last night, and she'd realised that had they gone camping properly, they would have needed better bags than the one-season cheapies they'd brought along this time. She closed her eyes and drifted back to sleep.

When she woke again, she was alone and the pungent aroma of frying bacon drifted into the room from below and she sniffed appreciatively. Coffee, too. I wonder, she thought, if I just stay here, will it find its own way up here? She didn't want to risk missing it, so she struggled out of the double sleeping bag and into her clothes and hurried down the stairs to the kitchen where Mickey was serving French toast to Miranda at the same time as spooning baby cereal into Luke. Bacon was sizzling and spitting in the pan and two mugs of coffee steamed gently without their lids.

"I was just about to nip up with your coffee," Mickey said. "Did you sleep well?"

Isobel picked up her mug and rammed on the anti-spill lid.

"Mostly," she said, taking an appreciative slurp. "Once I got used to the absolute absence of street-lights and traffic noise, I was fine. If it were ever this quiet at home, I'd wonder if the Rapture had happened and I'd been left behind, except I don't believe in that sort of thing. There was an owl too, that woke me up, I think. But other than that I slept great."

Mickey had sat Luke on one of their folding armchairs rather than at the folding picnic table, so that he couldn't fall over backwards, but Miranda was sitting at the table, an empty bowl that was smeared with the remains of cereal in front of her as well as the plate of French toast. Isobel sat down opposite her daughter, who didn't look up from tearing the small pieces into even smaller ones.

"You are going to eat that," Isobel said. It wasn't a question.

"I'm sharing it out," Miranda said. "These bits are for the fairies."

"I think the fairies have already had breakfast," Mickey said. "They eat at daybreak, you know."

Miranda looked scathingly at him.

"Then it must almost be lunchtime for them," she said with annoying but impeccable logic, but she did begin eating the toast, only leaving a few shreds on the side of her plate.

Mickey served up the bacon between himself and Isobel, and they enjoyed that true gourmet breakfast of bacon butties with brown sauce.

"I need to find a supermarket today," Isobel said. "We need a whole host of things I didn't pack, as well as food. It's just as well it isn't so hot now as it was a few weeks back, as there isn't a fridge for the milk and butter and stuff. I was thinking it might be worth buying an extra bucket and then we can put the milk in cold water and maybe get an extra day out of it. It'd make more room in the cool box, which is almost useless once the ice blocks have thawed. Funny how you take such things as fridges and freezers for granted."

"Whatever," said Mickey with his mouth full of bacon sandwich. "Then what?"

"Don't know yet," she said. "Probably more cleaning, but if it's as nice as this, it'd be a shame to waste it. Maybe we can have a look around and see what there is to see. Find an information centre. If we take the cool box, we can make sure any chilled food stays chilled."

"Have you made a list of what we need?"

"I did, but it doesn't seem to be where I left it," Isobel said. "I thought I left it on that cupboard. That's odd. My pen is still there, but the list is gone. Have you moved it?"

"Nope," said Mickey. "Haven't seen it either. Maybe Miranda has taken it to draw on?"

"If she had, we'd have seen it again complete with masterpiece," Isobel said cynically. "It must have blown away when the door opened. Damn, I bet I'll forget stuff. I'll make another one before we go."

They drove to the nearest town after breakfast and found the library open and collected a whole sheaf of information leaflets, and since the sun was still shining, they headed instead for a country park complete with stately home, calling at a superstore on the way back. When Isobel struggled into the kitchen with Luke under one arm and a lot of shopping, the first thing she saw was her list, lying on the floor near the door, with a muddy footprint on it.

"Will you look at that!" she said as Mickey came in with the bulk of the shopping. "We must have walked over it and never even saw it. Shows how stressed we've been, I reckon."

She parked Luke on the folding armchair and began unpacking the shopping, though there wasn't a lot of cupboard space. Miranda came into the kitchen clutching her bottle of pink bubble bath.

"Later," said Isobel before Miranda had a chance to say anything. "Go and put it in the bathroom and go and play in the living room."

Miranda wandered out singing to herself.

"I need a cup of tea before I do anything," she said and Mickey grinned, and put the kettle on.

They took Luke and his chair through to the living room where Miranda had built herself a nest with the spare blankets and her own sleeping bag and pillows and was curled up pretending to sleep, so they took the chairs down to the far end of the room, and sat with the French doors open. The green velvet curtains still lay where they'd fallen, and Isobel kicked them.

"I think when we've got some space out there, I think a bonfire would be in order," she said. "I don't think there's any chance of getting these clean without them falling apart. I was going to ring one of those numbers and see about getting some hatchet men in to clear the garden."

The breeze blowing into the room was cool, and few leaves skittered in with it, and Isobel sat happily drinking tea and cuddling her drowsy son, watching the trees swaying gently and listening to the soft whispering sound in the leaves.

"It's nice here," she said. "Beats the hell out of a damp camp-site in Wales."

"Yeah but you don't have to scrub out the bathroom in a Welsh camp-site," Mickey said, bursting her bubble somewhat. "You'd be asking for a refund if you had to do that."

"True," she conceded. "But at least we're dry here."

When she'd finished her tea, she put Luke down on the rug and left Mickey in charge while she went to try and clean the bathroom properly. She found that the so-called lime-scale remover did very little to remove the accumulations under the taps but an enormous amount of elbow grease and a scouring pad did the trick. The whole room took her till it was fully dark, and then she ran a pink bath for the children and went to have a shower while Mickey bathed them. She opened the shower door and saw that the bottom of the shower was full of water, dirty water at that.

"Oh God, Mickey, the shower's blocked," she called.

"That's why I brought a sink plunger," Mickey said. "I reckon the plumbing here is a bit odd. I reckon that's backwash from last night's bath."

Isobel dragged her clothes back on and went and rummaged through the toolbox until she found the sink plunger and returned to the bathroom and stepped barefoot into the foul water and located the drain and began vigorously pumping at it with the plunger. After a few fruitless minutes, there was a noise like a giant raspberry or worse and the water began to drain away. Lying at the edge of the drain was another bunch of twigs like the one she'd found in the bath, slightly larger this time, that had obviously been blocking the drain. She picked it up with distaste and tried to look at it closely, and she could see that it was woven loosely together rather like one of those arty garden ornaments made of spheres of woven willow wands. It stank of standing water and the leaves that remained on it had browned and had begun to decay.

"Yuck!" she said, and showed it to Mickey before chucking it out of the window. "That was what was blocking the shower. I wonder how it came to be there. It's too big to have come up the plughole so it must have blown in or something."

Mickey said nothing and carried on washing Miranda's hair, so Isobel stripped off and got into the shower.

"It is so good to be clean," she said five minutes later as she stepped out of the cubicle and wrapped herself in a towel. "Give me two minutes to get dressed and I'll take Luke up and feed him and put him in his cot."

Isobel curled up in her armchair and fed the warm sweet smelling baby before carrying him upstairs and tucking him warmly into his bed and then went and looked in on Miranda to say goodnight while Mickey was reading her a story. When Mickey came down to join her, she handed him a glass of wine.

"This is all right, this is," he said, toasting her. "Bit chilly though. I thought I'd shut those doors before we went through to the bathroom."

He got up and went to shut the French doors.

"They must have blown open," Isobel said.

Mickey examined the catch carefully.

"Must have done," he said. "If I didn't click it properly shut it would pop open quite easily. I'll bolt it now and then it's secure. Shall I light the fire?"

She thought about it for a moment.

"No," she said. "It'd take a while before we get the benefit anyway and I can think of a much better way to stay warm. Just wait till the kids are fully settled and I'll show you!"

"That sounds more fun than sweeping out the hearth and mucking about with matches," Mickey said and came and sat down in his chair. "It's a shame they don't make camping sofas."

"They do!" Isobel said. "I saw one at the camping show. Not a patch on the real thing, though. Just wait till Saturday. We'll be getting sofa and chairs to slob about on, not to mention a few other creature comforts. Simon did say he's bringing Katy and Jodie, so at least the Fairy Princess will have a friend to play with while we're all moving furniture."

She felt a sudden wash of sadness.

"It's going to be very odd seeing Mum and Dad's things here," she said, uncertainly, and Mickey came over and knelt at her feet.

"I know," he said. "But it won't be the same as having them at home. It'll look very different here."

She snuggled into his warm arms.

"I think the kids have gone to sleep," she said. "Drink up and we can go and get warm the fun way."

Chapter 7

By Saturday morning, the cottage was looking a hell of a lot cleaner, and the firm Isobel had called to clear the garden had been in and cleared the front, so that it was possible to park on the paving that had emerged. They had also put down weed-killer on the stumps of brambles and nettles that peeped up between the slabs, so at least there would be a substantial delay before they sprang back to life again. At nine o'clock, Isobel reversed their car up the lane and parked it on the main road so that the van Simon was bringing would be able to get as close to the house as possible. The contractors for the garden were supposed to be coming as well so she had no idea how they were going to fit both the removals van and the contractor's lorry on the cleared area in front of the house. Still, she didn't think it was her problem; it would sort itself out somehow. Things like that always did.

When Simon rolled up the lane, in his own car, she had a sudden pang of concern, before she saw the big Bedford van following him, and she ran down to greet them.

"I thought you were getting a proper van," she said, gesturing to the Bedford van.

"Hello to you too," said Simon. "I've had a hell of a job finding this place; we must have missed the turning to this lane three times. No, the guy at the hire place reckoned we didn't need anything more than a Bedford, so I've got Bill from school to drive it for me. You remember Bill?"

"Of course," said Isobel, racking her memory. "Physics teacher, yes?"

"Well done," said Simon. "The back of our car is packed with the small stuff that wouldn't fit in the van. It's all the stuff you said you wanted. This looks a pretty place. Very nice. Garden could do with a bit of work though."

"That's the other thing," said Isobel. "I've got some contractors coming in to make a start on the back. I'm not sure where you can all park so you won't be in each other's way. There's a bit of room at the front but not enough for two vans and a car."

It took some manoeuvring and a certain amount of subdued swearing to get Simon's car turned round so he could unload and then drive back down the lane to let the Bedford van park on the hard standing, and they were still easing the van up as close to the cottage as they could when the gardening contractors arrived. With a skill that astonished Isobel, herself a good driver, the driver managed to ease his van next to the Bedford, so that they could unload their machinery and wheel it round to the back. Simon had walked round to the back, while they were doing this, and had returned looking impressed.

"That's a lot of land back there," he said. "Pity we can't let the rug-rats out there just yet; Jodie could do with a good run around after the drive we've had."

It was a truly chaotic day, with people bumping into each other, furniture and tools being dropped, children being knocked over, and over all was the sound of the heavy-duty strimmer to set everyone's teeth on edge. The smell of trampled undergrowth filled the air and bits of leaf and twig somehow got everywhere. The van seemed as though it would never be empty; every time Isobel went in to lift something else out, it didn't seem as though they'd touched it. Then suddenly it was empty but for a rolled up rug. It came as a slight shock that after all the lifting and shoving and adjusting there was nothing left to unload. Isobel made tea for Bill first as he was in a hurry to get home, and when he'd gone, went and sat down in the living room with her brother and sister in law.

"Where are the kids?" she said, suddenly noticing their absence.

"Mickey took them out for a walk," Katy said. "As soon as the van was empty, he went."

"I'll make us some tea then," Isobel said, and got up. Simon had stretched out on the sofa and looked very much as if he were about to go to sleep. Katy got up and came with her.

"It's a nice cottage," she said, when they were in the kitchen. "Be a bit lonely up here in the winter though, I'd think."

"Probably," Isobel said. "But I'm only expecting to be here a day at a time, maybe not even stay the night, during the winter, if at all. There's no heating except open fires, so I'm not expecting to spend a lot of time here at a stretch during the winter."

"So you are going to come up here to paint, then?" Katy asked.

"It was the general idea, yes," Isobel agreed. "Miranda is starting play group as soon as there's a space. She should have got a place at the start of September, but you know how it is. When she does go, I'll have a few hours a week with only Luke, and he's a lot less hassle than she is. I'm intending to stop breastfeeding soon, so when I do, I can at least leave him with Mickey when I need to get work finished. But I am hoping that maybe one day a month I can come here and get on with work."

"I think it'd do you good," Katy said. "You need that sort of time, sometimes."

Isobel kept silent for a minute, debating with herself.

"Sometimes," she said. "Sometimes I just want to run away from it all: the phone, the doorbell, the kids, Mickey. I never seem to have a minute to think, let alone paint. The usual stuff is just about manageable, but the real work takes more than just standing and transferring an image from photos to canvas. The real stuff comes out of me, and sometimes I just don't think there's enough of me to be able to stick any of it down in paint. I'm really tired, Katy and I don't mean just from broken nights and that sort of thing. I'm deep down, bone weary exhausted. I keep feeling scared I've sort of dried up inside, that the inspiration has gone. I don't know who I am any more."

Katy said nothing and busied herself with cups and tea bags.

"You're the same as you always were," she said, finally. "There's just a lot more baggage than there was. You've got to learn how to translate that into images."

Isobel rubbed her eyes that were suddenly wet.

"I know," she said, helplessly. "I just don't know how to do it."

"Give it time," Katy said. "I think it's great you've bought this place. I think it's got real atmosphere, and once you've settled into a routine, I think you'll find everything changes."

Isobel shrugged and made the tea.

"You're probably right," she said, and gave Katy a rather watery grin. "You'd better wake Simon; he was always scary to wake when we were kids."

"He still is; sits bolt upright like something from the Curse of the Mummy," Katy said. "I usually yell from a distance."

She went into the hall and called,

"Tea, Simon?"

A moment later, making them jump, the gardener stuck his head through the open front door, and asked,

"Was someone offering tea?"

Isobel came through.

"We've only got three cups," she said. "If you wait ten minutes, I'll make you some when we've had ours."

"OK," he said and wandered off again.

"Actually, it isn't quite true," Isobel said to Katy as she brought through the tea to the living room. "We've now got Mum's mugs, but I'd forgotten about them for the moment. Still, ten minutes won't hurt, and I'd rather they had the unbreakable camping mugs out in the garden."

When Mickey got back with the children, Isobel went out into the back garden and gazed at the devastation. There were a number of bonfires smoking away and a huge swathe had been cut through the matted undergrowth, but there was a lot to go still. The older of the two contractors, the father by the looks of him, came over and grinned at her.

"It'll look worse before it looks better," he said.

"I'm sure it will," she said. "I was wondering if you'd found any sign of a barrow. Someone in the village told me this used to be called Barrow Cottage on account of a wheelbarrow in the garden."

He laughed, startling her.

"Wrong sort of barrow, love," he said. "There's your barrow, over there."

He waved a dirty hand over towards the tree-covered mound at the end of the garden.

"I don't know whether it's really a barrow at all," he said. "But that's what people have always reckoned it is. Now, did you offer tea earlier, because we're about parched just now?"

"Yes, yes, of course," Isobel said, dazed. "Milk? Sugar?"

She went back into the house, so preoccupied by what he'd said that she didn't hear Simon asking her if she'd seen his car keys till he'd asked her twice.

"I put them down on the mantelpiece, I'm sure of it," he said, patting at all his pockets frantically. "I was wanting to get off just now, and now I can't find my bloody keys."

"Does Katy have spare set?" Isobel asked.

"Well, yes but that isn't the point," he snapped.

"We'll all have a proper look for them," Isobel said soothingly.

She poked around in the kitchen while she made tea for the gardeners but couldn't find Simon's keys anywhere, and by the time she got back into the house after delivering the tea, Simon was getting more annoyed by the minute.

"For goodness' sake, Si, get a grip," Isobel said. "Just go; I'll send them on if they turn up."

He gave an exasperated sigh and gave up looking.

"I hate it when this happens," he said.

At the car while Katy strapped a tired and grumpy Jodie into her car seat, Isobel felt an uncharacteristic urge to hug her brother. He stiffened and then relaxed when she did so.

"Thanks ever so much for helping with this, Si," she said. "And thank Bill for me. If you could get him a bottle of whatever is his favourite tipple, I'll pay you back."

Simon laughed.

"And what's my reward?" he asked.

"Virtue is its own reward," Isobel said. "You can come and use this place for the odd holiday, if you like. Thanks. I'll see you all soon?"

"I think we might come over to you for Christmas," Simon said. "Boxing Day anyway. OK, take care."

He got into the car and drove off, Isobel watching the lights in the deepening dusk until she lost sight of them, and then walked back up the lane to the cottage. Mickey came to meet her at the door.

"Have they gone?" he said. "Because I just found his keys. They must have fallen off the mantelpiece and onto the hearth. Funny how we all missed them."

"Yeah, very funny," said Isobel, not amused. "I checked all over the hearth, you know. I wonder if one of the girls had hold of them and dropped them back there once the fuss was over. Oh well, I'll pop them in the post for him tomorrow."

As they were standing at the door, both the gardeners came round, hefting tools.

"I've left the mugs by the French doors," said the older one. "Nice cuppa. Thanks. We'll be back Monday, but we're getting there, we're getting there. I reckon you're going to need to reseed if you want grass. I can give you a good deal on grass seed if you fancy it."

"I'll see what it all looks like when the scrub has been cleared," Isobel said. "I want to keep costs down as much as possible."

"Cheapest way to get a lawn is by seed," he said. "If you aren't in too much of a hurry that is. If you are in a hurry, I can get you a good deal on turf, as long as you don't want a bowling green. It'll cost more than seeding it, obviously."

"Seed is probably the best bet," she said. "But let's just see how much grass is under that lot."

He gave a snort that might have been amusement and then again it might have been disgust.

"Right you are," he said. "But I can tell you now there isn't a lot of grass there at all."

Isobel shrugged.

"See you Monday," she said. "And thanks for working so late."

"No problem, missus," he said, and they too were off.

Inside the cottage, the air felt cold and smelled of wood-smoke and greenery.

"Let's get a fire lit and we can at least be warm when we've had supper," Isobel suggested.

In the living room, the hearth had been swept clean of ashes and bird bones, and it took her about twenty minutes to get the fire lit, scorching her fingers twice with matches, and getting her hands filthy into the bargain. Miranda came and stood behind her to watch, not saying a word; sometimes her sense of self-preservation told her when a running commentary was not the best of ideas.

"You're not to go near the fire," Isobel said once she'd got it lit and had put the funny little guard over it. It was only there to stop any coals or sparks flying out into the room and certainly had no value as a child safety device as it wasn't secured in any way.

"No, mummy," said Miranda, calmly, the picture of obedience.

Isobel went through to the bathroom to scrub her hands clean of coal dust and newsprint from the papers she'd used to try and get the fire started. The air in the bathroom was icy and she went to shut the window. Maybe I should light the fire in here too, so it's warmer for bath-time, she thought.

Miranda was sitting a judicious distance from the fire, which had caught properly and was blazing away nicely. She had her doll in her lap and she was singing to it, a wordless croon that Isobel could barely hear.

"Are you hungry, sweetheart?" Isobel asked.

"Yes, mummy," said Miranda.

"Let's get you some supper then, and then you can have a nice bath and get to bed," Isobel said. "You must be tired after playing with Jodie all day."

Miranda shrugged, which just showed how tired she must be, as she usually only needed the slightest provocation to launch into endless chatter. Isobel took her through to the kitchen where Mickey was spooning slop into Luke, who was sitting with his mouth open, very like a baby bird.

"Baked beans on toast all right?" Isobel asked and Miranda nodded.

Once her daughter's dinner was on the table, Isobel slipped away to try and get the fire in the bathroom lit, and was astounded to find that the window was still open.
"I could have sworn I shut that," she said, and slammed the window shut, taking care that the catch had fastened properly before laying the fire and setting a match to it. Once it was going, well, at least the fire-lighters and newspapers were blazing away merrily, she began running the bath, tipping in the dreadful pink bubble bath and leaving it to run.
When both children were asleep, Isobel sat on the hearth rug and gazed into the coals of the living room fire.
"I found the barrow," she said, as Mickey came in with hot chocolate.
"Oh yes?"
"It's the other sort of barrow," she said. "It's that mound thing at the bottom of the garden, not a wheel barrow at all. I don't know if it really is a burial mound or not. Perhaps it's just local folklore. It didn't say anything about it on the deeds; there isn't a preservation order or anything mentioned anywhere. I would have thought it would be mentioned if it really were a proper barrow."
"Maybe not," Mickey said, kneeling down next to her and putting her mug on the hearth. "Sometimes that sort of thing is ignored altogether. There are huge numbers of unrecognised sites, I reckon, just waiting for someone to discover them. Just because this one hasn't been documented doesn't mean it isn't genuine. A lot were ploughed out in previous centuries, either because no one knew or no one cared. Look at the sort of stuff that happened to places like Avebury: stones pulled down and broken up for building. That mound looks as if it's had trees growing there for a long time; they look big old trees. Once the gardeners have got a bit closer we can have a proper look. There's nothing we could do with that end of the garden even if we wanted to; trees that big should be left alone, in my opinion. There are too few of them left."
Isobel picked up her mug and inhaled deeply, and then sighed in contentment.
"I think one thing I may do when I've saved up enough is to have double glazing put in," she said. "I keep fastening windows and they keep popping open again; I reckon the catches are shot."
"I'll have look at them tomorrow," he said. "Those French doors need to be bolted every time. I've found they seem to spring open again if I don't bolt them. With the weather getting cooler, I don't want to waste heat if windows are opening themselves because of faulty catches."
Isobel sipped her drink, warming her hands round the sides of the mug.
"It's going to be funny sleeping in Mum and Dad's bed," she said. "I'm glad we're still in sleeping bags though. It would be really weird with a proper duvet. I don't think I'm going to leave any bedding here over the winter, in case it gets damp."
"Probably a good idea," Mickey said. "Until we get some sort of rudimentary central heating in here, it is going to be consistently cold here, especially if we aren't staying

here that often. If you're here every few weeks, at least that'll mean you can keep an eye on things. It's probably a good idea to have those gardeners come along every fortnight in the summer to cut the grass, unless you want to buy another mower and leave it here and cut the grass yourself."

"Not a chance, mate," Isobel said. "I cut the grass at home, and that's enough. No, I don't mind paying someone else to do the hard work here; I don't think there's anywhere to store a mower here anyway, and it'd cost a fair bit to get one big enough to cope with all that land. Overall, probably best to pay them to do it. Only problem is making sure they actually do it and don't try and fleece us. I suppose if I let them know when I'm coming they can at least make sure it's done before I arrive each time. Maybe I can sort out a way of payment that means they have to see me to get paid. I'll have to think about it. Right, I think I'm ready for bed. What about you?"

"I'll just finish this and I'll be up," Mickey said.

Isobel struggled to her feet; her back and arms were hurting from all the lifting and carrying and she was so tired she could scarcely keep her eyes open. Bed was possibly the nicest place in the world she could think of right now.

She was the first to wake the next morning; she woke cold and shivery and headed downstairs to put the kettle on to try and warm up. When she got to the foot of the stairs she had a slight sense of shock to see the front door standing wide open, dead leaves and small twigs swirling around the smooth stones just inside the threshold as a brisk breeze banged the door softly against the wall behind it. No wonder the house was so chilly, she thought and went to shut the door. It obviously hadn't shut properly last night, she said to herself and went to make tea.

Chapter 8

Back then; back to the dull reality of life as mum to two small and demanding children. Back to the incessant ringing of the telephone, to the continuous ringing of the doorbell and the never ending round of housework. Back to falling into bed each night so damned exhausted that all she could think of was sleep and what she hadn't managed to get done that day. Back, in fact, to her life as it had become.

"Where did I go?" she asked her reflection most mornings as she went through her truncated beauty routine, that most days consisted of running a comb through her damp hair, rubbing her face with moisturiser and cleaning her teeth.

One small mercy though; a place had become available at the local playgroup so Miranda had three mornings a week to go and wear out someone other than her mother.

The first morning, Miranda had run in without so much as a backwards glance and Isobel had sauntered off whistling the tune from The Great Escape, breaking off mid-bar when she saw one of her acquaintances leaning against the door-frame sobbing inconsolably.

"What's the matter, Emma? Are you OK?" Isobel asked, concerned.

Emma looked up and rubbed her eyes. She was a little older than Isobel and today she looked it; there were lines around her eyes that surely hadn't been there last week.

"I'm fine," she said, hopelessly. "It's just... This is Sam's first morning."

She broke off, looking appealingly at Isobel, obviously hoping she would understand without the necessity of long-winded explanations. Isobel felt suddenly horribly guilty and hoped Emma hadn't heard what she'd been whistling.

"It's OK," she said. "Sometimes it's tough to let go. Especially the first time. But you know, they do still need us. That isn't going to stop. This is just for a few hours a week."

"I know," said Emma. "But then it'll be nursery and then school and then..."

She tailed off, tears welling up in her eyes again. Isobel felt helpless and actually rather irritated; she wanted to get home and get on with some painting while Luke had his morning nap but she knew she couldn't just walk away. Emma was really hurting, even if she couldn't quite get her own head round why.

"Come on," she said, and took Emma's arm firmly. "You're coming home with me. There isn't much in life that can't be improved by a nice cappuccino and a plate of chocolate Hob Nobs. I'll even let you push the buggy!"

It became clear that half the reason for Emma's tears was the simple fact that her son Sam was likely to remain an only child; they'd had to resort to IVF to get him and there was no way they could afford a second try. So Emma was pouring a huge amount of her hopes and energies into her one lamb. Isobel felt guilty again and had to remind herself that she had struggled against the odds herself, having thought at one time she would never have a child, when one miscarriage after another had carried away her hopes.

Miranda had been the child she'd never thought to see, named because she was in effect simply something to be wondered at, and given thanks for. At home, Isobel made them both coffee with frothy milk and shook out a generous amount of chocolate biscuits onto a plate.

Emma wasn't a churchgoer and was gazing round the vicarage living room in some anxiety but could apparently see nothing to alarm her. She smiled damply at Isobel as she brought in the coffee.

"This is nice," she said, gesturing to the room. "I've never been in a vicarage before. You never struck me as being very religious."

"I'm not," said Isobel, sitting down. "One is enough in any family. Mickey does for both of us."

"But your little boy has a Biblical name, though," Emma said, cautiously.

"Only by accident," Isobel said. "It's a bit silly, really. Miranda was called that because it means to be wondered at, but Luke got his name because I misheard the midwife."

"Sorry?"

"It's a silly story," Isobel said. "But for some obscure reason, my second labour was much harder than the first, and when the baby was finally born I nearly passed out with tiredness. I had a midwife with a strong Northern accent and she sort of held the baby up to me and said, "It's a boy: look!" But her accent made it sound like she'd said Luke, so I thought, oh, that's a good name, how clever of her. By the time I realised what had happened, he was Luke. I told you it was silly!"

"It's a nice name," Emma said, obviously relaxing now it turned out Isobel wasn't really religious at all.

It was a pleasant couple of hours, certainly, but Isobel couldn't help feeling a twinge of resentment as they walked back up the road to the playgroup to collect their children. Like so many mothers who had put their careers on ice or even abandoned them altogether, Emma seemed to be living through her child, hence her grief when he made his first forays into the world without her. Isobel had never felt like that about her children.

She took care not to get drawn into the cycle of going always to someone's house while the children were at playgroup or having someone come home with her; there was plenty of time outside those precious few hours to do the mother and toddler type socialising. Those few hours went far too fast as it was and she always craved more time. Luke began crawling early in November, which meant that she was no longer able to rely on him staying put when awake, so her sessions while Miranda was at playgroup ceased to be reliably free for her to paint. If Luke was awake, he needed supervision. Only for a few minutes at a time was it possible for him to be entertained by toys in front of him; he'd quickly decide that something further off was of far greater interest and would crawl off to investigate. It did mean that he was fully tired come bedtime and he slept better but she suddenly had no opportunity to get on with work during the day. She took to trying to get work done after they'd both gone to bed, but if she really got into her stride it was sometimes three in the morning before she'd collapse into bed and three hours sleep was only enough when you're eighteen and used to it. She found her mind wandering when she was doing those repetitive tasks that so grind you down; wandering back to the cottage, and she realised she was craving solitude the way some people might crave drugs or alcohol and she herself sometimes craved chocolate.

"It's no good, Mickey," she said finally. "I'll have to go and have a day at the cottage. I've got commissions to finish before Christmas."

He looked at her in some amusement.

"I thought that was mostly why we'd got the cottage," he said. "I was wondering when you'd be going back."

"I'm a wimp," she said. "I don't like the idea of how cold it's likely to be. And I'd hoped I might have been able to get on better at home with Miranda going to playgroup but that hasn't quite worked out as expected. And I've been putting off weaning Luke. The amount of calories I've been expending feeding him comes to quite a lot of Hob Nobs, you know and I don't like the thought of dieting."

Isobel was lucky and had a fast metabolism that meant she rarely put on weight and lost it easily, but it had taken her months to lose the weight she'd put on carrying Luke.

"Look, why don't you head down there next day off," Mickey suggested. "If you get Luke down to just a bedtime feed, you can be home for that. Set off nice and early and you can have a whole day to get on with what you need to get done. It'll be nice to have the kids to myself."

"Fibber," Isobel said, but she smiled. "If I've got the car, you won't be able to go anywhere much."

"That isn't a problem," he said. "The park is only a short walk away. Will you do it?"

Much to her own surprise, Isobel burst into tears.

"I feel so guilty," she wailed.

"Guilty? Why?" Mickey said, holding her against him.

"Because I wanted the kids so much and sometimes I can't wait to get away from them," she said, sniffing. "Some of the other mums are so much more devoted than I am and I keep thinking of that portrait I did for the lady whose grandson had died and I think, what would I do if I lost them?"

Mickey pushed her hair away from her eyes; she was in need of a haircut, he thought, or else she was growing it.

"It's only natural to feel like you need some space," he said. "I know you love them. You don't have to smother them in soggy affection to show that. Some of your pals are living through their kids, you know, and I'd hate for you to be doing that. You're an artist; that's who you were when I met you and it hasn't changed. It's got harder for you, but that's still what you are inside and if you don't go and do something with it, you're going to end up climbing the walls. Or painting them maybe."

She blew her nose on his hanky and smiled grimly up at him.

"You're right of course," she said. "How'd you get to be such a clever bugger anyway?"

"Hard, devoted work," he said. "Not to mention natural talent and eating my greens. Now, I suggest you either go and have a haircut or else let me lend you one of my bobbles so you can tie that hair back. You're starting to look like a Shetland pony."

She snorted in derision at that but took him at his word and made an appointment at the hairdressers for the day after, and when she came back, Luke burst into screams when he saw her and Miranda looked at her sternly.

"You've cut off all your hair, Mummy," she said. It was obviously the cardinal sin; Miranda craved hair long enough to sit on and was continuously frustrated in this desire by the slowness of growth, not to mention the fact that sometimes Isobel had to cut bits off when they got so tangled that it seemed far kinder to just get the knots out the easy way than make Miranda sit still for minutes at a time to ease them out.

She'd asked the hairdresser to cut her hair really short, so that for the first time in years her ears were on show. None of the piercing scars showed any more. She'd also had the hairdresser henna her remaining hair a deep coppery chestnut colour that seemed to restore her eyes to their original colour. Now they seemed to be once more that vibrant shade that seemed to match the Baltic amber beads that Mickey had bought her for Christmas, though he didn't say this in case he gave away the surprise.

"It looks wonderful," he said.

Miranda sniffed.

"Fairy princesses have golden hair down to here," she said, gesturing to her bottom.

"They might," said Isobel. "But I'm certainly not going to. I went blonde once when I was fifteen and I looked like a freak."

Miranda just stared at her and then ran off. Mickey grinned.

"You'll never convince her," he said.

"I don't like to tell her that she's never going to be blonde unless it comes out of a bottle," Isobel said. "At least this isn't very far from my real colour."

"It looks wonderful," he said again, and nuzzled into it. "It really suits you; your face has a lot more colour and your eyes are glowing."

She buried her face in his chest and sighed.

"I'll go tomorrow," she said. "If you can manage without me, that is?"

"What can be so hard about having two small children for the day?" he said, sarcastically and was rewarded by a sharp kick to the shins.

*

Isobel rose at five, in the pitch darkness of a winter morning that made her shiver almost uncontrollably from a mixture of guilty glee and frost. The heating hadn't yet come on for the morning so the bathroom was icy as she showered and when she sneaked out to the car, crystals of ice sparkled on the roof and windscreen and made the pavement slippery. She had packed the car the night before so that her comings and goings were less likely to disturb the family as she got ready to go, but she had heard Miranda's sleepy voice as she had padded down the stairs carrying her shoes, and had ignored her, hoping she would just assume from the darkness that Mummy was going for a drink of water and go back to sleep. She didn't like to think how tired Mickey would be if Miranda got up at half past five, because it tended to mean that she would go straight through and wake Luke and then there was no going back. But as she started the sluggish engine, she glanced back at the house and sighed with relief that no lights had come on.

The roads were not as deserted as she had expected, forgetting the numbers of people on early shifts, night workers clocking off, and later in the journey, milk lorries and the like. She even had to stop once to let a herd of cows cross the road on their way to be milked. She also had to drive more slowly than she would have liked as the grit lorries had not been out the previous night, a frost of this severity not being forecast and she shivered in anticipation of how cold the cottage was going to be, after six weeks without so much as a coal lit in any of the hearths. She'd packed an extra jumper and one of the heavy duty sleeping bags so that she might nap if she needed to, but even so, all she could think about was getting that living room fire lit while she made herself her jump-start morning coffee.

As the lanes narrowed, she found herself getting more and more excited, almost as though she were going to meet a lover, not going to work for the day. She couldn't wait to see what the cottage looked like again after these weeks away, or how the garden seemed now that the gardeners had finished the clearance as they had assured her on the phone the other day. Maybe today she would actually get a chance to have a proper look at that mound.

When she pulled up in front of the gate, she was red-faced from the car's heater blasting warm air at her, and she shuddered with the shock of the cold air when she got out to open the gate. The paving stones were white with frost and ice had formed on the small puddles still present from the rain the day before, making black circles on the whitened surface. She unlocked the front door and hurried in to light the fires before bringing in her canvases and equipment. There were dead leaves on the stones of the hall floor that must have blown in as they left the day their holiday ended, and a smell filled the house, not of leaves or sap this time but that curious insubstantial fragrance that made her think of snow on the ground and evergreens.

There was soot on the hearth when she went into the living room, as though a bird or something had tumbled down the chimney, but there was no soot elsewhere so she assumed that soot had simply detached itself and fallen down, splattering out onto the hearth. She had swept the grate clean the day they had left, but she had set no fire ready so she had to fumble with cold fingers to set out coal and fire-lighters and it took several tries with matches to get one to stay alight long enough to infect the slabby whiteness of the fire-lighter with tiny tongues of flame. She went through and lit the camping stove they'd left behind and put the kettle on and hunted out the cafetière from the now dusty welsh dresser. She had brought milk with her and fresh coffee and while the kettle began to steam she went back to the car to unload.

She dumped her easel and canvases on the sofa and took her bag with provisions through to the kitchen where the kettle had begun to whistle softly and she joined in for a moment, again whistling the tune from The Great Escape. A big grin was tickling the corners of her mouth and after trying guiltily to suppress it she let it split her face and she let out a chortle of anticipation.

A whole day, to get on with what she wanted to do; no nappies, no cooking, no laundry, no telephone and best of all, no bloody doorbell. She made coffee and took it through to the living room where the fire was starting to catch properly and the faintest traces of warmth began to steal across the room. She set her coffee down on the mantelpiece and set about putting up her easel at the far end of the room by the French doors, and then sat down to enjoy her coffee while the fire crackled and roared into life. This is the life, she thought, enjoying the heat of the coffee through the thin walls of the mug. I wish I'd brought some biscuits, though.

She started work as soon as she'd finished her coffee, finding her focus within moments of starting. She rarely got the chance to just go at it without interruptions and it was some hours before she became aware of certain discomforts that when she stopped to assess them she managed to name as a very full bladder and a totally empty stomach and plummeting blood sugar levels. Sticking her brush in a jar of water, she trotted off to the bathroom to deal with the first and then to the kitchen to deal with the rest.

She had packed half a loaf of bread and a packet of bacon, and she was touched to find that at the bottom of her food bag, Mickey had put a packet of chocolate biscuits; not Hob Nobs, but chocolate coated ginger biscuits, which had to be her absolute favourite of all time, hard to find and usually so prohibitively expensive they were an occasional treat only. While the bacon spat and sizzled in the pan, she munched three, crunching them down with great care and was still chewing on the bit of ginger that always seemed to get stuck in her teeth when she remembered she'd promised to phone home and let Mickey know she'd got there safely.

The answer phone took the call, which must mean he was either out or so tied up he couldn't get to the phone, or else, since it was his day off, he was avoiding answering the phone at all.

She ate her bacon sandwiches with greedy speed, washed the grease from her hands and went back to her easel. She only stopped again when she realised she was freezing cold and her hands were trembling. The fire had burned down to embers glowing in the ashes and the room was colder than she'd thought it could be. When she looked up, she saw why. The French doors had slipped open and she'd been so involved with her work she hadn't even noticed. She went and fastened them again, making sure she slid the bolts firmly into place and went to coax the fire back into life. It took another cup of coffee and the rest of the biscuits before she felt warm again. She'd finished though, all the paintings she'd promised to have done for Christmas, and she wasn't sure she remembered the last time she'd worked that fast, or that well. It would take a few hours before the paint was dry enough for her to move them, so she washed her brushes and sat down to think what to do. She could start another painting but she had no more commission work with her, only her sketch book and pencils, seldom used these days. She washed up her lunch plate and the bacon pan and thought about what to do next. She couldn't go home yet, not for a while, and somehow she didn't want to. The near-perfect quiet of this place was soothing and her memory of the noise of her home did not inspire her.

I'll have a walk around the garden, she decided, have a look at that mound for myself.

She fetched her extra jumper and coat and opened the back door; the day was drawing on towards dark, but the last threads of pale sunlight were streaming through the trees as the rooks headed home overhead, calling to one another in their rough resonant voices. The ground was rough, scarred by machinery and studded here and there with the stumps of saplings cut off at ground level. It really had been on the brink of reverting entirely back to woodland, the young scrub trees had been starting to outgrow the brambles and nettles, and there was hardly any grass to be seen now the scrub had all been cleared. Maybe it would be worth seeding it after all. That was a job for the spring, though. She stumbled a few times over uneven ground and bits of wood as she made her way over to the end of the garden and the surprisingly large mound. The boundary of the garden was made up on barbed wire fence on chestnut palings that leaned drunkenly in places and had fallen over entirely in others, and was there simply to stop the incursion of cattle or sheep from the neighbouring farmland, but no livestock were to be seen today and she suspected that the cattle at least would be in for the winter now.

Arriving at the mound, she was struck not only by the size of it but also of the size of the trees that covered it. Mickey had commented they were large old trees, but she hadn't taken it in herself, not really. The sheer size of the trees was not readily seen from the house, but here, up close, she had a small lurch of shock. They weren't just large, they were massive, silver skinned beeches for the most part with a few rougher barked oaks, their roots spreading out like gigantic serpents to get a grip on the stony soil of the mound. She hesitated, almost unable to make that first tentative step, as if it were somehow irrevocable to set foot on the frozen earth.

She took a deep breath, though she couldn't have said why, and bounded up onto the hillock and reached the summit at a run. The trees stood very tall and silent around her, their trunks like the legs of unimaginably huge elephants. The ground was frozen hard, and there were dead leaves scattered thickly all around that rustled when she moved, sounding like distant voices on the very edge of hearing. She could still hear the rooks, but they had moved off to a far away copse. Somehow she had thought they would roost here, but as she gazed up through the naked branches she couldn't see a single nest or roosting bird and the air seemed very still as though the breeze she had noticed earlier simply didn't reach these trees. She found the remains of a tree stump, covered with buff and bronze leaves and sat down, cautiously, expecting to feel damp seeping through her jeans. She was feeling very strange, almost as if she were in a church waiting for something to happen. But nothing did. She continued to sit, and gazed around her at the silent trees and the carpet of dead leaves, feeling that weird sense of expectation growing stronger. It was almost like that awkward pause at a gathering or party where no one can think of the right thing to say, and so, no one says anything at all.

A wood pigeon clattered suddenly in one of the trees near the mound, startling Isobel to awareness of the increasing chill and the deepening of the blue of the sky. She glanced at her watch; she was shocked to find she must have been sitting here for a good half an hour without realising it. The sky was a slate blue, and the faintest tremor of a star could be seen trying to twinkle bravely above her. She remembered she had intended to count the trees, but somehow it didn't matter any more, and she went on sitting until her mobile began vibrating in her pocket. With a sigh, she answered it.

"How's it going?" asked Mickey. "I got your message but I thought I'd just let you get on."

Isobel got up from her stump and began walking off the mound, kicking away leaves covered with the first lacing of the frost that was forming.

"It's gone really well," she said. "I'm going to clear up and head home just now, though. There's a heavy frost starting to fall already and I'd rather be on my way before the roads get totally frozen. It's pretty cold in the cottage, as you'd expect but I've managed to keep the chill at bay, mostly. I'll see you in a few hours."

At the back door, she turned and glanced back; the boles of the trees seemed to gleam silver in the light of the moon she could now see rising, and she hurried in to make the place secure for the duration. The fire had died down to a few tired embers, so she poured water on them to make them safe, and a great tar-smelling steam rose into the room and then was sucked back up the chimney. She wrapped the precious canvases up in bubble wrap and stowed them in the car before washing and drying her cup and the cafetière and making sure everything was locked and bolted before shouldering her bags and heading towards the front door. As she turned to say a silent farewell to her haven, she saw a tiny movement out of the corner of her eye. She turned back to look properly and saw that it was just a small twig covered with dead leaves moving in the draught from the door, so she stepped out of the door and shut and locked it carefully behind her.

As she drove home, strange images floated in front of her inner eye, of trees with roots that burrowed down through the stones and soil into great empty caverns, filled with silence and years and memories.

"Concentrate, you moron," she snarled to herself as she narrowly missed a car coming the other way, having drifted into the centre of the road. "This is no time to go daydreaming."

The roads were not especially busy but they were beginning to be slippery and she was relieved to get home with no serious incident beyond skidding in a near complete circle at one junction. She knew she'd been lucky she had been the only one at the junction and no one had been coming the other way, but even so, she'd been sweating when she regained control of the car. When she got home, Miranda careered into her arms shrieking with delight that her mummy was home and Luke, slower but no less enthusiastic, crawled into her lap and began tugging at her shirt.

Mickey grinned at her, his own relief and delight as evident all over his face.

"Shall I unload the car?" he said. "I thought we'd have fish and chips for supper; I'm too tired to think about cooking and I bet you are too."

"Good thinking, Batman," Isobel said.

He paused in the doorway, and glanced back at her. She looked somehow different, as if she had been away far longer than one day, and her cheeks were pink with the change in temperature.

"I've missed you," he said. "I don't know how you cope with these two every day."

"Nor do I," she said, grinning back. "But today has been great. I can't remember when I got so much done in one day; I'm not even sure I used to get so much done before children."

When Mickey had unloaded the car, Isobel took the canvases upstairs to the spare room and unwrapped them.

"They're brilliant," Mickey said after a few moments silent assessment. "You obviously need the space to work well."

Isobel gazed critically at the row of paintings. They seemed to have a flavour of otherness that she hadn't seen before; for bog standard portraits from photos, they seemed to have a lot more life and vibrancy than usual.

"I am pleased," she said cautiously. "I've had some ideas though for proper paintings, and I think I'll go up again after Christmas and see what I can do with them. I have some ideas I might sketch, though."

Later that evening, the children in bed and the house smelling of vinegar from their fish supper, Isobel settled with pencils and sketch book to try and capture the images that had so distracted her on the drive home. After an hour of frustration, she put the book down and sighed.

"It's gone," she said, as Mickey looked up from his book. "I've lost it. I'm going to bed."

She lay in bed, trying to remember what she'd seen in her mind and the images that had filled her mind like a waking dream and like a dream that dissolves in the sunlight and activity of a new morning, the images were gone, leaving her with the faintest of uncomfortable memories and a few threads of meaning that disappeared the second she tried to seize them, and in her mind was the scent of fallen snow and frozen evergreens.

Chapter 9

The smell of snow stayed in her mind like a persistent virus until the first of the real snow fell in early January, timid flakes more like icy scurf than real snow that merely peppered the pavements and lay like tatty lace on rooftops, and got Miranda appallingly over-excited at the prospect of making snowmen and going sledding.

"Bloody television," Isobel said under her breath as she watched her child try to scrape up every scrap of snow that had fallen in their back garden and failing to gather enough to make anything more than a muddy snowball studded with bits of twig and dead grass. "Come in, love," she called. "There's not enough fallen yet for that."

Miranda stayed out till her hands turned a shade of blue that outdid the colour of her nose and Isobel felt guilty for not simply scooping her up and bringing her in anyway. The tears of a tantrum couldn't possibly have been as bad as the tears and screams from the pain of warming hands and feet and face.

"Terrible twos," she said to Mickey when he came out of his study to see what the noise was about. "Not to mention self-inflicted frostbite as a side effect."

The weather turned wet and windy, effectively trapping Isobel at home until the school term started and the local playgroup also opened up again. One morning, with Miranda at playgroup and Luke asleep upstairs, Isobel realised the anniversary of her parents' death had passed her by and she had not remembered it at all.

"I must be getting over it," she said to Mickey that evening. "I just sat down and started drawing and forgot all about it again."

She didn't show him what she'd been drawing though. While the scent of snow had faded and vanished with the arrival of the real thing, the images that had haunted her on the drive back from the cottage had returned, but this time vivid enough to startle her into trying to capture them with a pencil. The monstrous trees, their roots like tentacles gripping the earth and plunging down into it, probing and piercing the mound below filled her pages like some sort of medieval bestiary illuminations and when she began to fill the images with colour from pencils, they sprang to startling and disturbing life. There was something fleshy about the texture of the bark, and something oddly watchful about each tree, as though it had eyes that were turned away. She didn't show Mickey what she had been drawing because she had a sense that the images were still incomplete and she felt unusually protective of them, as though they were unborn children. They might still miscarry or yet be stillborn and it felt kinder to keep them concealed in her mind-womb until they might be born successfully.

Christmas had passed in a frenzy of food and guests and chaos and now the decorations were finally down and forgotten, she began to feel bereft, and berated herself for it.

"I don't even like Christmas much," she said to Mickey when he asked what was wrong. "But this year I'm stupidly sad it's over and done with for another year. It was fun having Simon and Katy and Jodie here for Boxing day, but it felt as if something was missing, and I can't think what."

Mickey said nothing. It seemed pointless to point out that what had been missing had been her parents, when she was so determined to deny that she was missing them at all.

"Why don't you go and have another day at the cottage?" he suggested. "It'd do you good."

"I do have one or two commissions I could be getting on with," she said, thoughtfully. "But nothing pressing. I suppose I could go and maybe try and see if I can do some of the other stuff."

"Other stuff" Mickey knew to be her paintings that bordered on the surreal, or visionary even. She had done very little since Miranda had been born, her energy taken up with first one baby and then another, and it was more than three years since her last exhibition. The website she'd had done for her brought in a steady stream of commissions, but nearly all of them were for the portraits that she were her bread and butter staples. Only a very few had enquired after her other work, and that usually after a specific piece she had already created; only the woman who'd asked her to combine images for the portrait of her dead grandson had even mentioned her less conventional work.

"OK," she said finally. "I'll go in a couple of weeks, if you're happy with that. I could do with some space, really."

It was a bit of an understatement. She'd found herself somehow inundated with visitors, many of them women she knew as a result of the children, and some of them people from Mickey's congregation, but nonetheless, she'd found there was a constant stream of people coming to the house for any one of a dozen reasons. It wasn't that she didn't enjoy the company, or appreciate that the children enjoyed the company. It wasn't even that she minded taking messages for Mickey or making tea for his visitors, or any of it. It was more that at the end of the day, when she was cleaning her teeth or sorting laundry or whatever tasks were needing doing by the finish of the day, she found herself dimly aware there had been something she'd been meaning to do, something important and now she couldn't even remember what it had been. Her thoughts had been broken in on by the doorbell or the phone or by a crying child or some domestic crisis, and now she couldn't recapture what she'd been thinking about. It was immensely frustrating, not least because she couldn't even begin to explain to anyone what she felt because she couldn't even explain it to herself, or justify why her thoughts had such a value that to disturb them might be such a problem. It was very like one of those mornings where you wake from a powerful dream that has such meaning that it might just change your whole life. Yet by mid-morning the pressure of the day has driven the dream and its power away leaving you with a few shreds of memory and a sense of feeling foolish for having been so seduced by a mere dream that blew away once the world was awake.

*

Isobel reached the cottage on the first day off Mickey had in February, and unlocked the door with that same furtive excited anticipation she'd felt on the earlier trip. She was met by a stench of decay that made her retch and choke until she had to step back into the garden and take a number of deep breaths. She tied her scarf over her nose and mouth and plunged back inside in search of the source of the terrible smell.

It didn't take long. Lying half on and half off the hearth was a rotting mess of feathers and maggot-infested flesh that had been a rook; the splatter of soot around the hearth and the floor around it showed how the bird had got there, but she could see no sign of how the bird had died, though in all honesty she couldn't bring herself to look terribly closely at the writhing mass of maggots. The bird looked as if it may have broken its neck falling down the chimney but that seemed somehow unlikely, but she could see no other possible cause of death. If it had been trapped here and had starved, then surely there would be feathers against the windowpanes, droppings and soot everywhere.

She fetched a plastic bag from the kitchen and managed to scoop up the horrid mass of heaving feathers and took it outside. There were no gardening tools here, so she fetched the little coal shovel and somehow managed to scrape a hole deep enough to put the remains in and cover it with loose soil and leaves; that would be at least enough to get rid of the sight and the smell of it.

In the bathroom she ran some water into the sink and scrubbed obsessively at her hands, before going to clear up what remained by the fireplace and light the fire. With the windows open, the smell dissipated fairly quickly and by the time the fire was giving off any appreciable heat, the stench had been blown away by the brisk wind that filled the room with the scent of approaching rain. I am definitely going to bring some joss sticks next time, she thought, closing the windows and doors again and rubbing her hands together in an attempt to warm them. A brisk walk in the garden seemed in order while the room warmed up, so she set up her easel and headed out into the garden to be buffeted by the rising wind.

The trees on the mound seemed much as they had before and it occurred to her that while for her the weeks had seemed long, to the trees, those weeks would have been more like a few hours in their long lives. She reckoned some of the largest must be hundreds of years old, and wished she had a means of reckoning their age; she'd heard that every inch of trunk circumference equalled approximately a year, but then she'd also heard this didn't work for some species of tree as the growth rate of individual species varied so wildly that such a general rule could not hope but give a hopelessly confusing result. There were a few oaks mixed in among the beeches, their trunks less awesomely massive but huge nonetheless.

She sat down on her stump and tilted her head so that she could look at the grey sky through the bare branches. The wind whipping through the high branches made them clash together like the antlers of battling stags. A few leaves skittered about her feet, rattling mournfully as if for attention and she glanced down. A twig fell and caught her on the shoulder and as the first of the rain began to fall, she decided that sitting out here in both a rising gale and pouring rain was unlikely to be good for either her health or her inspiration, and she got up and ran back to the cottage.

In some annoyance she found that the living room was still icy cold because the French doors had burst open with the wind, and had toppled her easel, which had leaves blowing over the watercolour board she'd fixed on it. She stared at the board, her eyes hardly seeing what was really there, before righting the easel and slamming shut the doors, ramming home the bolts really firmly.

She'd chosen to use watercolours as a deliberate move away from her usual acrylics, partly because she needed to use something that would dry quite quickly, and partly because she craved the kind of translucency that was impossible with either acrylics or the more inconvenient oils. The images that haunted her were misty and insubstantial and while they had a kind of vibrancy, it was not one of solidity. What she saw in her head was not concrete, steadfast or definable; it shifted like the leaves of a gale-tossed tree, refusing to be pinned down and nailed to a moment in time and space. She drew out her pencils, selecting the softer ones, but wishing she had thought to buy more charcoal as her one remaining piece would last all of about three minutes.

She took a deep breath, almost as if she were going to dive into deep water, and began sketching, half-closing her eyes the better to see the images in her head. From time to time, she glanced up and out the window at the trees waving in the wild wind; the light in their naked silvery branches seemed to be brighter than anywhere else on this grey, dreary day.

It was the headache that finally drew her to a halt; pounding insistently at her forehead and temples until she dropped her pencil, and straightened up after retrieving it to clutch at her head in sudden surprised pain.

She swore, in irritation and pain. I shouldn't be surprised, she thought, I haven't had so much as a sniff of coffee today, I was bound to get withdrawal symptoms before too long. But she was annoyed enough to resent stopping and reluctantly went to put the kettle on. When she came back through to drink the resulting brew, she assessed the preliminary sketch and wondered how she could put colour to this tangle of lines that would have meant little or nothing to anyone else gazing at it.

She began again while the mug was still warm, and the fragrance of the coffee still filled the room. For the translucency, she used regular watercolours, and to get those touches of vivid vibrancy, she used watercolour pencils and the darkness of her softest pencils.

The light was beginning to change before she stopped again, almost in pain from her bladder and still in discomfort from the headache. She looked up at the sky through the window and saw the dark clouds scudding rapidly across the sky, like sheep running from the sheepdog, and realised the daylight was almost gone. She went to the bathroom and when she'd been to the loo, she splashed her aching head with cold water and groaned with the shock of the chill on her hot forehead. There's no way I'm going to be able to drive safely with this bad a headache, she thought. I'd better have a lie down for an hour or so before setting off.

She went through to the living room and gazed at the painting with reluctant satisfaction. The finished product rarely ever lived up to the inner vision that had inspired it but she'd come a lot closer today than she sometimes did. She'd managed to capture some of the feeling of mystery and wonder about the trees and the mound, and also some of that shivery feeling of almost-fear; the roots had an organic but sinister look about them as they snaked down between rocks and wove themselves into the very fabric of the mound that she'd tried to create. It probably didn't have anything much to do with the real mound, barrow or not, that lay at the bottom of the garden, but it was a real attempt to recreate on paper her own feelings about the mound. The ground below the trees in her picture had a dark and empty look about it, suggesting empty rooms, echoing caves and a dim sense of the forgotten past; there were half seen hints of something that might have been treasure gleaming golden in the shadows, and even less well defined images that might have been bones, but then again might also have been rocks and roots and yet more shadows. She'd painted an entrance to the barrow that wasn't really there, a dark passage way lined with rocks and held up with tree roots like a rabbit's burrow, and the whole thing showed the interior of the mound as well as the exterior, but not as some cutaway diagram in a child's book. It looked more like a visionary's view, showing the inside and the outside without a barrier between the two realities to help orientate the viewer. Isobel felt suddenly rather drunk looking at it, and a bit sick; it was a bit like how she felt when viewing those weird drawings by Escher, where your brain got boggled by trying to see how a floor became a ceiling, and tried to work out which way was really up and which way was down.

"Bugger that," said Isobel and grabbed her sleeping bag and burrowed into it before stretching out on the sofa, tucking one of the musty-smelling cushions under her aching head.

As she closed her eyes in some relief, she thought she saw movement at the French windows but decided it must have been a leaf or something whipping past in the wind, and she fell asleep with surprising speed considering the pain she had been in a few moments previously.

It was some hours before she woke, and only then because her mobile woke her. Mickey had called to see how she was getting on, but it was just as well since she had been so deeply asleep she reckoned later she might not have woken till very late that night.

"I had a headache," she said. "I'm going to set off shortly, though."

"Is your head all right now?" he asked.

She moved it experimentally; a faint ache still lurked at the back of her neck but beyond that she was fine.

"Yes," she said. "Mostly fine, anyway. I'll get packed up and then I'll be on my way."

"I've missed you," he said, softly. "Did it go well?"

"I think so," she said, and her uncertainty seemed not to go unnoticed.

"You only think so?" he said.

"It's a bit, well, different," she said, struggling to free herself from the sleeping bag. "You'll see what I mean when I get home. I'll see you later."

She gazed around the room when she'd rung off; the only light was from the final embers of the fire, glowing like small reddish eyes in the hearth. She got up and turned on the light, banishing the shadows that seemed to fill every corner, but making the view beyond the window suddenly invisible. The wind was still high, gusting at the house and when she went out to the car with her wrapped painting, it tried to wrench the board from her hands.

"This is going to be fun," she said once she'd locked up and left the house.

All along the lane, trees were creaking dreadfully as the wind threw them this way and that and the lane was littered with fallen branches, some of them alarmingly large. As she turned off the lane and onto the road proper, a small branch thudded down onto the roof of her car, making her jump, and the rest of the drive was no better. When she finally got home, to find Luke screaming for her, she was exhausted. There had been whole trees come down on her route home; she'd once had to come to a screaming halt barely in time when she had come round a bend to find a large branch blocking the road. With the help of the man in the car behind her, she'd managed to drag it off the road, but now she was safe home, she felt more than a little frayed round the edges. She fed the frantic Luke and put him sleeping into his cot while Mickey unloaded the car for her. Miranda was already fast asleep.

"I was pretty worried about you when it took so long," Mickey said when she came downstairs. "The news was full of reports of falling trees and pylons and so on. I thought about ringing you and telling you to stay put but when I did ring, your phone was off."

"I had to get home for Luke," she said. "Mind you, he's nearly bitten my nipples off, so I think I'm calling this a day soon. He's a year old; I've given him six months longer than I originally intended and I'm not going to turn into one of those women who only wean the kids when they finally go to school."

"Can I see what you did today?" he asked, eagerly and silently Isobel unwrapped the board and held it up for him to inspect.

He was silent long enough for her to become uneasy.

"Don't you like it?" she asked.

"I'm not sure I understand it enough to like or dislike," he said, thoughtfully. "It's amazing but you must admit it is a bit, well, disturbing."

She shrugged, and said nothing.

"Well, it is," he said defensively. "I mean, have you had a proper look at it?"

"What do you mean, have I had a look at it? I painted the bloody thing, I've been looking at it all day," she said crossly.

"Have a good long look at it now," Mickey said. "Now you've had a bit of time to detach from it. Look at the shape of the mound and the way you've got the interior showing as well as the exterior. What does it look like now?"

Isobel stared at the painting for some minutes, blankly, until with a reeling sense of shock that she had not seen it before, she finally saw what Mickey was trying to show her. Even though it hadn't been at all what she'd painted, she could see now that the entrance to the tunnel and the shadowy depiction of the cavern inside had the look of great hollow eye sockets, and the bare pale frost covered surface of the mound had the look of ancient bone, weathered and scarred by time. With growing horror, Isobel saw that what she had painted had the look of a skull, an ancient flensed head, crowned with monstrous trees that writhed and wriggled their roots down into the skull like burrowing maggots or worms.

Chapter 10

Easter came with a sudden burst of unseasonally warm weather, the sun like that of June, though the nights were still cold enough to pinch any new growth on tender plants, and Mickey had managed to get the week after Easter day as some of his official leave, so they headed off to the cottage straight after the service, stopping only at their local supermarket for supplies. Isobel drowsed in the car, musing on the whole Easter story. The word Golgotha had dredged up her shock at the painting; her surprise that she had unwittingly painted such a terrible image had made her hide the painting at the back of a stack of canvases she'd been saving for her next exhibition, but even so, she had mentally named the painting The Place of The Skull, and tried to forget it had been created.

Both children snoozed on the journey, at least once they'd eaten the sausage rolls Isobel had passed to them after their stop at Sainsbury's, though she suspected that much of Miranda's had ended up being passed to Luke. Luke had begun walking, and as a result of his extra activity he seemed to be eating like never before and she was very glad she had stopped breastfeeding him; watching him devour a bread bun was enough to make her shudder now.

"Nearly there," Mickey said, waking her with a touch to her arm. "It looks like we might get decent weather this time."

Isobel nodded and rubbed her eyes. The bare countryside had begun to put on green growth, but not enough yet to cover hedges or woodlands with anything more than the faintest veil of green, and the ploughed fields looked like chocolate icing still. She wondered if there were any bulbs showing yet in the cottage garden, as she had seen a few tentative spears of green. At home, the snowdrops were fading and the early daffodils were open and rank upon rank of green buds waited their turn. Mickey got out and opened the gate and then eased the car onto the paving.

"We're here! We're here!" Miranda shrieked and tugged at the restraining harness of her car seat.

"Anyone would think it was Disneyland," Isobel said cynically but her own excitement was growing too as she undid her own safety belt and slid out of the car.

The usual chaos ensued for the next hour or so as they tried to unload the car without losing sight of either child or for that matter knocking one of them flying as she and Mickey tried to carry in all their belongings in as few journeys as possible, and it was only when they'd got everything sorted and the kettle on that Isobel managed to assess how the cottage seemed after her absence. There was a dispiriting amount of dust, and the inevitable spider in the bath, but other than that, it seemed much as it had done. She was relieved there was no dead bird to deal with this time, and was pleased when she wandered out into the garden to see that all across an expanse that had been bare and pitted with stumps and twigs new growth of grass showed through, tender and fine as baby hair. She wouldn't have to pay to have it reseeded then; obviously there had been far more grass lying under the scrub than the gardener had thought and now the spring was here, it was shooting up with new vigour.

"Shall we have a look at the barrow then?" Mickey said, coming up behind her with both children and making her jump.

Luke toddled resolutely at her side while Miranda ran on ahead, whooping with all the energy of a child who has been cooped up in a car for hours. Mickey caught her spare hand and they meandered across the greening expanse that might one day be termed a lawn.

At the foot of the mound, Mickey stepped back in amazement; Miranda just hurtled onto the mound and began throwing handfuls of leaves into the air.

"It's an awful lot bigger than I thought," Mickey said. "Those trees are stupendous."

"That's one word for it," Isobel said, wryly and followed her daughter onto the mound. "Don't do that, darling."

"Why?" Miranda demanded, not stopping.

"Because you're getting dirt in your hair," Isobel said. "And that means a hair wash later."

Miranda narrowed her eyes as she thought about this; she had decided she hated having her hair washed at all, but found that attitude cut no ice with her mother, who carried on just the same. A compromise was eventually decided upon by Mickey who ruled that she only needed to have her hair washed if it really was dirty, so as a result Miranda insisted on having a scarf over her hair if she was doing anything remotely mucky, and she had become far neater eating her morning cereal than she previously had been. Isobel still insisted on regular hair washing but if Miranda didn't get it visibly dirty, it only got washed once a week.

Having thought about it, Miranda dropped the handfuls she'd been holding and ran off down the other side, and then proceeded to run round the perimeter of the mound until she flopped into her mother's lap, panting. Isobel had settled on her stump and was gazing up at the buds high above her that were beginning to unfurl like tiny flags. Mickey was walking slowly from tree to tree, touching each trunk almost reverently, and Luke, unconcerned about forthcoming ablutions was flinging handfuls of half rotted leaves into the air where he sat and watching them falling around him like clouds of confetti, and then seizing them again and repeating the performance with as much glee as the first time.

"I reckon I could rig up a swing on one of these tree branches," Mickey said. "If I can get hold of a ladder, that branch over there would be perfect. Put in a couple of metal staples or rings, and then rig the ropes from there."

Isobel said nothing but a sudden, inexplicable chill ran down her spine at these words. There wasn't a lot of point saying anything because the chances were it might be years before Mickey actually got round to doing it.

"I think the kids are a bit little for that yet," she said after some consideration. "Maybe it'd be worth it in a few years time, when they're older."

He nodded absently and continued to prowl around the trees, thoughtfully touching the trunks. After a while, and only when Miranda had finished running round madly, he came and sat down on the ground next to them.

"It's getting cold," he said, suddenly, and Isobel could see he was shivering.

"It is still only April," she replied. "Come on, let's go and get the fire lit and get some supper on to cook. Daylight's going fast."

That evening Isobel wished they had managed to put up curtains in the main living room. Once the children were in bed and asleep, she found herself staring frequently at the black emptiness of the windows, and fancying she could see things moving out in the garden.

"It's either your imagination or the trees moving their branches," Mickey said when she'd got up to go and peer through the glass for the eighth time. "We don't even have any neighbours to speak of, we're off the main road, so who or what do you imagine might be in the garden?"

He sounded more than a little irritated.

"I don't know," she said, exasperated by her own jumpiness. "A fox, maybe. Or deer. I reckon we probably get both through the garden. I'd like to see them if they do."

He seemed to accept her answer though it wasn't entirely true. She wasn't at all sure what she was looking for, but the blank glass drew her eyes nonetheless.

"Tomorrow we'll have look through that heap of curtains from your parent's house that Katy brought along and see if any of them will do for these windows," Mickey said. "You're too used to towns, love. You could wander round this house naked and no one would ever be near enough to see."

Isobel let out a squawk of laughter.

"Don't try this at home," she giggled and peeled off her shirt and bra and then the rest of her clothes.

Mickey stared at her first in amusement then catching her mood, shed his own clothes and chased her round the fire-lit room until he caught her, tripped her up and carried her to the sofa.

"You Tarzan, me Jane," she gasped, half hysterical with laughter.

"That's funny, I could have sworn your name was Isobel," Mickey said and dropped her onto the cushions and fell on her.

Later, dressed again and warm with lust, Isobel crawled around on the floor, patting the rug carefully as she did so.

"What's the matter?" he asked.

"I can't find my pendant," she said, plaintively. "It came off when I took my shirt off and now I can't find it at all."

"Which one was it?"

"That bit of amethyst set in silver, you know," she said. "Polished purple stone in a Celtic knot setting. I expect it'll turn up in the morning when I can see properly. You can never find anything at night. Glass of wine?"

"Yes, please," Mickey said, appreciatively. "I assume that means you want me to get it?"

"If you would," she said, continuing to search on the floor. "I got two bottles of red, since we don't have a fridge to chill any white, though I suppose we could just leave a bottle outside and that'd chill it a fair bit."

She topped up the fire while he went to open the wine, and turned on the lights, hoping to see her pendant glittering on the hearth or further away from the sofa, but she saw nothing, though her eyes were continually being drawn by the blackness beyond the windows. This is being silly, she told herself, there's nothing out there but trees and maybe deer and the odd fox or two. So why am I gazing out there like I'm expecting to see a mad axe-man heading this way?

"Wine, madam," Mickey said, handing her a glass and brandished the bottle at her in mockery of the obsequious wine waiter.

"A very fine year," she said, in her best BBC accent and held out her glass for him to fill. "Seriously though, I think you're right about putting up some curtains. I am far too much of a townie still to be able to relax with bare windows and not worry that someone will be able to see in. I dare say I'd not care if we lived here all the time."

She eased herself back onto the rumpled cushions of the sofa and drew up her feet and tucked her long skirt around them, wishing she'd brought her sheepskin slippers. The stone floors downstairs were icy to bare feet, which would be wonderful when the temperature soared in the summertime but now as a light frost was forming outside, she decided she'd have to make do with woolly socks. Mickey flopped onto the sofa next to her, slopping his wine over his hand.

"I'm shattered," he said.

"You're getting old," she teased him. "Next thing, you'll be cutting off that ponytail and getting a blue rinse instead."

"I think one of us with artificially enhanced hair is probably enough for the parish," he said. "They sort of ignore that fact that I've got long hair. Though I wonder if they just excuse it because Jesus is always depicted with a hippy hairstyle, so they reckon it must be all right. I'm not sure I'd get away with dyeing my hair."

Something in the way he said it made her bristle defensively and she took great pains not to let her anxiety overwhelm her voice.

"Has someone said something to you about my hair, then?" she asked.

He shrugged, looking suddenly uneasy and a bit shifty.

"One or two comments," he said, neutrally.

I can just imagine, she thought bitterly but bit her lip.

"I don't suppose they realise it has to cut both ways," she said in a careful voice. "They were pleased enough to have a new vicar juvenile enough to have a young family; surely they must accept that if we're young enough for kiddies, we're young enough for a host of other things."

He sighed, obviously wishing he'd not said anything.

"It was only one or two of the real old guard," he said. "They aren't anything to worry about. I don't think anyone else has even noticed you've coloured you hair. Just forget it, love. They probably don't approve of anything past nineteen twenty, anyway."

Isobel ground her teeth in silent annoyance, and then sipped at her wine.

"I don't really care," she said. "It isn't as if it matters anyway."

She snuggled next to him, burrowing her hands under his heavy sweater to try and get her hands warm.

"Get off," he said, laughing. "Your hands are like bloody ice."

"I know," she said, holding onto him. "That's why I'm trying to get them warm."

He struggled and then gave up, letting her place her hands on his stomach.

"What shall we do tomorrow?" he asked. "Are you going to paint?"

"I don't know," she said. "It depends how I feel."

She hadn't said to him how much she had been unsettled by what she had painted last time she was here, and she wasn't sure how much he had guessed.

"We could go out for a picnic or something," he suggested. "If the weather holds, that is. Or we could just stay here and maybe do a bit around the house or the garden. I brought a few garden tools, just secateurs and hand tools. Some of the little borders right next to the house need some work. That's not too bad; if we prune and feed up that rose round the door, it'll give some lovely flowers, I reckon."

"Yes, good idea," she said, hardly listening any more, but leaning her head on his chest so she could hear the drumming of his heart.

"I think we can take it in turns to mind the children," he said. "If we stay in the house, that won't be a problem at all."

She closed her eyes.

"No, that's fine," she said, sleepily.

"You're not listening to me, are you?" he asked and she lifted her head and looked at him reproachfully.

"Not really, no," she said. "Let's go to bed."

"What a good idea," he said, draining his glass and setting it down on the floor. "Come on then, Jane. The tree-house awaits us."

With some difficulty, he scooped her up and staggered to the door, where he lowered her to the ground again.

"They make that look so easy in films," he said. "Can you just pretend I've swept you off your feet and carried you up to my lair?"

Isobel smiled.

"I've got a good imagination," she said.
"That sounds promising!"
"Just one question, though?"
"Yes: what?"
"Who the hell is Jane?"

*

Isobel woke in a pleasing tangle of limbs and gently extricated her own from Mickey's and lay back to gaze round at the sunlight that filled the room. Luke had been banished to the other bedroom, and so far no noise emerged either from his room or Miranda's, so Isobel stretched and turned over to slide back into sleep. As her head touched the pillow, her cheek touched something cold and hard, and she sat up abruptly to have a look. She stared in stunned wonder at her pendant, the purple stone gleaming in the bright morning light. It must have been round my neck all the time, she thought, and saw that the cord was indeed undone, as if she had been wearing it all night and the knot had gradually come unravelled. Well, there you are, she told herself, sometimes you can look in all the wrong places. She heard the murmur of voices and knew that both children were now awake; she heard faint footsteps running along the landing and then Luke's voice rose more loudly as clearly Miranda opened his door and went in.

So much for a lie-in, she said to herself and wriggled out of the double sleeping bag without disturbing Mickey, dragged on her dressing gown and went to investigate. When she got to Luke's room, she was surprised to find him alone, standing up in his travel cot, swinging from side to side.

"Where's Miranda?" she asked him and he just smiled at her toothily.

It wasn't a big room and there really wasn't anywhere to hide so she left Luke for a moment and padded down the landing to Miranda's room, and cautiously opened the door. Miranda lay sprawled out on her bed, clearly fast asleep, that faint pink bloom of deep sleep across her face. She shut the door again very quietly and stood silently pondering.

"It must have been the boards snapping back into place that sounded like footsteps," she said to Mickey at breakfast. "Old houses are like that; all sorts of funny noises and things."

"What about the voices?" Mickey asked.

"It did sound like both kids," she admitted. "But then that was what I was expecting, I guess, so I must have heard it like that and it was really only Luke chattering to himself."

Mickey nodded, his mouth too full of toast to comment.

"I suppose so," he said eventually. "If you're expecting something, that tends to be what you hear or see."

Isobel didn't add that she had no idea how the door came to open the way it had; she presumed it was simply the result of another faulty catch and a stray breeze.

They headed out into the garden after breakfast, and spent the morning doing not very much beyond desultory pruning of the shrubs that grew next to the house. Time and again, Isobel found herself gazing at the mound, as she played ball with the children, and wondered yet again if it was a real barrow at all. They had an early lunch, the fresh air apparently giving them all a huge appetite, and spent the next hour or so sorting through the neatly folded heaps of curtains that Katy had crammed into the boot of their car when they'd come with the furniture. Much to Isobel's surprise, she found some suitable for every window that urgently needed them, even if the ones she found for the living room trailed on the floor when she managed to hang them. I'll take them up one day, she told herself and then forgot all about it as Miranda rushed in wearing as a huge cloak the deep magenta pink curtains they'd selected for her room. She was wearing on her head a wreath made of twisted ivy.

"I'm a fairy princess," she squealed. "Look at my crown!"

Isobel looked at the wreath. It had been made by simply twisting a spray of ivy back on itself and tucking the ends in.

"Did Daddy make it for you, sweetheart?" Isobel asked, and Miranda looked at her with faint contempt.

"No," she said. "The fairies left it for me."

Isobel shrugged and said nothing; Mickey must have made it from the ivy he'd snipped away from the wall near the kitchen and left it for Miranda.

"Let's go and get those curtains hung," she said, and was met by wails of anger.

"No!" said Miranda firmly. "This is my cloak; I can fly with it."

Isobel just ignored her and got on with fixing the curtains first in Luke's room and then in her own, and once Miranda had discarded the curtains because they were too hot and cumbersome, she hung them too. Her throat was full of dust from the curtains and when she got back downstairs, Mickey was making some tea.

"Both the kids look fit to drop," he said. "I thought they might have a nap. What do you think?"

"We can but try," Isobel said, and much to their shock, both children went to sleep with almost no protest. The bedrooms were in newly created twilight from the curtains, which were heavy duty ones that excluded a great deal of light, and the afternoon was warm.

"I think I might join them," Mickey said when the silence from upstairs had become sufficiently profound.

"I don't think I will," Isobel said. "I think I might go and have a walk, explore the area a bit. I'm sure there must be a river at the bottom of this valley. I'll head that way."

"We must get a map soon," Mickey said, sleepily as he stretched out on the sofa. "Have a good walk, love. Take your mobile in case you get lost."

"The cheek of it!" Isobel said, and went to put on her boots with an eagerness that surprised even her.

The sun was golden and warm, and she had to screw up her eyes to be able to see properly, until she got further down the valley and into a tree-lined footpath that led inexorably downwards, winding this way and that according to the contours of the land. I wish I'd brought my sunglasses, she thought. The route didn't seem to be descending very rapidly but when she stopped and looked back she could see how far she had actually come and began to dread the walk back; she wasn't used to walking these days, except along pavements pushing a buggy, and even if you went miles like that, it simply didn't use the same muscles as walking up even a minor hill.

Her hunch that she would eventually reach the river at the bottom of the valley was quite right; as she seemed to reach level ground, she caught a faint glitter of sunlight on moving water, and getting closer, she could hear the water, that wonderful gurgle and splash of a swift moving stream, and a few minutes later she stepped out into brilliant sunshine and found herself of the banks of a small river, swollen still with the rains of a week or two ago. She sighed with contentment, and went to sit down on a sort of bench constructed out of a split log nailed across two smaller pieces sunk deeply into the earth. The wood was worn smooth and felt surprisingly comfortable, and she relaxed and watched the rushing water.

The sunlight dancing on the rippling water was almost hypnotic and she had begun to feel so sleepy that when she glanced up and gazed horrified at the two children in the water being swept along, she thought for one moment that she had been dreaming. They were swept past her, and any last remaining doubts as to their reality were destroyed by the sound of their voices raised in frantic screams. Isobel looked round, trying to see if there was some sort of lifebelt in sight, or a large branch or anything, or anyone but there was nothing and no one there, only her, standing paralysed on the bank as the two heads seemed to be swallowed up by the water. You'll never live with yourself if you do nothing, Isobel said to herself harshly and struggled with the laces of her boots, hauled them off, and peeled off jeans and lumberjack shirt, and bracing herself for the chill of the water, ran along the bank and did a dive that, could she have seen it herself, she would have been proud of it. The water was a lot colder than she'd anticipated and it nearly took her breath away, so that it took a moment or two for her to orientate herself and began to strike out with the flow of the water in pursuit of the two children.

She found she drew level with the children quite quickly but the current of the river was strong enough that she knew she would have trouble getting out again even alone. She could see the children now quite clearly: both of them boys, aged maybe ten or twelve years old, with hair that would be fairish when dry. As she gazed at them trying to work out how on earth she could ever rescue both of them, she saw with a shock colder than even the water, that both were grinning at her, and then she saw that they both seemed to be far more buoyant than she'd have expected, but before she had a chance to try and understand, she saw that they were being swept towards something concrete that straddled the river. It must be some sort of bridge or weir, but it barely cleared the water, and there were small channels in it for the water, some rather clogged now with debris. Before she had a chance to think anything else, she was bashed rather hard against the concrete and came to a stop with bruised body and a mind that was increasingly livid with anger. The boys had scrambled out onto the bridge, and she saw now why they had been so much more buoyant than she had been: each carried a luridly decorated body board that they must have been using as floats. They were both laughing at her, and she hauled herself out onto the concrete, exhausted and full of rising fury. The sound of the water filled her ears and she got to her feet finding she was quite shaky.

"What the hell did you think you were doing?" she demanded, pointing at the older boy. "You could have drowned. I could have drowned."

The boy tried to look abashed and failed miserably, his face erupting into a smile of almost pure mischief.

"We didn't ask you to come in and rescue us," he said. "We're perfectly safe; the bridge stops us going any further."

Isobel felt both angry and stupid and hated the kid for making her feel either.

"You stupid little moron," she said, her voice rising into a scream at the end. "I could have been killed due to your water-sports. What do you have to say about that, you selfish little toe-rag?"

In unconscious imitation of Miranda's words to the police, the kid grinned at Isobel and said loudly and insincerely,

"Sorry!"

"Where the hell do you live?" she demanded. "I'm going to have words with your parents and you'll be grounded till you're thirty."

Isobel hadn't noticed the other kid had run off while she had been shouting and he was now returning, a woman following him. She glanced up at the sound of footsteps to see the woman gliding to her side, all ethereal trailing scarves, long curly blonde hair and bead necklaces glittering.

"Is there a problem?" asked the woman with a smile.

"Yes, there bloody well is!" Isobel snarled. "These little maniacs fooled me into thinking they were drowning and I went in to try and save them."

"I am so sorry," said the woman. "You must be freezing cold. The boys don't seem to feel the cold. Tristan, would you run back and fetch this lady's clothes for her?"

The older boy started to argue but soon gave up when he saw the look on the woman's face and ran off downstream, his bare feet seeming not to notice the thistles and stones along the path.

"You must come back to the house and have a hot drink to counteract the cold and the shock," said the woman and she started to move away from Isobel who was feeling very unhappy standing there in nothing but her bra and knickers.

"I'd like to wait a moment for my clothes," she said, and the woman stopped and stared at her in surprise.

"I'm not going anywhere like this!" Isobel said.

The woman smiled, rather condescendingly, Isobel thought.

"And yet, on a beach, you would walk round wearing much the same as that or even less," she said musingly.

"I haven't worn a bikini since I was ten," said Isobel defensively. "Anyway, it's quite obvious these are my undies and I would far rather not be arrested for indecency."

The woman gave that faint supercilious smile.

"I think it very unlikely there are going to be police lurking between here and the house," she said. "Ah, here are your clothes."

The older boy, Tristan, handed Isobel her clothes and boots and looked at the woman in query.

"Yes, you may go back to swimming," she said and both boys raced off down the riverbank.

Isobel struggled into her clothes, hating the feel of her clammy underwear, and wishing she could have had the courage to shed them before pulling on her clothes.

"Better now?" said the woman.

"Warm anyway," Isobel said. "Don't you worry about them, playing in the river like that?"

The woman shook her head, making the bow of the gauzy scarf tied round her hair sway like a pair of early butterflies mating.

"Not at all," she said. "They are perfectly safe."

She turned away and began to walk up the slope and Isobel felt she should follow; not because she was really in need of a hot drink, she told herself, but rather to try and get some sort of apology or explanation. As she walked alongside the woman, Isobel realised she was heavily pregnant, something not immediately evident; the voluminous Kaftan type dress she wore disguised the bump, and the scarves trailing round her neck hid it still further. It was only when the breeze flattened the dress against her and fluttered the scarves away that Isobel was sure. She wasn't pleased; somehow or other bawling out a pregnant woman for her poor parenting skills seemed a rather dangerous thing, remembering how easily upset and unreasonable she had been towards the ends of each of her own pregnancies.

After a short distance, the woman opened a wooden gate in an overgrown hedge and gestured for Isobel to follow her, and she soon found herself in a huge park-like garden, strewn with play equipment, everything from swings and slides to bicycles for every age from what looked like adult size to tiny tricycles. The grass was mown though, and the shrubs that clustered here and there were well cared for and neatly pruned. The garden sloped so that it was quite an effort to reach the house that stood at the far end; the woman must have been at the bottom of the garden when the younger boy had gone to fetch her, for her to have reached Isobel so quickly. Isobel was faintly surprised by the size of it, a great rambling old farmhouse, with some sort of huge extension that looked like an old barn that had been joined to the main house with a sort of tunnel of glass.

The woman headed for the barn, seeming to waft along gracefully. I never looked graceful when I was that pregnant, Isobel thought resentfully and then cheered up with the thought that anyone can glide around in a hippy kaftan. It takes real grace to move beautifully in jeans and walking boots, she thought, and followed the woman into the building.

For a moment, Isobel thought she had walked into some sort of nursery, as the huge high ceilinged room was filled with more children's toys than she'd ever seen outside of a toy superstore, and an indeterminate number of kids milled around, few of them wearing much by way of clothes and all were barefoot. She blinked in surprise.

"Are all of these yours?" she asked the woman.

"Good gracious, but no!" said the woman. "Only half the children here are mine. Now what would you like to drink?"

Isobel stifled the impulse to ask for a double brandy.

"A hot chocolate would be nice," she said, suddenly feeling very shy and uncertain of herself.

"Certainly," said the woman. "I won't be long. Please make yourself comfortable."

Isobel found herself alone in the huge room but for a horde of small children who didn't seem to have noticed her. She saw that at the far end of the room was a big leather sofa that faced a huge television screen and made for that. The television was off and no children were close to the sofa so Isobel sat down there. It was a huge sofa, the leather buff coloured but when she put her hand down to touch it, she noticed that there was a certain tacky almost sticky feel to the leather, and when she surreptitiously ran her hand over a greater area, she realised that the whole sofa was sticky. It had the same sort of feel as spilled juice on her own leather sofa, and as she looked more closely, she saw there were darker marks on the leather, as of spills that had been allowed to dry without being wiped up. There was a carpet, a huge Persian style rug, and when she reached down to touch that, she found it too had the same sticky texture. Unconsciously, she shifted herself so that the minimum amount of her jeans was in contact with the sofa.

The children carried on with their games, playing strangely chaotically, and took no notice of Isobel till the woman returned carrying two mugs on a tray, and then they swarmed closer so that Isobel was obliged to slide further onto the sofa to avoid being trampled by them. There were five children present, the eldest of which must have been about four or five and the youngest about Luke's age and they shoved and fought each other to climb onto the woman's lap, and Isobel nearly fell off the sofa when one little boy with dirty golden curls undid the buttons on the woman's Kaftan and fastened his mouth greedily onto her nipple. He was at a guess about three and a half, older than Miranda certainly and Isobel had gone cold with the shock of this sight when the woman spoke.

"Here's your drink," she said, apparently oblivious of the child happily sucking at her breast, and mutely Isobel took the proffered mug.

The drink was certainly hot and dark brown in colour but it certainly wasn't chocolate at all. Isobel set it down on the tray after her first sip, so confused and unsettled she really wanted to bolt for the door.

"I don't know your name," said the woman. "But I think you must be the woman who has bought Barrow Cottage. I'm Maggie Broadbent."

"Isobel Trelawny," said Isobel but didn't offer her hand to shake but then neither did her hostess.

"Is there something wrong with the drink?" said Maggie suddenly. "We don't have chocolate here but carob is pretty much the same just no caffeine."

Oh, that's what it was, thought Isobel in huge relief.

"It's just a bit hot still," Isobel said and picked up her mug again and made a show of blowing on it to cool it.

"And how are you liking the cottage?" asked Maggie. "I gather you have just got it as a holiday cottage?"

"Not precisely," Isobel said. "I use it to work from, but I haven't been able to get here as often as I'd hoped, at least not yet. But we're here for a holiday this week."

"You have a family, then?" Maggie asked.

"Husband, two children," said Isobel, feeling uneasy. "Obviously I don't usually bring them when I'm working."

"What is your work, then?" asked Maggie, without a great deal of enthusiasm.

"I'm an artist," said Isobel, somewhat shyly. She'd barely got used to saying it anyway, as it always seemed so pretentious but it seemed even harder to say it now for a reason she couldn't quite fathom.

Maggie's face seemed to light up, interest sparkling all over her features.

"Really? Really?" she said. "What an amazing coincidence! I am an artist too. I knew the moment I saw you we were somehow kindred spirits and now I have that confirmed."

She pushed the child sucking at her nipple off her breast and did up her buttons to an enraged wailing, and leaned towards Isobel.

"This is so amazing," she exclaimed. "I knew something was going to happen today. Oh, we shall have such a good time! I just know it. What sort of art do you do, Isobel?"

"Painting, mostly," Isobel said uncomfortably.

"I have talents in many of the disciplines," said Maggie. "But I do adore painting! I have a gallery in the village, you know. You must come and have a look; obviously apart from pieces in progress, I don't have a lot here."

Isobel felt that horrible sinking feeling she usually got when cornered by someone who felt themselves to be her soul-mate or something. She drank her carob drink hastily.

"I must be getting back," she said. "My husband will be worrying that I've got lost."

"You must let me drive you home," Maggie said. "It's the least I can do when you put yourself to such trouble and risk to try and save the boys."

At last, an acknowledgement of her heroism! Isobel grinned wickedly at that thought.

Maggie led her out to the front of the house, where a garden stood that either had never been finished or was in the process of being rearranged, so that beds stood empty with spades still embedded in the soil, and pot-bound plants languished waiting to be planted out. There was a small sports car standing there, and Maggie folded back the roof and beckoned Isobel to get in, though Isobel had her doubts that Maggie would ever fit her bump behind the wheel. She was barefoot too, something that by now didn't surprise Isobel, and she didn't bother with her seat belt either, but the way she drove made Isobel very glad of hers.

At the bottom of the lane leading to her cottage, Isobel said,

"Just drop me here, there's no need to take me to the door or you'll have trouble turning round."

"Not a bit of trouble," said Maggie, clearly not listening, and drove Isobel right to her gate.

"I'd better get back," Maggie said. "Otherwise I'd have loved to come in. But my partner and my friend are both out and I really shouldn't leave the children alone for too long."

Isobel bounced out of the car, horrified at the thought of leaving so many small children unattended.

"But now we've met, it'll be so good to get together properly," Maggie said. "I shall pop over tomorrow. Bye!"

She reversed down the lane, scarcely looking behind her and waved as she did so. Isobel stood at her gate and waved back, somewhat feebly and had this terrible sinking feeling in the pit of her stomach that she was going to have trouble shaking off this new friend.

Chapter 11

Mickey came to meet her in the hall, his thin face so full of concern that she felt immediately guilty that she had been gone so long.

"We really need to talk," he said, his voice strangely low and urgent.

"I wasn't gone that long," she said defensively.

"No, not about that," Mickey said. "I assume you had a good walk?"

"Interesting, anyway," Isobel said. "But I'll tell you about that later. What's the problem? The kids are all right, aren't they?"

"They're fine," he said, his voice taking on a reassuring note. "It's not that at all. I don't really know how to start this, because it seems a bit barmy in all honesty. You know you managed to worm out of that estate agent that the people who viewed this house before us felt it to be somehow a bit spooky?"

"Well, yes," Isobel said, curiously.

"I've been wondering about things for a while, but today, being here alone while the kids slept, it got to me rather," he explained.

"That's not like you," she commented.

"No, I know it isn't," he agreed. "When you went out, I was about to settle down on the sofa for a snooze, but then I thought, I'll just go and make sure those French doors are secure. I didn't want Miranda coming down while I was still asleep and sneaking out; I know she can't manage the handle on the front door or on the one from the kitchen, but the one on the French doors is low enough for her to turn easily. So I shut them nice and tight and then for added security, I put the bolts across too. I dozed off for about half an hour, and then when I woke up cold, I saw why: the French doors were open again. Now, if we'd been in a gale, then it's faintly possible that those doors might have blown open, bolts or not, but when I looked, the bolts had been slid back, and they weren't damaged in any way whatsoever. And there wasn't much of a breeze."

He rubbed his face with a shaking hand.

"I tell you Izzie, I was scared, really scared," he said.

"OK, I get that," she said. "Maybe Miranda had managed to get them open. Did you ask?"

"I went up to check and she was still fast asleep," he replied, worried. "I don't understand it at all."

Isobel shrugged.

"Nor do I," she said.

"But that's been happening a lot; or things have gone missing and turned up where I know I didn't put them," he said. "And another thing," he went on. "Did you by any chance weave an ivy wreath for Miranda?"

"No, I thought you must have done that," she said. "Did you ask her about it?"

"She said the fairies had left it for her on her bed," Mickey said.
"I reckon she must have made it herself," Isobel said. "There's no point asking her too much because at her age the distinction between fact and fantasy is very blurred."
"I suppose so," he said, unhappily. "I'm just worried. What if the doors come open while no one's here, or if a coal comes off the fire when we've gone to bed?"
"I don't think it's worth worrying," she said. "I think it's all a coincidence. I think that maybe the catches on the doors and windows are a bit faulty. Maybe when you put the bolts across you didn't put them all the way across, and the wind forced the doors open. As for losing things and having them turn up, well, no one would accuse us of being exactly tidy and organised at the best of times."
Mickey shook his head.
"No," he said. "Not to that extent. There have been too many things for it to be a coincidence. Do you want to know what I really think is going on?"
Isobel raised her eyebrows.
"You're going to tell me anyway," she said, wearily.
"I think we have a poltergeist."
She stared at him and then began laughing.
"That is a bit ridiculous, isn't it?" she said, and Mickey looked hurt.
"It's the only thing I can think of that might account for what's been happening," he said. "Why should it be so ridiculous?"
"Oh, I don't know," Isobel said, infuriated. "It just is. In this day and age, a poltergeist?"
"It's an old house," he said.
"Yes, and so is the one we live in."
"Only late Victorian. This one must be a good fifty years older."
"I don't know," Isobel said, suddenly very tired. "Look, I need to have a shower. Can you find me some clean undies? Mine are soaked. Oh, better make it clean clothes throughout."
"How come your underwear is wet, or shouldn't I ask?"
"It's a long story and it doesn't involve losing control of myself, I should add," Isobel said. "Where are the children?"
"Playing in Miranda's room."
Isobel plodded up the stairs and showered while Mickey fetched her clean clothes, and she told him briefly about her afternoon while she got dry and into her clothes.
"It might be nice to have a local friend," Mickey said, tentatively.
"Not sure about this one, though," Isobel said, putting her head through the shawl collar of her big jumper. "She was well and truly weird, believe me. She's an artist though and she does have a gallery in the village, which I didn't notice when we went into the village centre before but then why would I? Maybe if I get to know her, I might

get some of my work up in her gallery. She must be fairly successful to have her own gallery. Remind me to Google her when we get home."

She felt much better to be out of her cold and clammy undies and she looked in briefly to check on the children, who were playing admirably in Miranda's bedroom.

"I'm starving," she said as she made her way down the stairs behind Mickey. "I could eat a horse, should it be offered."

"No such luck," he said. "I've made some pasta and some cheese sauce, and there's some of that cooked ham that can go in and some tinned pineapple. If I make it look like a horsey on your plate, will that do?" He was grinning manically at her

"Anything," Isobel said, suddenly aware that she was positively ravenous. It must be the effect of a long walk, a shock, a swim and the smell of dinner wafting up the hallway.

"I've fed the kids already," Mickey said. "So all this is ours if we want it."

He set about chopping up ham and pineapple and adding them to the pasta mix, and Isobel sat down at the table with her elbows resting on the scarred wooden surface of her Mum's old kitchen table.

"Mickey?" she said after a minute. "What if it is a poltergeist? What can we do about it?"

He glanced up at her; she had a thoughtful and rather unhappy look on her face.

"I don't really know," he said. "I think I'll have to ask around. It isn't something they covered at theological college, and so far it's never come up at all. But don't worry. I seem to remember it's not that much of a problem."

"Good," she remarked. "I knew it'd come in useful one day to be married to a clergyman!"

*

Somehow or other, Isobel was certain that if Maggie turned up at all, it wouldn't be first thing in the morning; she didn't strike her as a morning person. She also had no intention of altering their plans if the day was again lovely enough to go out and enjoy the sunshine; staying in because someone she really didn't want to see might come round was not on her list of things to do. But as it turned out, the morning was cloudy and by midday, a grey mist had swept across the valley, and rain began to fall in uncertain showers, so they stayed in anyway. Isobel set up her easel and got on with trying to finish a commissioned portrait she needed to get done, while Mickey played on the floor with both children. He looked a lot more relaxed than he had done last night; evidently admitting to his fears had helped in some indefinable way, though for her, she was struggling even with the thought of what he had suggested. She'd stared at the darkness in their room as she'd gone to sleep and had a tiny shiver of unease when she finally made herself close her eyes and try to go to sleep. But the night had passed without disturbance and she had begun to revert to her original conclusion that all of it was a combination of over-active imagination, coincidences, and perhaps even the insidious effect of having been told that others had found the place spooky. This is my house, she thought fiercely. I'm not having anyone or anything ruin that for me. So any lurking ghosties can bloody well bugger off.

There was a sudden rapping at the front door, which made her jump, and Miranda went running out into the hall before Isobel or Mickey could call her back. Isobel put her brush down and followed her child, but to her huge shock, the door was opening and Maggie was entering, calling as she did so,

"Hello, hello, it's only me," much as if she had called here every day for the last ten years.

Miranda looked up at her in wonderment; Maggie was wearing a long silk dress in shades of purple and pink and wore a gauzy pink scarf around her hair. A huge string of multicoloured beads reached almost to her navel, and her hands were covered in rings made of silver and coloured stones, one of which Isobel recognised as turquoise. Isobel suddenly felt dowdy, and wished she had put on her amber beads; they were so lovely and they didn't make her look like a superannuated Christmas tree.

"Hi," Isobel said, smiling. "Miranda, say hello to Maggie."

"Hello," said Miranda. "Your dress is very lovely." Her voice sounded awestruck.

"Why thank you," said Maggie and beamed at her and then at Isobel.

Mickey came through into the hall, carrying Luke, and held out his spare hand for Maggie to shake.

"Shall I make some coffee?" he suggested.

"Please," said Isobel.

"I hope it won't be too much trouble," said Maggie. "But do you have any decaffeinated?"

"Er, sorry, no," said Mickey. "At home we do, but since we tend to drink coffee for the caffeine, we don't have any here where it's only us to think of. I think we have some chamomile and some peppermint tea though."

"Chamomile would be lovely," said Maggie graciously.

"Er, come and sit down," said Isobel, and tugged her shirt straight. "I must just put my brush in water, though."

She led Maggie through into the living room and went to wash her brush. Maggie had seated herself on the sofa, and Miranda had come and sat next to her, gazing at her as though she would vanish.

"Are you a fairy?" she asked, presently, in a breathless excited voice.

Maggie laughed; a very tinkly and fairy-like laugh, which Isobel couldn't help thinking was rather affected.

"Oh no, my dear," she said. "But I appreciate the compliment."

"My daughter is very taken with the idea of fairies," Isobel said, rather unnecessarily. "I don't like to disillusion her, I'm afraid. Time will do that for me."

Maggie put her hand to her heart.

"How sad," she said. "I take it you are not a believer?"

Isobel floundered. What the hell was that supposed to mean?

"I'm sorry," she said apologetically. "I don't quite understand you."

"You don't believe in fairies?" Maggie said, patiently.

What the hell is going on? Isobel thought wildly. Have I strayed on to the set of a remake of bloody Peter Pan?

"No, sorry, I don't," she said.

Maggie gazed at her with sad and soulful eyes.

"You poor dear," she said, and before Isobel had the chance to say anything, Mickey came through.

"Would you like honey in your chamomile tea?" he said. "We usually do."

"No, thank you, just as it comes," Maggie said. "All sugar, even honey, is addictive and damaging."

Mickey looked at her and then at his wife.

"I'll get the coffee," he said.

When he'd gone, Maggie said,

"I am surprised you aren't a believer. This area is well known as a haunt of the Fair Folk."

"I had no idea," Isobel said.

"I suppose you wouldn't, no," said Maggie. "But it is mentioned in a number of books."

Her eyes ranged round the room and lighted on Isobel's easel.

"May I see?" she asked and Isobel couldn't think of a polite way of forbidding her.

"Be my guest," she said and watched as Maggie struggled to get off the sofa, and then walked to the easel with her, watching her face closely when she gazed at the almost complete portrait of a group of children enjoying a picnic.

"Very nice," she said, but without any warmth or enthusiasm. "I work in a more abstract way myself."

Isobel tried not to bristle.

"This is what pays the bills," she said. "I do other stuff too, a lot more adventurous. But this is what pays."

Maggie smiled at her.

"Not something I ever worry about," she said. "My muse is free to inspire me without any taint of money."

Lucky bloody you, Isobel thought, and managed to smile at her and hoped her thoughts didn't show on her face.

"It makes people happy," she said. "Me, for one. I don't think I've ever had someone who wasn't delighted with their picture. It says more than a photo ever can."

"Of course," said Maggie and Isobel felt horribly belittled.

They went and sat down again, and Miranda sat next to Maggie, still staring as if she might grow wings and fly away. Mickey came through with mugs and Luke came toddling after him, a biscuit in his hand. Normally, seeing her brother with a treat she had not herself been given would have inspired Miranda to rage, but she didn't seem to notice at all. Her whole being was concentrated on Maggie; Isobel found this a touch disturbing and then rather irritating but evidently Maggie thought it charming.

"When is your baby due?" Isobel said after a lull in the conversation.

"In the merry month of May," said Maggie, almost singing it. "I do so love being pregnant. Don't you?"

Isobel had suffered from morning sickness the whole nine months she'd carried Miranda, and was the only person she knew who was several pounds lighter after the baby was born than she had been before she'd become pregnant. The midwife had been worried that she had failed to gain much weight at all through the whole nine months. While carrying Luke, she had been much less sick but from about five months he played football with her internal organs to such an extent that she had trouble sleeping, and by the time her due date arrived, she'd felt like a barrage balloon and had trouble with even the simplest of tasks, so unbalanced had she become with the immense bump.

"No," said Isobel, shortly. "Not much anyway."

"Perhaps you are too tense about it," Maggie suggested. "I find that if I simply go with the flow, it's all a beautiful experience every single day."

"How many children do you have?" Isobel asked.

"This will be my fifth," Maggie said proudly.

Isobel swallowed hard, trying to restrain any trace of her horror from showing on her face.

"Who do the other children belong to?" she asked.

"To my friend, Cassandra, who lives with us," Maggie said. "She's minding the children today; my partner has gone away for a few days now. He's facilitating a workshop."

Isobel could sense Maggie wanted her to ask what sort of workshop, but she waited in silence until Maggie began to explain, anyway.

"My partner runs courses for men to rediscover their manhood; we have so few rites of passage now, and many men pass through their lives without ever truly becoming men. It accounts for so much hurt and suffering we see; boys trying to do the work of men, boys trying to be men without truly passing through the portals that *make* them men."

There was a small noise of stifled amusement from Mickey, on the floor again with Luke; but Maggie either didn't hear or register the smothered laugh as having anything to do with her comments. He rolled Luke onto his back and blew into his tummy, making the baby squeal with laughter. Maggie looked from one child to the other.

"Are you having more?" she asked.

Isobel felt horror-struck at the question; it wasn't one she would ever have expected a stranger to ask.

"No," she said, quietly. "I had enough trouble having these. I don't think there'll be any more."

Maggie gazed at her soulfully, which made Isobel feel quite sick suddenly.

"You poor love," she said. "Only two little ones to pour all that love into."

Isobel shrugged; she could feel herself going red from embarrassed anger.

"I have my work," she said with some dignity, and felt even more annoyed when Maggie shook her head sadly.

"Your work does not live and grow and breathe like children," she said.

Isobel couldn't take this and she knew she was likely to be rude if it continued.

"Can I just ask you something?" she said, casting around frantically for a new subject. "How can you be so sure there really are fairies? I thought only kiddies believed in fairies."

Maggie smoothed her scarf and settled back, folding her hands over her bump.

"Well," she said, as if taking a big run-up to the subject. "*Well!* I suppose it's because I've experienced their involvement in my life. Some lucky, lucky people have been blessed by the fairies allowing them to see them; but I have yet to be worthy of that blessing. The most common way of knowing they are present in a place, is when they play with our belongings; especially pretty things. Have you never had a necklace or a ring go missing and then turn up days or even weeks later in a quite different place from where it could ever have been put naturally?"

Isobel went cold inside, but shook her head.

"Nope," she said. "I don't need fairies to lose things for me; I'm pretty good at losing things myself."

"Or perhaps doors and windows that won't stay shut?" Maggie suggested. "Or perhaps little gifts of leaves or flowers or feathers that turn up out of nowhere? Sometimes little voices, half heard?"

"Nope," said Isobel again.

Maggie gave her a surprisingly hard stare.

"The people who owned this house before you had many of those things happen to them," she said. "In the end, they couldn't stand it. While it was just a holiday cottage, it was OK, but when they retired and came to live here all the time, well, within six months they had moved to their daughter's home and put this house up for sale. Such a shame, really, as the fairies really only want a bit of love and they're fine. I told

Muriel, leave them some sugar every day and they'll not trouble you, but she wouldn't listen. They even got a priest in, would you believe it? Not that he was much use, I never expected he would be, bigoted old fraud."

Mickey swung Luke up and sniffed at his nappy.

"Time for a change," he said and smiled at Maggie as he went out.

"So good to see a father shouldering his responsibilities," she said and Isobel grinned.

"He's a real new man," she said.

"Perhaps he would like to come on one of my partner's weekends," Maggie suggested. "To help ease him through the initiation of fatherhood and find his true manhood."

I should imagine that'd be the last thing he'd want, Isobel thought, but smiled politely and non-committally.

"I'll mention it to him," she said.

"What is it your partner does?" Maggie asked, suddenly curious.

Isobel fell back on a tried and tested lie she always used when she wanted to conceal Mickey's vocation.

"He's a community worker," she said. "Does a whole range of things, from youth work to visiting the elderly."

"How interesting," said Maggie, losing interest at once. "Well, this has been so lovely. You must come over and have a meal with us when we're all home."

She rummaged in the little bag she carried, and pulled out a tiny diary.

"How about Friday?" she asked.

"Sorry, we're heading home again on Friday," Isobel said, with some relief.

"What a terrible, terrible shame," Maggie said, but without much evidence of sorrow. "Ivan won't be back until Friday, and you really must meet him. He would help your partner so much, you know, to complete himself and find his true path."

"Another time, then," said Isobel. "We may be back during the summer, sometime, but I don't know when yet."

"Oh, well, why don't you give me a tinkle when you're next here, or when you're planning to come along," Maggie said, and rummaged in her bag again and handed Isobel a business card, the letters embossed in gold over swirling multicoloured card that looked like it had been tie-dyed. Isobel held the card without looking at it.

"Thank you, I will," she said.

There was a significant pause while Maggie obviously waited for Isobel to offer her a card or something in return, but when she realised it was not going to be forthcoming, she stowed her diary away and again struggled to get out of the sofa. It was a mark of how keen Isobel was to get rid of her that she took her arm and pulled her gently but firmly to her feet. Miranda, much to Isobel's disgust, held onto Maggie's skirt and began to cry, saying how she didn't want her to go. Maggie swung her up, so she clung to Maggie with her legs round Maggie's waist, such as it was at this stage.

"Oh, can I take her home with me?" Maggie said in a high, rather childish voice. "She is such a little darling."

Isobel took Miranda rather firmly from Maggie's arms.

"You'll have your hands rather full in about four weeks or so, so I don't think it would be a good idea to have Miranda as well," she said briskly and to wails from Miranda she showed Maggie to the door. Maggie hugged Isobel and kissed her on both cheeks; Isobel was astonished to see tears in the other woman's eyes.

"I do feel we have known each other before, that we are kindred spirits," Maggie said, and dabbed at her eyes with a shred of tissue. "Farewell and well met, my dear."

Isobel stood at the gate with a howling Miranda thumping at her chest to be let down, and watched Maggie vanish down the lane, in reverse, and waving all the way.

"Pack that in, right now, young lady," Isobel said firmly, and much to her surprise, her daughter stopped hitting her and subsided into a damp grizzle.

In the hall, Isobel put her down and saw her run away into the living room, apparently having forgotten Maggie in only a few seconds. Mickey was sitting at the top of the stairs, watching.

"Is it safe to come out?" he asked.

"Have you changed that nappy, then?"

"Didn't need to," he said. "I just wanted to get away and that seemed the best excuse I could find at such short notice. What an awful woman!"

Isobel couldn't help agreeing.

"We're going home Friday," she said. "Unless you want to go over to them for dinner? She tells me that her partner will help you find your true manhood."

Mickey looked horrified.

"I didn't know I'd lost it," he said and stood up abruptly and peered down his trousers. "Phew, it's still there!"

"Idiot," she said fondly.

Chapter 12

When they got home on Friday evening, Isobel bathed and put both children to bed straight after supper, and headed for the computer. Mickey was in the middle of sorting out the various crises that had occurred during his break, and it was only after she'd been glued to the screen for more than an hour that he thought to ask what she'd found.

"Well?" he asked. "Is she an internationally known artist of great repute?"

"Hell's bells; no!" Isobel said, and he could hear both the relief and the scorn in her voice and it tickled his curiosity no end.

"What is she, then?" he asked.

Isobel shook her head as if in disbelief.

"She's a lottery millionaire," she said. "About five years back, she won about eleven million quid. She bought herself art lessons as well as that house, and then she bought a gallery for herself and filled it with stuff that even the kindest critic couldn't find anything complimentary to say. The not-so-kind critics have written such reviews that I wonder she can sleep at night. I'd have killed myself if I'd got that sort of review. There's more; she's hovered on the celebrity fringe for years too, buying her way in, or so it goes, with all the C-list celebs. Her partner is called Ivan Manners and he runs a company on her money, called Manners Maketh Men, and guess what, it purports to initiate men into their true manhood, but there have been some very dubious rumours about that, as you can imagine and as a result, the ones they originally started for boys have been stopped, though nothing has ever been proven; the minimum age for the courses now is eighteen. They advertise in various New Age magazines and websites and they seem to have quite a take-up rate, whatever the courses are actually like. Here's the other juicy bit; they're actually a three-some. The third member is a woman called Cassandra Collins; she and Maggie apparently share Ivan, and they each have four children by him, Maggie with her fifth on its way. There's a lot of information but frankly, I've seen enough."

Isobel clicked off the site she'd been looking at.

"I had a look at her website, and her art is truly awful," she said. "All floaty fairies and stuff like that; it looked rather like the pictures of the Cottingley fairies, except she isn't very good at drawing and it's all fairly luridly coloured and some of it's quite explicit too. Not something for the kids, I can promise you: fairies fucking in the flowers. Or even fairies fucking the flowers, just for a bit of variety."

She turned away from the computer, and Mickey was alarmed to see she was looking rather sick and upset. He came and put his arms round her, and felt her lean into him for comfort.

"It's all right," he said.

"I know," she replied. "I'm just determined to avoid her at all costs. She's vile, however much Miranda liked her."

"I'd be willing to bet that if you put her in jeans and tee-shirt, Miranda wouldn't look at her twice," Mickey said. "It was those clothes and the hair that did it, I reckon. She looked like something from a story book, or from a fairy tale."

"Yeah, one of Grimm's," Isobel said, nastily. "Anyway, if I go up on my own, I shan't be calling round for a cup of sugar, not even for the bloody fairies."

"Anyway, you needn't worry about her," he said. "If she's that poor an artist, she won't be making anything from it."

"She doesn't need to," Isobel said. "And contrary to all sensible expectations and all the reviews, her stuff sells. I can't imagine why; I suppose it must appeal to a certain mentality but if I ever meet anyone with that said mentality, I shall run as soon as I twig! I can't help thinking it's cheating, using her money as a leg-up in the art world."

"It's better than using the leg-over technique," he said. "You're just jealous!"

Isobel went very red at this, and said nothing for about a minute, getting more and more cross, until she burst out,

"You bet I'm jealous. I had to work my socks off to get anywhere; it does annoy me that she's bought her way in and worse that she's succeeding despite everything to the contrary."

"You're successful yourself," he said, mildly.

"Only in a very minor way," she said. "I couldn't live off what I earn. It's a very useful second income but it's never been enough to manage on, not even when I was living in a one-room bed-sit and living off the end of the day special offer food from the supermarket. I've seen what sort of prices she asks for her work, and people *pay*!"

"I'd still rather have one of your pictures on the wall than fairy porn," Mickey said.

"Even that morbid one?"

"Even that one, yes. It was still very beautiful even if it was a touch disturbing. Are hers really that awful?"

"Let me put it like this: I shan't for a long time look at a rose in bloom without a slight shudder," Isobel said.

"Yuck!" said Mickey. "I've been thinking about the poltergeist thing."

Isobel glanced at him curiously.

"Oh yes?" she said, cautiously.

"I think I shall ask Les about it," he said. Les was his team rector and therefore his boss.

"For goodness sake don't tell him it was us," Isobel said.

"What kind of an idiot do you take me for?" he said. "No, don't answer that. I'll mention it at our staff meeting on Monday and see if he has any useful general advice. I don't think I want him to know it was us who were having such experiences; somehow I'm not sure that'd go down too well. I shall think of a cover story."

"Do that," said Isobel. "Are you hungry? I'm starving; shall I put some toast in and we can have some supper?"
"I am pretty hungry now you mention it," he said. "And tired too. Supper and then bed, I think."
Isobel went through to the kitchen to obliterate the sour taste in her mouth with toast and honey and by the time she went to bed had managed to forget most of her bitterness, even though she still had reservations about living in range of someone who managed to push all her metaphorical buttons all at once.

*

On Monday, Mickey came home from his staff meeting uncharacteristically tense and irritable and it took Isobel some minutes before she could get him to calm down enough to tell her what was wrong.
"It was Les," he said, finally. "I mentioned I had come across a case that seemed very much like a poltergeist and you'll never guess what he said. He said: his theology didn't include poltergeists. I couldn't believe it. He asked me where I'd come across it and I said it was something happening in the parish of a friend and that as it was confidential I couldn't say any more than that. He said he blamed the mass media and horror films for the sudden proliferation in these things and said it was simply the product of over-active and over-stimulated imaginations and nothing more than that. Hell, I was so angry I almost told him it was us being affected by it. I thought at least he'd know who the trouble-shooter in this area is and maybe pass on the number. I'm right back at square one and haven't the foggiest what to do now."
"I seem to remember Chloe has an uncle who's a priest," Isobel said. "We met him at Clifford's ordination if you remember and he seemed pretty sound and sensible. Why don't you ask Clifford?"
"Why not?" Mickey said. "I think it's Clifford's uncle anyway, not Chloe's. I'll ring him then."
Isobel went back to ironing while keeping an eye on both children, currently staring rapt at cartoons on video, and after about half an hour, Mickey came back through to her, looking much happier.
"He said he'd ring his uncle Peter and ask for advice," he said. "He didn't say it wasn't in his theology, but then I didn't think he would. He said he'd ring back when he's managed to have a word. Good thinking, Batman!"
Isobel just grinned at him.
"I'm like that Victorian household manual: inquire within for all knowledge," she said.
"I wouldn't go that far," Mickey said. "You might be pretty clever sometimes but you sure aren't omniscient."

"Shhh!" Isobel said. "Don't let the children hear you say that! They still think I know everything and can see through walls."
"I was going to make a cup of tea," he said. "Want one?"
"Is the Pope a Catholic? Do bears sh-"Isobel said but Mickey put his hand over her mouth, and gestured at the oblivious children.
"That's something neither of us wants her ladyship picking up," he said, grinning. "I can just imagine the ladies who run the church crèche having the vapours when Miranda uses the latest addition to her vocabulary."
"I wasn't going to say what you think I was going to say," Isobel protested. "Oh all right, I was, but they aren't listening anyway."
"They're always listening, just like cats always sleep with one eye half open," Mickey said.
"Shut up and go and make me my tea, you sanctimonious low life scum," Isobel said, and kissed him.
They were about to start drinking the tea when the phone rang again, so Mickey took his through to the study to answer the call and Isobel drank hers while waiting for the iron to cool down enough to put away; it wasn't safe to leave it alone while it was still hot and she couldn't put it away while it was hot, so she was obliged to sit and watch cartoons till Mickey came through again.
"That was Clifford," he said, looking pleased. Clifford had been Mickey's closest friend through theological college and in the time since they'd all left, Mickey had yet to find a replacement buddy.
"What did he have to say?" Isobel asked.
"He rang his uncle, who is in the process of retiring, and explained what I'd told him," Mickey said. "He said that his uncle said he'd send me some books that might be of help. I'm quite relieved to be taken seriously after this morning. He also said that if things weren't easy to sort out, he'd be happy to help, if we need it. Clifford said his uncle had come across this sort of thing quite often and was pretty unconcerned by it."
"I still think you're barking up quite the wrong tree," Isobel said. "So any books Peter sends will just confirm it."
"Woof, woof!" said Mickey. "At least I'm only *barking* up a tree!"
"Watch it, mate, walls and children have ears."
"I never said a thing," he protested, and she just laughed.

*

About three days later a parcel arrived, and Mickey got immersed in various books, which Peter had marked the relevant sections with post-it notes, to save him trudging through the whole of each volume. That evening after supper when the silence upstairs strongly suggested that both children had gone to sleep and therefore would not be interrupting, Mickey opened the conversation. Isobel was curled up with a much-needed glass of wine, and was feeling quite mellow again.

"I've had a good read through the bits Peter marked about poltergeists and I'm going to have to concede that it almost certainly isn't a poltergeist," he said.

"Yay!" Isobel said and punched the air in mock triumph.

"Grow up, won't you!" Mickey said irritably.

"If I grow up, you won't be able to play with me any more," Isobel said, unperturbed. "OK, tell me why it isn't a poltergeist, then. You seemed to be quite sure before you started on those books."

"I know, but I was basing my conclusion on false information," he said. "You see, the common idea of the poltergeist as an actual ghost is erroneous."

"But that's what it means, noisy ghost, isn't it?" said Isobel.

"So I understand," said Mickey. "The Christian Exorcism Study Group-"

"The what?" Isobel interrupted. "Is there really such a thing? Wow!"

"As I was saying, this group prefers the term "poltergeist phenomena" to just simply "poltergeist"," Mickey said. "Because they don't see the whole thing in terms of a ghost being involved, but rather as being a psychokinetic transformation of emotional energy into physical energy. Someone in the house is doing it; someone alive that is."

"Bloody hell!" said Isobel, setting her wine glass down and sitting up straighter. "That's some jump; what was it, psychokinetic transference of energies. I bet most people would prefer a ghost to being told that was what it was."

Mickey grinned at her rather ruefully.

"I know, I know," he said. "In some ways, they just exchange one concept that people sort of understand for one hardly anyone understands. The idea that somehow or other people can unconsciously transform emotional upsets into actual physical movement of objects or whatever, is almost as huge a thing to swallow as the idea a malevolent ghost chucking stuff around the house. Anyway, that's what the experts reckon it is."

"And what do they say that makes you certain that it isn't what's happening at the cottage?" Isobel asked.

Mickey looked a little uncomfortable.

"They give a list of what they call predisposing features that may lie behind a poltergeist case," he said. "Such as bereavement, menopause, a death or a birth in the family, puberty, changes in employment. A lot of things basically which seem to be lifestyle changes and stresses."

"Well, apart from puberty, which I think you and I have probably passed, and menopause which I suspect is an annoyingly long way in the future, we've probably got most of the stresses available," Isobel said. "Why couldn't it be one of us that's doing it, unconsciously of course? Not that I'm that stressed out or anything, but you never know."

"I know," said Mickey. "And believe me, I would have wondered about you and your parents' deaths, if I hadn't read earlier that the disturbances go along with the person who is triggering them. If either you or I were the trigger, then it would be happening here as well as at the cottage."

There was a silence while Isobel let this sink in.

"It's a shame we can't just put it down to that," Mickey said. "Because the phenomena usually fizzle out after about six months whether or not any action is taken; sooner if the person triggering it gets some sort of help, either by having the stresses removed or by some sort of counselling. And the list of things known to happen so fitted our circumstances; doors opening and closing, things being moved, things appearing out of nowhere, noises you can't explain, all that sort of thing."

He sounded quite absurdly sad, and Isobel began to feel quite sorry for him.

"So what do you reckon it is?" she asked.

"I don't really know," he said. "I'm going to have to read the rest of the books to see if anything seems to make sense, but I'm pretty fed up of it already."

"Why?"

"Because the whole thing is rather unnerving even to read about it in some scholarly tome," Mickey said. "Each of the books Peter sent is very low key and non-sensational, but even so, I get the shivers when I read about a lot of things. Not, I might add, things I am likely to ever come across in my usual work. I don't know. Anyway, what I think may be best, is next day off, if we all go up to the cottage for the day, and we say some prayers in every room in the cottage, it certainly won't do any harm and might just get it sorted without any need for further investigation."

"Sure," agreed Isobel. "That seems a sensible idea, but you know I wasn't convinced anyway, and nothing that has happened has been more than irritating as far as I was concerned. It would be good to go for the day anyway; I'd like to do some work there. I was thinking of having a go at painting those trees."

"That seems like a nice idea," Mickey said uncertainly, and Isobel just laughed.

"I shall try and eliminate all ghoulish quirks of paintwork," she said. "They were just starting to come into leaf so it'll be a lovely moment to try and capture."

"If the weather is good, you could even paint outside," he suggested. "Oh, by the way, while you were putting the kids to bed, Chloe rang. I forgot to mention it."

Isobel sighed and looked at the clock on the mantelpiece.

"It's not too late to call back," she said. "I'll use the study and then you can relax without wondering what I'm talking about."

"I didn't ring for anything much," Chloe said when Isobel got through. "I just haven't heard from you recently and wondered how things were going. I've been run off my feet recently and haven't had much time for anything beyond the basics, but things are a bit quieter now."

"Everything's fine," Isobel said, but something in her voice must have triggered concern in Chloe.
"It can't be," Chloe said. "It never is; so what's wrong?"
She sounded her usual blunt self and Isobel relaxed.
"All sorts and nothing," she said. "It's all a bit complicated and rather silly, actually."
She explained first about the happenings at the cottage and then her encounter with Maggie. By the end, Chloe was very quiet.
"I mean, though: fairies!" Isobel said, laughing rather scornfully. "The woman would have been ridiculous if she wasn't so awful. But *fairies*, though!"
Chloe was silent for a moment, and then said, rather unexpectedly,
"My grandmother was a great believer in fairies."
This threw Isobel into some quite natural confusion. She could either say, well, your Gran was as barking mad as this woman, and therefore risk upsetting Chloe or she could ask quite what she meant.
"What did she mean by fairies, though?" she said finally.
"I've never been entirely sure, actually," Chloe said. "She used to say that most folk beliefs had some basis in truth, though sometimes it was quite hard to see it. I think what she meant by it was spirits. Spirits of the natural world, I guess. I've often tried to classify Gran's spirituality and usually failed. She said that she saw that God was in everything and everything was in God, so that sort of adds up to panentheism. She said in many cultures there are traditions of spirit beings aiding life, which is perhaps where the idea of flower fairies comes from. She reckoned that if you worked with the spirits of a garden, everything went better. I was too young to understand it while she was still alive; I tried to ignore it, actually, in case she was going strange in the head. But over the years since.... Well, I've begun to think she may be right about that and so many other things. One of my current clients, if you like, though that makes me sound like a lawyer not a gardener, is an old lady who has a garden that she cultivates using various ideals, including organic and bio-dynamic principles, and she has said on a number of occasions that if you work with the garden guardians, as she calls them, your results are always much better than if you ignore or work against them. Her garden is fantastic, too. Biggest raspberries I've ever seen and the flowers smell amazing."
"If she's got it so sussed, what does she need you for?" Isobel said.
"Brute force, I'm afraid," said Chloe. "Certainly not any subtlety. She reckons she's not up to the heavy stuff or lawn cutting, so I go in to trim hedges and anything like that. I have to say, I usually try and arrange it so she's my only client that day so I can take my time. She comes out and we chat. I think I've learned more useful stuff from her than I did on my course. She doesn't call them fairies, though but I think what she means is the same as what Gran meant. And there are plenty of Biblical references to the existence of things seen and unseen, not to mention the whole company of Heaven.

Just because some things have ceased to be recognised as real doesn't mean they ceased to exist."

"Hmm," sad Isobel, thinking hard. "I don't know what to say."

"Then don't say anything," Chloe said. "Just 'cause this dreadful woman is a painter doesn't mean all painting is by definition also bad; so what if she believes in fairies? It doesn't mean they aren't real; what she thinks they are isn't necessarily the truth either. But I would steer clear of her, though. I'd want to put a fist in her face, myself."

Trust Chloe to put it like that. Isobel smiled.

"Tempting," she said. "But I can bet she can afford a better lawyer than me and six months in prison for ABH isn't on my to-do list, thank you very much."

Chloe chortled.

"Maybe you can ask the fairies to go and hide some of her stuff instead," she said. "I'll give you a call in a week or two and see how your next trip went. Take care! Bye!"

Isobel sat at stared at the blank screen of the computer on the desk in front of her and found a smile starting at the corners of her mouth and she went back through to Mickey and her unfinished glass of wine. She looked on the coffee table for her glass and saw that it was no longer there. For one horrible moment, she began to think that it had vanished the way so many items had vanished at the cottage and that perhaps either she or Mickey was the unwitting trigger for the strange events. Then she saw, first with relief and then with annoyance that her glass was now in Mickey's hand and apart from the crimson stain on the bottom of the glass, it was now empty.

"Hey!" she exclaimed. "No fair! Mine! Wah!"

"Like I said earlier, do grow up!" Mickey said grinning evilly. "There's plenty more in the bottle. I thought you'd finished with it."

"Since when have I ever left wine in a glass?" Isobel asked, and whisked through to the kitchen to fetch the bottle and another glass.

"Is that one for me?" he asked, looking up as she came in.

Isobel glared at him.

"Do you think you deserve it after nicking my drink?" she asked, and then passed the empty glass over. "Don't think you're getting anything in it though!"

"I may be obliged to pull rank and order you to!" he said, holding out his clean empty glass and her smeared one.

"Oh, yeah! And what rank would that be? Grand High Wombat of the first Order?" Isobel said, snatching her own glass back and hugging the bottle protectively.

"I've been promoted!" Mickey said, exultantly. "That calls for a celebration; I was only Grand High Wombat Second Class last week. Break out the wine!"

Isobel poured them both a glass full and then looked puzzled.

"I think I may have just been bamboozled," she said reflectively. "Anyway, I meant what right have you to order me around? I don't recall I ever vowed to obey you because you wouldn't worship me."

"I just meant in my capacity as head of the household," he said, sipping his wine.
"Head of the household, my arse!" Isobel snorted. "Head of something else more like!"
She took a gulp of her wine and gazed fondly at him.
"You really can be such a prat," she said.
"I know," he said. "I am so good at it, I did it for a career. What did Chloe want?"
"Nothing much," Isobel said. "We haven't spoken for weeks and she wanted to check I was OK. I told her about what's been going on, and about Maggie, and she reckons we shouldn't be too hasty to dismiss the existence of fairies. Apparently her Gran had some thoughts in that direction. Hard to argue with the Gospel according to Gran, and I don't intend to try."
"I always thought her Gran sounded pretty sensible, from what she's said of her," Mickey commented.
"Usually," Isobel conceded. "But I am going to take a hell of a lot of convincing that any of it is real, you know."
"That sounds alarmingly like famous last words," he said. "More things in Heaven and earth Horatio, and all that. Can the world really be limited to what the great Isobel Trelawny manages to get her head around?"
"My world is," she replied stubbornly and then grinned at him. "OK, I know I'm being stupid but I really can't accept that anything that woman ever said can really be true. And that may well be because it was her saying it and no better reason than that. Chloe more or less said that. But I'm comfortable with my prejudices and if Maggie's an example of being open minded, I'd far rather mine stayed closed than ever be tarred with the same brush as her. Her mind is so open I bet birds would nest in it if she didn't wear those silly bloody scarves."
"There's the rub," said Mickey. "You don't want to be tarred with the same brush. Would you stop being an artist just because she's one too?"
"She only claims to be one," Isobel said. "She's about as artistic as a loo brush!"
"You know what I mean," he persisted.
"No, I wouldn't stop being an artist. But I would be very careful about who I said it to round there. My current nightmare involves finding myself at an exhibition with my paintings alongside hers and the critics getting us mixed up," Isobel said, and shuddered at the thought.
"No one who saw any of your work could ever mix it up with hers," he said, gently.
"I did say it was a nightmare, not that I thought it might really happen," she said. "Anyway, if it makes you happy, I'll admit I don't know everything there is to know about this world, and maybe some of the stories about fairies have some basis in some sort of reality, maybe tree spirits or something like that. But I absolutely refuse to believe in someone else's version of that reality, especially-" and here her voice rose in

pitch and volume, "especially not that dreadful woman's version. I think I'd rather believe in Elvis being abducted by aliens first."

Mickey grinned at her.

"Don't you see the link? Elves and Elvis?" he said and she threw a cushion at him.

"Why don't you grow up for a change?" she said, and he began laughing.

"I can only think of one good reason to be a grown up," he said.

"Yes, so can I," she said. "And it involves being able to go into an off-license and buy booze without having to prove my age."

"That wasn't the reason I was thinking of," he protested.

"Not a chance, mate!"

"Aw, why not?"

"Why do you bloody think?" Isobel said and suddenly Mickey realised why she'd been so tense and easy to upset lately.

"Oh well," he said. "At least it means you aren't pregnant."

"At least when I was pregnant I didn't go round in such absurd clothes," Isobel remarked, and Mickey agreed, rather fervently.

"I don't think you even possessed a maternity dress," he said.

"I did. Just the one. It made me look like a tent that's been blown away in a gale, so I didn't wear it very often," she admitted. "OK, I will stop obsessing about that woman. I'm beginning to feel a little less manic now I've started."

She thought about it.

"That is one good thing about pregnancy," she said. "No PMS. But beyond the baby at the end, there's bugger all to recommend it. Can't imagine going through it five times. Damn, I'm obsessing again. Shoot me if it continues."

"Don't like to tell you this, but no, I won't," he said.

"Why not? I probably deserve it."

"No, it isn't that. We don't have a gun!"

"Excuses, excuses," Isobel said, and drank more of the wine.

"Have you got any further with figuring out what's going on?" she asked presently.

"I'm beginning to think it may be some sort of ghost," he said. "Attached to the cottage: unquiet dead, the book calls it. That makes the hairs on the back of my neck stand on end; this is just too creepy for me. Can't think why anyone would take this sort of thing on as part of their ministry; you'd have to have nerves of steel, not to mention good bladder control."

Isobel laughed.

"So you don't fancy a secondary ministry as an official ghost buster?" she asked.

"No more than you fancy a career as a broodmare!"

Chapter 13

It was May before they managed to get to the cottage again; minor illness had created a delay that seemed to extend indefinitely, but then whinging children were not exactly conducive to a prayerful atmosphere, as Mickey said. Both children had picked up colds, and Isobel, as always, was astounded at the amount of mucous one small nose could produce in the course of a day. Then, of course, both she and Mickey fell prey to the same virus, and clear breathing and nights not racked by coughing became distant memories for the unpleasant duration of both illness and convalescence.

When they reached the cottage, a fine rain was falling, making everything seem slightly misty, and the new green of the opening leaves was silvered over with moisture. The grass had allegedly been cut a few days ago, and she was relieved to see damp grass clippings on the paving at the front of the house, and thick chunks of matted mud and vegetation moulded in the shape of the pattern on the tyres of a sit-on mower lay at random down the lane. She would have been cross if it hadn't been done as she had sent the gardener a cheque to cover mowing the grass regularly.

There were threads of cobweb across the front door, but no sign of a spider, and she unlocked the door while Mickey got the children out of the car. The plan was to get the children settled in one room while he and Isobel went round and said prayers in each room, but Isobel very much suspected that they might well find that both children would be more interested in following their Mum and Dad and offering their own unique contribution to the proceedings. Mickey had brought his vestments and had produced printed sheets containing the suggested prayers for the blessing of a house, which had taken him several snuffly sessions at the computer to produce while he had been recovering from his cold.

Isobel sighed and pushed opened the door, and hesitated before stepping inside. She could hear nothing and there was no noxious smell to greet her, and apart from the accustomed swirl of dead leaves around the door as she opened it, there was nothing to see. It occurred to her that she had no idea how the leaves got there; when she left each time, there was the odd leaf of two, but nothing like the tangle that was here now. Perhaps they blew in from other rooms. Yeah right, said a small sceptical voice, and just how could that happen when all the windows are shut? Even assuming there are leaves in corners and so on, how can they have blown to the hall when all the windows are shut? Just shut up, Isobel told herself firmly. There's probably a rational explanation, if I could just think of it.

She had yet to become accustomed to seeing Mickey in full liturgical vestments and found it vaguely funny and vaguely disturbing at the same time; she was hard pressed today to keep a straight face when they began their tour of the house. She was also glad it was raining because they kept the front door shut, and that meant that since the blessing of the house began at the front door, no one was likely to pass by and see Mickey at work. She felt very uncomfortable at the thought of Maggie seeing their car and coming to call; her lie about Mickey's work was only a white one but it was still something she would prefer not to be caught out on. She could tell Mickey was nervous too as he kept stumbling over words, and hardly looked at her.

"Lord, you gave to your Church authority to act in your Name. We ask you therefore to visit what we visit, and to bless whatever we bless," Mickey said. "And grant that as we enter this house in lowliness of heart, all powers of evil may be put to flight and the angel of peace may enter in...."

Isobel gazed at her sheet of prayers and remembered to join in with Amen at the end of this bit. After a while, she managed to relax and concentrate without wanting to giggle, and she watched with growing pride and fascination as Mickey got into his professional stride and stumbled less and spoke with greater confidence. They blessed water and then moved from room to room, Mickey saying the requisite prayer for each room and Isobel joining in with a sonorous Amen. Much to her surprise, the children stayed in the living room with the portable television they had deliberately brought with them to act as a distraction should toys fail to be enough of an incentive to stay put. She was touched with the prayers for the bedrooms of the children, and amused by the prayers for the bathroom, which Mickey had been obliged to make up as there didn't seem to be any existing prayers for the blessings of a bathroom, and she had real trouble keeping a straight face when he prayed in the utility room, and felt like asking what sort of ghost lives in a Belfast sink and answered herself immediately: a very clean one!

In the living room they rejoined the children and Isobel sat Luke on her lap and Miranda on Mickey's as they said the Lord's Prayer and finished with Mickey standing and saying,

"Lord God, holy, blessed and glorious Trinity, bless, hallow and sanctify this house that in it there may be joy and gladness, peace and love, health and goodness, and thanksgiving always to you, Father, Son and Holy Spirit; and let your blessing rest upon this house and those who dwell in it, now and forever. Amen."

"Amen!" agreed Isobel fervently.

The silence that followed was broken by Miranda, saying,

"I don't think we should say Amen."

"Why not, sweetie?" Mickey asked.

"It should be Ah Women sometimes at least. Otherwise it's not fair," Miranda said thoughtfully, and slipped off her father's lap to go and sit in front of the television again.

Isobel stifled a giggle.

"Cup of tea, vicar?" she said, and Mickey nodded.

"I'll just get out of this lot," he said, shrugging off his surplice.

Isobel went through to put the kettle on, feeling a sense of relief at having done the deed, even if she was still somewhat sceptical of the reasons for doing it. At least no one could now say they hadn't even prayed in the house. Then she felt a wave of irritation at this thought. Nobody had any right or need to even comment on her life let alone criticise. This is my house, she thought fiercely, and no one can tell me what to do in it. She fitted the new gas canister, the old one having given out the last day they had been there, and filled the kettle. Mickey came through, dressed in his usual casual clothes.

"I reckon that'll take care of anything," he said, fetching mugs from the dresser.

"You make it sound like a miracle elixir, Rev. Trelawny's Cure-All Potion," Isobel said, dryly. "Not that I'm objecting, mind. It's best to cover all the bases after all."

He didn't say anything and just rinsed the mugs under the taps and then said, loudly and with disgust,

"Yuck!"

"What is it?" she demanded and turned round. The water gushing from the tap was brownish in colour, but as she watched it steadily cleared and after a minute or two, the water looked fine again.

"I'd better empty the kettle," she said. "I forgot to run the water first, too. It's been stagnant in the taps for weeks; it's always like that at first. Best too if we boil water for the kids, just in case."

Mickey was staring at the taps, as if caught by some sort of vision and then he shook his head.

"Yes, of course," he said.

"Are you OK?" she asked, seeing him looking not quite right.

"It was just a bit of a shock, seeing the water like that," he said. "After the prayers, too."

"This is just plumbing and nothing else," she said firmly. "Honestly, Mickey, I think you must have watched far too many horror films when you were a teenager. Did you think it was blood or something? Some of the pipes are a tiny bit rusty, that's all."

He had the grace to look shamefaced, and she felt suddenly sorry for him, and went and put her arms round him.

"It's all right," she said. "I don't think we'll have any more problems that we can't solve, and you won't have to go trawling through all the creepy books again."

As soon as she spoke, the mug he had been rinsing crashed to the floor and shattered into a hundred shards of china. She gave him a stern look and said,

"Don't get ideas. You'd left it balanced on the edge of the sink; it was bound to fall. Now, where's the dustpan and brush. I don't fancy picking splinters of china out of anyone's feet."

Later, when she'd drunk enough coffee to get her mind racing, she set up her easel as close to the French doors as she could manage and stared hard at the greening trees on the mound for some time before she picked up her nice new piece of charcoal and began to sketch.

She sank into a sort of a waking dream, deeply absorbed in the changing shapes on the white surface before her, drawing and rubbing and standing watching, and to Mickey watching from the other end of the room, it almost looked as though she was listening to something she couldn't quite hear. When she was happy with the initial sketches, she began to paint. He loved to watch her paint; she became utterly focussed and oblivious of everything but the colours and the brush and the images taking shape in front of her. She spoke to the children if they approached her, but it was strangely disjointed as though she was answering a memory rather than answering what they actually said to her. Luke had begun talking, just the odd word, but he did prefer to be given proper attention, so when he began to squeal at her, Mickey came over and picked him up, and Isobel glanced at them, her eyes dazed and unfocussed.

"Was he crying?" she said, vaguely.

"Not really," Mickey said. "Didn't want him to start, though. How's it going?"

She stepped away from the easel and turned it to show him. The intense freshness of the new leaves had been reproduced quite faithfully, and they even seemed to quiver with an unseen breeze. The silvery branches seemed to contain far more shadows than a May morning would suggest, and when he looked closer, the shadows seemed disturbing, even though he couldn't see anything definite. Here and there was the suggestion of eyes watching from behind the leaves, and below on the mound itself the carpet of bluebells was wilting as if there had been no rain for a long time.

"Interesting," he said neutrally, and she turned back to it and began to add more details.

She worked till he brought her a cup of tea in the late afternoon and he prised the brush from her hand and replaced it with the handle of the mug. She gazed at the mug as if it were something she had never seen before and then seemed to snap back to reality. She took a sip of tea and then shook herself like a dog emerging from water.

The painting was really very lovely, Mickey thought, but odd, in ways he was unable to define. There were hints here and there of something beyond the scene of the picture, as if it held some sort of gateway to another scene that was subtly different and disturbing, the way mirror images can be. The longer he looked at it, the less sure he was that the odd lights among the leaves were eyes at all, but if he glanced back, his first impression was of hundreds of tiny impersonal eyes peering back at him from the painted canopy of trees. It was stunning; but it made him uncomfortable.

She sat down on the sofa and drank her tea far too fast, and he made more and gave her the biggest mug in the dresser, that held three quarters of a pint, and gradually she came back fully.

"I thought we'd give the kids a sandwich before we go," he said. "And find a chip shop on the way home for us."

"Sounds great," she said. "I could just eat a big bag of chips and a battered sausage. No visitors today, then?"

"None," he said. "Neither unseen ones or the kind that might bang on the door. I reckon Maggie's either had the baby by now or she's so huge she can't get behind the wheel of the car. And we aren't on the way anywhere, so she can't just happen by and see the car, not for one day. Anyway, if we make a start as soon as the paint's dry?"

"Yeah," Isobel said. "Would you load the car? I'm dying for a pee!"

*

When they got home, Isobel had a look again at her completed painting and was surprised by what she had produced; it was distinctly otherworldly in tone and while she could see something of the real trees and the real mound in the picture, there was something that set her nerves on edge. She gave a brief involuntary shudder and put the picture with the other one.

"I really should paint something a bit more saleable," she remarked to Mickey, who was bathing the children.

He glanced up; his hair was flecked with specks of bath foam that Luke had thrown at him and his sleeves were damp.

"I thought it was amazing," he said. "I think it would have to really grab someone though. Maybe when you have your next exhibition?"

"If I have another one," she said gloomily.

She perched on the side of the bath and Luke put out his hands to her and she lifted him out and onto the waiting towel. Miranda crowed at getting sole possession of the bath, and Isobel glared at her, in her mock severe manner.

"Don't be so pleased, young lady," she said, wrapping the wriggling Luke in the towel. "You're next!"

When the children had grumbled their way to bed, and the noises of protest at their incarceration had died away, Isobel relaxed, stretching out on the sofa. Mickey came and sat on the floor next to her and began rubbing her feet.

"Oh, that's so good," she said, wriggling her toes. "I'd forgotten what it feels like to be on my feet all day."

"I think you should go to the cottage more often," Mickey said to her.

"You just want to get rid of me!"

"No, seriously," he said. "I don't like you being away, actually. But what you've been producing there has a new edge to it, something unlike anything you've done before. Yes, I know it's a bit disturbing, but it's good. If you had the chance to work more often there, you'd soon have enough for a new exhibition. There's maybe something about the light or whatever there that seems to be giving you inspiration."

Isobel thought about it. If the two new paintings were anything to go by, he was right. She'd never painted quite like this before, and while her rational mind found them disturbing, deep down she found them intriguing at the very least.

"I don't know how I can get there more often," she said, finally. "I know what you're saying, but I don't like leaving the children and I don't like missing out on time with you. If I go on your day off, I don't get any time with you, even if you come along, and I know I'm more or less oblivious to the kids when I'm working anyway."

"Well, I still think you should go more often," he said. "I don't know how we can manage it, though. If we could maximise the time you have available, that might help. What about if you drove up the night before my day off, so you can just start first thing in the morning, and then come home in the evening? It would mean less time taken up getting there, if you've arrived the night before. That'd be dead time anyway."

"I'll think about it," she said.

"If you head off about the kid's bed time, you won't be depriving them," he said. "And if you come home again at dusk, you'll be home to see them before bed. And then we can have the rest of the evening together."

"It makes sense," she said, slowly. "All right, unless I change my mind, I'll try it next week. It would be good if you and the kids came along sometimes too. We could have some supper and head off after that; put the kids into bed when we get there."

"You're only saying that so you get your head cook and tea maker coming along sometimes," Mickey said, and began tickling the foot he'd been rubbing. "Not to mention having me along to rub your feet or you back or anywhere else that needs rubbing at the end of the day."

She squealed and twisted, trying to wrench her foot out of his grasp and ended up falling on the floor next to him before she could escape.

"It's a good time of year for this," she said, when she'd got her breath back. "I hardly have any commissions at the moment; it'll pick up as we get closer to Christmas. While the days are longer and the light's nice and bright, it's the ideal time to do some experimenting."

"That sounds fun," said Mickey, and kissed her.

Chapter 14

The night wind rose and Isobel's nightdress billowed out around her, making her look briefly either very fat or very pregnant. She clutched the fabric around her, and it stopped flapping around and fell still again as her bare feet picked their way across the rough grass of the garden. The grass was damp with dew and her feet were like ice, though the night had been warm enough when she'd gone to bed, and she wished she had a shawl or had thought to put something on her feet. Above, the sky was velvety dark and speckled with millions of stars, very bright and far clearer than they ever were in the city with its horrible orange street-lights and spot-lit buildings. The moon was a crescent of silver, but she couldn't tell whether it was waxing or waning, and it somehow seemed important, though she didn't know why. The soft scent of trodden grass filled the air around her, and other fainter fragrances: green smells of growing things and a hint of wood-smoke. The wind moved the leaves of the trees on the mound as she approached it, sounding like a far-off sea, the waves ebbing and flowing softly against shingle.

She hesitated before starting onto the mound; the bluebells were a faded, almost luminous colour, not quite blue and not quite white in the odd shifting light of the half moon and the stars. Under her feet the leaves and flowers were icy cold and silky to the skin as she trod them down. This is wrong, she thought. I wouldn't walk over flowers.

At the centre of the mound, the bluebells were gone, and the earth was bare, the soil beaten flat and smooth; to her bare, sensitive soles it felt coarse and slightly gritty. And it felt cold, so very cold. You would hardly believe this was almost summer; the air had a prickle to it as of frost forming and the ground felt as though it were frozen hard. She swung her head round, hearing footsteps behind her, but it was just the echo of her own heartbeat.

The swirling of the leaves sounded more and more like a distant seashore, and she wished the wind would drop so she could be quiet and go to sleep; the creaking of the branches and the way they clashed against each other made her think of stags fighting, battling against each other for possession of the females. She gazed at the stars through the canopy of leaves so newly opened they were still wrinkled and tender; the seashore sound grew until she looked at the ground again. At the edges of the mound, white-tipped waves were brushing lightly against the bluebells, and as she watched, very slowly, the flowers disappeared under the sea-foam.

Above her, a barn owl launched itself off its perch and gave its eerie cry as it swooped silently down, its wings seeming to skim her face as it passed, and its wide unearthly eyes looked implacably into hers. The touch of soft feathers sent a shiver down her spine and she sat up in bed and looked wildly around her.

The room was dark, but at one end where she had failed to close the curtains of the window that overlooked the garden, silver light streamed in. The owl called again, and she slid out of her sleeping bag and padded over to the window. The night wind had filled the room with chill air scented with forest smells but when she gazed out, there was no sea lapping at the skirts of the mound, and though the trees had a sheen of silver, the branches were only swaying gently in the wind and not clashing as in a gale. The breeze blew against her face, making her shiver, and she thought she caught a glimpse of movement on the mound. As she watched, the owl passed in unearthly silence across the garden and was gone. She pulled the window shut and scuttled back to her warm sleeping bag and dived into it, pulling it close around her and shivering.

When she woke again, it was dawn. The light streaming into the sparse bedroom had that newly minted look and the sound of the birds confirmed that it was still very early. In town, the birdsong seemed half-hearted by comparison; now she could see why people went out at dawn to hear the dawn chorus. She lay and listened to it for a little while, expecting to slip back to sleep, but found that she grew steadily more alert and awake. At home, the very thought of rising at dawn would have made her shudder, but today, it seemed very different.

Downstairs, waiting for the kettle to boil, she opened the kitchen door and gazed out at the garden, the grass still greyish with dew. There was no sign of frost; her dream had been no more than a dream perhaps induced by a draught on her face. She made coffee and went to drink it in the living room. It had been quite late when she arrived last night, not far off midnight, and she had simply unloaded the car, had a glass of water and gone to bed. Driving through the night had at first been exhilarating and then just plain boring and she'd been glad to get out of the car and get settled. It certainly had felt weird going to bed alone, like that.

The coffee warmed her and she began to feel properly awake after the second cup. She'd brought some provisions but she decided not to bother eating just yet; it was still hours from when she would normally have breakfast, so she opened the French doors and set up her easel on the small area of paving stones, just outside the doors. All round the house a row of slabs formed a path next to a small border close to the house itself, and the area in front of these doors had a double row of slabs where the border would be elsewhere. She brought out one of the camping chairs to put her equipment on, and a second for her to sit on while she was thinking. The early morning sunlight streamed through the leaves of the trees on the mound, turning them greenish-gold and translucent, but her mind was still in the dark, with the starlight and the moonlight on the garden that had not slept at all and had seemed in her dream far too awake, too alert and aware for comfort.

How do you draw what you can't describe? How do you chose colour for what had been without colour and form? How can anyone draw a dream?

I can try, Isobel thought, and picked up her charcoal.

*

The light had grown stronger and the air had become warm before she realised that the pain in her belly was hunger, and she glanced down at the painting with a small smile before walking back to the kitchen to raid her food bag and make a hot drink. Carrying a doorstep of a cheese sandwich and a shiny apple in one hand and a mug of tea in the other, she went back to her easel and sat down in her chair and sighed with sheer contentment. She sank her teeth into the sandwich and began to chew eagerly, taking a swig of tea to wash it down, her whole body suddenly crying out for attention, and small aches from standing so long made her stretch in ways that would have had an onlooker in giggles as she eased all her muscles in turn, pulling faces and rotating her head to ease the kinks in her neck, trying to stuff down her sandwich at the same time. She nearly choked when she looked up and saw that there was someone on the mound; two bicycles were being ridden up and down as thought the mound were part of a BMX course. She was too stunned to react for a moment; then she swallowed her last mouthful, very carefully put down her mug and leapt out of the chair and pelted across the garden, almost incoherent with rage.

It was the two boys, Maggie's boys that she had dived into the river to save, each with an expensive mountain bike. They were oblivious of her as they careered over the mound, crushing the fading bluebells as they rode, yelling and screaming with enjoyment, so that they didn't even hear her approach until she reached the top of the mound and stood like a pantomime demon, appearing to them as if out of nowhere. The older boy actually rode his bike straight at her, expecting her to jump out of his way, but she stood firm, arms folded on her chest and he braked in time.

"And just what do you think you're doing?" she demanded, as the younger boy slammed on his brakes and brought his bike to a halt only a foot or so away from her.

The older boy looked nonplussed.

"Riding our bikes, isn't it obvious?" he said, staring at her.

Isobel could see every freckle on his unremarkable face and made herself remember this was still a child.

"This is private property," she said. "It's my land and no one can use it without my permission."

He stared at her, considering his options. Then he did the last thing he should ever have done. He held up his hand and extended one finger to her in an unmistakeable gesture.

"Do you see that?" he said. "Swivel!"

Isobel took a sharp involuntary breath, and again told herself this was still a child. If he'd been even half way polite, she might have felt a great deal less angry with them for being here in her garden; but this was way beyond acceptable behaviour, and she was struggling to keep her temper from spilling over.

"Get off my land," she said in a cold menacing voice. "Get off my land now, you foul-mouthed guttersnipe."

He just stared at her, defiantly, without moving.

"Or what?" he said. "Or you'll cry? Or you'll call the police?"

"No," she said. "Or I may be obliged to do something your benighted parents should have done years ago and introduce you to a little discipline. Get off my land."

He stayed where he was. Isobel moved forward, very controlled, and leaned down so her face was level with his and only a few inches away, and then bellowed so loud he lost his cool entirely,

"GET OFF MY LAND!"

The change from her cold measured tones couldn't have been more obvious, but she hadn't actually lost control, though from the damp patch that appeared at the front of his shorts, he clearly had, and rather than wait to see what she might actually do, he leapt onto his bicycle and pedalled furiously away, his younger brother in close pursuit. They hauled the bikes over the nearest bit of collapsed fence and vanished away over the fields.

Isobel swallowed hard; yelling like that had hurt her throat and she felt slightly sick. She ran back to the house, collected up her easel and moved all the chairs and equipment inside. She had a feeling that she wouldn't be getting much more done for a while. When she'd got up, she hadn't bothered with a shower, but now, hot and flustered and sweating with emotion as much as from the warmth of the day, she went upstairs and had a cool sluice down in the shower, and she was dressed and was combing her hair when, as she had imagined, an almighty banging started at the front door.

Sighing, and mentally girding herself for the coming conflict, she ran down the stairs and opened the door. Maggie was there, as expected, wearing a mauve dress, a baby sling complete with infant mostly hidden in its folds, and an expression like a human volcano. She wasn't alone; at her side was a thin, weedy-looking man with a long ratty ponytail, another woman, dressed entirely in black and clanking with heavy silver Gothic style jewellery, and a child of perhaps six years old, whose hair looked like it had seen neither shampoo nor a comb in years and whose face was so grimy the tracks made by her running nose gave the only clue to her natural skin tone; a stench of unwashed child and clothes wafted to Isobel and made her feel at once furious and compassionate.

"Oh, congratulations," said Isobel with a big smile. "I see you had the baby safely. What was it this time, a boy or a girl? I can never tell just by looking."

This only slightly wrong-footed Maggie, who merely ignored Isobel's questions.

"What the hell do you mean by frightening two innocent children like that and threatening them with violence?" she demanded, her voice blaring and shrill.

"First of all, I asked them to get off my land, since they were trespassing," Isobel said, calmly. "They were abusive; or at least the older boy was abusive in a way that suggests to me he's far from innocent. So I raised my voice to get my message across."

"You deliberately humiliated him," Maggie snarled.

"Nope," said Isobel. "Don't blame me if your toilet training has been inadequate."

She looked deliberately at the child who was standing picking her nose assiduously; the aroma of partial incontinence was one among a bouquet of odours emanating from her.

"I was going to ring the police and report them as truants," Isobel went on. "Surely they should be in school?"

"We don't believe in school," said the man in a nasal, affected voice. "Children thrive better in a home environment, where they are lovingly educated and drawn on to fulfil their true potential."

"So the true potential of those two is to become hooligans, yeah? I see," said Isobel. "Well, I think I will call the police if I ever see them uninvited on my property again."

"All property is theft," said the other woman, in a flat, snide little voice that sounded very like a little girl who has just discovered the joys of sarcasm.

"Oh yes?" said Isobel. "Especially when that property is the weekly dose of hope for millions of people. Yes, I'd agree with that."

Maggie flushed with some unnameable emotion.

"You mean you didn't Google me?" Isobel asked, sweetly. "Amazing things, search engines. You can find out anything, pretty much. I am surprised you didn't return the compliment, but then I probably don't rate as a human being really."

"You threatened them with violence," Maggie said, coldly.

"No, I think you'll find I threatened them with discipline," Isobel said. "Quite a different thing, unless you only associate discipline with being belted half silly."

The child moved forward, and sniffed at Isobel elaborately, rather like an uncertain dog.

"The lady smells funny," she announced.

Isobel, fighting her rising bile at the child's stench, leaned down and said softly to her,

"It's called soap, darling. You could ask your mummy to buy you some."

Close to, she could see the lice clinging to the roots of the girl's hair, and she moved back again quickly. I know nits can't jump, but I'm not taking any chances, she thought.

"You should be ashamed of yourself, treating children that way," said the man. "Shouting at our boys. Who knows what damage you've done their psyches with your abuse?"

Isobel felt her own rising tide of fury, and held it back.

"If it's shame we're talking about, what about this poor little specimen?" she said, indicating the little girl. "How can you treat a child this way?"

"Celeste has decided not to wash," Maggie said. "We have chosen to respect her decision."

Isobel shook her head, in horror.

"I can't make up my mind whether you're all bad or just mad, or maybe both," she said. "Children need care; not this abuse and neglect. Now, get off my land or I will call the police and report you for threatening behaviour. I'm still in two minds whether I'll call social services or not."

Maggie stared at her, her eyes flashing with unspent fury, and shook her head in unconscious imitation of Isobel, shaking loose the purple gauzy scarf that she wore round her hair, and Isobel saw that the curly blonde hair it covered was almost certainly a wig.

"I thought you might be a true fellow artist," Maggie said, drawing herself up to her considerable full height to look down at Isobel. "But you're nothing but a bourgeois housewife with pretensions. Your art is nothing but a dull pandering to the tastes of the middle classes, without skill or vision or imagination."

"Yes, maybe, but it does pay my bills, and I've never been accused of producing tasteless New Age pornography," Isobel said calmly.

"Erotica," snarled Maggie. "Get the terms right, you Christian cretin. Erotica!"

"I seem to recall the critics all called it porn," Isobel said. "I'm only quoting a higher authority. I also seem to recall asking you to leave. You seem to be still here."

She slid her mobile out of her pocket and began to tap in a number; she hadn't turned it on but they couldn't see that, and they started backing away, so rapidly that Maggie trod on the toes of her partner who had been standing right behind her.

At the gate, when safely off the property, Maggie turned and screamed back at Isobel,

"Marriage is only institutionalised prostitution. You're nothing but a tart, Isobel Trelawny."

"Better a tart than a flake," Isobel called back and went back into the house, where out of sight, she began to shake.

More than anything, she wanted Mickey. She had very seldom endured conflicts like the one she'd just experienced, and it had made her feel sick and alone. It was all right being defiant while they were standing there, but now she was alone, she knew the little voices of doubt would begin to creep in, and she would start to wonder if any of the abuse Maggie had hurled at her might have any foundation in fact. Was her art without imagination or vision? Was she bourgeois and pretentious? She could hear the doubts begin, sharp metallic barbs that hurt as much to pull out as they had done going in.

"Bugger that for a game of soldiers," she said to the empty hall. "I need tea; hot tea, with sugar in it."

She would have gone straight home then, once she'd had the tea, but for her pride telling her she couldn't allow such people to drive her from her own home. She would go when she'd originally intended to go home and not before, so she went back through to where her easel stood near the French doors and looked hard at her completed painting and felt the glow of self-esteem warm her doubts away; it was a bloody good piece of work. Vision, well, it was there in spades. Imagination, by the bucket-load. No one could call this dull. Feeling suddenly much better, Isobel wrapped the board up and went to put it away in the boot of the car, but as she went down the hall to the front door, she saw that on the stone flags where a doormat should be, a whole pile of dead leaves had appeared. They had not been there earlier, and she thought that in fact they must have appeared while she was making and drinking her tea. The only way they could have got there was through the letterbox, and she yanked the door open, expecting to see two boys on bicycles disappearing away down the lane, laughing and jeering at her. The lane was silent and still, no one in sight at all. They'll be home by now, she thought; it only takes two seconds to stuff leaves through a letterbox and run away. I should be just glad it was only leaves. Town kids could teach you a thing or two about revenge.

She brushed the leaves out into the front garden with the side of her foot and put the painting in the car. She wondered what she should do now, and decided that she deserved a bit of a break, and lay down on the sofa, sticking her feet over the armrest so they were higher than her head. The sounds of the summer day filled the living room; the calling of doves, soft and mournful, the occasional raw croak of a rook, and a bumblebee buzzed just outside the open window. The late afternoon sunshine spilled into the room and she felt herself grow sleepy and she closed her eyes. I could probably do with a rest, she thought, I was up at dawn after all. Just half an hour, and then I'll wash up and head home. Just half an hour.

It never is half an hour, unless you set an alarm. Isobel woke with a chill and sat staring round her in puzzlement, heavy-eyed and dull with sleep, not able to take in the fact that she had slept for hours and hours, in a deep dead slumber, and now the sky was growing dark. The kids would be long in bed before she could hope to get back. Damn and blast it, she thought. How could I be so stupid? She rushed through her few chores of washing up and putting away the few bits and pieces she'd used, ran round shutting and locking doors and windows and hurriedly stowed away her equipment in the boot with the painting. As she stepped out through the front door, she saw that there were more leaves just inside the door and she felt cold at the thought of those children prowling round her house while she had slept the sleep of the dead; they might have put lighted paper through the letterbox rather than dead leaves. The idea of them peering through windows as she lay helpless and unconscious on the sofa, was a truly nasty thought, and as she pulled the door shut, she thought she saw movement in the hall and stopped for a second. No, it was just another leaf being swirled around by the draught from the door. She shut the door with a resounding crash and turned the key firmly in the lock.

"Stay safe," she said to the cottage in a whisper, echoing the prayer of generations as they left their homes unattended.

She opened the gate first before going to the car; the car was over-hot and smelt of the baked plastic of the car seats, and a hint of stale bread; probably a half eaten crust or bread bun had wedged itself unseen in a corner under one of the child seats, and would emerge either semi-fossilized or blue with mould the next time she had a good clear out. It was always scary what turned up when she swept the car out properly; little lost treasures of the children's, odd socks, hard bits of food or gooey chunks of fruit turning to compost in the safety of the dark crevices under the baby seat. Sometimes her own belongings turned up, an earring that had fallen out, a book or a tube of hand-cream. It was a sort of domestic archaeology, though without the glamour.

She turned the engine on and opened the windows, to try and blow away the heat and the smell, and eased her way onto the lane and went to shut the gate, again making that silent heartfelt prayer for the security of her cottage. I'll kill Maggie if anything happens to this place while I'm gone; and if there's dog muck on the doorstep next time I come, I'll make her eat it, Isobel thought savagely and began the long drive home as the sky darkened from deep blue to full black and the stars emerged and twinkled kindly overhead as she drove.

The roads seemed pretty quiet and she made good time, sinking into that dull state of mind of the long distance driver, eating up the miles and counting the time till she could be home and comforted. She was about an hour or perhaps a little less from home, and was passing through an area where the road surrounded by high wooded banks, the trees that loomed high overhead made the road ahead dark even at noon, when she caught a movement out of the corner of her eye. A fraction of a second later, she hit the deer that had leapt out in front of her. Too late she slammed on the brakes, setting the car into a skid, the deer bouncing away from the bonnet and into the darkness. Her head whirled as the car spun briefly out of control, before she managed to wrench the wheel straight and brake properly.

Her heart pounding, she turned the engine off. Everything was suddenly totally silent, except for the blood thundering in her ears. She scrambled out of the car, trying to locate the deer. In the dense shade of the thickly grown trees, she could see nothing, so she went back to the car, turned on the lights, so that even though the headlights were broken the rear lights and the hazard warning lights were on and shining enough to give her some light as well as warn any approaching traffic, and rummaged in the glove compartment for the torch she knew was there. Trying not to look at the bloody mess that was the front of her car, Isobel quartered the ground, searching methodically until finally, yards further away than she would have expected she found the deer.

It lay limp at the side of the road, a big red deer stag. She couldn't look at its injuries, and she knew it was dead. Its eyes were wide open, staring wildly at her, though the light was gone from them. Unable to stop herself, she knelt down in the muck at the side of the road and put her hand on the animal's flank. The skin was still warm, the hairs surprisingly soft and smooth. The heat of its body was a shock and she ran her hand up to its head, and touched its muzzle, moist and slightly bloody. She pulled back her hand in horror, staring at the blood, bright in the light of the torch and the rear lights and the hazards, and felt a sob welling up in her throat, coming out of nowhere and breaking like a wave that brings untold flotsam and jetsam to the shore in its wake.

"What have I done?" she whispered, and laid her head on the cooling neck and began to cry.

Chapter 15

Mickey glanced at the clock for the third time in almost as many minutes and fought the desire to ring Isobel on her mobile. I mustn't be clingy, he told himself firmly. But it is after midnight, and she hasn't rung to say why she's been delayed, he thought, allowing himself a pang of worry. I'll give it another half an hour and then I'll ring her. The house was very still and silent, the day's detritus of toys and food cleared away and all the dishes washed and put away in his restless attempt to fill the quiet hours after the children's bedtime. He'd tried television; he'd tried reading. Nothing worked.

"Bugger it, I'm ringing," he said, and picked up the phone and dialled her number.

It rang and rang until her voice-mail picked it up.

"Isobel, ring me back as soon as you get this," he said. "You've probably lost track of time, but I'm getting worried. Call me."

He cradled the phone after he'd hung up, his sense of disquiet growing every minute. Something was very wrong, but he had no way of finding out exactly what.

At half past three, the phone rang; he snatched it up before it had finished that first blaring ring.

"Mr. Trelawny?" said an unknown male voice.

"Yes," breathed Mickey.

"Everything's all right. Your wife's had an accident but she's absolutely fine," said the voice. "She's at the hospital; you'd better come and fetch her."

"What happened?" Mickey said, strangely breathless.

"A deer ran out in front of the car," said the voice. "She's unhurt but pretty shaken up."

Shaking with relief and shock, Mickey took details of which hospital Isobel was at, and then tried to think what to do. Isobel had been driving their only car, and even if there were another car available, he'd have to do something about the children. In the end, his mind seemed to freeze, and he phoned his boss, Les, who was at first annoyed at being woken, and then genuinely worried. He drove round shortly afterwards, with his wife, who had volunteered to sit up for the children and then drove Mickey to the hospital and waited in the deserted car park.

Mickey walked into the bright lights of the casualty department and asked for Isobel, and was directed to a curtained cubicle, where he found Isobel lying on a bed and crying like a small child. There was blood on her clothes, on her face and in her hair, but it was dried now to a shade like rusty mud, and he knew it wasn't hers. She looked at him almost without recognition and then flew into his arms, more like Miranda than own self. He was truly shocked; this was so unlike her usual calm pragmatic self, who took even tragedy in her stride. She'd cried briefly at her parent's funeral, but never like this, never so wildly and with such abandon.

"You'll dissolve," he said after a minute, and passed his handkerchief to her, and obediently she mopped at her face and blew her nose, her breath coming in little sobs and whimpers.

"What on earth happened?" he asked, when she seemed a little calmer.

"It just appeared, I had no time to even try to stop," she said, in a whisper. "The noise, oh God, the noise when I hit it. I've never heard anything like it. It was like a hundred blunt meat cleavers hacking at a side of beef all at once. The car's pretty bad. The police said they'd arrange to get it off the road. They were so nice."

He held her again, feeling the little muscle tremors that ran through her whole body every few seconds. The curtains twitched and a white-coated doctor put his head round.

"Ah, I see your husband's here to take you home, Mrs. Trelawny," he said, in the hearty voice of someone who has been working for far too long and can see the end of the shift approaching. "Can I have a word with you, Mr. Trelawny?"

Mickey detached himself from Isobel.

"Back in a minute," he said, and followed the doctor to an empty cubicle a short distance away.

"What is it?" he asked, when he was sure they were out of earshot.

The doctor looked a bit uncomfortable.

"We're a bit concerned about your wife's state of mind," he said. "Is she usually very volatile and emotional?"

"Not unduly so, no," Mickey said. "She's usually the one who doesn't panic or get upset."

"That is worrying," said the doctor, biting his lip. "The police were called when another car stopped to help and she didn't respond. The policeman who came in with her said they'd found her cuddling the dead deer and not answering when she was spoken to, so they called an ambulance thinking she might be badly hurt. She's hardly said a thing, just cried the whole time. She's in a mild state of shock, medically speaking, but it seems to go deeper, but since she isn't talking, I can't explain it. I just thought you ought to know, so you can keep an eye on it. Is she a strict vegetarian? That might explain her extreme reaction."

Mickey shook his head.

"We've toyed with it sometimes, but she always reckoned the true test was the smell of frying bacon and neither of us can ever resist. She's not even sentimental about animals normally, just very pragmatic. She'd always try to avoid hitting rabbits or whatever, but it does happen and she's never got in a state before," he said.

"As I say, keep an eye on her," said the doctor. "She's physically unhurt, though there may be some whiplash, as you'd expect, but I am more concerned about her mental state. If she doesn't recover in a week or so, please ask your GP for some advice. There may be something deeper at the root of this."

Once the formalities were done with, Mickey took her out to the car park, where Les was dozing in his car.
"We'll both sit in the back," Mickey said.
"How are you feeling, Isobel?" asked Les, but Isobel said nothing and just slipped into the car.
"She's feeling pretty rotten, Les," Mickey said. "I think I just want to get her home. Before the kids wake up and find us gone."
"Yes, of course," said Les, and started the engine.

*

When they got home, Isobel ran upstairs to her room and burrowed fully clothed under the duvet and lay very still and refused the offer of tea, saying she just wanted to sleep, and after a little while holding her hand, he saw that she had slipped off to sleep. While she slept, Mickey made arrangements about the car and got breakfast for the kids, and somehow managed to keep his daughter from crashing into their bedroom to bounce her mother awake.
"Mummy's a bit poorly," he explained. "We need to let her sleep."
"But it's morning," Miranda said, puzzled. "People don't go to bed when it's morning."
"They do if they've been up most of the night," Mickey said, wistfully.
He was hoping that he might get an hour or two while Miranda was at playgroup, if Luke were cooperative enough to have a nap too. He felt almost drunk with tiredness. He looked in on Isobel when he was about to leave to take Miranda to playgroup, and she was still asleep, so he left her alone. When he came back, Luke had no intention of having a sleep; he'd really outgrown daytime sleep now, though once in a while he would have a sleep in the afternoon if his sister would let him. Mickey made a few phone calls, cancelling all his engagements that day, and hoped that Isobel would be back to normal by the morning, as he knew he would find it hard to find cover for more than a day or two.
At lunchtime, he took a mug of tea and a cheese sandwich up and gently woke his wife.
"What is it?" she said, pushing the covers back from her face. She'd been sleeping with the duvet over her head, and her face was dripping with sweat and her hair clung damply to her skull.
"Lunch," he said.
She struggled to sit up, and took the mug from him, taking grateful gulps, but she wouldn't take the sandwich plate.
"I'm not hungry," she said.
"When did you last eat, then?" he said.

"Yesterday lunchtime," she said. "I feel a bit sick still. Sorry. Maybe I'll eat them later."

"No worries," he said. "The kids are longing to see you; Miranda was hoping you'd be up when she got back from playgroup, and I had trouble stopping her bouncing in here when I came in just now. I said you'd probably prefer a gentler awakening."

She managed a weak smile.

"Go on, let her in," she said, and when he opened the door, there was a race between the two children to see who could get to the bed and onto it the fastest. Isobel found herself swamped by squealing children, hugging and kissing her and shrieking. Fortunately, neither child had actually missed her much and each had the attention span appropriate to their ages, and within a few minutes they had dispersed, Luke having laid claim to Isobel's uneaten sandwich.

"We'll be finding bits of escaped cheese all over the house," Isobel said, her voice sounding weak but a great deal more normal.

"I'll round them up later," Mickey said. "You'd not think he's just had his own lunch. That kid could eat for England."

"It was the size of a small horse, you know," she said, unexpectedly. "I'd never seen one close to, before. I had no idea they were so huge."

Her face was very set and still, and almost without expression; her eyes seemed to see things he could not, as if she were gazing into the far distance through a window.

"I'm going over later to have a look at the car," Mickey said. "If it's still drive-able, I'll bring it home, and if not, then I'll have to arrange for it to be brought a bit closer to home for repairs or whatever. Is your stuff still in it, or did you leave it at the cottage?"

"In the boot," she said. "Will you bring it home, for me?"

"Of course," he said, gently. "Did you have a good day, before the crash?"

"Till about lunchtime, yes. A very good day," she said. "It just went wrong after that."

"What happened?"

Isobel said nothing, trying to remember. It seemed so long ago, that awful row, and it didn't seem at all important even, now. It seemed utterly trivial and futile.

"I had a row with Maggie, because I yelled at her kids," she said, dreamily. "It doesn't matter any more."

"Tell me about it, anyway," Mickey asked, relieved that she was talking.

Isobel described how she had had strange dreams the night before and how she had sought to translate some of the images and emotions from her dreams into her painting that day, and how furious she had been to see the boys on the mound.

"They really didn't care that it wasn't their garden," she said. "They really didn't care at all. I was pretty shocked at that, to tell you the truth. I must be getting middle class or something, expecting all kids to have at very least an inkling that their behaviour may be unacceptable. These boys knew as soon as I appeared and told them off that they were doing something wrong and they didn't give a monkey's about it. I made the older one piss himself with fear, though. Probably not something to be proud of, and I think it was that which made Maggie go ballistic. I'd go ballistic myself if anyone threatened my kids. But they all came along, the three adults and the smelliest child I have even seen, so unless they have a nanny or something, there were seven kids left at home unattended, and I wouldn't trust that oldest boy not to harm the younger ones just for something to do."

"What were her partner and her friend like, then?" Mickey asked.

"Unremarkable to look at, I suppose; they'd go totally unnoticed in somewhere like Glastonbury," Isobel said. "He's rather creepy, actually, and frankly I can't see why he's managed to get two women to himself, unless there really is more to him than meets the eye. The other woman must be a good ten years younger than Maggie, and I'd eat my hat if she were actually called Cassandra by her parents. I also reckon that blonde hair of Maggie's is a wig; I think I saw the seam when her scarf slipped. They were so horrible and I felt terrible after the row, so I had a rest to try and calm down before I headed home. I was considering phoning social services about those children; that child is in a state no decent parent would let a child get into."

"How bad? Just in need of a bath?"

"Delousing, for starters. I don't think you could ever untangle the hair; it had gone to a sort of foul smelling felt," Isobel said with a shudder. "I think she was quite probably a pretty child underneath it all. I can't think how no one has spotted it, but then, if they don't go to school at all, who would ever notice? They seem to have their own self-contained little commune up there. I doubt they're even registered with a doctor's surgery. I even wonder if they bother registering births."

"That's pretty awful," Mickey said. "I think maybe a call would at least alert someone to what's going on. Just because they're rich doesn't mean they should get away with stuff like that."

Isobel passed her mug to him and then looked at herself in some shock.

"Dear God," she said. "I didn't realise I was still in these clothes."

She eased herself cautiously out of bed and stripped off her clothes as she went to the bathroom.

"Are you feeling better, now?" he asked, sitting on the side of the bath while she showered.

"Weird," she said. "I feel weird, as if I'm not here, really."

"Will you be OK for a few hours while I go and sort out about the car? I've managed to get a lift," he said.

Isobel nodded.

"I think so," she said. "Just as long as the kids are moderately well behaved. My head hurts, and my neck's really sore too, but I think I'm OK, now. I can't think what came over me to get so upset last night. It must have been the shock, I suppose."

"Not surprising," he said. "I'd have been shocked too."

When he'd gone, Isobel dressed and went down to sit with the children and lost herself in children's television, laughing mindlessly at the cartoons and doing the usual things she would have normally done at this time of day, fetching drinks and changing Luke's nappy and all the time feeling as though she were working solely by automatic pilot and her mind was somewhere very far away indeed. She kept getting flashes of memory, or perhaps it wasn't memory at all but imagination, seeing the deer in ways she knew that she hadn't. It had happened too quickly for her to have seen it gaze at her, the brown, liquid eyes full of emotion as she hurtled headlong at it. She could even see the long, thick eyelashes that she had actually seen on the half-closed eyes of the dead animal, but in her mind they blinked at her. Cross, she shook her head and cleared away the images for the moment, but every few minutes they recurred; things she hadn't seen, couldn't have seen even. She saw the deer detach itself from the herd and walk towards the road, listening to her approaching car, listening to her thoughts and to her heart before leaping out very deliberately in front of her car.

I'm going stark staring bonkers, Isobel thought, horrified. They'll lock me away and throw away the key if they know what I'm seeing. Oh God, what am I going to do? The little voice that was her own practical self gave the answer: go and cook the supper, that's what you're going to do, you silly woman. Leaving the children watching the television, Isobel slipped through to the kitchen and found she was sweating profusely. I'm terrified, she thought, I am so very scared, and I don't know what I'm scared of even. Later, when Mickey got back, she struggled to remember what she had cooked for the children, and it was only by going and checking the plates by the sink was she able to tell Mickey she'd cooked them pasta shapes with tomato sauce; the act of cooking was a big, accusing blank in her memory.

She let Mickey bath the children and put them to bed, coming through to kiss them each goodnight, when they were drowsy and contented and mesmerised by the story Mickey had read to them. They smelled of sweet-scented soap and baby shampoo, small warm bodies hugged close to hers and she felt the tears welling up again, but somehow managed to hide them till she was downstairs again.

"This isn't like you, love," Mickey said as he patted her shoulder rhythmically as she wept softly against him. "You don't get this upset over things."

"I know," she said, hoarsely. "I don't know what's the matter with me. And before you ask, it isn't that time of the month either. I just feel so sad."

After Mickey fell asleep that night, exhausted by two long days and a sleepless and anxious night, Isobel lay next to him listening to his breathing and felt the silent tears sliding down the sides of her face and steadily soaking her pillow. It was a long time before she finally slept, her mind racing itself in frantic circles. She didn't want to close her eyes, in case the deer came back. Did I fall asleep at the wheel? Is that why I didn't see it in time? She asked herself questions she knew the answers to, knowing she had not fallen asleep, that there had been no time to stop. As she finally fell into a deep sleep, the heavy head of the stag raised itself in front of her, but again she couldn't stop, and ploughed straight into it and slept.

*

The sun was filling the room when she woke; Mickey had opened the curtains so that she would wake to brightness, and she could hear the rest of the family in the kitchen: Luke's banging on the tray of his high chair meant that breakfast wasn't coming quickly enough, Mickey's voice, slightly frazzled saying something she couldn't quite hear, then Miranda's screaming in anger over some imagined slight. She's probably been given the wrong spoon, Isobel thought, and struggled out of bed. She was surprised to find how stiff and sore she was; bruises she didn't know she'd got were starting to show, and hurt rather a lot. She must have been very tense in the night; her hands ached with the effort of clutching a dream steering wheel and trying to regain control of the spinning car.

Staggering down the stairs in her nightie, Isobel felt that horrible surge of out-of-control emotion again and swallowed back the tears she felt forming. I don't know what I'm crying about, even, she thought and walked into the kitchen and went to hug her children in turn and then Mickey. He was back in his clerical collar, and looking hassled.

"Sorry I over-slept," she said. "Shall I take over?"

"Please," he said, so she took the cereal spoon from him and began feeding Luke.

"Are you very busy today?" she asked as he made more tea.

"Fairly. I've got stuff to catch up with from yesterday, but I'll be in and out all day," he said. "So if you start feeling ill again, I'll be around sometimes. I'm sorry I can't take more time off; but there's stuff this week that's not so easy to pass on or find cover. There are a couple of evening meetings that I really can't get out of. Sorry."

"It's OK," she said, but dully. "Did you bring my things in from the car?"

"Yes; all in the spare room as usual. The car is going to be out of action for a week or two; the insurance people debated about whether to write it off altogether but decided that it was cheaper to have it fixed. It's going to be pricey though, so I'm glad we got fully comp. Can I have a look at the new painting before I head off? I didn't like to look last night," he said.

"Help yourself," she said and wiped Luke's mouth with his bib and hauled him out of his high chair and let him run off to play.

Mickey glanced at her; she looked unwell, still. There were huge dark shadows under her eyes, and her eyes themselves had no lustre and were reddened by all the crying.

"Tell you what," he said. "You can show me it later when I've got time to appreciate it."

She shrugged, and began washing the bowls from breakfast.

"Did you not want this tea?" he asked, gesturing at the pot.
"I didn't notice you'd made it," she said.
"Are you all right?" he asked, worried.
"Fine," she said, and burst into tears again.

Chapter 16

"I don't know what to do," Mickey said to Simon as they sat in the corner of the back room at the pub nearest Mickey's vicarage. "She's not herself at all, but I don't know quite who or what she is. She's there and not there. She bursts into tears for no apparent reason; and when I ask what's wrong, she says that nothing's wrong, that everything's fine, and I can't get through to her how worried I am."

Simon took an experimental sip at his pint, stalling for thought.

"Is she coping with the children?" he asked. "Katy was a bit low after Jodie was born. Maybe that's it."

Mickey shook his head.

"I don't think so," he said. "She had some baby blues after they were both born, but this isn't like that at all. I mean, Luke's fifteen, sixteen months now. This is quite different. She's sort of coping with the children, but she won't answer the door in case it's parish stuff and she's stopped answering the phone at all. The kids seem OK, or I would be frantic by now. She looks after them, feeds and baths and plays with them and all that, but all the time she seems to be elsewhere. You should see the paintings she's been producing though: weird but brilliant. Last week, she went up to paint as soon as the kids were in bed every evening. I was a bit shocked when I saw what she'd done. You'd have to see it to get the full force of it. It's sort of an island, in a lake or something but you can't see clearly the surroundings. There's this sort of muddy lakeside beach, all washed up bits of twig and stuff, and lying there, obviously gasping its last is this fish. It's a salmon, I think, and it's got a rip in its lip as if its been hauled off a hook and left to die on the mud. You can almost see the gills moving and the fins and the tail flailing around trying to get itself back into the water. The colours are so vivid and it's so animated and so heart-rending. I asked her about it, and she said, that's how I feel sometimes."

"Ouch!" said Simon. "Have you suggested she see the doctor?"

"I did," admitted Mickey. "But she said she felt fine, that there was nothing wrong. That's why I rang and asked you and Katy to come and stay this weekend, to see if you had any ideas, either about what's wrong or what I can do about it. I tell you, Simon, I am so bloody worried about her. She's lost weight and she's lost colour and everything, and she seems so shut away, lost inside herself. It's almost like having a relationship with someone living on the other side of the world; there's a delay every time I speak to her, as if what I say takes time to get to her, and then a delay while she thinks about what to say."

"She's always been a bit moody," Simon said. "When we were kids, she'd get in a strop about something and sulk for days. Mum and Dad just ignored it though, saying she'd get over it if we left her alone. She does seem a bit, well, I suppose she seems dislocated, as if she's lost the plot. Do you think Alzheimer's might be hereditary?"

"Bloody hell, Simon, don't say things like that!" Mickey said, in an explosive whisper. "I can't imagine anything worse."

"Puts it into perspective, though, doesn't it?" said Simon with an apologetic grin. "Look, I'll have a word with Katy tonight when we go to bed. She's spent the evening with Izzie, so she might have something to add, and then if you and I sneak off Sunday afternoon, take the kids to the park or something, I might have a few thoughts by then. Do you fancy some crisps, or do you reckon supper will be ready when we get back?"

*

Isobel chopped onions and fried mince while Katy sat on a tall stool and sipped red wine, keeping a weather eye on the children in the next room, who so far had been playing nicely.

"You've lost weight," Katy said, as Isobel tipped the onions into the pan.

"Been busy," Isobel said.

"I've been busy but I just seem to gain weight. You must tell me the real secret," Katy said.

"I just haven't felt hungry," Isobel said. "I think I am, and then after a few mouthfuls it goes."

"Are you fully recovered from that crash?" Katy asked.

"I wasn't really hurt," Isobel said. "The car was fairly mangled, though. Thank God for insurance. I sometimes wonder if collisions with deer are acts of God."

It was such a strange thing to say that Katy almost missed it.

"What do you mean?" she asked.

"Nothing, really. Just that some things like gales and floods and stuff like that you can't do anything to prevent. Most car accidents are someone's fault, somewhere or other. Something leaping out at you is different. You don't have time to brake or swerve or anything. It doesn't matter if you're going at thirty or sixty; just the amount of damage to the car is less if you're going slower. It's the same to the deer; it dies anyway," Isobel said, stirring the onions as they browned. "Just ignore me, I'm being silly."

Katy saw with horror that Isobel was crying, and just as she was about to come over to hug her, the front door opened. Simon and Mickey were back from the pub. Isobel blew her nose on kitchen roll and wiped her eyes as Mickey came into the kitchen.

"Bloody onions," she said. "Supper will be about an hour, I think. You could have stayed at the pub, you know."

"Just thought you might need a hand, with the kids," Mickey said.

"Everything under control," Isobel said. "No need to panic."

"I've got some bottled beer in the fridge," Mickey said, to Simon. "If you fancy one while we're waiting?"

"Go on then," Simon said. "We'll leave the wine to the ladies, eh?"
"Can I show Simon your latest paintings, love?" Mickey asked, and Isobel glanced up without much interest.
"Yeah," she said.
"Can I nip up too, while the kids are quiet?" Katy asked. "I haven't seen any of your work for ages."
Isobel just nodded and opened a can of plum tomatoes.
Upstairs, in the spare room that served as a storage place for Isobel's work, the double sofa bed had been opened for Simon and Katy, so there wasn't a lot of room for the three of them. Isobel had stored her paintings in the big wardrobe that dominated the room, and Mickey opened it and began bringing out the paintings.
"This is the one she did the day of the crash," he said, and they gazed at the board in some wonder.
It was a night scene, the colours strangely misty and indistinct. The mound they recognized, but none of the surrounding scene was familiar. The trees were waving in a strong wind, and all around the mound, the sea was rising. Silver flecked waves licked at the flowers on the sides of the mound, as if tasting them, and on the mound itself, amid the tree and the wisps of mist, a figure stood. It was a strange figure, that seemed almost a woman in a long white gown, but when you looked again, you could see that it was really a sea gull with its wings half folded and trailing slightly as if injured, its beak dropped against its breast so that it looked almost like clasped hands.
Simon and Katy said nothing, and Katy's eyes had filled with tears.
"This is the most recent one," Mickey said, bringing out the one with the stranded salmon.
"That's so sad," Katy said, horrified.
"It gets worse," Mickey said. "She said that's how she feels sometimes."
The colours of the salmon, and its evident distress were so vivid that Mickey put it back almost immediately.
"Fish out of water, she calls that one," he said, wrapping it again.
"I don't know what to say, mate," Simon said, helplessly.
"You wait till you've seen the others," Mickey said grimly, and pulled out the one she'd named The Place of the Skull.
They looked through Isobel's work and after ten minutes, Katy shook her head.
"She's not well," she said. "This isn't the cheerful, pragmatic, hopeful Isobel we all know."
"I know," said Mickey. "I'm worried sick."
From downstairs, the wail of an irritated child rose fretfully.
"Better go down," he said. "The kids are getting hungry and grouchy. Maybe we can talk later when they're in bed. Though I doubt she'll admit anything's wrong. I mean, this stuff is some of her most gifted work, but even she admits it's a bit disturbing. I'm

so scared she's going a bit mad, not to put too fine a point on it. She wouldn't be the first artist to go that way, after all. I don't like leaving her on her own, but what choice do I have? I have to get on with my work. I can't take any more time off to be with her and the kids. She won't go to the doctor's, won't admit anything is wrong even, so what can I do?"

"I'll think about it," Katy said.

Another cry came from below, an enraged bellow that had to be Luke's protest at being excluded by the older pair from some game they considered him too little to be allowed to join in, and reluctantly, they trooped down to rejoin both the children and Isobel.

"What do you think, then?" she asked, but without much interest.

"You need a shrink, Izzie," said Simon, tactlessly. "How about going back to painting puppies and children? I'm never going to look at another salmon sandwich again after that Fish out of Water picture."

Mickey held his breath, expecting Isobel to react, but she didn't, and just smiled and shrugged and turned back to the cooking.

"Can't please everyone," she said, apparently unconcerned. "Does everyone like sweetcorn?"

*

After supper, Mickey and Simon put the children to bed, and Katy sat down next to Isobel.

"You do know we're all worried about you, don't you?" she asked.

Isobel looked at her, rather blankly.

"I don't quite see why," she said. "I'm fine. It was just a silly smash, and I wasn't even hurt, and it was ages ago now. I don't understand why everyone keeps going on about it. I wish you'd all stop nagging me and just leave me alone."

She got up, her movements jerky and abrupt, and paced around the room, her hands fluttering unconsciously at her sides, hands opening and closing, reminding Katy of the gills of the fish in the painting.

"Sorry," said Katy. "I didn't mean to upset you."

"I am not upset," said Isobel harshly. "I am irritated, annoyed, hassled and frustrated. But I am NOT upset."

She burst into tears, and walked out of the room. Katy sat where she was, wanting more than anything to go after her but knew it was a bad idea. Before very long, she was called to say goodnight to her daughter, who had been put to bed in their bed so that she and Miranda would not keep each other awake for hours; the idea was that they would carry her through to the camp bed in Miranda's room when they went to bed later. Isobel had gone to her and Mickey's bedroom and shut the door; Mickey went and asked her to come and say goodnight to the children and she came through obediently to hug and kiss Luke and Miranda and Jodie, but Katy could see her eyes were still full of tears.

"I've got a really nasty headache," she said, by way of explanation. "I'm going to go and lie down. I'll see you a bit later."

After a while of waiting for her to come down, Mickey slipped quietly back up, and when he came down again, he was still alone.

"She's gone to sleep," he said, shutting the living room door. "Oh well. I didn't think she'd talk anyway, but it would have been good to at least try."

"She's losing it," Simon said brutally. "She's definitely going Van Gogh."

"Simon!" Katy said crossly. "That's hardly helpful, is it?"

"It's one of the things Mum and Dad used to worry about, for her," he said defensively. "They never could quite understand her interest in art. They wanted her to become a pharmacist, or something. They really got in a stew when she went to art-college, and an even worse stew when she went off to live in that bed-sit later and try and make a living out of painting people. Mum was terrified she'd get into some sort of trouble, the way she'd go round the cafés and places offering to draw people; she thought she'd end up going off with some dangerous maniac."

"She did," said Mickey with a grin. "Me!"

Simon looked briefly embarrassed, having forgotten how his sister had met her husband. Mickey had seen her in the cafés around the coastal town where he worked at the time, and had been working up the courage to ask her to draw him, just to get the chance to be close to her when she'd approached him. She'd had a terrible week, hadn't had a proper meal for days, and she'd noticed Mickey watching her. He'd been elated when she'd come over and asked if she could draw him for the price or a meal. She'd never got round to drawing him; he'd bought her lunch and they'd got talking and never really stopped since. Until now that is, Mickey reminded himself.

"Sorry," said Simon. "You know what I mean. Mum used to worry that she'd get hurt or something by someone she approached; or she'd be made homeless because she'd not paid the rent or something. And I'm sure you know how much they hated the way she had her hair and all the earrings and nose-rings and everything. You can imagine how quiet they kept about their daughter at the golf club and with all their social set, at least until she began making some sort of name for herself. Dad was quite proud of that; Mum was more proud of the fact that she'd married you, and when you went off to that college, she was even more proud. She never had a moment's worry about how it might affect Izzie."

There was an awkward silence.

"Sorry," said Simon again. "I do keep putting my foot in it, don't I?"

"Both feet," said Katy firmly. "Just shut up a minute, Si. You're depressing Mickey."

Mickey shook his head.

"She was fine about what I do," he said. "All through my curacy, she was fine. I know she didn't enjoy the time at college, and it was a bit tricky at times, but once we weren't living in that pressure cooker, she was fine. I know she isn't the stereotypical clergy wife, but I don't think such a thing exists any more if it ever did. Since I was ordained, she's been OK about what I do. She comes along to church and she even goes to some of the social events and bazaars, and she answers the door and the phone and things. She's never once said she was unhappy or even uncomfortable about any of it. So I just don't understand what's going on any more."

He was alarmingly close to tears himself, and Simon shuffled uncomfortably.

"She's just a bit weird, mate, always has been," he said. "I bet this'll pass, you know, give it a few weeks and she'll be back to normal."

"I don't think so," said Katy, and Simon glared at her, annoyed.

"Be really optimistic, why don't you, love?" he said, irritated.

"Do shut up, Simon, before you show yourself up," Katy said harshly. "I am trying to be realistic. Something has happened to Isobel and it had affected her so profoundly, not only does she seem not to be herself any more, but also she's been producing some of the best and most challenging work she's done in years, maybe in her whole career. I have some thoughts, but this isn't going to be easy. Stuffing it all down and hoping it'll all go away is just going to make things far worse."

"What are you getting at, Katy?" Mickey asked.

"I've noticed a few things even in the short time we've been here," Katy said. "I'd noticed it before, but it didn't occur to me how strange it was because I'd only been talking over the phone or that time we came with the stuff for the cottage. Simon mentions his Mum and Dad all the time, refers to them and what they thought and did and so on. I have hardly ever heard Isobel even mention them; in fact some times she seems to go out of her way not to speak of them."

"So?" said Simon. "She wasn't as close to them as I was."

"That was only because you were geographically closer to them for so long," Katy said. "It's quite natural that you spent more time with them, living nearby. But Isobel was close to them too, though not in the same way you were. Do you remember the day they died, and you called Isobel immediately and she drove straight over?"

"I don't think I shall ever forget," said Simon.

"She never cried," Katy said. "If she did, it wasn't when we could see her. I know she was told to try and stay calm, what with being pregnant and all, but I know if that had happened to me, pregnant or not, I'd have been hysterical with grief. You were, Simon."

"What are you trying to say?" Mickey asked.

"Just that I think that Isobel has been putting her grief to one side till she's got time and space to deal with it," Katy said. "All those paintings are full of images of death and grieving and loss and dislocation. You can only contain emotions for so long, you know.

They find a way out eventually. What I am trying to say is simply that she can't put it off any longer. This is all about grief."

There was a long silence and then Simon said heatedly,

"That's absurd. Mum and Dad have been dead more than eighteen months. Why on earth should she still be grieving now? That is ridiculous!"

"No it's not," said Mickey slowly. "It makes sense, it really does. She seemed to shrug it all off. I was puzzled, and I waited for her to start to react and she never did. I mean, she had Luke to cope with only six weeks or so after they died, and then we moved house and areas and everything. You seem to have grasped it, Katy. But what can we do about it? Do we just ignore it, and hope she gets better of her own accord?"

"I've been thinking about it," Katy said. "I think given Isobel's intense nature, if this goes on in dribs and drabs, it could take a very long time to work through, and I don't like to think what damage that might do to you and your relationship, not to mention the children."

"Intense? Izzie?" Simon said incredulously. "She might be a bit moody but she's about as laid back as you can get."

"Shows how well you know your sister," Katy said, irritably. "She's one of the most intense people I know. When she goes for something, she goes for it hard. If it matters, she's in there like a shot. Take her and Mickey: married in under six months from first contact. If something doesn't matter, she doesn't make an effort. That's not laid back; that's having priorities."

Simon thought about it and finally nodded slowly.

"When you put it like that, it does sort of add up," he said. "So what's your advice, Dr Katy?"

"I think we should make space for her to go at it good and hard," Katy said. "She said she wanted people to just stop nagging her and leave her alone, and that's what I think we should do. She needs to be alone, to paint, to cry, to think. She can't do that here, with the doorbell going ten times a day and the phone twice that sometimes, or with the children needing constant attention."

"And if she doesn't get that? What then?" Mickey asked.

"I don't know," said Katy honestly. "She may just manage to fit it all in round the edges of other people's lives. I don't know. She may have a complete breakdown, go barmy and need to be hospitalised. She may even run away."

"Dear God," said Mickey and put his head in his hands. "I didn't realise it might be this bad. I wondered if another holiday might fix it."

"I don't think so," said Katy. "It might even make it worse. Being on holiday and under pressure to enjoy yourself can make things worse. Just think of Christmas. How many huge family rows happen over the Christmas period?"

"What can I do?" Mickey said, straightening up, his eyes wet with tears.

"This is just my thoughts, so please accept that I am not an expert, just an interested amateur," Katy said. "I think she should be allowed to go and live at the cottage on her own for a while, to get through this in her own way."
Mickey gazed at her, hopelessly.
"I don't know how I can manage that," he said. "I can't do my job and look after the kids. I don't know how it can be done. And what if she gets worse, out there on her own? There's be no one to help her if anything happened."
"She's not likely to harm herself if that's what you mean," Katy said. "And if you insist that you communicate by phone every day, on the understanding that if too long passes without communication you'll drive straight there."
"But what can I do about the kids?" Mickey asked despairingly. "I don't think I can find anyone to come in and mind them, not all the time, even if I could afford it."
"They could come and live with us, for the duration," said Simon.
Katy beamed at him.
"That was what I was going to suggest," she said. "We could bring them over at weekends, or you could pop over when you could. Who better than me? I'm only working part-time, at the moment. My child-minder has been complaining she's not got enough work now Jodie's at nursery in the mornings when I work. She'd welcome the extra work; we'd pay for it, you needn't worry about that."
"That's very kind of you, but-" Mickey said.
"Yes, you can accept it, you moron," said Simon. "Look, it won't be forever, anyway. Isobel's the only sister I've got, and she's looked after me over the years. If she's in danger of going totally Van Gogh, and there's stuff we can do to help her, we'll do it. A few quid a week extra for childcare and so on isn't going to break the bank."
"I can't just strand Isobel out there with no means of getting around if she needs to," Mickey said.
"Then she can have my car," Katy said. "It's her Mum's old one. Roy gave it to me about six months before they died. He must have been concerned about Wendy's mind even then, but he *said* her eyesight wasn't up to driving. It wasn't part of the estate anyway because of that and I've felt guilty about having it. Isobel can have that for the duration. I can walk to work, anyway. It'd do me good."
"This is so very kind of you," Mickey said, his voice shaking. "But there is just one snag."
"Which is?" Simon asked.
"Isobel," Mickey said. "I don't know if she'll accept it. Her best friend Chloe wanted to come over when I said Izzie wasn't so good; Izzie wouldn't let her even visit. She won't talk to her on the phone even. She's pushing everyone away; she won't accept help. She'd feel terrible about letting the kids down, about leaving me on my own."
"We can ask her," Katy said. "Then the choice is hers. That's all we can do: make the offer and let her choose. After that, it's back to Plan B."

"And what is Plan B?" Mickey asked.
"I've no idea," said Katy. "I'll think of it if I need to."
"Will you run it past her in the morning?" Mickey asked. "I'm doing an eight o'clock communion and then a ten thirty family service, so I'll be home by lunchtime. If she seems interested we can talk about it over lunch. Don't mention what we think it's about; it'll just set her against it. She hates mentioning her parents."
"I was going to stress the art and inspiration side of things," Katy said. "I've always believed in her work, so if I emphasize that, I think she may accept the offer. If not, well, we've tried. She may change her mind, anyway, whether she accepts or not."
"Thank you both so much," Mickey said. "It won't be for too long, will it?"
"I have no guarantees, I'm afraid, Mickey," said Katy. "It'll take as long as it needs, I think. But this way, I feel sure it'll be less painful all round."

*

"Yes," said Isobel without a second's hesitation. "I'd really love that. Don't get me wrong; I love Mickey and the kids to bits. But sometimes, I think I'm just not cut out for motherhood and all this. It doesn't come easily, and I'm not very good at it. I don't think KID all the time like most of my friends and acquaintances. When the doorbell goes, I don't think, ooh what wonderful visitors am I having now? I think, oh just fuck off and get a life and stop bothering me. I'm intrinsically selfish, I think, and sometimes, all I can think of is what's going on inside my head and how much I need to paint it." She stopped and rubbed her eyes with a handkerchief. "But what I want to know is why. Why have you made this fantastic offer at all?"
Katy had stayed awake half the night trying to think of an answer to this predictable question that wouldn't wind Isobel up and set her to refusing the offer out of irritation.
"Because I think you need it," she said. "I've always believed in you, you should know that by now. I've liked your portrait work, obviously, but I've always found the other stuff more intriguing. It says things that sometimes a whole load of words can't, and this new stuff seems to me to be important, not just for you. I think it's your best work yet and I truly think you should have a real chance to explore it to its limits."
Isobel was silent, for a moment, thinking.
"When I was younger," she said. "I used to wonder why there were so few great women artists, of any discipline: so few women poets and writers and all the rest of it. It really used to puzzle me when I was at college. Lots of the girls were so clearly brilliant, better than most of the men. So why was there such a discrepancy later in life? When I got married I began to understand. When I had Miranda, I really started to get it. There's only so much emotional energy one person can hold and use; and kids and husbands take a lot of it, running a home takes some more. And it's emotional energy that fuels art: not skill, nor time, nor any other thing. It's like living over a great

seething cauldron of energy; but if some of it goes on broken nights, and worrying about teething or bills or laundry or whatever, there's so much less to throw at your art. So even if you have great skill or talent, if there's nothing to fuel it, you just produce forgettable stuff. It can be technically excellent, attractive even, but there's no soul to it really. And when the lives of most women in the past were filled with the domestic cares and concerns, even if they were also truly great artists, they never achieved their potential. I used to think that it'd be easier with all the labour-saving devices, but that isn't the point. It's the emotion going to the wrong things that wastes the energy, not the sheer slog of running a home and a family."

She glanced at Katy.

"Am I making sense?" she asked.

"Yes," said Katy simply. "Please accept our offer. It isn't made out of any thought that you're failing or anything. I think you've done amazingly well: blindingly well actually. But you're stretched to your limit now and you need a break to work through whatever is driving you."

"I'd miss Mickey and the kids," Isobel said.

"There's no rule that says you can't come home and visit, or come over to us," Katy said. "Do what you need to with the time. No one's going to be looking over your shoulder and complaining."

"Then, yes, I'll do it," Isobel said. "I can't tell you how grateful I am. You are sure you'll be OK with both my kids?"

"Miranda and Jodie are like sisters, and Luke's a little love," Katy said. "My child-minder is great, and Simon is a real New Man. It'd be good to get into practise. We're thinking of having a second child, you know. This would be a trial run for how the whole thing might go."

"You don't think I'm unnatural and a bad mother, do you?" Isobel said suddenly and with some anxiety.

"Good God, no, you silly girl," Katy said. "If you were a bloke, no one would blink an eye at you needing to go off to develop your career. I think this is the best thing you could do for your kids. If you have the chance to explore this, you're going to be lot less restless and unhappy, and that's got to be good for everyone, hasn't it?"

Isobel nodded, but her mind had already raced ahead to wondering how it would be not to have her usual daily concerns fighting with the images and feelings and concepts that flooded her every day, making her slow and distracted as she tried to give enough time to everything. It would be good to fall into bed not utterly exhausted and guilty with unfinished tasks and neglected work, not to feel continuously as though she were short-changing everyone, especially herself.

"I can't wait," she said. "But don't tell Mickey I said that. He'd be hurt if he knew."

"Just think," said Katy. "He'd be able to nip up on his day off and you could actually get some time together without being interrupted all the time."

"I don't know how to thank you, you know," Isobel said.

"Just make sure you mention us when you make your acceptance speak for the Turner Prize," Katy said. "No pressure, mind! Just do it!"

"Thanks," said Isobel and for the first time in a long while, she felt as though there was a glimmer of light at the end of a very dark tunnel.

Chapter 17

It took longer than Isobel expected to make all the necessary arrangements for moving her children to her brother's house, as well as a good deal more upsetting than she had expected. The children seemed quite happy at the thought of a prolonged holiday with Auntie Katy and Uncle Simon, though Isobel had her doubts whether either of them really understood that it would be mostly without mummy and daddy. Miranda probably understood more, but quite how she would feel the first night was anyone's guess. Alone with Mickey for her last night at home, Isobel waited unhappily for the phone to ring, to tell her both children were inconsolable without their parents, but it didn't come, and perversely she was briefly disappointed. She and Mickey had stayed one night with the children at Simon and Katy's house, and then gone home; Mickey in their own car and Isobel in Katy's car, so that she could set off the following day to the cottage, and have most of a day to get herself settled in. That last morning, Isobel felt sick with nerves as she packed the boot of Katy's small car with everything she thought she might need.

"You can come back for stuff if you need to," Mickey pointed out as she gazed unhappily at the full boot. "You'll have to come home to do your laundry, since there isn't a washing machine at the cottage. I'd doubt very much if there's a launderette anywhere nearby."

"I'll probably hand wash for a while," Isobel said. "If it's only me, it won't take too long. Are you sure you're happy for me to do this?"

"Yes," he said, quietly. "You followed me to college without complaint; and that wasn't exactly to your tastes either, but it was necessary. So is this. We can get together when I have my summer break, all of us. I am going to miss you so much."

"Me too," said Isobel. "What does Les think of all this?"

"I don't really think he understands," Mickey said. "I think he thinks you're leaving me but we don't want to say so yet. I don't think he quite gets what you're about anyway. He seems to regard your painting as some sort of fairly profitable hobby. I'll let you know if you get any commissions either by phone or email, by the way."

"Won't be much till the autumn," she said. "Summer time is pretty dead for that sort of thing. People tend to start inquiring when they start thinking about Christmas. But I could be surprised. There are sometimes a few. OK, I think that's everything. I'll stop off at a supermarket on the way for perishables."

They went inside to say their goodbyes without half the street watching and Mickey stood at the door and waved her off as she manoeuvred the little car out of its parking space and began the long drive. She was feeling very confused as she set off. First she felt guilty for abandoning her children; then she felt guilty for not feeling halfway guilty enough. Then she felt resentful that Katy seemed so much better at the mummy stuff than she was; then she felt guilty for thinking that when Katy had been so kind to her.

You are such a selfish cow, she told herself, and then retorted, OK, so I'm selfish: get over it!

The day warmed up pretty quickly and she wound down the window, enjoying the breeze that blew her hair around her face. She should really have had it cut but she hadn't found the time, so it would just have to do. It was now two-toned; where it had grown at the roots, it was its normal warm brown, but the longer strands were still coppery with the henna. It wasn't quite long enough to tie back yet so she reckoned she would have to pin it back if it started annoying her. Maybe I should buy a scarf, she thought and laughed out loud at that thought, imagining herself with one of the gauzy fairy scarves that Maggie favoured. Not on your life, she thought. If I get a scarf, it'll be a bloke's bandana or one of those bright tie-dye things from India.

She stopped at a superstore to buy some groceries and also some ready-made sandwiches, so she could just eat lunch when she got to the cottage without having to mess around preparing food. The sun was hot when she pulled into the lane and approached the cottage and she was feeling hungry and sleepy. Once she'd got the car onto the paving, she saw that the rose around the door was in full bloom: heavy, fluffy pink flowers, heady with scent in the noontime heat. Other plants were coming into flower too and the front part of the garden at least looked lovely. She unlocked the door and pushed it cautiously open, half expecting to find something horrible where the doormat would be had she ever got round to buying one. Instead of the usual pile of dead leaves, there was a pile of dried petals, as if someone had pushed a handful of roses through the letterbox and they had dried and separated in the early summer heat. Further along the hall there were dead leaves, but scattered as if blown around by an uninvited wind. She carried her shopping through to the kitchen and stowed everything away before putting the kettle on and going back to unpack the car while it boiled.

It was whistling away frantically by the time she'd managed to unload everything into the hall, and the sound made the house seem somewhat less lonely. She hadn't expected to feel so alone; she told herself it was to be expected that she should feel a bit strange at first. It was years now since she'd lived alone, and while she had craved solitude recently, it had only come in brief controlled bursts, always followed by a return to frenetic family life.

She sat out in the sunshine to eat her lunch, enjoying the breeze that stopped her becoming too hot, and found, as always her eyes and her mind were drawn to the mound and the trees waving in the wind upon it. The leaves had opened fully now, and had lost that tender translucency they had had when they had first opened, and the ground underneath was more heavily shaded and the bluebell leaves were dying away into the thin grass that covered most of the mound like sparse hairs on a balding pate. Leaving her plate and mug, she wandered over the garden, noting the grass would need cutting again soon, and came inevitably to rest on the mound. The air under the trees was cooler and the earth felt cool to the touch when she sat down at the very top of the mound and lay back to gaze at the sky through the few small gaps between the moving leaves. The sound of the wind in the trees was so like a distant sea murmuring against a shingle shore that she found she was remembering that dream and sat up again rather abruptly to look for the waves creeping up the sides of the mound.

"This won't do," she said out loud, and got to her feet, brushing away bits of dead leaf, grass and beechnut casings that had stuck to her clothes and managed to drag herself away from the mound and back to the cottage to unpack.

The rather Spartan bedroom looked better once she had unpacked her belongings and set out her hairbrush and toiletries on the dressing table and left her dressing gown on the back of the door. She unrolled her sleeping bag and put her pillow at the head of it and gazed round the room, wishing that Mickey's dressing gown were next to her own and that he would be arriving in a few hours. This is silly, she told herself firmly. You came here to be alone and get through this work and all you can think about is how lonely you are. Do grow up; you can't have it both ways.

Loneliness and isolation were both swept away once she set up her easel and began to work. She was drawn into her own visions and only when she was in actual pain from cramped muscles and complaining bladder did she stop to rest and look at what she'd done.

Standing on the mound, surrounded by the smooth boles of the beech trees, was a stag, fine and strong and unafraid, the shape of its antlers echoing the barely seen branches above. The ground at its feet looked more like skin than earth, and in places it seemed to have ripped or cracked open, the crevices showing what lay beneath the surface. Closest to the surface the cracks showed heaps of carcasses of deer, piled up and rotting, some newly dead, others in advanced decomposition. As the eye was drawn down to deeper layers, the cracks showed bones and skulls, the antlers still attached and as the very deepest layers were revealed, the bones were crushed, by time perhaps or by simple weight of the corpses above, till at the very bottom, only bone powder remained that blew out of the crevices in clouds like the smoky vapour from an autumn puffball. Above it all, the stag stood proud and alive, and unaware or uncaring of the horrors below it.

"Bloody hell," breathed Isobel when she saw what she had produced. She had been so absorbed by the work that she had been unable to see the whole, the complete picture till now. Obviously she had seen it but she had not taken it in, had not registered the finished images.

The light was fading now, the day almost over and she realised that she was bursting to go to the loo, starving hungry and aching from top to toe. She dragged the easel inside, and bolted the French doors before rushing to the bathroom. Food was a trickier matter; she had brought along food that was quick to cook but not immediate, and not actually very exciting. That didn't matter; she had very little interest in food these days, seeing it as only fuel that stopped her keeling over. She cooked some couscous, added raisins and sunflower and pumpkin seeds and a hefty dash of olive oil and ate ravenously, washing it down with a pint of water. The light was too poor for painting and her eyes were hurting with tiredness, so she went through to the bathroom and began running a bath. She had often thought she perhaps ought to sit down to paint, but never felt quite right about it, needing to move around as she worked. Every muscle ached, or that's what it felt like. A good hot bath should do it, she thought, and went back to put in some of that pine-scented bath oil that de-knotted the tensions in her neck and shoulders at home. She stopped at the side of the bath, puzzled.

Bobbing around in the water was a funny little tangled ball of leaves and twigs that she could have sworn hadn't been in the water when she'd started running it. Fishing it out, she stared at it in bafflement. It was almost perfectly round, the fine twigs woven together cleverly, like the ones she'd found before that had vanished when she'd come to have a closer look later on. The soft leaves dripped onto the stone floor, making tiny puddles. She put it carefully on the window ledge and tipped her bath-oil into the water, and set about lighting tea-lights and putting them round the edges of the bath and round the room. The deep bath took some time to fill and she sat on the side of the bath rubbing her aching neck with one tired hand. The fresh foresty aroma of pine rose with the steam from the water; Mickey claimed it smelled more like toilet cleaner than a real pine forest but she liked it anyway. As the bath reached the required depth, she shed her clothes and slipped into the hot water with a sigh half of pain and half of contentment, and let the water support her and ease away the aches.

The darkness outside the curtain-less window deepened and as the candles flickered, Isobel felt her eyelids growing heavier, half mesmerised by the wavering lights and their shimmering reflections in her green-tinted bathwater. She drowsed pleasantly without slipping into sleep properly, her eyes closed. This feels so bloody good, she thought, and then froze as a tiny noise outside the window made her open her eyes again. The window was thick with condensation running down it, but distinct against the glass was a figure close to the window. She sat up in the bath, alarmed, the water sloshing noisily around her and the figure moved, vanishing silently.

She leaped out of the bath, aches forgotten in sudden fear and dragged on her clothes and ran from the room, round to the front door and out into the garden. In the cooling night air, she could hear nothing but her pounding heart: no footsteps running away, no voices, nothing. Forcing herself to be calm, she walked carefully round to the back, and to the bathroom window. There was no one there. Well, of course there wasn't. Anyone would be gone by now, hearing her moving around the house.

She circled the house and to her horror, she found the French doors had swung open. I could have sworn I bolted them, she thought, her mouth dry with fear. She went inside and shut them again, then went from room to room to make sure nobody had sneaked in while she was prowling round outside. Nothing. Her hair dripped pine scented water as she walked, and once she was sure the house was secure and she was alone, she returned to the bathroom to wash her hair. The bath water was tepid, and she didn't fancy getting back into it, so she rinsed the dirt off her bare feet in the cooling water, and pulled out the plug before giving her hair a quick wash in the sink.

I must have imagined someone being there, she said to herself. It must have been a shadow or something. If it had been a real person, they couldn't have got away so quickly and so quietly. Later, when she was curled up in her sleeping bag, it occurred to her that it might well have been one of Maggie's boys; she could just imagine a boy like that Tristan finding it something of a draw to peep through a frosted glass window in the hopes of seeing her naked. He would have been light enough to get away quietly and quickly, and she felt herself go hot all over at the thought that he may have been spying on her in the bath. Bloody little animal, I'll have his bollocks if I catch him at it again, she thought and fell asleep shortly afterwards.

*

She knew she was dreaming when she passed through the window without opening it. It was like easing through a waterfall, some cold resistance and then she was through. The air beneath her was cooler than she would have expected on a late June night, and as she soared up into the starry sky, she told herself not to think about it. If I think about it too hard, I'll fall, she thought. Let's just enjoy this anyway.

The mechanisms of flight just didn't exist: no flapping, no wings, and no machinery. She just thought, up! and she went up, or down! and she went down. It felt wonderful, though she wished she were wearing pyjamas rather than a nightie, since the fabric billowed around her as she flew. She headed into the countryside around the cottage, circling, trying to keep her bearings. The mound was lit by faint lights; and when she swooped closer, she saw the lights were tea-lights and candles, set around the roots of the trees. As she flew further, she saw that there were other lights on the ground, set around what must be mounds, though most were virtually flattened or destroyed. If she had seen them from the ground, she would not have known they were mounds or barrows like her own. Maybe they aren't real, she thought. This is a dream, after all. She swirled round in mid-air, losing track of where she'd come from, and with the thought that she couldn't find her way back came throat-clenching panic and with a huge rush of descending air, she found herself back in bed, cold and shaking, and the room dark around her.

The thudding of her heart gradually slowed until she could sit up without feeling dizzy, and she managed to get out of bed and drag on her dressing gown. Her mouth and throat were horribly dry, and her head was pounding. I need some tea, she thought, and remembered there was no one here to disturb, that she could get up at any time of day or night and make as much noise as she needed. She padded down the stairs, her feet warm in sheepskin slippers, and saw why she had been so cold. The front door had swung open and the breeze was ruffling and swirling the leaves on the stone flags.

"This is absurd," she said, and slammed the door shut, sliding the bolts across.

In the kitchen, the fluorescent strip light seemed glaring and unnatural, and when she'd made her tea, she went into the living room to drink it, without turning on the light, and sat in darkness, curling up on the sofa and pulling her dressing gown down to cover her legs. Once she felt better, she went back to bed; the warmth of her sleeping bag soon lulling her back to sleep. Outside, an owl called unheard and she rolled over, deep in dreams again.

*

She woke and stretched lazily, reaching over to Mickey's side of the bed to share the heat of her dreams with him. Her arms touched an empty expanse of mattress and she remembered she was alone, and she sat up and rubbed her eyes, feeling stiff and aching all over. She'd planned to make a trip to the nearest town today for more supplies, this time of paints and paraphernalia, having noticed as she'd cleared away yesterday that she was running low on a variety of stock. If she had found the time before she'd set off, she would have replenished everything but the concerns for getting the children settled had driven those thoughts from her mind, and now she would have to take half a day away to try and find an art supplies shop somewhere relatively nearby. She had a craving for something sweet and sticky, and nothing that quite fitted the craving could be found in the cottage so as soon as she was up and dressed, she locked up and headed out in Katy's little car in search of paints and pastries.

It was sometime after lunch when she got back to the cottage, both quests successful. When she went to open the gate, so she could bring the car in, she got a bit of a shock.

Sitting on the doorstep, looking so woebegone that she immediately forgot to be angry, was Maggie's oldest boy, Tristan.

"Are you all right?" she said, at once.

He'd been sitting huddled up, knees to his chest and his head pressed to his knees as if her were cold or simply trying to seem as small as he could, but when he heard her voice, he looked up, his head tilting back to be able to see her clearly. He had marks down his face that looked like bruising not quite showing yet, and one eye was cut and swollen almost shut.

"What the hell happened to you?" she asked, coming forward.

He got up and tried to turn his head so the bruising wasn't as obvious.

"I'm sorry, I didn't know where else to go," he said. "Mum said you'd threatened to call social services about Celeste so I figured you might care, even if I have been horrible to you."

"Who hit you?" Isobel said, unlocking the door. "You need to get that cleaned up and a cold compress on it to stop the swelling. Who hit you?"

"Mum," he said, and followed her in.

"What for?" Isobel asked.

"I said I wanted to go to school," he said, surprising Isobel who had expected him to say he'd been rude to his mother or he'd hit one of the smaller children.

"That's a bit extreme," she said. "She could have just said no."

"I said I would just go anyway, and tell them what she's like too. That's when she hit me," he said, and followed Isobel into the kitchen.

She ran some water into a bowl and started to clean up the cut round his eye; he winced a little but didn't cry as she thought he might.

"I think I have some butterfly stitches in the first aid box," she said, and rummaged around till she found them. "These just hold the edges of a cut together while they heal. A lot less painful than real stitches too. Keep still."

"What are you going to do?" she asked him when she'd dealt with the cut round his eye.

"I've run away," he said. "I've had enough."

"Where will you go?" Isobel asked, not at all sure what she ought to be saying.

"I want to get to my granny's," he said. "I haven't seen her for years, not since she and Mum fell out about the money and Ivan. Do you think I might phone her from here?"

Isobel nodded, marvelling at the transformation from vile, rude mini-yob, to polite little victim.

"Why did you come here?" she asked. "Weren't you afraid I'd just send you on your way?"

"Yes," he said. "But Mum hates you, so I figured you must be so different to her and you might help."

"What about your dad?" Isobel asked. "Did Ivan not try and stop her hitting you like that? She really hit you hard and with rings too."

"Ivan's not my Dad," he said. "I don't know who my father is. Mum says she doesn't remember."

"Well, why didn't Ivan stop her?"

"I don't know, he was laughing so much I guess he thought it was funny," he said. "Can I ring my granny please?"

Isobel passed him her mobile but he hesitated.

"Can you speak to her, please?" he asked, helplessly. "I don't know what to say."

"What's her name, then?" Isobel asked.

"Broadbent, same as Mum."
He gave her a grubby old envelope with a number written on it and Isobel tapped in the number and waited. After five rings, the phone was answered by a woman's voice, quite plummy but kind sounding.
"Hello?" said Isobel. "Is that Mrs. Broadbent? Yes, good. You don't know me at all, my name's Isobel Trelawny. I have your grandson Tristan here with me; he's wanting to come and visit you."
There was a brief surprised intake of breath at the other end of the phone and then the woman asked,
"Is everything all right?"
"Not terribly, no," said Isobel. "I think Tristan should tell you himself."
She passed the phone to the boy, who took it looking terrified.
"Hello, granny," he said. "No, I want to come and live with you. Mum's hit me and I want to go to school and have a proper home."
He sounded much, much younger than his years and Isobel could see tears spilling down his face and splashing onto his dirty tee shirt. After a few minutes, he passed her the phone.
"She wants to talk to you," he said.
"Hello, Mrs. Broadbent," said Isobel. "How may I help you?"
"I need to know what's been going on," said Mrs. Broadbent. "I haven't spoken to my daughter for some years so I am rather lost about what's happening."
"I think you would be better coming to see for yourself," said Isobel. "But I think your grandson needs rescuing first, at any rate. His mother has hit him quite badly, and I have a feeling it isn't the first time. I'd say all the children are quite neglected. I've only just come here myself so I don't know much about it, I'm afraid."
"We'll certainly take care of Tristan," said Mrs. Broadbent. "I had no idea things had become so bad. But then, my daughter and I haven't spoken since she won that money and accused me of wanting to steal it from her. It isn't even as if we had a good relationship before then. Would you be able to put Tristan on a train and I shall pick him up at the other end? I shall reimburse you of course."
"Yes, certainly," said Isobel and for a short time, they discussed arrangements.
When she rang off, Tristan was crying properly, with relief, she thought. She didn't know what to do or say; he was too old to hold as she would have done her own children, and though she felt very sorry for him, she still had more than a few stirrings of the memories of his awful behaviour.
"I'm putting the kettle on," she said. "It'll be a while before there's a train for you to catch, so do you want tea or coffee? I don't have any decaffeinated, before you ask, or any carob, but I may have a few chocolate biscuits I was saving for an emergency if that's any help."
She passed him the roll of kitchen paper and he blew his nose and wiped his eyes.

"Sorry," he said. "And I'm sorry about everything else too. Ivan told us we should challenge authority at every opportunity; Mum told us to go and ride around in your garden."

"Did she now! Why?" Isobel asked.

"I don't know," he said. "She just wants me and Gareth out of the way all the time. She's only interested in babies. She doesn't like me or any of the older ones, and she doesn't like us in the garden in case we hurt one of the little ones. She just lets them crawl around and never checks what they're doing. Cassandra's pregnant again too."

"What was it like before you came here?"

"Before Mum won the money you mean?" he said, with a sudden very adult grin. "We lived in this horrible old bus, and travelled all over the place. There were different people coming and going all the time, and there was usually someone around who could be bothered with us, even if Mum never was. Ivan and she got together a few months before she won the money, I think, but Mum and Cassandra were together off and on for years before that."

Isobel blinked, and hoped her shock hadn't shown on her face.

"Why do you want to go to school? I thought you must be having a great time, just running wild?" she asked.

"Do you know how boring it is, not having anything to do?" he asked. "Being told we are free to do whatever we want as long as it isn't anything even remotely like what other kids do? I don't want to stay there my whole life. I want to do something else. And I want to be able to read and write and all the rest of it, and not be trapped there all the time, minding the kids Mum or Cassandra have discarded."

Isobel said nothing, for a while, and then she said,

"When you get to your granny, tell her everything that's happened. Then she can decide what to do about it. I reckon she'll call social services. Do you like your granny?"

"I don't know her very well, but I think that if she doesn't like Mum and Ivan and Cassandra, and she does like me, I'll like her," he said.

"Word of advice," Isobel said. "However cross you get about things, never tell anyone to swivel again. It really doesn't make friends. Is that what Ivan told you to say?"

He nodded.

"And did he explain what it meant?"

He nodded again and Isobel felt slightly sick.

"Has he hurt you at all?"

He nodded again.

"OK, make sure you tell your granny that too. Right, I have a clean tee shirt upstairs that you may borrow so that your granny doesn't get too much of a shock seeing you for the first time in years," Isobel said. "You don't look too dirty otherwise. Your little sister Celeste would really freak out your grandmother. Why did she stop washing?"

He shrugged.

"Don't know," he said. "Maybe she thought she'd get Mum to take some notice of her. It doesn't work. Once she stops breastfeeding a kid, Mum doesn't notice anymore."

Isobel fetched a tee shirt of Mickey's that had been left behind last time he'd been here, and Tristan wrenched off his own filthy one. Isobel couldn't help noticing the bruises all over his body: new ones and old faded ones blurring and blending into each other. The tee shirt was too big, obviously, but it was at least clean, and Isobel put the old one into the bin.

"Right, did you want that cup of tea and biscuits, then?" she asked, and set about making them both tea.

"Just one thing, Tristan?" she said as he munched biscuits like a starving dog. "Have you or your brother been up here putting leaves through the letterbox?"

He shook his head vigorously.

"Were either of you up here last night, just after dark?" she asked. "I was a bit alarmed as there was someone wandering round the garden but I couldn't see who."

"No," he said. "Mum talks about there being fairies up here, but I reckon there's ghosts or something. Mum has fairies on the brain. Have you seen her pictures?"

Isobel nodded and pulled a face.

"They're rubbish, aren't they?" he said and she giggled.

"And very rude, too," she added.

"Mum says you aren't a proper artist," he said. "So I reckon you must be very good, then. Can I see your pictures?"

Isobel considered for a minute.

"OK," she said. "If you've seen your mother's work, then none of mine is going to be a shock."

She'd brought all her recent work with her, and showed him them in silence. He gazed closely at all of them and then said, thoughtfully,

"No wonder Mum hates you!"

"What do you mean?"

"She hates anyone who's better at things than her," he said. "That's why she and Cassandra are having babies all the time. Mum think she's a better mother; Cassandra thinks she is so they're having this barmy competition to see who can have the most."

"I think they should stop confusing quantity with quality," Isobel said dryly and he laughed.

"She said yours were rubbish," he said. "But they aren't. These are brilliant. They are scary though."

Isobel glanced at her watch.

"We'd better go," she said. "Come on; I'll let you sit in the front."

"I'll even put on a seat belt," he said, and Isobel marvelled that a kid should be rebelling by choosing to do conventional things.

Isobel got him to the station with plenty of time to buy a whole picnic's worth of sandwiches and drinks for the journey, and to have a word with the guard on the train, to make sure Tristan got off at the right station, since he couldn't read.

"Ask your granny to give me a call when you're there," she said, as she stepped off the train, and winced as the shrill whistle sounded too close to her ear.

She watched him from the platform, go to a window seat and sit down, uncertain as a dog in a cattery, and waved at him till the train vanished from view. Then, much to her own surprise, she burst into tears.

Chapter 18

Back at the cottage, Isobel tried to stem the tears, telling herself not to be so bloody silly and get a grip and all the encouraging things we say to ourselves at such moments, but all to no avail. It didn't matter that she'd done what she could, patched up the poor kid and sent him on his way with all the best wishes and ham sandwiches in the world. She sat on the sofa and howled, until she felt dim and sick with it, and a kind of strange contentment came over her, and she went to the easel and set up a new board and began sketching despite the fact that the sun was long past its zenith and she wouldn't finish until after dark.

Her phone brought her back; to a darkened room and a stomach long empty of the morning's Danish pastries. It took a moment to recognise the sound, and then she struggled to get it out of her pocket in time. It was Mickey.

"How's it going?" he asked.

"Uh, a bit weird, today," she said, wandering across the room to the light switch and flooded the room with bright yellow light.

It took a while to explain all that had happened and when she'd finished, Mickey whistled softly.

"Poor kid," he said. "Do you reckon his Gran will do anything?"

"I don't know," Isobel said. "Maggie is her daughter, after all, so she wouldn't want to see her in court, I suppose. Some of those children are her grandchildren and she can't want them all to live like that. I reckon if the lad tells her everything, she'll have to do something. I'm pretty sure he didn't tell me everything, either. That Ivan chap is not good news, but the women are worse. Urgh! I feel sick just thinking of it."

"I just hope Maggie doesn't find out you were involved in the kid's vanishing act," Mickey said.

"I'm waiting to hear from the Granny," Isobel said. "I did suggest to Tristan that he phone his mother when he gets there to let her know where he is, but he reckoned she probably wouldn't have noticed he was gone for days. He's only twelve, for God's sake. What sort of a start is that to life? All that money and no care."

When Mickey rang off, she went to the toilet and as she was coming back through to the living room the phone rang again. It was Mrs. Broadbent.

"Is that you, Mrs. Trelawny?" she said. "Sorry it's taken me a bit longer than I intended to ring, but the poor boy was in such a state, I had to get him clean and fed first. He even had lice."

"You should see one of his sisters," Isobel said. "Lice capital of England, I reckon."

"I just wanted to thank you for helping out," said Mrs. Broadbent. "He's told me how he was less than polite to you, even when you went into the river to help him. I can't imagine how my daughter has escaped investigation for so long. I am utterly horrified by it all, and I have made a number of phone calls already and I have been assured of action. My concern extends beyond those children who are my own blood kin, naturally, but I am sixty-two and the prospect of taking on so many children is more than I can cope with. I am hoping that the families of this other woman may be persuaded to do their duty too."

"You're going to take Maggie's children?" Isobel said.

"I shall certainly be looking after Tristan," she replied. "Whether the powers that be deem me suitable to be guardian to the younger ones remains to be seen, but they cannot remain where they are. I have a strong suspicion that my daughter may well be in need of psychiatric care, and this may be the case for the other woman."

Nutty as a fruitcake, both of them, Isobel thought, but didn't say so aloud.

"You may well be right," she said instead. "Anyway, I'm glad Tristan is safe at least. He's going to be a handful, I think, but give him time and I think he'll turn out well."

After she rang off, Isobel felt the tears welling up again and for solace went back to her painting, and despite the poor light provided by the electric bulbs, continued work till she began to feel somewhat faint and went in search of food.

*

It was past midnight when she rinsed her brushes out and stepped back to gaze at what she'd done as if she had somehow been absent the whole time she'd worked. The mound rose up like the belly of a pregnant woman, the trees seeming to struggle to hang on to the soaring hillock as it broke apart in places like dough stretched too far over too large a pie dish. Beneath the broken surface were glimpses of what lay inside: babies. Babies curled up tight waiting to be born, hundreds of them, packed as tight as sardines, small feet pressed into the faces of others, tightly scrunched faces, little fists, bottoms, legs, all jumbled together in one heaving mass of infants tucked into an earth womb: waiting.

It shocked her and warmed her all at the same time, and she shook her head in wonderment at it. All that life, just waiting to be born. She locked up and went up to bed, aching and weary, too tired to have the bath she probably needed. So tired, so very, very tired.

She woke at dawn with the first warm rays of sunshine hitting the house and the slight breeze filling her room with the smells of dew wet grass and flowers. I need a bath, she thought, and padded downstairs. The sunlight filled the kitchen and she opened the door onto the garden, breathing in the cool morning air as she waited for the kettle to boil. Already the sky was a clear azure blue, without a single cloud to mar it; it was likely to be hot, she thought, and decided not to bother with a bath but to start work immediately so that she would be able to knock off during the heat of the day.

Last night's work seemed strange in the morning light but perhaps it had always been strange. The babies seemed neutral when she looked at them; they were not cute, as she would have thought, but oddly dignified and full of hidden potential. Too often babies were depicted as cherubic, all plump innocence and superficiality. These were *deep* babies; symbols that stood for so much more than they depicted. The secrets of the womb and the unborn life were not light ones, after all. Isobel shook her head and put the painting to one side and set out a fresh board, and stared at the blankness of it for some time, lost in thought. Finally, she picked up a piece of charcoal and began to draw.

She lost all awareness of time and of anything going on around her, focussing inward on the visions inside her head and trying to translate them onto the board in front of her. She drew and then painted with her eyes half shut, all the time trying to match the tangle of colours, lines and emotions that filled her mind to what she was trying to get down on the surface in front of her. Sometimes she found she was breathless, as if she had been holding her breath so that she could hear better sounds that hovered on the very edge of her hearing; she had to stop then and take long slow deep breaths or she would find her vision becomes fuzzy and her knees go weak. Once, years before, at college, she had actually fainted while painting. At the time, her tutor had put it down to her having missed breakfast but it had really been caused by her failing to breathe properly.

Her head was hurting when she finally stopped and stared at her work. The air streaming in through the French doors was as hot as if she had opened an oven door, and the scent of baked earth and drying grasses streamed in with it. She flopped into a chair and made herself breathe, long and slow, and gradually her head eased a little. Her stomach growled like a grumpy dog, so she made herself a sandwich and ate it sitting out in the garden, trying not to think about what she had just painted.

It wasn't disturbing in the same way the other paintings had been; but what had puzzled her was where the images had come from and why. She'd painted a warrior; probably Bronze Age or earlier, she was unsure about those details. He wore a mixture of skins and rough textiles and carried a spear. A knife, dull and grey, hung at his belt, and in his other hand he carried what looked like a brace of hares, limp and dead. A crude helmet made mostly of cracked and blackened leather covered some of his head, but the face underneath, cut and bruised, was that of a boy rather than the man she would have expected to wear the costume and weapons. The eyes were tired and resigned but still defiant, the dirty face, with its traces of blood old and new had a set to it that said, go on, just give me an excuse. He was standing under trees, leaning somewhat on the spear as if tired or just fed up. The clothes were probably out of some lost memory of Stone Age hunters, but the face was Tristan's.

She brushed the crumbs from her lunch off her lap and wandered idly over to the mound, and lay down at the top, feeling the gritty soil under her and the stray beechnut casings crunch as she did so. Above, the leaves waved in the wind and the sound soothed her like the sound of the sea. There were tears forming in her eyes again, and she let them flow unhindered, running down the sides of her face and soaking into her collar or splashing down onto the parched earth. The trees sighed above her and she drifted off to sleep.

The day had changed somewhat when she woke; the air was much cooler but had a sultry feel to it as of an impending storm, and the trees were being lashed by a rising wind, and as she made her way back to the cottage she felt the odd drop of rain hit her, heavy and ponderous, but as she shut and bolted the French doors and went round shutting other windows, only a few more drops seemed to fall. The paving outside the window remained dry but for those few spots of rain.

"All mouth and no trousers," she said, looking up at the darkening sky. The thickening clouds with their cargo of rain and the heavy feel to the air promised a storm but nothing happened for another half an hour or so. The sky had darkened to such an extent that she turned on the lights, even though it should still be daylight for some hours yet, and she had sat down with a cup of tea, when the first sharp flash of lightning made her jump and slop the tea over her hand. She counted; and an alarmingly short time later, the roll of thunder followed. It was close; she'd never had a problem with storms before now, but this time, on her own here and in the midst of empty fields and hills, it seemed far more personal. You could almost believe in thunder gods out in the wilderness, away from roads and cars and technology.

She fetched a blanket and snuggled up on the sofa, watching the flashes and trying not to count the gap between the flash and the rumble of thunder. The room was as dark as if true dusk had fallen, and the beating of the rain drowned out her own thoughts. The sound of the thunder filled the whole house, making the old windows rattle alarmingly. Isobel pulled the blanket up to her chin huddled and further down as another brilliant flash lit the room up, and then the lights went out altogether.

"Bugger!" she said, and flung back her blanket and went in search of candles.

At home, she would have gone outside and had a look at the street-lights and the houses along the street to see if they too had lost their power, or phoned a crony in the same area. She hadn't even got the phone number of the power company to see if the power was really out or whether the storm had blown out the main fuse. I don't even know where the fuse box is, she thought, irritated with herself. She found a big bag of night lights in the kitchen and lit a few on the living room hearth; there was no point in lighting more; if the storm blew out, there would still be a bit of daylight maybe. She had no idea how long the power would be out so the few candles were more as a token, a brave little gesture. She curled back up in her blanket and shut her eyes against the glaring flashes of lightning and tried to ignore the thunder as it rolled overhead like some sort of celestial war. The rain drummed on the roof and against the windows, a frenetic tattoo that slowly mesmerised her into an uneasy sleep.

She woke with a jerk, alarmed and unsure what had woken her till she saw that the French doors had burst wide open. They were banging together, the latch rattling but not catching as the wind and the rain tugged at them. I know I shut them, she thought. I know I bolted them. Her mouth was suddenly dry with fear and as she watched, all of the tea-lights blew out as if blown with one breath.

"I am not having this," she snarled, and marched across the room to wrestle with the swinging doors, slamming them shut so hard the windows at the other end of the room rattled as if in sympathy. The sky outside was properly dark now, and though the thunder seemed to have passed, the rain still fell in intermittent torrents; the gutters were gurgling wildly and she could hear water splashing down the sides of the house walls where the gutters were failing to channel the rain fast enough. The room was cold, and she fetched a jumper as well as the blanket and toyed with the thought of lighting a fire, but the coal bucket was empty and there was no more coal in the bag in the utility room. As the rain continued to hammer down, Mickey rang.

"It's pouring down here," she said when they'd exchanged greetings. "The power's out and I am so glad we've got a camp stove. I'm out of coal and it's cold now."

"But other than that, you're having a great day?" he said, amused.

"Actually, yes," she said.

"Admit it, you're missing me!"

"I am. But it's going well," she said. "Are the kids OK with Katy still?"

"Fine. I'm going to go over next day off and spend the day there. Is that all right, or were you planning to come home for a visit?"

"Not just yet," she said, feeling guilty again for her absence. "I'm just getting into the swing of things, here. The bloody doors are playing up though. I'm dead sure I bolt them as well and yet they come open. It must be a building fault or something. Maybe the house shifts or something."

"If the house can shift to that extent, it'd have shown up on that very exhaustive and expensive survey we had done," Mickey said, reasonably. "It must be the locks or something like that. I'll come and change them all when I come up. If you're worried, put a chair hard against the door-handle, and that'll stop it coming open in the night."

"I love you," Isobel said suddenly, and felt the tears prickling at her eyes. "Thank you for letting me do this; I miss you so much."

"You can come home any time you want to, you know," he said. "I love you, too."

After he'd rung off, she mopped her face with a tissue and looked round at the dark room. It wasn't worth lighting more candles; she wanted to go to bed now and leave the day behind. She fetched a kitchen chair and wedged the back of it under the door-handles, thinking that what it really needed was a bungee. She gathered up a few candles and the matches in case she needed them, reminding herself to go and buy a nice big electric torch when she next went shopping as well as a few bungees, and slipped upstairs and into her sleeping bag without undressing. The rain sang its wet lullaby to her and she fell asleep quickly.

*

She woke after deep and wondering dreams took her far from herself and she looked that morning on the wet world as if on a new one, her eyes strangely cleansed by the night. When she brought her tea into the living room, she found the chair that she had wedged against the doors had fallen over, but the doors were still shut and bolted. Her hunter portrait of Tristan still rested on the easel and she gazed at it with the mixed feelings her own work always provoked in her; satisfaction at war with discontent. Sometimes the vision was so much more vivid than the result, but this time as always, some flavour of the original was there, even if she had not managed to translate it all onto the blank white of the board.

She glanced at her diminishing stock of watercolour board and reckoned another few days and then she would have to go and forage again. She couldn't recall the last time she had worked this fast, this well or if she ever had, in fact. What anyone would make of it she really had no idea, but at the moment she truly wasn't even interested. She hitched up her jeans, and noticed that they were much looser than they had been. Nice way to get rid of the post-baby fat, she thought. I hadn't even noticed.

She made herself toast under the camping gas grill, and checked the lights had come back on. She hadn't bothered with a shower this morning yet, so after she'd eaten her breakfast, she went back upstairs to shower. She stood in the warm water as it cascaded around her, and it was only when she felt the water lapping round her ankles did she realise the water was not draining away.

"Damn!" she said, and turned the shower off.

The drain seemed to be blocked, and she felt around amid the soapy tide at the bottom of the shower till she found the drain and found what was blocking it. She pulled hard at the mass of twisted leaves and twigs and they came free with a rude noise and the water and foam began to drain away freely. She turned the shower back on so she could rinse the last of the shampoo from her hair, and also to rinse the scum from the ball of twigs that had blocked the drain. It was another of those weird balls, flattened slightly this time; a matted sphere of woven twigs and leaves, slippery and slightly decaying as if they had been in the water for weeks. She dropped it in the bin and wrapped herself up in a big towel and went to get dressed.

She'd left her dirty clothes on the bed, but she'd put her amber necklace on the dressing table and when she'd pulled on fresh clothes, she went to put the necklace back on. It wasn't there. She knelt on the floor, and felt around for the beads; she shook out her dirty clothes in case she'd managed to drop them in there. She even shook out her sleeping bag. Nothing. The beads were gone.

That morning, she painted a magpie.

It perched on a beech branch, its clever bright eye fixed on something out of view, and in its claws it held not a necklace of amber beads but a necklace of shells and bones, hung in the centre with a stone arrowhead. Its feathers were gleaming and iridescent but in the eye turned to the viewer, a hut was reflected, too small to see any detail beyond the round shape and the threads of smoke rising from the roof.

She grinned at her picture, and went to make tea.

*

Isobel lost track not only of hours but of days; she reckoned the passage of days at first by how long her milk lasted, and then fed up with going out to buy fresh milk, she had started drinking her tea and coffee black despite the fact that it had always made her feel sick before. She knew a day had passed only because Mickey phoned at much the same time each day, to check she was all right. Otherwise there was only the changing of light to tell her time had passed. Her watch had stopped working. She reckoned she had dropped it in the water when she washed her dirty clothes but it had stopped before then; she just hadn't noticed. She was very relieved when a few days after it had vanished, her amber necklace reappeared, on the hearth.

"I must have dropped it there after all," she said, but the truth was that life at the cottage defied explanation.

So too did her pictures. They came in a torrent of creativity, a massive rush of jumbled images in her mind that had to be teased apart and separated and made sense of. Some days she painted two or three pictures; often she didn't know quite what would emerge onto the white boards as she put them onto the easel and picked up her charcoal. Only when she finished did she have a real idea of what she was doing; she could not have said beforehand, today I shall paint a woman wearing a cloak of owl feathers, or the sparks of a fire becoming butterflies in the dusk, because she did not know that was what she was about to paint. It was exhausting, exhilarating and utterly absorbing. She did not question anything that happened around her. She did not ask who could be putting the balls of twigs and leaves into sink or bath or toilet, or who was hiding her jewellery or her pencils or who opened doors and blew out candles. She didn't question the odd feeling of not being alone here, or the moments at dusk when the shadows in the garden seemed to move towards the house, or the glimpses caught from the edge of her vision of something moving fast as a scurrying mouse where no mouse would be seen.

There was a tiny part of her mind that spoke in the voice she used to her children, and told her to eat and to drink, to sleep and to wash and to change her clothes. It told her how to drive when she sat at the wheel of the car, suddenly unable to remember what to do. It told her when she needed to buy food and what to buy, it made lists for her that she didn't quite remember writing. It told her when she should go back into the house when she'd been sitting outside in the garden watching the stars far above her and losing herself in the depths of the night sky; she would go inside and realise she was shivering with cold from lying on the damp grass and would go and change into dry clothes.

Three weeks after she'd first come here, Mickey came to spend the day with her, and it was like waking up after a long feverish sleep when she saw him getting out of his car and she ran to the door and flung it open and rushed into his arms. Later, in the tangle of blankets and pillows and clothes, she woke from the deep sleep she'd fallen into and saw a sudden furtive movement at the very corner of her vision, somewhere near the window. She slid silently off the bed, taking care not to disturb the sleeping man next to her and crept naked across the room to where she'd seen the movement. On the floor was a leaf, brown and cracked and still. Nothing more. The window was shut against flies; the door was shut. The day itself was windless. There was nothing that could create a breeze, a draught, and move the leaf. But it had moved, and moved fast at that, like a mouse or an insect or spider, and now, just as she had been able for weeks not to question, she found she could no longer ignore or fail to see that something odd was going on and she had no more answers than when she had first bought this house.

She bent down and picked up the leaf and stared hard at it. It was a beech leaf, years old, and virtually skeletonized by insect life and decay. Holding it up to the light, she turned it over to be sure there was no spider or beetle clinging to it anywhere. The pattern of veins showed through like fine lace but there was nothing else, nothing to explain its movement. Cross and irritated, she crumpled the leaf, and opened the window and threw it out. The sound of the window woke Mickey, who sat up smiling lazily and held his arms out for her.

"Come here," he said. "I think I need to tell you again how much I've missed you."

Isobel shut the window again, and shivered slightly as she ran back to the bed.

Chapter 19

The sound as she shut the door behind her seemed far louder than it ever had been before. It sounded more like the heavy iron-bound door of a castle slamming shut than the door of a cottage; a great echo seemed to ring through the empty house and she felt like picking up her phone and calling Mickey on his mobile and asking him to come back. He wouldn't have gone far yet, barely out of the village; she'd watched him drive down the lane, had stood at the gate until even the distant sound of his engine had been lost amid the birdsong and the soft soughing of the wind in the trees. The rose around the door had been shedding petals on the path, pink and fragrant still but soon to become first limp and then clammy, browning at the edges as they began to decay, and the cloying scent of wilting roses seemed to fill the hall as she stood uncertainly, trying to decide what to do. She had an almost overwhelming urge to grab her car keys and drive after Mickey, to be anywhere but here.

Don't be so bloody silly, she told herself sternly. There's nothing wrong that a cup of tea and a couple of chocolate Hob-Nobs won't make better.

She went through to the kitchen to make some tea, and found she needed to turn the light on. The sky outside had become heavy with purplish clouds; she'd hardly noticed the day changing. They'd been too busy to notice anything bar a major explosion in their vicinity. When she'd stood at the gate to wave Mickey off, she had noticed the strange yellowish cast to the light but had not really registered it. She had not registered either the heaviness of the humid air or the stillness of it. She opened the kitchen door onto the garden and felt the air press down on her and the first squally gusts of breeze whipped her hair around her face and a few leaves scuttled in like animals seeking cover. Abruptly she shut the door again and went to hurl a teabag into a mug and to hunt down the elusive biscuit tin.

As she nibbled on the edge of her biscuit, she could feel the hairs on the back of her neck begin to prickle. There must be the mother and father of all storms brewing; she was even feeling slightly sick and faint, and she hoped Mickey would have the sense to pull over somewhere at a service station or something if the storm burst while he was still driving home. She walked over to the French doors and bolted them and wedged the chair she'd taken to using to ensure the doors didn't fly open at night, and at that memory, she baulked suddenly.

She pulled the chair away and unbolted the doors and as the slightly sickly air gusted in, she knelt down to examine the fastenings on the doors, playing with the handles until she was sure they could not open themselves short of being kicked hard and accurately open. Shutting the door, she slid the bolt backwards and forwards, assessing the surety of its closure. The bolt was, if anything, a little stiff. It couldn't just come undone all by itself. Which left the question: who was opening the doors?

You're alone here. You have been for weeks. There's no one else been here but that kid and he's at his granny's now. There's no one else here but you. So who is doing all these things?

The questions raced through Isobel's mind and she shuddered involuntarily. How did I manage to take no notice of all this? How did I not ask what was happening?

Because if you had, you'd have been so scared you'd have gone home straight away. The answer came in her own voice, the one she used mostly to the children: her reasonable, sensible rational voice. But for this, there is no reasonable, sensible rational explanation and so I have been ignoring it while I worked, she thought, because if I hadn't I'd not have been able to work. So what has changed?

Me. That's what's changed. *I* have. I've been in a trance or something for weeks, and today, the trance broke. Maybe it was Mickey or maybe it would have happened anyway. I don't know. But whatever has happened, I can't pretend I still don't notice any of the weird things that keep on happening.

She stepped back from the door, and wedged the chair firmly back under the handles. Whatever was going on, she wasn't going to stand for it. She'd get to the bottom of this in the end, and she wasn't taking this shit any more.

As she thought this, the first burst of lightning lit up the room as bright as a camera flash, and was rapidly followed by a rumble, and the rain began. Huge drops hit the window, a few at a time, then faster and harder. The paving outside the French doors became dark with water, and then as the rain fell faster the surface seemed to boil as the drops hit and bounced and fell again.

"I hate thunder," she said to the room, and went to turn the lights on.

The electric light made everything in the room seem sickly and yellowish and she drank the rest of her cooling tea sitting watching the rain hitting the windows. The trees were being whipped around by the wind, swaying wildly and the sound was so like a stormy night at sea that she shuddered and almost felt seasick. After a while, she felt her bladder ache and she hurried through to the bathroom.

The stone floor was awash with dirty water full of twigs and leaves and unnameable muck. The toilet was gushing over with foul smelling water.

Oh hell, the damn thing must be blocked or something, she thought furiously, and rolled up her jeans and waded in barefoot. The stench was pretty horrible but then so was the thought of plunging her arm into that dark water, if it even *was* water. She rolled up her sleeves and held her breath as she gingerly eased her hand and then her arm into the toilet bowl. The water was too dark to see through, and a small part of her mind that was managing to be rational told her that though the water was filthy, there was very little actual sewage. Most of the muck was decayed leaves, mud and unidentifiable slime. Her hand met the blockage straight away and she had to yank hard to dislodge it. She gazed at the offending mass with distaste; another of those matted twig balls, this time so foul with mud and filth that the twigs looked more like a mass of rotting bones, as though a number of dead animals had been squished up together and had rotted into this peculiar ball. The toilet made a great sucking, belching noise and began to drain away. Experimentally she flushed it and the water in the bowl ran clear again.

Her bare feet were icy on the flooded floor, and she could feel stuff squishing between her toes, and the touch of something slimy. She fought her rising nausea, grabbed the mop and began to sweep the dirty tide back down to the little drain in the floor, sweeping and sweeping till the dark flood was gone. Then she rinsed her feet in the shower, and fetched a bucket and disinfectant and began to swill the floor down, bending to dislodge the odd scrap of twig (or was it bone? She didn't want to look too closely.) The disinfectant was scented with a synthetic lilac fragrance, but it didn't seem to shift the heavy scent of rotted vegetation and mud, like the sludge from the bottom of a neglected pond and the damp odour filled the house, touched by the lilac scent only enough to make it nauseating.

She used the toilet but somewhat reluctantly even thought she'd cleaned it. She felt filthy, inside and out, and no matter how much she scrubbed at her feet and at her arms and hands, the scent of mud seemed to cling to her flesh. It was the smell of a waterlogged graveyard, and she wondered how she knew that and told herself not to be fanciful. The drains had not coped with the deluge, and the toilet had somehow become blocked. Then how, said that little voice, did that twig ball come to be in the loo in the first place? It couldn't have come *up* the toilet, since it couldn't go down it. So where did it come from?

It wasn't it the bin where she'd chucked it, and that, more even than the foul odour that filled the house, that was what made her shiver. The twig ball, like all the others, had simply vanished.

She stood amid the scent of mud and decay and began to cry, rather hopelessly. The sound of rain drumming on the roof and windows, gurgling down gutters and hammering on the soaked garden filled the house, louder even than the beating of her own heart that had become absurdly loud in the last few minutes. Far off, or so it seemed, she heard a thump, and she ran through to the living room to see the chair she'd wedged under the handles of the French doors fallen on its side. The door was still closed but she could see that the bolt was no longer across.

"Oh *Christ*," she whispered and the lights all through the house faltered and then went out as another flash of lightning ripped across the sky.

Her mouth had gone as dry as if she'd been eating sand, and she fought to wet her lips with a tongue that felt like old leather. She wanted to swallow back the terrible fear that was rising in her, but she had no saliva left. She remembered reading once that the very lack of spit was what made you afraid, so she drank a glass of water and tried to make herself calm. Breathe in slowly, breathe out slowly; you're quite safe, she told herself.

Upstairs, a floorboard creaked and she had to bite her lip to stop herself screaming. It's an old house, she thought, boards settle and make a noise. Get a *grip*, girl. What could there possibly be that could hurt you? It occurred to her then that Mickey wasn't the only one to have watched too many horror movies in his teens. At least I don't have a basement to go down into, she thought, her sense of humour briefly putting its head out from under the blankets.

"That was not footsteps," she said, aloud. "There is no one here but me."

She got hold of the bag of night lights and the matches and took them through to the living room where she lit half a dozen and put them around the room and dragged her discarded jumper on; it had begun to feel oddly cold, rather like being underground, in a cave or a cellar or somewhere dank and chilly.

The trouble with candle-light when you're alone and scared is that it isn't romantic or atmospheric at all; it creates a whole host of imaginative shadows, flickering across walls and ceilings, bouncing off mirrors and window glass and making the whole room full of furtive, elusive movement. She watched the shadows the candles created and made herself ignore them. She ignored the sounds of the storm, telling herself it was only a storm, that short of a bolt of lightning hitting the roof or the chimney, it couldn't hurt her. All the time, she was shaking with a visceral primitive terror that she'd never have explained to her friends; she would have neither the right words nor would they have the imagination to make that leap of intuitive comprehension.

Imagination. It's all my imagination, she told herself, and tried to stop her teeth chattering. Hell's bells, she thought, I only thought that happened in Scooby Doo cartoons.

Upstairs, something creaked again and she shut her eyes. If I don't look it'll go away.

"Dear God, that was the stairs," she whispered, eyes still tightly shut. "It's coming downstairs."

What's coming downstairs? I am alone here, her rational voice said. All the noise is the stresses of a storm on an old house. I am imagining things; that's all. I do: I am an artist. Imagining things is what I'm supposed to do.

Nonetheless, she crept out into the hall, holding a tea-light on a saucer. She gazed into the black emptiness at the top of the stairs.

"Is there anyone there?" she called, softly, not sure what she would do if there were to be a reply.

Nothing, of course! She was alone; there was no one up there. Of course there was no one up there, stupid cow.

She felt her heart rate slow a little, and her breathing settle. Her knees were feeling quite wobbly, as if she'd not eaten in days, and her chest was hurting a bit, probably from not breathing properly.

It's all right, she said to herself, as if soothing a small child or a frightened pet. It's all right.

With the suddenness of pantomime, the front door flew wildly open, the rain and the wind gusting in and bringing a smell of flooding rivers and disturbed leaf mould. She stared at the door as it banged against the wall, as the rain splashed in, soaking the stone flags and making puddles amid the leaves that had blown in. She had not screamed; she had been too scared to open her mouth even. The door had been shut and locked, the bolts firmly fastened. And now, it crashed back and forth, unlocked and unbolted, and the rain streamed in.

Her heart was beating queerly, banging on her ribcage like a trapped bird, and all her senses were telling her to run, to leave and to leave *now,* but she managed to hang onto her sanity long enough to find her battered old boots, and went to the kitchen to pick up her car keys, from the Welsh dresser where she always left them. They weren't there; the china dish where she put them was conspicuously empty. She could feel panic rising fast as a flooding river, and she went to check her pockets: only her door-keys and her mobile.

I know I put the car keys in that dish, she thought, frantically. So where the fuck are they? She could feel her chest heaving as she tried to breathe properly, tried to think properly. The sound of the wind from the open front door sounded like someone sobbing, lost and sobbing on her doorstep, until she realised that the sobbing was from her. Upstairs, a window burst open and finally her nerve gave way and she flung herself out into the storm, pulling the door shut behind her and running towards the car.

Useless, she thought. I can't even get into the car and hide there. My keys, why my fucking keys? She didn't bother to open the gate, just swung herself over it and out into the lane where the torrential rain had turned the rough unmetalled road into a rushing stream, the water like café au lait as it churned up mud and clay in its wake, small twigs and bits of rubbish bobbing madly along. It came almost over her boots, and she splashed along, feeling her clothes already more or less soaked through as she ran.

Where am I going anyway? I don't know any more. Away and away, and that's all I need to know. She felt the odd relief and release of flight that perhaps all pursued animals may feel: the relief that after the waiting there is action and the release of tensed muscles and strained nerves into movement at last.

When she reached the end of the lane, she turned down into a footpath and began running down it. The overgrown grass of the path was partially submerged like reeds on the edge of a marsh, and the water was again cloudy with mud as it flowed more sluggishly now. Her breath was coming in ragged gasps and she blundered and slipped on the wet surface of the path. It was surrounded by high and overgrown hedges of hawthorn and other low trees, but many branches had put their new growth right across the path at head height so she was slapped and thumped by sodden leaves, and scratched by thorns as she tried to force her way through. Nettles had grown almost as tall as she was and they too slapped at her, stinging her arms and even her neck as she pelted along. She felt sick with a stitch and she couldn't think with the rain hammering on the top of her head but still she ran, her boots floundering in the mud and muck.

She knew she was crying, but she couldn't seem to stop, the tears lost amid the water running down her face and neck. She must have trodden on something extra slippery, perhaps a patch of smooth clay unseen under the water, and she fell headlong, measuring her length on the path For a moment, she lay with her face in the water, her breath coming in gasps and whimpers and then she hauled herself upright and sat amid the soaked grass and leaves and tried to get her breath back as the storm raged on overhead. The wind hadn't lessened, and even the low trees around her were being thrown this way and that, lashing their branches around as though possessed by some unholy demon and fighting their domination all the way. She sat in the stream that had been a path and sobbed and gasped until she managed to wipe the mud from her face and get back to her feet.

Think, she said to herself. Just think! Where can you go? There are houses round here; you've noticed them when you've gone out to the shops. You could go into the village; there's maybe a pub you can go to, see if you can get shelter there till this is over. Just calm down! Her breathing slowed as she calmed and she walked now instead of running helter-skelter. When she came to the end of the footpath, she realised she didn't know where she was at all. In theory, she should be down near the river, and there ought to be a road down here, but there wasn't. The footpath ended instead in a strange little clearing, like an unkempt park, and there was nowhere to go but back.

She trudged back up the path, the strain of the slope pulling at her calf muscles, and when she got back to the top where she'd joined it, she could see no sign of her own lane. It wasn't there. It simply wasn't there at all. She couldn't seem to think properly, and night had fallen properly so it was doubly dark apart from the occasional flash of lightning as the storm moved slowly away, though the rain continued pretty well unabated. She was soaked to the skin; even her skin felt waterlogged and she was utterly lost. At a guess she was probably no more than half a mile from home; but she was completely lost.

Chapter 20

Lost, a few hundred yards from home; it wasn't possible. But she had to face the fact that however ridiculous it seemed, she hadn't got a clue either of where she was now or how she could get home. Nothing around her looked remotely familiar; she'd backtracked twice, and each time, she had thought she'd found the right way, only to come back to where she'd started or find herself in a completely new place. There were no signs to help her, no landmarks visible in the darkness or the pelting rain. She tried to remember particular trees or shrubs, but she became quickly confused and even when she broke the ends of twigs to mark where she'd passed, she never found them again, or found other incidental broken twigs that had nothing to do with her at all and got more and more hopelessly lost. The little lanes and footpaths might as well have been a maze designed to confuse her.

She'd stopped running when she realised she was lost, and now she settled into a steady plodding pace that she knew she couldn't keep up for very much longer. Her legs were hurting, her jeans clung icily to them and she had blisters from her boots rubbing bare heels and toes. The constant pounding of the rain on the top of her head was making her drowsy and confused, and she was developing a headache just to round things off nicely. She wondered if she would just wander till dawn, and maybe then she'd be able to see where she was, when she saw a light. It flickered, as the branches of trees and shrubs lashed around, but it seemed real enough, though the trick was going to be getting to it. There was no way of forcing a straight line through the hedge, so she began walking back up the path she'd just come down, trying to keep her eye on the light and try, just try, to somehow reach it.

It had the yellow glow of an electric light, but not that awful orange colour of street-lights that polluted the skies around cities with a dirty terracotta light and hid the stars. She didn't think there were street-lights here, so it might be a house. It stayed still, so it couldn't be a car, though if it had been she might have at least found her way to proper road and thence homewards. She pushed through a heavy branch of hawthorn that had been broken by the storm winds and lay draped across the path, and caught her wrist on one of the thorns. Blood sprang up and was washed away immediately by the rain, but Isobel clasped the wound with one hand, feeling the sting of the thorn deep in her skin, and held it firm, trying to slow the blood that fell onto her jeans.

This is not amusing, she thought, but she wasn't crying any more. She rounded the end of the path and saw she had come closer to the light, and headed off more directly towards it, through another overgrown lane not unlike her own. It briefly occurred to her that she might actually be returning to her own cottage, that the power might be back on and she was heading back to whatever had driven her from the cottage. A bit further on, she saw a gate; but not her own. This one was done in neat wrought iron, and wasn't fastened with bailer twine. She had to struggle with the latch, but she was soon at the source of the light. In a tidy rustic porch, out of the wind and the rain, hung a black Gothic style lantern, with an electric bulb inside. Here at last was the light that had drawn her like a moth in the night.

In the shelter of the porch, she watched the water and mud stream off her clothes and onto the stones of the step. Her wrist was bleeding quite badly, and she felt sick but she hesitated. This was the door of an utter stranger; she could be knocking at the door of a psychopath for all she knew. Her sense of humour had been cowering somewhere deep inside her, and now surfaced long enough to comment that no one could be that unlucky in one night, not even her. She wondered whether it was still today or perhaps after all her wanderings, it was actually tomorrow now.

Oh well, nothing else for it. I can't stand here all night bleeding like a stuck pig. I can at least ask for directions, if nothing else.

She raised the knocker and rapped sharply on the green surface of the door. She waited a moment, and then hearing nothing, rapped again a number of times. Still nothing. Overwhelmed by disappointment and exhaustion, she felt herself sliding slowly down onto the step, tears streaming down her face. I'll just rest here a minute, she said to herself, and then I'll go on. She let her face rest against the smooth paint and as she did so, she heard movement within. In a second she was back on her feet, and rapping smartly on the door again.

"All right, I'm here now," came a voice, muffled by the door, and the door swung open.

It took her a moment to adjust, because the face peering at her was not at her own level, but much lower and she saw that its owner was in a wheelchair.

"I'm so sorry to trouble you," she said, abjectly. "I'm lost."

"I should say you are," said the man in the wheelchair. "It's Ms. Trelawny, isn't it? You'd better come in and tell me what on earth had happened to leave you in such a state."

He backed the wheelchair away from the door and Isobel stepped inside the hall with some relief. Already it felt better not to be pounded continuously by water, but she looked at the floor, stone like the hall of her own cottage, as the water ran off her and formed puddles on the worn flags.

"Sorry," she said, suddenly horrified about how she must look.

"What are mops for?" the man said lightly. "Come through to the kitchen and let's see what we can do for you."

He swung the chair round neatly and rolled it down the corridor to the kitchen and dripping, Isobel followed. He was reaching into a tumble drier when she caught up with him.

"Here," he said, and threw her a big green bath towel still hot from the drier. "That might help, though I should perhaps offer you clothes. I suspect my wife would take it much amiss if I did, though. You're bleeding. Let me see."

He'd taken her wrist before she had a chance to do more than rub her face with the blissfully warm towel.

"Nasty," he said, letting go. "I think you've still got the thorn stuck. One moment while I find some tweezers."

The whole kitchen was set out so he could get to most things from the chair; work surfaces were at two heights, so that he could use them as well as his wife, wherever she was. He opened a cupboard and extracted a red first aid kit, and with great care and dexterity, pulled out the wicked looking thorn from Isobel's wrist and clapped a pad of lint over the wound.

"Hold that and press hard," he said, and dazedly Isobel obeyed, draping the towel round her shoulders awkwardly.

"Now then, Ms. Trelawny," he said. "Tea or brandy? I wonder which."

"Brandy," Isobel said. "How do you know who I am?"

He smiled at her.

"Everyone knows all about you now," he said. "Fall foul of Maggie and everyone knows it round here."

He opened another cupboard and fetched out a brandy glass.

"One moment," he said and wheeled away, out of the kitchen.

Isobel leaned exhaustedly against the cupboard behind her and waited. He was back in a few moments, bearing a bottle of brandy. She managed to look at him properly while he poured the spirit into her glass and found herself reassured by what she saw. He was old, white hair swept back off a high forehead, and blue-green eyes like the far off sea watched her kindly if somewhat ironically. His hands, she couldn't help noticing had joints that were twisted and swollen, the skin across them shiny and red as though they had been scalded and healed over and over again.

He let her sip the brandy in silence and laughed quietly as she spluttered over the first taste.

"Not a brandy drinker, I see," he said as she cradled the glass against her.

"Not much of a drinker at all, any more," she said. "I have probably kept certain vineyards in France in business, though, over the years. Thank you for this."

He nodded, thoughtfully.

"Now, come through to the warm and tell me how you got into such a state," he said. "No, don't worry about dripping everywhere. It's only water."

"Mud too," she said but followed him anyway.

She found a wooden chair in the living room and sat on that. The room was dimly lit, but she was aware of walls of books and CDs, a stereo system that she would guess cost about half of Mickey's yearly stipend, and old, heavy furniture that gleamed in the firelight with years of polishing. There was a small fire lit in the grate, and it crackled and spat sparks as if he'd only just topped it up.

"I have a fire most evenings," he said. "I feel the cold, even in the summer. My wife thinks we should move to the south of France but I cannot make that transition yet for all my travels. Now, tell me how you managed to get lost less than a quarter of a mile from your own home."

It felt silly now, here in the comfort and safety of this room, to remember how she had run in panic from shadows and noises, but he was watching her with eyes that seemed to see a lot further than most.

"It seems daft now," she said, hesitant. "I don't know how to start. Once I got lost, I just couldn't find my way back, no matter how I tried. I must have been hours wandering around."

"It doesn't surprise me," he said. "The lanes and footpaths here are somewhat notorious for misleading walkers. How did you come to be out on such a night?"

"That seems even sillier," she said, taking another sip of the brandy and enjoying the heat as it slid down to her stomach. "I got into a panic. I don't quite know why, now. Things haven't been right at my cottage, stuff I can't quite explain; things keep on moving, doors won't stay shut. This evening, I panicked. I thought there was someone in the cottage with me. I was scared and I ran away."

She ducked her head down, not wanting to meet his eyes or hear the derisive laughter that was bound to follow. When he said nothing, she looked up to see him nodding with understanding.

"I wondered if it would happen," he said and Isobel was astounded.

"What on earth do you mean?" she said, almost spilling her drink.

He made a vague but expressive gesture with his hands: one of mysteries unanswered and unanswerable.

"There are many things in this world we know so little about," he said. "What you have been experiencing is only one of them."

"You mean, I've not been going bonkers?" she asked, and he laughed, a light musical sound.

"Not in the slightest," he said. "Quite the contrary, in fact. I have my own theories, but no fool proof answers that cover every eventuality."

She stared at him and then buried her face in her glass, finishing it in a few gulps, and feeling the tears prickling at the back of her eyes again.

"Maggie puts it down to the fairies," he said. "But I don't think she'd really know a fairy if it came along and bit her on the behind. She'd give a substantial sum of money to have experienced what you've been experiencing, by the way."

"She talks about the fairies as if she's on first name terms with them or worse," Isobel said, and he laughed again.

"I gather you have seen some of her insalubrious attempts at art," he said. "No, I can assure you that she has never had anything happen at that tarted up farmhouse that you couldn't put down to her over-fertile imagination or to the antics of that horde of children."

"Then how come she thinks she knows all about it?" Isobel asked.

"That's just Maggie for you," he said. "Now, I know who you are but I don't think you will know who I am, unless you were a follower of classical music about fifteen years ago. My name is Guy Franklin. I came here about fifteen years ago when my career, as such, ended, and I had the same sort of welcome in this cottage as you have had at yours. So I know quite how frightening it can be; and I, as you can see didn't have the option of running away, and simply had to sit it out."

Isobel felt the hot splash of tears coursing down her dirty face and she buried her head in her hands. He wheeled across to her and put his hand on her head, very gently.

"You're quite safe, my dear," he said. "They can't hurt you, you know. Nor do they want to."

"What are they? What has been doing this? You can't expect me to believe in fairies at my age?" Isobel said, trying not to wail like a three year old.

"What we believe and what actually *is,* can often come to blows when they don't match," he said. "That's the tragedy of most religion. In the face of a strongly held belief, truth is very often a casualty. Here, we need to put aside what we think we know and examine the evidence. In the absence of much else to occupy me, that is what I have been doing off and on for the last fifteen years."

"Examining the evidence?" Isobel repeated, stupidly.

"Indeed," he said and passed her a beautifully ironed and folded white handkerchief. "I had hoped to come and call on you before too long. Maggie has tried without success to gather herself a little group of her own acolytes, but unknown to her there is already a loose association of artists and poets and musicians in this area who try, I am afraid, to stay as far as possible away from her. She would have us as a group, such as the Inklings or such as existed in the lakes during the time of Wordsworth, but we are not such people as that. When she first came here, Maggie sought to cultivate me, since I still retained some trappings of my former celebrity, but she soon found me too critical and has been distant with me since."

"I'm sorry," Isobel said. "I probably should know you, but I don't."

"I wouldn't expect you to; it has been many years since I was truly famous," he said. "I was a flautist; a very great one, in fact. Unless you were a fan of classical music, you would not remember me, though. I had a serious car accident some fifteen years ago that rendered me unable to walk more than a few steps. That would have been enough of a disaster had it not also been followed by the onset of severe arthritis, and my hands, as you can see can barely hold a pen let alone play a flute. I still take master classes once, maybe twice a year, for aspiring musicians, but mostly I live here in quietness and peace. My wife, alas, still misses the bright lights and spends a good deal of her time at much more exciting locations than here."

"I don't know about that," said Isobel, with a flash of a smile. "It's probably been too exciting for me recently. So what is going on? Am I about to meet Titania and Oberon?"

"Both culture and popular fiction and art have greatly confused perceptions of fairies," he said, with a brief smile. "Personally I would have every flower fairy book and painting locked away for the next hundred years; and extra taxes on each and every performance of A Midsummer Night's Dream, but I am probably in a minority."

"So what are fairies, then?" Isobel asked.

He poured her some more brandy before replying.

"Tell me what has been happening at your house?" he asked. "Indulge me; I need to be sure that you have experienced much the same as I and many others."

Isobel shrugged.

"I suppose it's always possible I am an hysterical idiot and nothing real has ever happened," she said, rubbing at her eyes with the handkerchief. She was horrified that it came away filthy with mud and blood.

"Is my face bleeding?" she asked, anxiously.

"Just some scratches; nothing deeper," he said. "A few days and nothing will show."

"Good," she replied. "What's been happening? Good question. When we first bought the house, I was very taken with its atmosphere and character. I really liked it. We had last year's holiday there, getting it clean and sorted for the furniture."

"I gather you actually live somewhere else," he said, and that reminded Isobel that he didn't know much about her beyond anything Maggie might have told him and none of that was necessarily accurate.

"Yes," she said. "The cottage is our holiday home; somewhere to retire to. There's never been any way we could afford our own home; my husband's a clergyman and I don't earn enough with my art for much beyond a few extras. But when my parents died, I got half of their house and a bit extra, so we could afford to buy somewhere. I have two small children, and it was getting tricky managing to work at home with them around, even on my bread and butter stuff, portraits and that sort of thing, let alone anything a bit more adventurous. So we thought I could come here from time to time and have a blitz on any outstanding work and hope I get inspired for something a bit more creative. I came down a few times, and found I got on brilliantly. It was almost like being reborn, creatively speaking."

He was nodding, as if he understood what she was going on about.

"But when we spent the holiday here, last summer, we noticed odd things, like jewellery going missing and then turning up again, doors not staying shut. I know I convinced myself if was coincidence and my imagination, but Mickey, my husband, got a bit spooked by it," she explained. "There were things at the edge of vision that sort of flashed past, moving so fast you couldn't quite see them. Funny little balls of twigs kept turning up in the bath or the shower, and they'd always have vanished when you went to have a closer look. All sorts of odd things happened; nothing very scary, just a bit unnerving."

She rubbed her eyes again; feeling more tears streaming down and was desperate to stop them.

"And then, I had this car crash," she said and stopped, abruptly, remembering what had happened to him.

"Go on," he said, smiling.

"I hit a deer, and killed it," she said. "And I have no idea why, but it just turned everything upside down, utterly."

She stared at her hands as they twisted and turned the dirty handkerchief.

"After that, nothing was quite the same," she added. "I seemed to go into a bit of a state, though I denied there was anything wrong. I just had so much going on in my head: masses of images and colours and ideas. I just wanted to get it all *out*, to get rid of it, or use it up or something, and I never got the time or the space. I was working into the evenings when the kids were in bed; any spare moment. And the bloody door-bell kept ringing or the phone or someone wanted something or the washing needed doing and I was *knackered*, totally exhausted because when I went to bed, it would all be going through my head as I went to sleep and I dreamed. Oh boy, did I dream! I could have dreamed for England if it were an Olympic sport. I just didn't seem to get any peace, ever. The minute I got one lot of images down, another would just come boiling up, demanding attention."

She let out a deep sigh.

"I think I understand," he said. "So what happened?"

"My family conspired," she said. "I still can't quite understand it. My brother's wife is a really lovely woman, and between her and my brother and my husband they came up with the idea that Katy and Simon would take my kids for the duration and let me come and live here till I was myself again. At least that's what I think now. That wasn't quite how they put it. I have had one hell of a good time; and beyond the occasional passing thought, I haven't missed my children at all. I don't suppose I should admit that, should I?"

He just smiled and said nothing.

"I've not been what you might call a natural mother," she went on. "I love them, obviously, but they don't enthral me the way I see other people's children enthral them. Well, mums anyway. I don't see so many dads. I watch other mums and I sometimes wonder what's wrong with me. I stand a bit to one side, observing, I guess. I'm not caught up in it, for all the broken nights and everything. Even when they were very tiny and needed constant attention, I always had a part of me that was separate, desperate for them to sleep so I could be me again. I don't suppose this is at all relevant, but when I hit the deer, and everything inside me changed, one of the things that changed was that I began to notice that I resent the time other people took from me. I began to feel I was in the wrong world. A fish out of water."

She got to her feet, wringing her hands and walked about the room, trying to ease the pain she felt. When she felt calmer, she sat back down.

"So when I got this chance to just come here and work, I was obscenely grateful," she said.

"Why obscenely?" he asked.

"Because I should be so grateful simply to have the family I do," she said. "I never thought I'd have kids. I had a series of miscarriages, and I had more or less resigned myself to being childless. And now I was finding I was only thinking about being alone and able to paint all these images that were blinding me. Like visions, but they never quite go away; they're always there under the surface, waiting."

"I understand," he said. "While I was still a star, I only thought of my family when they were there in front of me. The rest of the time, it was almost as if they didn't exist. Now, I can see I did what I had to do. Sometimes great talent needs the space and time to be itself."

"I don't know about great talent," Isobel said.

"I do," he said. "I don't agree with some of the things that are said about the needs of great artists and performers, but some of it is true. We are not quite as other people are; and that is as it should be. So you came here to work. What then?"

"I've never worked like it," she said softly. "Never, not even when I was younger. Not in scope or in execution or volume. I don't know what anyone else will make of it. It was like being alive again after being half dead. As if I suddenly had full vision again after being partially blind. You get the idea. I was in my element again, you might say."

"A fish *in* water," he suggested, and she nodded vigorously.

"I didn't notice or care about the things that happened," she said. "They were no more than an irritation. Even the doors weren't a problem. I kept dismissing it, assuring myself that it was my imagination or faulty catches, or that I'd put things somewhere else and then forgotten about it. I dreamed such vivid dreams each night, and each day I poured out the dreams and visions into paintings. Then, yesterday it must be now, my husband came for the day. I'd not seen him since I set off here weeks ago. When he went home, it all seemed to have changed."

She thought about her sudden pang of unease that had flowered into fear as the evening drew on.

"So what are they then, these fairies you say are what has been tormenting me?" she asked, briskly, trying to put aside her memory of her own panic. "Surely you can't believe in tinselly winged fluttery things with little magic wands?"

He smiled at her, patiently.

"No, that is the fault of Victorian artists and writers trying to sanitise folklore," he said. "They sanitised so much, cleaned the good earth from it and packaged it for the children. Fairy tales! Have you ever read the real unexpurgated Grimm's Tales?"

Isobel shook her head.

"No, most people haven't these days," he said, rather sadly. "They wouldn't pass muster through the censors now; tales of blood and guts and sex and natural justice; not to mention monsters and demons and so on. It's many years since I looked at them; we would not read most of them to your children now. Many of our most popular fairy tales are cleaned up versions. Granny was eaten by the wolf, really eaten, not just swallowed to be freed later. Sleeping Beauty was wakened by more than a kiss!"

He sighed.

"The fairies of real fairy stories are not *nice*," he said.

"But if they are real, what are they?" Isobel asked, infuriated.

"I have heard many theories from many people," he said. "One idea, that has plenty of credence among the New Age aficionados, is that fairies are nature spirits."

Isobel remembered her friend Chloe's comments about what her grandmother had thought, and nodded.

"They are usually referred to as *devas*, a Sanskrit word meaning shining ones," he went on. "They are seen as some sort of essential part of the natural world, helping trees and flowers grow. Some people even claim to have seen them and work with them. There is something in it; the gardens of such people are often spectacularly lovely and productive, beyond what the soil and conditions should logically be able to produce. But these beings are seen as useful, helpful, and never aggressive or mischievous in the way fairies have historically been seen. People in the distant past were frightened of fairies, terrified even. A whole system of folklore has sprung up around the appeasement of the fairies. You still find some of it practised in remote rural areas. Ireland in particular, and the Isle of Man have a culture of the Little People. It seems quaint to visitors, but there are tales galore of people who have scoffed at it, been disrespectful and been inexplicably punished by mishap."

"I've heard those sort of stories too," Isobel said. "I just thought they were silly stories for the tourists."

"Many may well be just that," he agreed. "But there are too many for them all to be just stories. There are some claims that in antiquity, the Little People may well have been just that: the remnant of a pygmy race, pushed to the margins of society and scavenging from the richer invaders to stay alive. For me, this is the least likely option for the true identity of the fairy folk. For a start, people in general were smaller. For a race to be truly small enough to merit the description, they would have to have been almost a race apart, which is what some people claim they were. We have no archaeological evidence of such a people coinciding with our people. The

Australopithecus, an early hominid would have been much, much smaller than modern man, but they died out millions of years ago, and even the gracile form who were much more delicate than the robust form, would have seemed monkey-like to any modern human. The tales of the fairy folk speak both of great beauty and great ugliness, but I cannot believe in a hidden pygmy race on the fringes of civilisation. For a start, I cannot imagine them staying hidden long; our ancestors would have hunted them all down as soon as possible. They were not likely to tolerate theft and mischief for long. No, without either archaeological or anthropological evidence I am afraid that theory is useless; though it would be interesting should evidence show up, I cannot think that such a race might exist still in our over-populated land."

"So what or who do you think the fairies actually *are*?" Isobel said, mesmerised by his voice.

He smiled again.

"It is only my theory," he said. "One, I may say, shared by many people over the years. They are the spirits of the dead."

Chapter 21

Isobel stared at him in horror, and then began to laugh somewhat hysterically.

"You must be joking," she said. "You're telling me that ghosts have been doing all this?"

"Not ghosts, Ms. Trelawny," he said, still smiling. "The spirits of the dead. It's quite a different concept, actually."

"Sorry, I must have been off school the day they did that one," Isobel said. "Is this more than a question of semantics, then?"

"Considerably more," Guy said. "It's almost a case of being divided by a common language. I say spirits and you think: ghosts. It isn't the same thing at all."

"I don't understand," Isobel said, feeling lost again.

"We use the words as though they are synonymous and they mean quite different things," he said. "And these days, our understanding of such matters has been eroded by the decline of organised religion and by the mass media. Not that many were experts in such fields in any time. But at one time, more people had a rudimentary knowledge of these things. When you were a child, was there a taboo on going into graveyards at night, one that most children dared each other to break?"

"Yes," said Isobel slowly. "I always thought it was a bit daft. The dead can't hurt you. I suppose though nowadays it's more to do with keeping kids safe from the kind of people who hang round such places."

"Graveyards have always been considered littoral places," he said.

"Literal? I don't follow," she said, puzzled.

"You misunderstand. Littoral; as in on the shoreline. A place on the borders between one place and another. There are times like that too: times of the day like dawn and dusk that are not quite night and not quite day. Times of the year, between times, the transition times, like Hallow E'en: not quite winter and no longer summer either. Graveyards in Christian tradition are waiting places where the dead remain waiting for the Day of Judgement," he said. "Have you ever been in a modern cemetery though, one that has been started in recent years, after the decline of the church had begun in earnest?"

She thought about it for a minute and then said,

"Yes, I have. It was horrible, actually. I don't know why, really, because it was clean and tidy and there were lots of benches and the graves were all well-tended. Some people go there and talk to their loved ones, sit at the grave and talk. It made me shudder."

"Why?"

"Because there's no one there," she said. "It's just bones and stuff. The person is gone. And those new ones don't have any atmosphere; they might as well be a park or something."

"Why do you think they don't have any atmosphere?"

She thought about it and shrugged.

"No idea," she said finally.

"Have you ever been in a really ancient cemetery or even a crypt?" he asked and when she shook her head, he went on. "I have, in a number of places. Ossuaries, too. As you say, it's just bones and stuff, but down there, there is a sense of something else being there, watching and listening. I used to put it down to having watched too many Hollywood horror films, until I came here and began to make sense of it."

He gazed at her, and she saw there was sympathy in his eyes.

"You see, we aren't very good about death, you know," he said. "It's always been the last great taboo. I've read a great deal about how in modern times we are too divorced from death and how we shy away from all mention of it, but I think that has been the case for a long time. Yes, people lived close to it, in the past, but it was never something that was courted or welcomed, and in modern times, even more than ever before, people try to convince themselves that it will not come for them. In the very distant past in some cultures, people buried their dead beneath the floors of their houses, to keep them close so they could continue to care for them, making offerings to them so they might continue to share in the life of the family. The Romans had their cemeteries outside their city walls, and made offerings of wine and food at set intervals to stop the dead seeking out the living and feeding off their vital essence. Our custom of leaving flowers at graves may stem from this same practise."

"I hate to see teddy bears and things stuck on a kiddie's grave," Isobel said, her voice husky and heavy with tears. "The kid's gone; give the teddy to some child who's still here."

"I know; I understand," he said. "But for many it gives them comfort to do such things. And it isn't far from the practices of the Egyptians who buried their dead with everything they thought they might need in the afterlife."

He sighed.

"This is not easy to explain," he said. "Because it may well challenge your personal beliefs to such an extent that you will refuse to accept anything. These are profound mysteries; not something we are used to. This land of ours is so full of the past that sometimes it seems to me there's hardly room for the present. This area is far richer in archaeology than almost anywhere in Britain, and yet most of it remains to be investigated, and is untouched, and ignored. The amount of barrows that have been ploughed out even in recent years is a shock to the system. Here they are scattered everywhere."

"I saw them," Isobel said softly. "In a dream, I flew and I saw them. Little candles lit at every one and there were dozens and dozens of them. But in the day, I could see almost none of them."

"Exactly," he said. "Your barrow was a special feature when the cottage was built. In fact, it was why it was built at all."

"I don't know anything about the cottage," she said apologetically. "I should but I never got round to asking anyone."

"I have been amused by Maggie's attempts to form a collective of artists and poets," he said. "Not least because it isn't the first time it was tried here. At the height of the popularity of the Romantic poets, a small group of artists and poets came here. No, you won't know any of their names. They were simply wannabes, I think we might describe them. The bored sons of rich men in the main, waiting for dead men's shoes and posing as they waited as the successors to Wordsworth and to Lord Byron and Shelley. They dabbled in art and poetry and never achieved much. My cottage and yours were built for them; a few others have since crumbled and been lost. Their work never achieved anything, partly because they were only playing at it and partly due to lack of any real original talent. For every Mozart there are a thousand, thousand Salieris; most think they are Mozarts till they die despite evidence to the contrary. So it was with the little community here; a few years later they drifted apart and left only the cottages as evidence of their existence. So whenever Maggie phones me to invite me to an at-home, I smile and decline and think of them."

"So did no one ever try and excavate the barrow?" Isobel asked, fascinated.

"I believe the original owner intended to have the barrow fully excavated but lost interest," Guy said. "There was likely to be a great deal of hard physical labour involved and none of the locals would get involved. The expense of shipping in navvies to do the actual digging proved to be a sufficient disincentive, apparently. The great days of archaeology were yet to come; the gentleman treasure hunter still ruled, and a muddy old mound in the middle of England didn't have the glamour these men craved. I suppose we should be glad they didn't, though it doesn't look like anyone will even now. I suppose it would be extremely expensive to do a proper excavation on the off chance the barrow might contain something worth the effort. And our museums are stuffed full of artefacts they don't know what to do with; the chances of this being the equivalent of another Sutton Hoo are so small as to render the whole thing impossible."

"I'm glad," said Isobel dryly. "I can't say I'd like it dug up. Are you sure these poet guys didn't build the mound as well as the cottage?"

"Quite certain," he said. "There was a certain amount of fakery going on at that time but records show that mound has been here at least as long as the existing village."

"So it is real," she said. "OK, you've said that it isn't ghosts, but you haven't told me what the difference is between ghosts and the spirits of the dead. As far as I knew, the two terms mean the same thing."

He looked thoughtful, piecing together his words for a moment.

"Ghosts are like shadows," he said. "They have no substance, no consciousness. They may even be some type of accidental recording, like a video. Most sightings of a ghost have exactly the same descriptions; different people see exactly the same figure or hear the same sound. There are theories that suggest that events can become locked into the landscape, into the fabric of a building or room; certain conditions are needed to release the recording but once that is done, it follows the same familiar pattern. People who have tried to communicate with ghosts have met with singularly little success. The spirits of the dead have consciousness; have a need to communicate with the living for whatever reason. They often have the kind of power to affect material things still."

"When you came here, what sort of things happened to you?" Isobel asked.

"They affected the electrics and in particular, electronics," he said. "My stereo had to be taken back to the dealers several times with an intermittent fault that the experts couldn't figure out. Things like the television and the fridge went on the blink but never broke. I had power cuts that the electric people couldn't explain. Oh, yes, and all the other little tricks of moving and hiding keys and spectacles and jewellery: shadows that moved, odd noises."

"We don't have many electrical appliances at the cottage but the lights did keep on flickering, now you mention it. And the power went out tonight. Or perhaps it was last night now. I don't even know what the time is. I am sorry. You must be tired," Isobel said, flushing with the realisation that she was probably keeping her host up.

"I don't sleep much these days," he said. "A mix of age and pain, I suppose. It's a little after four, by the way. Dawn will be quite soon, and then you will be able to see how close to home you actually are. Don't worry; I have appreciated this chance to meet, even under such circumstances. There is much to discuss, Ms. Trelawny."

"It's actually *Mrs*. Trelawny," said Isobel. "But I'd much rather you called me Isobel."

"Very well, then, Isobel," he said. "I think you will find that your home will seem less threatening when you see it in daylight. I must emphasize that they cannot hurt you, though they might frighten you enough to hurt yourself in panic. Let me ask you something you may find irrelevant: I assume Trelawny is your husband's surname?"

"Yes," said Isobel. "His grandfather was Cornish but Mickey was born in Kent."

"What, if I may ask, was your maiden name?"

Isobel blinked in surprise.

"Hunter," she said. "You're right; it doesn't seem relevant at all. What did you want to know for?"

"Just a hunch, that was all," he said, but looked pleased and that puzzled Isobel.

"I don't understand," she said.

"If I may be permitted to call on you later today, when you and I are both rested," he said. "I may be able to explain a little better. I don't sleep well, but I do need what little sleep I get."

"Would it be easier if I came back here?" she said.
He smiled.
"That's very considerate of you," he said. "But I think it is important for me to visit you at your own home and I have improved my health in the years since my crash, through physiotherapy and the like, so I am able to walk a little. Usually from the car to the house and back again but it does allow me a certain independence I previously did not have. My hands have more mobility than they did but not enough for me to play the flute again, just enough for domestic tasks and writing the odd note. It's astonishing how much improvement can be made when you're too bloody-minded to give in."
Isobel grinned, in sudden fellow feeling and liking.
"I bet you were too stubborn to run away when you first got here," she said. "Never mind not being able to, I bet you just wouldn't give in to the scare tactics."
He grinned back.
"You seem to have got my measure, quite well," he said. "Now, if I point you in the right direction, will you be all right now?"
"Yes," said Isobel, and then with greater feeling, "Yes, I'll be fine. It was the storm and the dark and all that weirdness that freaked me out. I usually just get a headache or get a bit jittery when it's stormy, but this just went beyond that. And in daylight, I think I'll be fine."
All dregs of panic had gone, soothed away by his reassuring manner, though she knew if she sat down and thought about it properly, she'd start feeling fairly scared again. All this talk of the spirits of the dead made her feel very creepy.
He wheeled his chair down to the front door and as she stepped outside, she saw the lane outside lit up by the very first glimmerings of daylight. There were shreds of mist and the grass and trees dripped, but the torrential rain had stopped, and everything smelled of water and bruised greenery.
"If you go down the lane a little, you'll find another path that leads downhill a little," he said. "Follow that and you'll find your own lane. You really are that close, a quarter of a mile if that. I can see the barrow from my landing window."
"Thank you," she said. "I feel such a fool, now. How could I get so lost?"
"Have you heard of the phrase, pixy-led?" he asked. "Sometimes they contribute to disorientation, so that we go around in circles and get more and more lost in land we know like our own faces. I will call on you later today, probably after lunch, to allow us both a little time to rest. Remember, you cannot be hurt, though you can be scared and irritated half to death."
Isobel set off into the growing light of morning and alarmingly soon found herself outside her own cottage. Rain still dripped off the greening walls and the paving at the front was awash with water, and the rose had lost all its remaining flowers, which lay in a soggy pink mass in front of the door, like a discarded, disdained bouquet. She hesitated before opening it, wondering what was inside, whether there were any extra

surprises waiting for her. What it is to be cursed with a vivid imagination, she thought and pushed the door inward, holding her breath involuntarily as she did so.

The door had the grace not to creak, and all that emerged from the hall was the smell of river mud that had filled it when she left, the residue of the stench from the flooded bathroom. She stepped inside, and listened, waiting for something to happen. Nothing. The house had a queer feeling about it, and it reminded her of a dog that knows it has been naughty and is being extra good in the hopes that you won't notice what it has done; a sort of cringing, tail-between-the-legs fawning feeling. She felt suddenly very relieved, and shut the door behind her.

She went round and checked all the rooms, making sure that windows and doors were secure, and when she got back to the kitchen, she glanced without surprise at her car keys in the little china bowl.

"Humph!" she said, and rattled them a little to reassure herself they were real.

In the new daylight, the house seemed benign and non-threatening and she could scarcely believe how terror-stricken she had been the night before. She looked down and saw the state of her jeans and decided that before she could sleep she had to get herself clean, and she emptied her pockets, stripped off all her clothes, and dumped them in the Belfast sink and ran some cold water into it, watching it turn a dirty shade of brown as the fresh water diluted the mud. She slipped naked from the utility room to the bathroom and into the most welcome shower of her whole life, watching filthy water cascade from her body and down the drain, scrubbing her skin and scalp till they tingled.

Wrapped in a thick towel she plodded wearily upstairs intending to pull on some clean clothes. Sitting on the bed to drag on warm socks, she leaned back against her pillow and gave a deep sigh, and was asleep in seconds.

Chapter 22

She woke feeling utterly ravenous, and pulled on the rest of her clothes, having fallen asleep wearing one sock and a towel, before running downstairs to eat toast and honey and drink tea. She was still wiping the crumbs from her mouth when she heard her phone ringing, and had to try and recall where she had left it. It lay on the shelf near the Belfast sink and when she answered it, it was Mrs. Broadbent.

"I just thought I should update you on what's been happening," she said, and Isobel could tell from her voice she was pleased.

"I'd love to know," Isobel said, quite sincerely. "I take it Tristan is behaving himself?"

"He's doing very well, for a boy who has had less attention in the last few years than a stray dog," Mrs. Broadbent said, with feeling. "I have hired a tutor so he can at least learn some of the basics like reading and writing before he goes to school and he has already made huge progress."

"He struck me as a clever boy," Isobel said. "What else has happened?"

"The social work people paid an unexpected call on my daughter," said Mrs. Broadbent. "And they were not pleased with what they found, though they didn't consider any of the children to be at actual risk of harm, though I would disagree. They have apparently been totally misled in the past. To home educate, it is only necessary to show that education is being offered to children, and Maggie has a whole room filled with computers and books and educational paraphernalia. The children have sometimes used all this, and the education people have never probed further. The fact that there was very little supervision or teaching as such doesn't seem to have been noticed. I think questions will be asked, and I suspect it is simply the fact that Maggie is rich and apparently well-educated herself that has been the main factor in this sorry state of affairs not having been discovered before. She has been given an ultimatum: send the children to school or we take things further."

"And I would guess that she would rather just send them to school," Isobel commented. "What about the state of that child, Celeste?"

"They told her to get her cleaned up properly, or they may be obliged to take her away," said Mrs. Broadbent. "So I would very much imagine that has been done. None of the children are apparently malnourished, and none show signs of anything more than the usual bumps and bruises of childhood, and none have spoken of neglect or abuse. Unfortunately, by the time a doctor saw Tristan's injuries, they had healed to such an extent that it was impossible to prove how they had been sustained."

"Apart from his word," Isobel remarked.

"They are looking into it, but I suspect that Maggie will just deny it and suggest the boy is being spiteful," said Mrs. Broadbent. "Anyway, I wanted you to know that Maggie knows it was me who blew the whistle, and she has no idea you helped my grandson to run away, so you shouldn't have any reprisals from her. I know how spiteful my daughter can be to those she perceives to have wronged her."

You don't like her very much, do you, Isobel thought, but didn't say it. Instead she said, "I appreciate that. I hope Tristan does well when he goes to school. Do give him my best wishes for his future."

She rang off. At least something had been done about those children, and done moreover without her having to get more involved than she needed. She'd been horribly afraid she would have to be the one to inform the authorities of what appeared to be going on. She went upstairs to find her hairbrush and tried to sort out the mass of tangles that her hair had woven itself into in the night. Maybe I should go back to dreadlocks, she thought as she tried to tease apart strands of hair that had become matted together forming something that more closely resembled felted wool than human hair. Despite the thorough washing, bits of twig and fragments of bark had become caught up and even a few of last summer's burrs had got caught up and had to be extracted carefully. In the end, once she'd got the majority of the tangles out, she went back to the bathroom and washed her hair again in the sink, soaking it with the conditioner designed for children's hair that she'd bought for Miranda and had left behind last summer. The scent of it made her hopelessly homesick and for the first time in a long while, she missed both her children to the point of tears. But her hair at least was behaving itself now even if her tear ducts were not.

She was drying her eyes and considering whether or not to phone Mickey and tell him all about what had been happening when she heard a car in the lane.

"Please God don't let this be Maggie," she said as she went to the front door.

It wasn't Maggie's natty little sports car, but a much less extravagant saloon car, and when Guy struggled to get out, she rushed to open the gate for him.

"Spoilsport," he said, waving one of his two sticks at her. "I was just getting ready to vault over it and amaze you."

She grinned at him, amused.

"Tell you what," she replied. "I'll shut it after you come in and you can jump it on the way back."

He made his way quite slowly up to her front door, where he stopped and leaned on his sticks so he could gaze at the building thoughtfully.

"I know, I know," Isobel said, defensively. "It could do with a coat of paint or whitewash or something. Another year I'll be able to afford that as well as everything else, or I might muster the energy to paint it myself."

"I was just thinking how nice it looks with the moss and algae," he said. "More organic, more a part of the landscape."

She hovered uncertainly while he made his way up the hall, placing his feet and sticks with care, and directed him into the living room, where he sank into a chair with obvious relief and gratitude.

"I was about to make some tea or coffee," she said. "Can I offer you some? It's not quite the same as a Napoleon brandy but then I don't think I'd have fancied tea last night, so maybe you won't fancy brandy now."

He smiled at her.

"Some coffee," he said. "That would be perfect. Are they your paintings?"

He gestured at the stack of boards and canvases at the other end of the room.

She nodded.

"May I look?" he asked.

She shrugged.

"I don't see why not," she said. "After all, the idea is they get looked at during exhibitions and so on. They aren't in any particular order. Feel free; I'll go and make some coffee."

Isobel always found it hard to stand by while anyone looked at her work; she was torn by her own need to both explain her work and the terrible need for affirmation that could cripple her own creative expression. It was all very well telling herself that it didn't matter if someone didn't like her work, that it was their problem if they didn't, but that didn't stop the almost dog-like need for praise and approval. I should wear a collar and lead, sometimes, she thought, and maybe call myself Fido. She stayed in the kitchen and brought the coffee through on a tray with a bowl of sugar and the packet of coffee creamer she'd bought on her last trip to the shops.

He was sitting on her camping chair, the one she used for her equipment, and all her pictures were ranged out on the far wall; he'd put his chair close enough to lean forward and peer at them. He glanced up as she walked in.

"Intriguing," he said. "These are truly remarkable, you know. I don't think I have ever seen anything quite like them. They aren't like any of your earlier work at all."

"You've looked me up," she remarked, pleased.

"As soon as Maggie started ranting about you, I took great care to have a look at your work," he said. "This is new, all this. There are shades of some of it, in some of your earlier pieces, but it seems to have come fast and furious recently."

"Tell me about it," she said wryly. "I don't think I have had a moment's peace in weeks, if not longer."

"All these have been painted since you bought the cottage?" he asked.

"Yes," she replied. "I have done other work, but it's been portraits and that sort of thing. I brought all the ones I did before I came to stay here. The first one I painted here is that one there, the one where the barrow looks like a skull. I think I was pretty shocked when my husband pointed that out; I hadn't seen it until he said."

"Curious," he remarked. "Very curious."

Isobel pushed down the plunger on the cafetière and poured coffee into each mug and carried a mug to where Guy was sitting.

"I don't have any fresh milk," she said apologetically. "Just this weird powder. It doesn't taste like milk exactly, but if you're fond of railway vending machine coffee, this is a close match for that funny taste you get from those machines."

"I love it," he said, gallantly. "I don't travel by train very often these days so I can afford to be nostalgic for such things."

They sat in companionable silence for a few moments, his eyes straying continuously to the paintings.

"I wanted to ask something last night," Isobel asked suddenly. "I forgot about it but it occurred to me just now. If it is the spirits of the dead doing these things, then why, given that the dead outnumber the living by millions to one, why are these things so rare? And why have I never come across it before? Surely if this was so then I'm have come across it before now? Is this due to the barrow?"

"I thought you might ask something like that," he said. "I did myself. It's obvious, after all; you only have to glance at a cemetery to see how thick on the ground the dead are and the graveyards and cemeteries are merely the resting places of the relatively recent dead. There are tens of thousands of years of human history and the dead of those millennia must be scattered everywhere. So I agree with your question, why have you never been troubled by this before now?"

He gazed at her, and she gestured for him to go on.

"It isn't a simple answer," he said. "And it's one that is still evolving. Let me ask you a few questions first. Who do you think were buried in the barrows and so on?"

"Important people," Isobel said, without hesitation. "Chieftains and kings, great warriors, queens and leaders."

"Why?" he asked. "Why are you so sure of that? Can you tell a man by his bones? Does kingship run through the bones like words through a stick of rock?"

Isobel snorted.

"If anything's written through my bones it'll probably be the words tea and Hob Nobs," she said. "No, seriously, I know what you mean. Partly it's because some of them got buried with treasure; you mentioned Sutton Hoo. No one knows for certain who was buried there but they know he must have been a king of some sort because of the treasures. And also it takes a lot of man-hours to build something like that. You don't do that for just anyone; it has to be for someone a bit out of the ordinary."

"But we can't tell that from their bones," he said. "There is no trace of who or what a person truly was. We can tell how tall they were; what they ate in early childhood, what diseases they may have suffered from, but nothing about who they *were.* Nothing at all; virtue leaves no trace in our dust, and nor does greatness or talent. Some vices leave traces, like the effects of syphilis on the bones in its late stages, but very little else. All we know of the people of the past are the stories that come down through the centuries. Pull the real Robin Hood out of time and the chances are he would be very little like the stories. What he may have believed of himself is a very different matter, though."

"Are you saying it's the belief of the dead that makes the difference?" she asked.

"In part, yes," he said. "Most ordinary people lived and died without making a mark on the world. It's still the same today; they touch the lives of their family and friends but rarely any further than that. That is how it should be. But the lives of kings and warriors, queens and chieftains, they were seen to change the whole world. We all know the myths and legends, even if most of it is fiction. When that barrow was built, which I would guess happened in the late Neolithic or early Bronze Age, whoever was buried in it, was a mover and a shaker in that far-off world, a person to be reckoned with. And they knew it too. Have you ever visited somewhere like Poets' Corner in Westminster Abbey? Or Kensal Green Cemetery?"

"No, but I once stood on the grave of Bobby Shafto," Isobel said.

"Did you feel anything?"

"Yes," said Isobel. "Cold feet!"

"Nothing else?"

She considered for a minute.

"Yes," she said after a while. "Disappointment and resentment. It's in a little country church in the middle of nowhere, and there's no one who visits the grave or marks it beyond a few words in a tourist guide."

He nodded.

"Sometimes even great men do not rest easy in their graves," he said. "Those who have in life believed themselves to be special, to be deserving of something greater than that allotted to the common herd, they do not always go to the grave and rest. It's less common since the days when Christianity became widespread; people were told they would either go to heaven or to hell, or purgatory for those in between. Their spirits rarely give cause for concern. The more powerful the person was in life, the greater their power after death, in general, though by powerful I don't necessarily mean having worldly power. The strangest place to visit is the King's chamber of the Great Pyramid. I am told that Napoleon spent a night there and emerged white-faced and shaken in the morning and refused to speak of what he had experienced. I think that those who have been promised that great things will continue after this life are the ones who do not pass away truly as I believe we are meant to, to whatever is after life, but they linger instead, hankering after greatness in this world. Hence the fear the Romans had of their dead, of vengeful and lonely spirits who needed to be fed and appeased to be kept from bothering the living."

"Are you saying that the spirits of whoever was buried in my barrow are troubling me now?" she asked. "Why? I'm nothing to do with them. I don't even know who they are. What might they want from me anyway? Maybe I should get Mickey to do an exorcism after all."

He shrugged.
"I don't think it would help," he said. "They crave contact with the living, and is that so very terrible? You have been touched by them and have produced some of the best work of your entire career."
Isobel opened her mouth to protest that it was all her own work, that she didn't need some spirits to inspire her and her eyes fell on her row of paintings and her protests died unspoken.
"You see, though they have no names that we know, they are still a part of our history," he said. "They are still a part of our national identity as much as more recent heroes like Nelson and Wellington, Elizabeth the First. I could list you many names, but we don't know theirs. Why should they be dismissed because we do not know their names?"
"Why do they pester me, then, if they were so great?" Isobel asked. "Why did they not vanish off into whatever after-life they believed in?"
"I don't know," he said. "I also don't believe it is that simple. The Egyptians believed in the soul as being a thing of many parts. You have probably heard of the *Ka?"*
"Bloody silly name for a motor vehicle," she said. "But yes, I have heard of it. There were other bits, too. I seem to recall a *Ba* as well."
"They saw the soul as something that had many layers, as I understand it," he said. "I think they were right too. Today we talk about the sub-conscious, the unconscious and the conscious, not to mention the supra-conscious and the collective unconscious. I don't pretend to understand it. But I do think that whatever element made someone great in their time is not something that dies in its entirety when the physical body dies. I think it may even be something separate to the rest of the soul."
"So I'm being beleaguered by some discarnate ego-maniac?" Isobel said indignantly. "Some forgotten would-be King Arthur who won't give up? What am I supposed to do? Leave flowers or something to keep him happy? Or sugar, like Maggie suggested."
"I don't know what you should do," he said. "But there's a reason why they have targeted you in particular, something that has made you susceptible to them. Not everyone is, you know. They don't bother with just anyone. I would be willing to bet that had Maggie bought either this cottage or mine, nothing would have ever happened to her. One of her children maybe, but not Maggie herself."
"Is that supposed to be a comfort?" Isobel demanded.
"No, a compliment," he returned, as quick as a flash. "You're special, Isobel. You don't have to be the ancient dead to see that."
Isobel surprised herself by blushing. She made a face, and then said,
"So what qualities do I have then that make me such a magnet for the attentions of the spirits of the dead. And don't say I must be a natural medium; I'm getting on for a small these days."
"There are a number of qualities that would have attracted them to you," he said.

"Such as?"
"Well, for a start, a minute ago you asked what you were supposed to do for them," he said. "You have already recognised that they are asking something of you; you just haven't managed to recognise it consciously."
"But you think I have recognised it unconsciously?" she asked.
"Well, obviously," he said, and gestured at the row of paintings.
"Those? I don't understand?" she said. "I'm a painter; I paint. What has that got to do with them?"
"I'm not certain," he said. "I am not certain about any of this. Much of what I feel and think seems contradictory, I expect. Some element of the ancient dead here remains conscious and powerful and for reasons that I have been trying to understand for years. I will say again, they mean us no harm. Much of the antics are aimed at catching our attention, to make us sit up and take some notice when they have been forgotten for so long. We need to be receptive to their messages whatever they may be, and I would guess from your work here that you have been very receptive indeed. The images you have painted speak of a world that no longer exists; you have been telling not so much their story but rather their identity."
Isobel stared into her empty mug and felt as if she couldn't swallow.
"What about you, then, what did they want you to do?" she asked.
"I have written music when once I only performed it," he said. "I can't even play it myself, but I hear it in my head and my pupils play it for me and I am content."
"Are you saying they wish to communicate with us, then?" she asked.
"Indeed I am," he said. "They have not ceased to exist when their bodies died, nor when their remains crumbled to dust, and they still have things to communicate with the living. What are books but the words and ideas of the dead, living on after their bodies are gone? What are our great works of art, of sculpture, of poetry, of music and architecture but the dead speaking on to us?"
She thought about it, again feeling that lump in her throat like the scar made by a careless fish-bone.
"These people had no written culture," she said. "Little or no art remains, no music, only post holes and barrows to mark their building achievements. OK, why me then? Why not someone like Maggie, who'd maybe welcome it?"
"That's an interesting question," he said. "Do you remember I asked what your maiden name was?"
"Yes," she said. "And I still can't get my head round that at all. Why?"
"Sometimes names can give a clue to someone's family history," he said. "Sometimes a name is an ancient one, like your own. The Hunter is a powerful archetype, an ancient image from forgotten times. Now we just think: fox hunting! But in a society where agriculture was still erratic, the Hunter was still an important figure."

"Are you really saying I must be descended from some Stone Age Hunter?" Isobel said incredulously.

"Not at all," he said. "But your name is part of that archetype; names can shape us in subtle ways we often fail to understand. You seem to be a person who is very determined and courageous, persistent and patient. When you hit that deer you spoke of, how did you feel?"

"Terrible," she said.

"Why? Surely you must have killed creatures on the road before," he said.

"This was different," she insisted. "I don't quite know why. But it was utterly different. I had dreams of it; where it stopped, saw me coming and then stepped out in front of me, very deliberately. And until then, I'd never seen a deer that close before."

"There are tales, hunters' tales at that," he said. "Of a moment when a deer steps into a clearing, and stops, and turns to look at you. It's the perfect shot; you just have to pull the trigger. I am told it's as if the deer is giving itself to you. I suspect these tales are truly ancient, going back thousands of years, to a time where the life of the land was seen as bound up with the life of the tribe."

"The deer gave itself to me?" Isobel said incredulously. "Is that what you are saying?"

He shrugged.

"I am not sure," he said. "But it had an effect on you that is hard to explain."

Isobel shivered slightly.

"OK," she said. "Let's leave that for now. You said I had a number of qualities that mean they are attracted to me. You've mentioned my artistic tendencies, and you've mentioned my maiden name. What else?"

"The other thing that tends to get their attention is what you might call unfinished business with the recently deceased," he said, and seeing her sceptical face, went on, "You see, when I came here, I was angry and grieving. The crash that robbed me of my mobility killed my sister who was driving. She was my manager and the day of the crash we had argued, and we were driving home in that awful icy silence where neither of you will speak except on the most mundane things. When I came round after the accident, she'd been dead ten days; I'd been unconscious and then sedated, and they only told me when they told me how bad my own injuries were. I was furious with them, with her and with myself. I couldn't understand why I'd been crippled and she'd got away. If anything I thought it would have been better if she'd been crippled and I'd been killed. I told myself I couldn't bear it, not being able to walk again, that I would have been better off dead, that it was all my sister's fault. You can imagine the things I thought. I was full of fury, mostly at my sister for allowing the crash to happen. When I began to recover, my wife bought the cottage and had it converted so that I could manage in a wheelchair, and when I was well enough she brought me there."

He looked a little haunted by it, his face paler than it had been.

"Within days, odd things began happening," he said, and then as if changing the whole direction of the conversation he went on, "I seem to recall you bought this cottage not long after your parents' deaths. Did you have cause to be angry with them, or to have other unfinished business with them?"

It was very like walking into the surf on a gently sloping beach and suddenly to find the sand dropping away and only deep sea remaining beneath your feet. You could sink or you could swim but whatever you did, it was still a shock. Isobel felt the question like a blow to the stomach, and she found she could scarcely breathe.

"No," she said. "I was just very upset. Not angry. Not angry. I wasn't angry; they did what they had to, how could I be angry? They did what they had to."

He reached across to her and patted her hands, soothing them as though they were frightened animals.

"I'm not trying to upset you, my dear girl," he said. "I feel sure you do have unfinished business with your parents but if you don't feel like discussing it, that's fine. It doesn't matter. It's simply the way in, for them. You have a wound, one that they can see and maybe empathise with; you have issues with your immediate ancestors and that makes you much more accessible to your more remote ones."

"They're dead," said Isobel through gritted teeth. "The dead are just that: dead. They can't reach us."

"I think you'll find that's not the case. Perhaps we simply can't reach them," he said.

"Why should they bother me? They had their shot at life, why can't they just leave me alone?" she said, scrubbing furiously at her eyes to beat back the tears.

"There's still a great deal they can teach us," he said.

"About what, precisely?" she demanded. "They aren't real, they're just... I don't know what they are. But how can anything they have to tell us be of any use whatsoever?"

"Why should the wisdom of let's say Goethe or St Augustine or Jung be of any less value now they are dead?" he asked. "I think the people who lived here were just as human as anyone living here now, and what they learned of life is just as relevant now as it was then. Perhaps it is more important than ever, in these days of rampant materialism and denial of our own mortality. Look at you own work, Isobel. See how it speaks of being human, in all its diverse and difficult facets: of death and sex and faith and hope, rebirth and pain, humour and bravery and sadness and love. These are the things that the ancient dead would speak to us of, the very things that seem to be in such short supply today. They are reminding us of what it is to be truly human and truly alive before we forget it altogether."

But Isobel was hardly listening to him, and just sat and stared at her hands as the tears fell one after another and splashed into her empty mug.

"I couldn't call them back," she said, softly, after a moment. "That's what I was so angry about, that I had no chance to say goodbye. I understand why they did it; I even think they thought they'd be doing me a favour by doing it. But I'd have liked to have been asked, or even simply told, so I had a chance to say what I needed to say. Things I should have said years ago and never dared."

He said nothing, and just held her hands gently with his twisted ones.

"They killed themselves, you see," she said, as if remembering for the first time that he was there. "They had good reasons, it was almost heroic really. But that's not how I felt about it. I felt about three years old, and I wanted to wail and scream and *protest*, because it was just so unfair. I couldn't, of course. I had to be strong, I had to be the big sister and be the calm one. And everyone kept on reminding me I was pregnant and tried to stop me doing anything that might have been useful, or might have made me feel better. I remember someone saying to me, "You've got to think of the baby," and I thought, yeah, right, and they were thinking of my baby when they did it, were they? Actually, yes, they probably were thinking of my baby. They knew it would have been impossible for me to look after two tiny tots, a terminally ill father and a mother with dementia. But I still wish they'd told me; given me the chance to say all the things I needed to say to them. Because now I can't ever say those things and dear God, I need to tell them what I feel."

Chapter 23

She cried herself to sleep that night, of course. Guy had been amazing: calm, quiet, gentle. He never once told her to pull herself together, perhaps because she told herself that often enough. He never tried to stop her crying; just sat by and passed her a packet of tissues, and when she'd reached that snuffling, hiccuping stage where she knew she looked like shit and just wanted to be alone, he left, quietly and unobtrusively, though slowly by necessity, leaving his card on the hall table so she had his phone number if she needed it. She almost didn't know he'd gone till she heard the engine in the lane and went to the door to see the car disappearing up the lane.

It was sheer nervous exhaustion, really, brought on by the events of the previous night and the lack of any decent sleep, and when Mickey phoned at the usual time, she had a hard job convincing him she was all right.

"You sound a bit nasal," he said. "Have you been crying?"

"No, I think I must be coming down with a cold or something," she said. "Or hay-fever maybe."

"You've never had that before," he remarked.

"It must be a cold starting then," she said, unwilling to tell him quite what she was feeling because she knew he'd probably want to jump in the car and drive straight there. Come to think of it, she felt pretty much like just going straight home now herself, but it wasn't a good idea, not this tired, this groggy. And when it came down to it, things were bubbling up again, images and visions and she knew she would have to paint them. Only then could she go home.

The cottage still had that chastened, repentant feel to it as she sat over a hot drink. No sudden shadowy movements unsettled her, no leaves rattling on the stone flags of the hall or kitchen to startle her with their resemblance to small animals, no keys or trinkets purloined and then returned. The air pouring in through the French doors that stood ajar as dusk filled the garden was soft and sweet, smelling of soaked grass and moist earth. She wandered over to stand at the threshold and gaze out at the still garden, violet coloured as the last rays of sunlight left the sky, and she fancied she saw tiny lights sparkling among the darkening leaves of the beeches on the mound. Raindrops, obviously, shimmering with the reflections of the sinking sun, but for a second she remembered the candles of her dream and wished she could soar above the trees in the cool night air and watch as the other candles flickered into life again, showing her where the ancient dead waited and watched, hoping to touch the living with their own stories again.

As she stood, the air seemed to have turned slowly cooler, and she held her arms out as if awaiting the embrace of an approaching friend, and then dropped her arms and shut the door, bolting it firmly and glaring at the bolt as though daring it to defy her. The hot choking feeling in her throat and chest had grown again, so she headed up to her room for the comfort of her sleeping bag and the release of endless sickening tears that soaked her pillow and hair and left her face looking like she'd been punched.

*

The next morning, she opened a box she'd not opened in many months and breathed the aroma inside like rare incense or a fine wine. These days she rarely used oils, the problems were so manifold that it had become pointless even trying; they took too long to dry, they were more expensive, she had to use proper canvases and the sheer hell of getting them off the hands or clothes of inquisitive kids meant that she would be so on edge if the children so much as entered the room that she could hardly concentrate on painting. But she loved using oils; the very smell and texture made her *feel* like an artist even on those days when she doubted her own talent enough to describe herself as simply a housewife and mother should anyone have the nerve to ask her what she did for a living.

Most of the rest of this sequence of paintings had been in watercolours; they seemed to suit the slightly soft edged texture of the images, a kind of misty vagueness that only enhanced the mysterious subjects, hinting at other worlds, other times, like a thread of dimly heard music that seems lost on the breeze. This one had to be oils; it needed the strength and permanency of oils to do justice to the subjects. And somewhere inside she must have known she would need to do this; she had bought a large canvas on her last buying trip, almost without noticing she had done it.

She worked much more slowly this time; she could not do this in a day the way she had done some of the others, working in a frenzy of visions and energy. This was slower, measured and careful, despite the rage of emotions and pain that swirled and whirled in her mind as she painted. She had to stop often to wipe her eyes, to sit and stare into empty, empty space as she tried to remember her parents' faces and somehow connect with them on a level she had never managed while they lived.

From time to time, she'd stop, to let the paint dry or to go and eat, or bathe or make a drink. Once she went out to the supermarket to restock her dwindling supplies of food; once she made another foray to the art supplies shop to replenish certain items, a new tube of titanium white, more linseed oil, more turpentine. Each evening, Mickey rang her, never once asking her when she was coming home, though she knew he was desperately lonely without her.

One evening he said,

"I was thinking of coming over in a week or so. I've got leave for a fortnight. I thought I might collect the kids and spend it with you."

He sounded so unsure of his welcome that she smiled through the tears that had sprung up at the sound of his voice.

"I'd really, really love it," she said. "I think I'm nearly done. Just this one picture that I'm working on that I've still got to finish. I've got so much to tell you about. I'll have finished it when you come, and then we can all go home together."

"Really?"

She could hear the break in his voice where his self-control had cracked, briefly but obviously.

"Yes, really," she said firmly. "I've been thinking about an awful lot of things. Now I need to act on them. I'm really looking forward to seeing you, and the kids of course. I bet they've grown."

"Must have. I think you'll notice more; I see them every day off, and whenever I can sneak over," he said, and she could hear the longing in his voice.

"It's all right," she said, gently. "It's all going to be all right, honest."

"Really? Really truly honestly?" he said, his voice teasing now.

"Yes," she said. "As far as I can see, anyway."

She had tears running down her face as she said it; how to tell of all she was going through as she painted this picture, of all the memories, sweet, bitter and mundane that went into it? She didn't have the words for it all.

After he'd rung off, she sat in the darkening room and gazed at the growing shadows and wished she understood all that had happened to her. I had it all under control, she thought wistfully. I had everything in hand. No surprises, no problems. I knew where I was and what I should be doing and suddenly, bang, everything changes and I can't do a bloody thing about it. It's like being swept away, caught up in a tidal wave and flung away with the flotsam and jetsam to wash up somewhere so different I don't even know where I am any more.

The days since she had run from the house in a blind panic had passed quietly, and she had started to feel that perhaps all the things that had been bugging her, the doors that wouldn't stay locked, the jewellery going missing and those tiny furtive movements caught from the corner of an eye, perhaps they were and always had been coincidences, imagination, or accidents. The odd, chastened, tail-between-the-legs feeling around the house continued, making her feel even more weepy than before, and that night, when she went up to bed a little after Mickey's call, she stopped at the door when she saw the bed.

Her sleeping bag lay rumpled and twisted like a discarded chrysalis when the butterfly has hatched, and her pillow was askew and dented as usual, but laid on the crumpled white of the pillow was a feather. She stood very still, and instinctively glanced at the windows at either end of the room. Both were firmly shut. She stepped cautiously closer to the bed and gazed at the feather. It was surprisingly large, and was a soft mottled tawny brown, with darker bars in places and when she picked it up, and stroked it, it felt unnaturally soft and downy, like perfect velvet, like the silvery pelt of pussy willow buds in the springtime. She'd painted feathers like it, woven into the cloak of a woman with the face of an owl.

It had lain there like the one perfect Belgian chocolate on the pillow, a gift from a repentant lover, begging for reinstatement and reunion. She stroked it along her cheekbones, feeling the whip of night air, feeling the high, far-off calls of bats that made her shiver even though she could only feel them in the bones of her skull and could not hear them, hearing the song of the clear stars above her and smelling the scent of venison roasting in the fire-pit and the wood-smoke curling through the reeds of the roof.

A slow, amused smile began to stretch her mouth wide and finally she began to chuckle.

"I get the message," she said to the shadows the ceiling light could not dispel. "You're sorry, right? Well, so am I."

She laid the feather on her dressing table and went back downstairs and rummaged in one cupboard for night-lights, and in another for a jam jar. Her torch she left on the table and she stepped out into the deep green-scented night holding the jam jar with the candle flickering bravely within, and walked steadily across the still uneven lawn until she reached the barrow and passed under the outstretched arms of the high beeches. The leaves above her whispered softly as she climbed the barrow, and they sounded like an audience trying to keep quiet and not quite succeeding, little mumbles and hisses of half-heard words, rustling clothes and sweet wrappers, wriggling in seats and stretching legs.

On the summit of the mound, the damp soil felt cool under her bare feet, and a few thistles that had sprung up when the bluebells had died down prickled at the sides of her feet and ankles.

"I remember you now," she said, though she had no idea why she said it, and she placed the lit candle in its glass jar on the earth amid the roots of trees like the trunks of elephants, and walked away silently back to the cottage and bed.

Much to her surprise, when she picked up her hairbrush, the feather still lay where she'd left it and hadn't vanished away as she'd more than half expected. When she crawled into her sleeping bag, pulling the edges up to her chin to exclude draughts, she was sure she saw movement at the far end of the room, but she closed her eyes unconcerned and untroubled and fell asleep so quickly she could hardly tell the passage from waking to sleeping, and her dreams were as vivid as the bright dew on the flowers and vanished as fast with the light of morning.

*

I didn't know you at all, she thought. I lived with you both for eighteen years and all I could think about was escaping, of pulling the wool over your eyes so I could do what I wanted to do with my life. I was so obsessed with myself I never once looked at either of you properly, nor asked myself *who* you were, what made you who you were, what you liked, what you hated, what you loved. You were both unique and I never saw it. Maybe my own children will do the same to me; I can just hear it now, the voices when they're in the teens: don't take any notice, my mum's a bit batty, but she's harmless, really. I'm just Mum, after all. Once they're grown a bit more, I'll never be God to them again like I am now, but only Mum, to be ignored, pitied and despised and discounted.

No wonder the dead are a bit miffed with me! I missed the lessons my own parents could have taught me; I had forgotten so much I should know. All because they did that one thing for me and for Simon that I could never accept and understand. How many parents can give their children their lives twice over?

She bit the end of her brush and pulled a face and had to spit into a hanky to get rid of the blob of paint that had stuck to the brush end and thence into her mouth.

My parents were heroes, leaders and chieftains, a king and queen of their own small clan. They don't deserve to be forgotten in the way I've shoved their memory to the bin of my mind, like curling sandwiches left over from the funeral tea.

A thought that had been brewing these last days reached a state of fermentation that meant she had to ring Mickey then and there, catching him on his way out.

"When you come," she said, breathlessly. "There's something you need to bring with you. It's important."

"Anything," he said. "Just tell me what you need."

"A kick up the bum for starters," she said, dryly.

"Anything to oblige!" he said, and she could hear him laughing. "I hope you don't mind," he went on, "But I've asked Simon and Katy to join us for a few days, our treat, you know. Wine them and dine them locally, that sort of thing. Well, OK, I know it'll be takeaways because we aren't going to find a babysitter round there, are we?"

"No," she agreed. "I think it'd be great to have them. I was going to ask about that as well but you've pre-empted me. Let me tell you what I want you to bring."

She explained carefully and he was silent for a moment.

"That sounds a great idea," he said. "But I really have to go; I think I may already be late."

When he'd rung off, she went back through and gazed at her partially completed canvas. The colours were as vivid as those of a newly created medieval tapestry, and the smell that rose from it and filled the room made her shiver with delight, and she picked up her discarded palette and brush and began again.

As she worked, she thought about her parents, about her own childhood and Simon's, letting all the resentments and slights flow out of her mind unchecked, and stood to one side, mentally commenting as if she were not involved. She remembered how she'd been forced to subterfuge to manage to do the A level in art, a fourth A level in addition to the three science subjects she'd hated, only Biology being of even the vaguest of uses to her; she'd aced the bits of her Art course at college that had focussed on anatomy and that was down entirely to the knowledge she'd already accumulated. Her father had been so cross with her, wasting her time on a subject he felt to be no use whatsoever if she were to do Pharmacy at university as he wanted.

"It might be a good way to unwind from the more demanding subjects," her mother had said, standing not between her furious husband and defensive daughter, but rather a little to one side. "It isn't as if it requires much work. Let it go, Roy. She needs some fun, you know."

Bless you for that, Mum, even if you didn't truly understand what it meant to me, thought the adult Isobel with warmth.

The row when he found out she had applied to the art college instead of the university that had already provisionally accepted her to study Pharmacy; well, that was something she'd tried to forget for so many years.

"You're throwing away your life, you stupid girl," he'd bellowed at her, and her mother, red-faced and silent nodded. "What did you think, that I'd pay for you to daub paint and mess about for three years with degenerates and drop-outs? I'd pay for you to do a sensible subject, one that would give you a decent life, a proper career, some self-respect."

"I'll do it myself," she'd snarled. "I don't want to mess about in a lab, or stand behind the counter at Boot's and hand over medicines to old biddies. I want to make my mark on the world."

"And you'll do that how?" he'd demanded. "Do you know how few artists ever make a go of it? How many live and die unknown? How can you be so stupid and stubborn?"

His voice had risen into a stricken wail, and now she heard it in her memory again, she knew what it meant. He had been frantic with worry that she was going to ruin her life all for what he saw as a whim. Oh, he'd paid her fees and her living allowance in the end; shamed, her mother said, by his cronies at the golf club, at Rotary and elsewhere. After all, they'd said, she's a girl; even if you pay for her to do Pharmacy, a few years down the line, she'll just give it all up to get married and have kids, so what's the point of her taking up a place a boy could have? Why not let her do this art course? It'd be a nice hobby when she does have children, and if she's good she might even make some pin money. Now, understanding that his rage had come out of concern for her, out of love even, she let those angry voices fade away and she could only see him holding the portrait she'd done for him of Miranda as a newborn and gazing at it with tears in his eyes and speechless with joy and pride.

"You really have done a lovely job of this," he said. "I can almost see her breathing."

Isobel gazed at her canvas and smiled through the tears, and thought of her mother, holding her hand after her first miscarriage, eight months after she'd married Mickey.

"It's all right," her mother had crooned. "So many of them come and go like this. There'll be others, you know, ones who'll make it and bring you more joy than you can imagine now."

She'd sobbed inconsolably at the time, but now she could hear what her mother didn't say out loud: I've been where you are now, and believe me it gets better. The sudden realisation that she and Simon had been born after at least one child had miscarried made her feel closer to her mother, who'd loved babies and had wanted a bigger family than the one she'd got. I never knew you, she thought, I never thought to ask about things I should have asked, and now I've lost you. You wanted me to be close and I pulled away all the time, not wanting it, and now I do, you've gone.

A sob rose in her throat and she let it out, a small keening wail ending in a hiccup, and she turned her face from her palette as more tears threatened to land in the bright pools of glistening colour. Now she saw her mother, holding Miranda the day she was born, a small white-wrapped bundle that snuffled and whimpered, and the smile on her mother's face was almost blinding in its joy.

"She's so like you were," her mother said. "So beautiful, so beautiful."

The unheard words of, "I told you you'd do it," sounded now in Isobel's mind and instead of the implied reproach she'd felt at the time, she heard only this paean of triumph, of delight and satisfaction. She could see now the great bunch of flowers her mother had brought to her, hot house flowers so unlike the English country garden flowers her mother loved that it seemed strange now to think of it. Perhaps she'd felt that this was a moment beyond garden posies. That was an accolade she'd not realised. Her mother had always given flowers from her own careful garden, maintaining that you couldn't beat proper flowers from a proper garden, but now, with odd clarity, Isobel saw that this was only a remnant of prudent habits from less well-off days when her parents had first married, too young everyone had said, her father barely qualified and nothing behind them and every penny had to be accounted for. Her mother's ingenuity in making ends meet, in making her own clothes, creating gifts at Christmas and birthdays, of eking out a joint of meat for three meals and using leftovers creatively, had long since lost its financial point but she'd kept those frugal habits anyway. That bunch of frankly florid and over-the-top florist's flowers was a sign that this birth merited discarding those habits and splashing out.

So terrible then that they had not been able to wait for Luke to arrive, but perhaps time had been so pressing, her father feeling the return of his illness and knowing they could not wait any longer or they would be overtaken by it and not be able to do what they did. She'd never managed to think about what would have happened if they had not died when they did, but she did now, letting her mind range over the possibilities and seeing with horrible vision what it may have been like: the pain of her father's death, fought every inch of the way by doctors, the slow death of reason and memory in her mother, the day when she failed to recognise her own children and lapsed into lethargy and then at times into violent, unreasoned energy. She saw the chaos of her home, her fear for the safety of her children, of the mess, the pain and the hopelessness, and the sheer *pity* of the situation. She felt the guilt of finally being forced to put her in a specialist home, unable to cope any longer, and the awful visits to a vacant eyed shell that had once housed her mother's spirit.

I wish they hadn't done it, she thought, but I know why now. That was what they feared; maybe only my father had those visions of what it might be like, but he knew we'd take Mum, that between me and Simon we'd try and take care of her and he knew it would be an impossible job and one he would not ask of us. Dad was always one for the worst-case scenario. The optimist sees the glass as half full, the pessimist sees it as half empty, but the dentist sees it and wonders if you'll clean your teeth after you've drunk all that Coke!

She laughed aloud at her own small joke and carried on painting, focussing so closely that by the end of the light that day, her eyes hurt and her neck and back felt as though she'd spent the day playing some vigorous sport rather than standing in front of a canvas and applying paint at intervals.

The following day, she finished the painting, and feeling oddly bereft and seeking to step away before she carried on adding touches here and there and ruining it, she headed to Guy's cottage, finding him at home and delighted to be visited.

"I was hoping you'd call soon," he said, pouring her a glass of white wine that had such clarity of taste that her whole being seemed to shiver with the pleasure of drinking it.

"Any particular reason?" she asked.

"Well, I was wondering how you're getting on, for a start," he said. "But you're looking a lot less *haunted*, for want of a better phrase. And also I have just received a recording one of my students has made for me of my own music, and I wanted to you hear it."

"I'm not terribly musical, you know," she said. "I'd like to hear it though, even if I am a pleb when it comes to such things!"

"Come and sit down and I'll put it on," he said, clearly excited about it and she followed him through to the sitting room where she'd dripped and shuddered that awful night more than a week ago.

He fumbled with the stereo, and the room filled with such music that she could never have imagined, and could not describe. The single flute soared high in plaintive trills, swooping low and harsh, and she seemed to see pictures in her mind, of ancient times, of kings and warriors, of the hunt and of the kill, of hearth and home, hounds and looms, the wolf at the edge of the forest watching and the babe in the cradle, sleeping. She closed her eyes and let the music take her, losing sense of time and forgetting the wine discarded on the table in front of her, until the silence of the room bought her back to herself and she jumped slightly.

"Wow!" she said, finding herself almost asthmatic with emotion. "That was truly amazing. I've never heard anything quite like it."

He was beaming with pleasure, his face flushed and warm with her praise.

"I could never have played it, of course," he said. "That's the gift of it, you see. Had I continued, I might have written music but only what I knew I'd be able to play. Now I can write for someone else's gift, not my own. Now, how have things been for you?"

"Quiet," she said. "Well, by that, I mean I've seldom been pestered by the tricks I was getting before. But in myself, it's been a real turmoil; so many things going through my mind. I started another picture, a real tough one, and I've spent a lot of time while I was doing it thinking about my parents and about myself and I must have wept buckets. I never used to be such a weepy person. I can't quite get over that. But you were right, I'm afraid. I'm sorry I lied, but you were right and I did have unfinished business with my parents."

He nodded.

"I know I wasn't coherent the time you came over," she said. "But you were right about that even if I didn't want to admit it at the time. I can't help wondering if all the tricks and irritations were to try and make me wake up."

"Wake up?"

"Yes," she said. "To wake up to some very hard truths that I didn't want to look at and had sort of shut down on. You see, when my parents died, I was very pregnant and so I couldn't grieve. And then I had a small baby to think of so I couldn't grieve. And then I was too busy and I couldn't grieve. And then, well, it was past so I must have grieved, and there was no need any more. Well, that's a whole load of bollocks; now I can see that! But the real thing was I was too angry to grieve."

She could feel her eyes prickling again so she took a sip of the wine and swallowed hard to dislodge the growing lump in her throat, like a bit of potato stuck in her gullet.

"I couldn't forgive them for leaving me when I had finally begun to need them," she said. "Or that finally my Dad had acknowledged my achievements in his suicide letter, that he'd kept a scrapbook about me that he never told me about and my sister-in-law had to tell me about. I felt so furious that he couldn't have *told* me those things to my face years ago. I was still hurting that they always seemed to reject me for what I was and what I had tried to do with my life, and then I find this wasn't so at all, that he'd always been proud of me. Silly old bugger just never got round to telling me, and I couldn't see that his final choice was intended to honour what he saw as my achievements (and my brother's too) by the simple act of letting us have our lives unhindered. Do you think that is why these people from the barrow, the fairies or the ancestors or whatever you want to call them, is that why they could get a foot wedged in my door, because I was aching to try and honour my parents and just couldn't manage to get my head round it?"

"I do," he said. "That's a part of it. Some of it is that the simple raw emotion of grief combined with a fair measure of anger is a beacon to them, a signal that here is someone who is hurting in the same way they hurt in life. Perhaps another powerful emotion like passionate love would act in the same way. I don't know. But I suspect that any powerful emotion is a kind of fuel or bait to them; something they can recognise and are drawn to. I don't think the lukewarm or the mediocre would cut the mustard at all!"

"Hence you reckon Maggie would be immune, yeah?" Isobel said. "It's made me realise I hardly knew them. They were always there, Mum and Dad. You never think about who and what your parents were. You just don't. Even people who are close to their parents don't question that, don't analyse it. Parents just *are*. And now I've thought about it, I can see they were special. My dad was a hero and a warrior. Just 'cause his enemy was tooth decay doesn't make him any the less heroic; after all, he wasn't cut out to be a blood and guts type soldier but he was a brilliant dentist. He used to get so annoyed about the fact that he'd patch up peoples' smiles, and give all this advice about dental care and people would promise, nay, they'd swear blind they'd brush twice a day and floss, and then six months down the line they'd be back with whatever problem they'd originally come with. That's why he wanted me to do Pharmacy instead of dentistry, because you don't have the same demoralisation. You dispense or whatever, and people have the instructions on the packet and you don't have to see what happens when they don't follow the instructions. As long as you do your job, everything's fine, there's no trail of decaying teeth and gum disease because people can't be *bothered* to do what they know is best. Well, that's what he reckoned anyway; I've no idea if it's true. He didn't get why I wanted to do art, but I think by the end he understood a bit what motivated me, and he knew I had a gift that would have been swamped by something so precise as pharmacy."

She took a sip of wine to moisten her dry mouth and grinned at him.

"And my Mum was pretty special in very different ways," she said. "She was much more domestic than I ever was. It makes me think that the original Anglo-Saxon words we get Lord and Lady from meant something quite basic."

He nodded, vigorously.

"Lord meaning loaf provider and lady meaning loaf kneader," he said. "We forget how important these things were to our ancestors, we live in such plenty."

"My mother was a Lady in many senses of the word," Isobel said. "I used to get irritated about it, seeing it as petty and bourgeois, all the things she'd do, like baking and making clothes and flower arranging and bridge and stuff like that. I could never see the *point* of any of it; it just seemed to be passing the time pleasantly, that's all it was to me. But now, now I can see some of it: the sheer pleasure of getting something right, for example. My mum could make the best chocolate cake in the whole world, but I know she'd got it so good because she'd had years of practise. My sister-in-law has the recipe and I think I shall ask for it and I can say to my little girl as she gets older and loves it like I loved my mum's cake, I can say, ah, but your granny made an even nicer one. OK, so once I despised some of what she did, but what have I ever done that's really any better, any more lasting? Maybe some of my paintings may last a while longer but on a scale of things, even that isn't much longer than a gorgeous moist cake that gives such intense pleasure at the time."

She found she had begun salivating at the very thought of her mum's chocolate cake and she licked her lips uneasily.

"No achievement can last for ever," she said finally. "Not here anyway. My mum did a good job of being a mum. My brother and I did well, and it was only my rebellious streak that meant I was at odds with them at times. They liked convention and normality and I challenged them. It's as simple as that; but now I know they still loved me and approved of what was really dear to me: my husband, my children and my work. All the rest is like smoke on the wind; all the rows when I was at school, and at college and when I was trying to make a living as a sort of artistic busker, well, they don't count any more. They were just sound and fury, signifying nothing. They *loved* me. And that's one thing that remains beyond time and everything and always will: love."

She scrubbed at the cascade of tears and he smiled wryly and filled up her glass again.

"I think you're right," he said. "When I came here, unable to walk, I blamed my sister for the crash. It took the onset of the arthritis that ruined my hands to reduce me to a state where I had no more distractions and I could begin to sit up and listen. The tricks were, as you remarked, intended to wake me up so I could face things. Once I began to forgive first my sister and then myself, the music began to flood into my head so I could hardly get it down fast enough. But it wasn't until I began to remember that I had loved my sister did the tricks quieten down and become benign entirely. Even now, when I have poured out that rush of music and it has finally been performed by someone who can do it justice, they sometimes come and leave me a small gift: a flower, a feather and this morning when I first played the CD my student sent me, I found a tiny whistle cut from an elder twig. I can't play it, of course, but I shall ask my student to play it next time he visits me. Of course, they still play around with things, steal and return things that catch their eye, but I don't mind that. I honour them how I can: with what I do."

Isobel looked at him and saw he had tears running down his face, and she grinned through her own.

"What a damp pair we are!" she said.

"Tears are a good part of being human; why should we not cry for joy as well as sorrow," he said, and unselfconsciously wiped his eyes. "I shall look forward to seeing your new exhibition, Isobel."

"I haven't even thought about that," she said, startled.

"Ah, but I have," he said. "I have a few contacts who have been interested in perhaps running an exhibition, showing your paintings and playing my music. It won't be the Tate, but it will be somewhere quite prestigious. What do you think, then?"

Chapter 24

Isobel paced up and down the hall, her ears straining for the sounds of an engine. The stone flags shone with scrubbing, the old stone smooth and still slightly damp, and the air smelled of recently cut grass, green soap and of the lavender she'd culled from the odd corner of the garden where a few straggling bushes contributed their flowers to the bright tangle of weeds and cultivated plants flowering in the overgrown borders round the cottage. She'd tied the lavender in bunches with garden twine in the absence of ribbon and hung bunches round the whole house, and the scent as the flowers dried was almost overpowering even when, as now, she had the front door open. The gate was propped open as far as it would go and her own car, Katy's car really, was parked as far over as careful manoeuvring could manage, so that Mickey could park their car close to the house. They had set off, she knew that because Mickey had phoned just as he'd got into the car, and she'd ended up doing unheard-of household tasks just to pass the time and stop herself from becoming impossibly anxious.

Would they remember her? Would they still know her? Her scrubbing brush had grated on the uneven stones and the scent of rough green household soap irritated her nose and she'd gone to have a shower and get changed, wishing that they had a real stove and oven rather than the camping stove, so that she could have baked something to welcome them.

I am not turning into my mother, she told herself firmly, but if I were imitating her in some things, it's not such a bad thing, is it? There was no answer from the quiet house, but she knew they were listening and she glanced again at the clock on her mobile. Any time now, she thought and sure enough, the sound of an engine filled the lane and Mickey's car swung into view and her heart beat faster, seeming to leap and jump beats like a cricket on hot stones. He pulled up neatly on the paving next to the other car and waved at her before getting out and leaning into the back seats to release the children. She could already hear their voices.

Would they hang back? It had been so long in their short lives. Would they be shy with her, not quite remember her, be scared of her even?

Miranda slipped from the car like a minnow evading a questing net in the shallows of a pond, and ran up to the house as Isobel stepped out of the doorway. Luke was following, almost as fast. God, how he'd grown! He didn't look quite like a baby any more. A second more and they were both clinging to her like sweetly scented monkeys, squealing, "Mummy! Mummy! Mummy!" in piercing, heart-breaking voices that made her eyes fill up and spill over.

She sat down hard on the doorstep, both children in her arms, and felt like this was the best moment *ever*. The sheer weight of them both told her without detail how much each had grown, the rest would have to wait; all the new achievements she'd missed, the new clothes and shoes she didn't recognise. Luke had had his hair cut for the first time; that was had made him look so much older, the cropping of his baby curls.

Mickey sauntered up and looked down at them, a huge smile stretching across his face.

"I think they're pleased to see you," he said, and helped her to her feet so they could go inside.

The children held tightly to her hands as they went inside, and sat close to her on the sofa so that part of each of them was actually in her lap. Miranda was oddly quiet, her eyes ranging round the room and back to her mother.

"Are there plenty of fairies still?" Isobel asked her, and Miranda gave her *such* a look.

"Mummy, I am three and a half, you know," she said, and after snuggling close to her mother for a minute, she detached herself and wandered off up to the room she would be sharing with her cousin later that day.

"She's still an odd little thing," Isobel said to Mickey, and hauling Luke to her hip she went through with Mickey to the kitchen to put the kettle on.

"She has missed you though," Mickey said.

"I kind of noticed!" Isobel said. "She's a bit of an odd one, though."

"She can already read a bit, you know," he said. "I was stunned. I thought maybe Jodie had shown her what she does at nursery but Jodie's not really much older. I thought maybe she was just remembering stories so I bought her a new book she's not seen before and with a bit of puzzling, she read that too."

"Dad would have been so proud," Isobel said and Mickey glanced at her.

"All right, all right, don't look so surprised," Isobel snapped. "I've been thinking about them a lot. Do you want to see the latest painting? I've put it in our bedroom as it isn't quite dry. All the others I've wrapped up and put in the boot of the car for safekeeping. There's only one more I need to do for the moment and I think I can do that either when we get home or if it gets a bit quiet later on this holiday."

"So you're coming back, properly?" he asked.

"I said I would be. Nothing has changed since I said that," she said. "This has been so necessary, you know. I can't say I have exactly enjoyed it because it's been a wild old ride lately. Come on, I'll make some tea when you've had a look."

*

Mickey stood alone in their bedroom, and gazed at the big canvas propped up on the easel. Isobel had taken Luke to the bathroom to change his nappy.

"I think I remember how," she'd said with some amusement before shutting the door behind her.

The paint was still at that tacky stage where it can smudge so easily, but the picture had an almost liquid quality to it anyway, like an image seen reflected in calm waters; a tiny breeze will ripple and ruin the image. It seemed to show a cave, carved out of a mix of earth and rock so that tree roots like the questing trunks of elephants reached down into the sudden hollow. All round the edges of the cave stood tall candles, the flames casting clear golden light that glowed and reflected on metal surfaces. In the centre of the cave were two biers and laid on the first was a man arrayed like an Iron Age warrior, his clothes made of leather and some textiles. He lay like a crusader on his tomb, his feet even crossed at the ankles, and his arms crossed at the chest and clutching what Mickey first took to be weapons. He looked more closely and saw that in one hand the warrior held a dental drill, enlarged to the size of a warrior's axe, and in the other, he held a toothbrush, again enlarged. Under the warrior's chin was something he realised was a dental mask, pulled down as if he'd reached the end of a job and had partially discarded it. At his sides on the bier beside him lay other things, that Mickey had at first taken as the weapons of his defeated enemies but were in fact things like golf clubs, a walking stick, and an umbrella. Mickey leaned closer still and saw that the face of the warrior was that of his father-in-law.

The second bier held a woman wearing a modern evening gown but wrapped as well in a heavy wool cloak fastened with a brooch patterned with Celtic serpents. Her feet too were crossed at the ankle, and rested on a velvet cushion. Her arms, again crossed at the breast held not weapons nor yet the spindle and distaff an Iron Age woman might have taken to the grave, but in one hand she held a giant egg whisk and in the other a pair of secateurs. Around her were things like cakes and oasis for flowers, sets of playing cards, packets of seeds and recipe books. Around both the lady and her lord were piles and piles of flowers, everything from Queen Anne's lace and childish bouquets of dandelions and daisies to extravagant corsages of orchids and lilies. He wasn't surprised to see that the face of the lady was that of his late mother-in-law. At the edges of the cavern were dark openings where the candlelight penetrated a little way, and there were suggestions of faces peering in at the lord and lady, faint faces that held some of the warm glow of the candles but so few details that it was impossible to see if they were male or female, old or young.

Mickey let out the breath he'd been holding and stepped back, unable to think even for a moment. The door opened and Isobel stood there, still holding Luke at her hip.

"Well?" she asked, but without concern.

"It's great," he said inadequately. "It's weird but amazing. The way you've got the candlelight is fantastic."

He paused, trying to think how best to say it.

"I think they'd have liked it," he said. "I don't know they'd have understood, but they'd have liked it."

"Good," said Isobel briskly. "Now, I wonder if you can give me a hand moving Luke's cot through here so I can get the air-bed set up for Simon and Katy. It's the only thing I haven't managed to get done."

"Will it be OK having Luke here, with the painting?" he asked.
"For the minute, yes. I was going to put it down in the utility room later and put the bolt across so the kids can't get in there," she replied. "It'll be a day or two before it's smudge free. There is some stuff you can spray on that speeds up the drying but I started seeing pink elephants the one time I tried it so I'd rather wait and let it dry by itself."
"Simon and Katy said they'd be here around lunchtime," he said. "Do you want to have something ready for them or shall we just play it by ear?"
"Knowing Simon, he'll stop on the way for lunch," Isobel said. "You did remember to bring what I asked for, didn't you?"
Mickey nodded.
"Good; I'll tell them about it tonight when the kids have all settled," she said. "Come on, I promised you a cup of tea. I even went to the shop for fresh milk!"

*

A second epiphany, a second tumult of emotions as Simon and Katy piled out of their car on the lane and Jodie hurtled at Miranda as if they'd been parted months not a few days; and a moment's pause while Katy and Simon looked carefully at Isobel as if checking for visible signs of madness and then there was another tangle of hugs and kisses, and Isobel found herself weeping with sheer joy at seeing them.
"You have lost so much weight, you selfish cow," said Katy, holding her at arms length before hugging her again. "I just seem to get fatter all the time."
"That's not fat," said Isobel. "That looks to me like you're hiding a baby bump under that dress."
"See?" said Katy to Simon. "I told you she'd guess!"
"Come on, let's get a cold drink or something," said Simon. "I was rather looking forward to a beer under those big beeches at the back."
They spilled out into the garden with folding chairs, trays of drinks and an entirely over-excited trio of children, who ran around the newly cut lawn squealing and shouting. Isobel was glad when Simon didn't want the bother of hauling the chairs all the way across the garden, which was bigger than he'd thought, and was happy to laze in the sun on the small area of paving outside the French windows. He looked a bit tired and confessed to having had a fraught term at the school he taught at.
"It's always the same," he said. "Exam term we always get kids bricking it because they haven't done the work, but the worst are the kids who have worked properly having the screaming ab-dabs that they're going to fail when you know they're up for A-stars. I seemed to spend half my time, not so much teaching, as staving off nervous breakdowns. Anyway, over now 'till next year. Shame you haven't got a fridge here yet, Izzie. This beer would be better chilled properly."

"Ungrateful, isn't he?" said Katy. "I bet you went out for it specially, didn't you?"
"Nah, I have it delivered by the crate load," Isobel said. "I bury the empties so no one knows I have a drink problem. Oops, I told! Oh well."
Katy took her glass of orange juice and began to saunter over to the mound, and a touch anxiously, Isobel followed. When she caught her up, Katy was sitting on the stump sipping her drink.
"How's it been, then?" Katy asked.
"Odd. But good," Isobel said. "I've done a lot of thinking and a lot of painting, and I've had a lot of weird things happening. But it's been worth it, and I don't know that I can ever repay you for taking over with my kids while I did it."
"Don't be silly!" said Katy, but looked pleased anyway.
"I was going to talk about it later, when we've all settled in and unpacked," Isobel went on. "There are still a few issues unresolved, you see, about Mum and Dad. Oh, and before I forget, do you have Mum's chocolate cake recipe?"
Katy looked bemused.
"At home, yes," she said. "Why?"
"It's just one thing I need to learn," Isobel said. "Anyway, I'll explain more later, when we've had dinner and got the kids settled."
"Whatever," said Katy, with a puzzled shrug. "It's lovely here. So peaceful."
She looked very peaceful too, so Isobel went back to where her husband and brother were supervising a game of chase, and sat back in her chair to enjoy the sight of her children running around, laughing and screaming with the sheer joy of being alive.
The chance to explain never came that night. They were all too tired, and once supper had been eaten, washed up and the kids put to bed they enjoyed a final glass of wine and went to bed themselves.
"What's this all about, Izzie?" Mickey asked as they settled down.
"I'd rather explain in one session," she said, her voice a whisper to remind him that Luke was still at that light stage of sleep where he might wake hearing voices and think he was missing something.
"OK," he whispered back, and she snuggled under his arm and closed her eyes and breathed deeply of his scent.

*

With small children in the house, no one got to sleep in and by seven they were all up, but not yet dressed. Jodie and Miranda were running round the garden in their nighties, but Luke was intent of consuming as much cereal as he could with minimum conversation.
"He's just like you," Katy said to Simon. "Not a coherent word till he's had breakfast!"
Simon just grunted and held out his mug for a refill of coffee.

"I wonder what this new one will be like," Katy said, patting her barely perceptible bump.

"Well, I can say for certain it'll either be a boy or a girl," Isobel said. "Simon, you pig, you've finished the coffee! Go and put the kettle on; I haven't had one yet and that's your third."

"I'm an addict," he said. "All teachers are. Coffee breath is all that keeps the kids from eating us alive. I thought you mostly drank tea anyway."

"Either and both, but not in the same mug," Isobel said, and wiped Luke's face with a wet flannel. "There; do you want some toast too, Luke?"

"Pease, mummy," he said, and Isobel buttered him a slice.

"It feels really weird having them back," she said as Simon filled the kettle. "I bet the girls will miss each other though."

"They'll get over it," Katy said. "Actually, it's been slightly easier with the two girls, because they play with each other all the time. The only problem was they used to leave Luke out something rotten, but he seems quite happy in his own company most of the time. I'd never quite seen the difference between little boys and little girls before; he seems to prefer playing with construction type toys and cars and stuff like that to interactive games with other children. He'd wail for a bit if the girls went off without him but then he'd just get on with something for himself."

"Sounds just like Simon!" Isobel said.

"Hey, is it pick-on-Simon this morning?" said Simon, scraping out the cafetière. "I'd have stayed in bed if I'd known."

They went through to the living room when they'd all eaten breakfast, though Isobel suspected that much of the toast the girls had taken out with them would end up feeding the birds. Simon on the sofa stretched out his legs and gave a sigh of deep satisfaction.

"Mum and Dad would have loved it here," he said. "There's that river down at the bottom of the valley. Dad would have been down there with his rods and stuff like a shot and Mum would have had such fun sorting out this garden."

Isobel glanced at Simon's feet, long and slender like their father's feet had been, and smiled.

"I'm glad you think they'd have liked it," she said. "I had something I was going to talk about last night but the right moment didn't come. You know I've still got their ashes because we couldn't think quite what to do with them? Well, what I was thinking was it might be a nice idea if we buried or sprinkled them on the barrow here."

Simon sat up as if startled, jerking from his boneless lounging into alert readiness.

"That's a bloody brilliant idea, Izzie," he said.

"Simon!" said Katy warningly as Jodie and Miranda ran by the window followed by a wailing Luke.

"Sorry, love," Simon said, but without much obvious contrition. "I don't think I can think of a better place. It's a fantastic idea. But what's made you think of it now?"
Isobel put down her half empty coffee mug and went and sat down next to her brother.
"I began to realise that I couldn't go on resenting their deaths for ever," she said. "Or their lives for that matter. It's all very well me going on and on in my head about how they never understood me, or appreciated my achievements. But it occurred to me that I'd done bugger all, sorry Katy, to understand them or even recognise their achievements. I was still behaving like a spoiled teenager. I thought that to put their ashes in that mound was to put them with whatever leaders and warriors and so on who were originally buried there, and that would honour Mum and Dad for who they were and what they did. OK, so it was nothing earth shattering they did with their lives, but they did what they did to the best of their abilities and no one can do more than that, not even kings and princes and so on."
Mickey gave her a curious look but said nothing.
"So I thought that today we might do it," Isobel went on. "I had thought of doing it when the kids had gone to bed but I felt it would be better if they were a part of it."
"You can explain then," Simon said. "No way am I going to tackle this with two rising fours and a tot of eighteen months! I shall be very interested to see how you do it."
"Coward!" said Katy. "I quite agree. We shouldn't exclude the children. They were their grandparents, even if the girls will hardly remember and Luke wasn't even born. I think they won't really understand, but I do think it's important they be included. They may remember it later."
"OK," said Simon, yawning again and dragging himself to his feet. "It's me for a shower then."
He sloped out of the room and Katy smiled at Isobel.
"I think it's a great idea too," she said. "I think I might go and share that shower with Si. Can you watch the kids?"
Isobel nodded and Katy went out of the room. Mickey came and sat next to her.
"There's a lot more to this that you've said," he said.
"There is," Isobel admitted. "But they'd think me mad if I told them even the half of what's been happening."
"Will you tell me, though?" he asked, anxiously, and Isobel smiled.
"This afternoon, I thought you and me could take all the children for a nice long walk and let Simon and Katy have a quiet afternoon together," she said. "And then I'll tell you about what's really been going on and why it's so vital that we do this."
"Fair enough," Mickey said. "Do you want me to do anything this afternoon, or shall I just be there?"
She knew he meant in his role as priest.

"Just be there," she said. "I've thought of what to do and what to say. It's mostly for Simon and me, and to a lesser extent you and Katy, and the kids, even if they won't have a clue what's happening. It won't be anything dramatic or complicated, just very simple and straightforward. You know I'm not into making a fuss about things."

He nodded.

"If Simon and Katy are in the shower," he said. "I think I'll go and use the bath. See you shortly."

"Don't call me 'Shortly'!" she said automatically and he laughed at the old joke and vanished.

She wandered out to the garden where the children were picking the daisies that had sprung up in the rough lawn as if overnight. The grass had been cut a few days before, and she'd thought the little white stars would not have reappeared so fast. Miranda was showing her cousin how to thread the stalk of one flower into a slit in the stalk of the next; her coordination and dexterity was amazing and much better than her older cousin's. She really is an odd little thing, Isobel thought and went over and sat down on the grass with them. She had no intention of doing this with the other adults around; she could just imagine Simon holding up invisible score-cards and mouthing "Null points!" at her. She also didn't feel quite confident of her theology in front of Mickey.

Luke scrambled over and sat in her lap, leaning back against her and butting his head against her. She closed her arms protectively around him.

"Girls, do you remember Granny and Granddad?" she said when the girls looked up at her expectantly.

"Granny and Granddad who went to heaven when I was little?" said Miranda.

"That's right, just before Luke was born," Isobel said, pleased. "What about you, Jodie? Do you remember them?"

"A little bit. Granny made nice cake; my other Granny doesn't," Jodie said.

"Good. I can tell you remember her; her cake was lovely," Isobel said. "Now, when people die, they don't need their bodies anymore."

"Like old clothes," said Miranda, and Isobel remembered explaining that at the time.

"That's right," she agreed. "Because your body is just what your spirit, your soul uses to get around. It isn't you. You know when you have dreams?"

Both girls nodded, but Luke was just snuggled up and almost asleep and said nothing.

"Well, when you dream, your body stays in bed and your spirit can go anywhere," Isobel said. "You are not your body. When we die, we don't need our bodies any more, so something has to be done with them as they go all smelly and horrible and fall apart. Some people are buried in the ground and their bodies sort of become part of the earth over time. Other people think it's neater and cleaner to burn up the body in a special way. It's called cremation. At the end of that, there's only fine ashes left. Well, before they died, Granny and Granddad wrote down that they would prefer to be cremated. So that's what happened. Now, I was given two special boxes with the ashes in, and I didn't know what to do. Granny and Granddad had written it was up to me, and your daddy, Jodie, what we then did with their ashes. I didn't know what to do, and nor did your daddy. So I didn't do anything. Now, we have this cottage and at the end is that funny hill."

"With the trees?" said Jodie. "It is a funny hill."

"It is," said Isobel. "You see, it isn't an ordinary hill at all. It was made probably several thousand years ago as a special place where the people who used to live here used to bury their kings and queens, all the important people."

"What about princesses?" asked Miranda, revealing that her interest in princesses hadn't waned as much as her liking for the fairies.

"Maybe for princesses too, though I hope most of them grew up to be queens," Isobel said. "We don't know exactly who was buried there but we know they must have been important. I thought, and Simon, your daddy, Jodie, thought too that we could bury Granny and Granddad's ashes in the hill. It's what's called a barrow, by the way. Granny and Granddad may not have been king and queen, but they were important to us and the rest of the family and everyone who knew them."

There was a long silence as the two little girls tried to digest what had been said. Isobel felt uncomfortable, hoping it hadn't been too heavy for such young children.

"Can I put flowers in with the ashes?" said Miranda suddenly. "Granny loved flowers."

"She did," said Isobel. "That's a great idea, darling. When we're all up and dressed, I think we can do it. So you go and get into your clothes and I'll get Luke dressed and get dressed myself, and then we can do it and maybe have a little party to remember Granny and Granddad tonight?"

The girls were off the grass in a moment and running back towards the house. Isobel hefted the sleepy Luke to her hip and padded barefoot back to the cottage. That hadn't gone at all badly; in fact, she felt quite proud of how she'd handled what was after all a hellishly difficult subject to broach with small children. Simon was down and dressed when she came in through the French doors, and Katy came through with wet hair and flushed cheeks.

"Bathroom's free now," Simon said. "It's just you running round in your nightie now, Izzie. Hurry up!"

"You might be bigger than me now but I'm still the big sister and don't you ever forget it," she said, and he laughed at her.

"Yeah right," he said. "Eight stone wringing wet these days, I'd guess."

"Watch it, matey, I can still do the nastiest of Chinese burns and I won't stop even if you squeal like a girl," Isobel said and Simon pretended to cower with fear.

Isobel had about run out of clean clothes a day or two before and had done as much washing by hand as she'd been able to manage and her clean but crumpled dress was going to be the best she would manage for this ceremony.

"I can just hear Mum saying "I hope you're going to iron that dress,"" Isobel said, trying to smooth the creases away with one hand as they walked across the lawn.

She held one of the urns containing ashes, and Simon held the other; the children had picked great armfuls of flowers both wild and cultivated and Mickey held a trowel. Katy held a single pink rose, the last from the climber round the front door, and a single petal fell unnoticed as they walked.

On the summit of the mound, they all took it in turns to dig a hole with the trowel. The ground was tough, baked as hard as clay by the bright summer sun, and the air under the trees was stifling. The hole took quite a bit of digging, and in the end, Mickey managed to bend the trowel and Isobel decided the hole was deep enough. The children were oddly solemn, even Luke, who often seemed immune to the emotions around him, was wide-eyed and silent, perched on Mickey's shoulders as Isobel and Simon stood on either side of the hole and undid the lids of their urns. They had not discussed what they would do or say, but as if choreographed, they began to pour from their respective urns at the same time so that the stream of whitish grey ashes fell as one, mingling and catching the light as they filled the hole. The very finest of the ashes floated as white smoke above the hole until a slight, unexpected breeze caught them and they were gone.

"Rest in peace," said Simon, looking awkward and uncertain.

"We love you," said Isobel, and smiled at her brother through her own tears.

Miranda and Jodie wordlessly tipped their flowers into the hole and walked away solemnly, hand in hand, and then Luke put his handful of daisies in and followed them. Katy placed the rose in and Mickey began to scrape in the dry earth on top. A cloud of the white dust rose as he did so and lingered a moment until it too was dispersed by the errant breeze.

"That's that, then," said Isobel, and turned to go.

Her foot caught on a stone and she nearly stumbled; on impulse, she picked up the rock and placed it on the wound in the soil and after a moment, the others searched for a rock too, and placed their too on the tiny grave. Then, as one, they turned and began to walk away, back towards the house.

"I thought we might take the children down to the village a bit later and buy some party food for this evening," Isobel said. "You know, fairy cakes and cocktail sausages and cake, and something bubbly to drink. You and Katy can have a quiet afternoon at home if you like, Simon."

"I'd like that," Katy said. "I could do with putting my feet up."

"Fine, that's settled," Isobel said. "Me and Mickey'll take the kids to the village and forage for provisions."

"Just one thing?" Simon said. "Take the cool bag and stick the beer in it!"

Chapter 25

"Are you finally going to tell me what the hell has been going on?" Mickey said as the wheels of the buggy bounced along the hot tarmac of the road.

Isobel grinned at him.

"I am," she said. "But you've got to keep quiet while I tell it. I'll lose track if you ask questions and confuse me."

"OK, fine," he said, and made a zipping gesture across his mouth and Isobel laughed.

As they walked up the road, taking care to keep the girls close and keeping a weather eye open for traffic, Isobel began telling Mickey the extraordinary events of the weeks she'd spent at the cottage, ending with her meeting with Guy and their subsequent conversation both that weird night and her subsequent meetings with him. By the end, Mickey was acting all boggle eyed with the need to speak, and Isobel finally finished by saying,

"I bet you think I've gone totally and utterly crazy."

He made mumbling noises, and gestured at his zipped-up mouth and Isobel mimed unzipping it.

"Phew!" he said. "There was a real danger I was going to burst with the need to speak. No, I don't think you're crazy at all. I don't fully understand any of it, but it makes a lot more sense than a poltergeist. What set it all off, do you think? Was it killing that deer? That was the point you seemed to change."

Isobel shook her head.

"I've thought about it a lot," she said. "The deer was important, yes, but it all goes back to that day when Miranda flooded the bathroom, called the cops and nearly ruined a painting. The deer was something different, but a part of it all."

"I don't quite understand," he said. "Well, I don't understand a lot of it. I sort of get this thing about the spirits of the dead, though for heaven's sake, don't tell the bishop! I understand that some of this has been about delayed grief and making your peace with your parents. But I don't get why this started with Miranda flooding the bathroom. Surely it started with your parents' suicide?"

"Yes and no," Isobel said gnomically. "Look, when I came in to the village last I spotted a play park with swings and slides. Shall we take them there before we go to the shops?"

"Good idea," Mickey said. "You lead the way."

"With my record of getting lost virtually in my own back yard, you're a brave man, Mickey Trelawny," Isobel said, wryly. "OK, I'll do my best. That way they can run around and I don't have to twitch every time I hear an engine."

When they reached the small, slightly shabby park at the edge of the village, the girls ran off to play on the small slide, and Mickey put Luke in one of the baby swings and pushed him back and forth.

"You were saying about Miranda flooding the bathroom. Why is that the starting point?" Mickey asked after a minute of silence.

"Because it was the first time I had any inkling I wasn't coping," Isobel said, thoughtfully. "I'd been so busy, so caught up in everything, I never had time to take stock. It was one thing after another. First your ordination, then Miranda being born, then Mum and Dad dying, then Luke's birth, then moving *again*. Finding a new circle of friends, getting used to a new area, getting used to having two children and two different sleep patterns, still trying to work as I always had done, cramming in more and more each day and never stopping to think. And the doorbell and the phone ringing constantly, always people around, never any peace. It was the day she flooded the bathroom that I first noticed I was missing."

"Sorry?" Mickey said.

"I looked in the mirror and I didn't see myself there any more. I was someone else, and I suddenly knew I wasn't coping. I didn't put it like that to myself, of course. It had been one of the worst days I've ever had, but it took a while to sink in that I wasn't coping. I'm not cut out for that sort of thing all the time. I really was feeling like I was out of my natural environment. I hadn't realised how much I need my own space. Not just physical space, but mental and emotional space, and dare I even say it, spiritual space. I suddenly couldn't hack it any more. I know it didn't show at first, I just kept on gasping and trying to breathe air when I needed water."

"Like that poor fish in the picture," said Mickey.

"Just like," she said. "It took a lot to make me finally realise what was happening though, that there was so much stuff I needed to deal with. The deer was the final straw, I suppose. I'd enjoyed working at the cottage, enjoyed it so much I felt guilty about it. And whatever you want to call them, the fairies or the ancestors or the spirits of the ancient dead, they were touching me even though I didn't know it, trying to tell me what it means to be human, and I wasn't quite listening because to be human is to *grieve* and I couldn't begin to grieve because I thought I already had. I had convinced myself that the reason I'd been so calm about Mum and Dad dying was because I wasn't actually that upset, that I had never been close and what little I'd felt was all there was to feel."

She grinned at him.

"I was so wrong," she said.

"What did the deer do, then?" he asked.

"I'd never seen something so recently dead before," she said. "When Mum and Dad died, the police made me go in another room when the bodies were taken out, so I wouldn't get upset about it, and presumably go into labour! I didn't want to see them when they were laid out at the undertakers. I've seen dead rabbits and stuff like that, but never something that big, something that until thirty seconds ago was alive."

She glanced over at the slide, to make sure the girls were all right.

"I couldn't get my head round the fact that even though I could see and feel the deer was utterly dead, *something* was still there. Not in the deer itself, though, but rather just outside it, hovering I suppose. I don't think I'd ever realised that before, that once life is defunct, *something* still lingers. It's the same feeling I get round the cottage sometimes but stronger and somehow a lot more personal. I suppose because the spirits at the cottage were human and the deer was, well, a deer. I don't know quite how to explain it and I know the theology is probably so cock-eyed I'd be a heretic three times over for even thinking it," she went on.

"Spirit is consciousness; soul is eternal," Mickey said thoughtfully. "I think I understand. The soul passes on but sometimes consciousness remains."

"That sounds a decent compromise," Isobel said. "I don't think I was ever much of a good Christian, and I've certainly never been a fundamentalist. Now I realise there's so much more to it than I ever suspected; I don't think I'll ever accept the easy answers now, because I've seen there are *always* more questions than answers, and all the answers do is make more questions."

"I think that's a very healthy place to be at," Mickey said. "When we get home, what do you want to do?"

"You mean, really home? I need to remember that I need my space; I need to value it and fight for it. I know you do a lot with the kids and I know you were pretty miserable with me away, but we need to carve out time for us too, as a family and as a couple. If I need my space, then so do you too. You mustn't let the parish or Les push you into doing too much, filling every evening with meetings," she said. "And I need to learn to be firmer with time-wasters, or at least to get the hang of who's wasting my time and who's really in need. There's a lot of things I need to learn, and I need to *stay* me and not try and be superwoman or something all the time; I need to be *human*. If the events of the last year and a half or so have taught me anything, it's that! I've found my natural environment again and I can breathe again, but it could be so easy to lose it all over again, so I have to remain vigilant. Hang on, Miranda, I'll catch you!"

She ran over to where her daughter had swung herself over the parapet of the slide and was hanging screaming for help, and lowered her down to the ground. It had only been a matter of maybe two feet to drop but Miranda had had sudden doubts about it and had not been able to climb back up.

"There you go," she said. "Now, do you want a go on the swings or shall we go and buy cake and biscuits at the shop?"

As they strolled out of the park and back onto the main street in search of comestibles, Isobel said,

"And Guy is arranging to stage an exhibition in London somewhere with my paintings and his music. He said he's going to ask a poet he knows who's been working with the same sort of area if we can include some poetry. He thinks we should call the exhibition Echoes."

"It sounds to me as if you really have found your proper environment again," Mickey said, pushing the buggy. "Not that you haven't been a great mum and all that. But there's always been something more to you and I'm glad you've really begun to realise it yourself. And I think I will learn to be a bit better at spotting the time-wasters myself. I have missed you so much; I'd hate for you to have to go away again for so long. The odd week I can about stand."
"I don't think it'll happen again," she said. "Just please get a doorbell fitted that rings in your study not the whole house!"

*

The walk back from the shops was a lot slower than the trip down, partly due to the load of shopping in the basket under the buggy but mostly due to the tiredness of all three children. Luke insisted on walking back most of the way and only the fact that Miranda decided she wanted to ride in the buggy made him get back into it. Mickey perched Miranda on the frame of the buggy, her feet in the shopping, and then Jodie began inevitably to whine that she was tired and her feet hurt, so Isobel hauled her up into a piggyback and struggled all the way home with bony legs chafing her hips and feet banging against her knees so she felt bruised all over when she got back to find Simon and Katy sprawled out on the sofa half asleep and looking suspiciously relaxed.
"I don't know how you managed all three," Isobel said, as she flopped into a chair. "I'm cream crackered."
"Sheer skill," said Simon and Katy elbowed him in the ribs.
"Oi!" she said. "You can't claim much credit; you were at work most of the time."
"OK," Simon said. "The secret is having a child-minder, actually. Even a few hours make all the difference."
Katy squealed in protest and began tickling him.
"No fair!" he said. "You know it's true. I have a theory that kids are energy vampires. If they drain someone else for a change, you have the chance to build up resistance, or at very least, reserves. I'd recommend it, Izzie. Even a few hours a week can make the difference."
Katy glared at him.
"He's probably right," she said. "But I don't like admitting it."
"We're having a party," said Jodie, coming over and sitting on her father's stomach.
"Oof, get off, that hurts," Simon said. "Where shall we have it, then, Miss Clever Clogs?"
"In the garden, in the garden," shouted both girls.
"The garden it is," said Isobel.
They dragged out chairs and a couple of blankets to and the picnic party extended towards twilight, when Isobel brought out candles in jam jars and they sat around until

the darkening sky brought night chills and sleepy children needed to be borne off to bed, protesting as children always have done, that they were, "not tired, not tired at all" and they, "didn't want to go to bed." But that not-withstanding, each child fell deeply asleep the moment they were tucked in and Isobel went back outside, her fleece jacket zipped up and carefully carried the jam jars across to the barrow and placed them around the barely visible stones that marked the resting place for her parents' ashes.

As she stood amid the deepening gloom, a light wind seemed to rise from nowhere and whipped a few early-fallen leaves around her feet. Despite the heat of the day, summer was waning now and she felt that familiar sadness that people have always experienced at the diminishing of summer. The candlelight flickered softly, and above her the first stars began to show, white against the navy sky; somewhere not far off, a bird was singing, a blackbird, perhaps. Then she turned and went slowly across the lawn, back to her family indoors.

*

Back then to the usual routine, the usual chaos and mess of family life. Back to the rush and muddle of mornings and the brief moments of calm. Back to familiar streets, familiar faces and shops. Back to the drudgery and endless repetition of housework. Back to the tyrants of phone and doorbell, though both were being diverted now.

On Mickey's first day off after they got home from their holiday, they had a day out at a child-friendly fun park, followed when the kids had flopped into bed, with a distinctly *not* child-friendly and fiendishly hot curry from the local takeaway, washed down with some ice cold lager. The week after, remembering her resolutions to make time for herself and her work, she took the day to work on another painting before the usual influx of Christmas commissions flooded her free time with portraits of other peoples' children and pets.

The light in the spare room wasn't perfect, but the light in her head still was and she worked hard, stopping only when Mickey came to bring her tea and sandwiches, and when she heard the bath being run for the children, she dropped her brush into the jar of water and stepped back to look at her work.

In a pool of water, surrounded by hazel bushes with the fruit ripening to golden brown, the sun shone on the rippling water and on the scales of a large salmon resting just beneath the surface. It was rising to take a fly struggling on the surface of the pool, and you could see that this was a clever salmon since the remains of a scar made by a fish hook was visible in the flesh of its lip.

Isobel grunted her satisfaction and began to clear away her materials, rinsing the brushes clean and leaving them to dry on an old tea towel. She heard the scampering of small feet and went through to say goodnight to her children, soapy-scented angels with impish giggles while Mickey read them a story, and then went to the bathroom to clear up the usual resulting mess.

As always, bath toys and damp towels lay strewn across the floor, now sanded and varnished to within an inch of its life against future floods, so Isobel began picking up and chucking the bright plastic boats back into the bath where they lay like wrecks amid icebergs of diminishing foam. She picked up one soaking wet towel that had obviously fallen into the water, and began wringing it out, and then spread it over the side of the bath to dry. As she straightened up, she caught a glimpse of herself in the mirror over the sink and she stopped, abruptly, as time seemed to shift on itself and she remembered another moment when she had done this same thing.

Her skin was dusted with gold from days in the sun, her eyes bright with achievement. Even her mad, two-toned hair seemed to shine with life.

"I'm home," she said softly, and went downstairs.

Acknowledgements

These days it doesn't seem to be enough to simply write a novel. If, like me, you have chosen the independent route there are a host of other things that demand attention and some of those have been beyond my skills to provide. Cover art was one of those things and my grateful and awed thanks goes to Andrew Meek who patiently read through my requests and suggestions for artwork for the cover and came up with some brilliant work. We went through a number of cycles of themes until my friend Mark Myers (thank you Mark!) mentioned how much the image of the magpie with the arrowhead necklace had struck him, and thus the decision was made. Andrew managed to translate the description in the book into exactly the image that had been in my mind when I wrote it. For his sheer brilliance and generosity of time I am profoundly grateful. He's also a wonderful writer as well as artist. Look him up.

My daughter Ellie deserves thanks for the endless mugs of tea and the odd sandwich she has delivered to my desk, not to mention encouragement and hugs.

The person who deserves most thanks of all is my husband Nigel, who has not only done wonders with the technical side of things but has also survived my moods and fits of depression with humour and love. Thank you, my love.

Also by Vivienne Tuffnell:

Strangers and Pilgrims

"My heart is broken and I am dying inside."

Six unconnected strangers type these words into an internet search engine and start the journey of a lifetime. Directed to The House of the Wellspring website, each begins a conversation with the mysterious warden, to discover whether the waters of the Wellspring, a source of powerful healing, can heal their unbearable hurts.

Sara: agoraphobic artist whose recent life has dealt her more trauma than she can recover from.
Gareth: transformed from gung-ho policeman to shattered recluse by more than a bullet.
Alex: academic whose promising career was ruined first by a convincing fraud and then by his crippling loss of self belief.
Ginny: sensitive rebel daughter of a Polish tycoon hospitalised for years for her belief in faeries.
Elizabeth: former nun who lost her vocation only days away from her final vows.
Mark: famous faith healer whose gift left him when he needed it the most.

Invited to spend some days at the House of the Wellspring each of the strangers come with the hopes of coming away whole again. But where is the Warden they all longed to meet and where is the Wellspring they all came to find?

(Available from Amazon UK, Amazon US, Amazon DE as a paper back or on Kindle.)

For news about Vivienne and her books, please visit her blog at

http://zenandtheartoftightropewalking.wordpress.com

Printed in Great Britain
by Amazon.co.uk, Ltd.,
Marston Gate.